What the

"Lachlan and Erin burn up the sheets together...DEEP IS THE NIGHT: DARK FIRE is the first story in this vampire trilogy. Readers will be eagerly awaiting the next installment to see what happens next. If you've never tried a book by Ms. Agnew, this may be a good book to start off with."
- *Denise Powers, Sensual Reviews*

"A masterfully scary story that's full of passion. The lovemaking between Erin and Lachlan is mind-blowing and highly erotic, together with enough suspense and tension to leave you breathless. I look forward with anticipation for the next installment. I hope I do not have to wait long. If like me you love sexy, scary, suspenseful novels then DEEP IS THE NIGHT: DARK FIRE is a must and a definite keeper. To be devoured again and again."
- *Gail Northman for Romance Junkies*

Discover for yourself why readers can't get enough of the multiple-award-winning publisher Ellora's Cave. Whether you prefer e-books or paperbacks, be sure to visit EC on the web at www.ellorascave.com for an erotic reading experience that will leave you breathless.

www.ellorascave.com

Ellora's Cave Publishing, Inc.
PO Box 787
Hudson, OH 44236-0787

ISBN # 1-84360-563-5

Deep Is the Night: Dark Fire edited by Martha Punches.
Cover art by Scott Carpenter.

DEEP IS THE NIGHT: DARK FIRE

Written by

DENISE AGNEW

Prologue

Darkness swirled around the vampire like a great, black cloak and masked him from the dangerous eyes of those who might see him. Standing in the shadows of the pine forest edging the quiet town, he knew it wouldn't be long now.

Soon Erin Greenway would arrive, and he would make an entrance. She would know he existed, and he would start her transformation from disbeliever to unable to believe anything else. Once he'd primed her for sex she would be in his power, enthralled by all he could give her, and all he could take. She would recall her life a thousand years before, and that she existed now through reincarnation.

He smiled at the pleasure it gave him to think his sweet Dasoria came back to him in the form of Erin. Erin might be human now, but he would assure her conversion back to vampire flesh.

He hated humans and everything they stood for.

They were lowly servants, these creatures. Except his sweet Erin, who drew him like a black widow to her prey.

Since he first saw her a month ago, he'd known she would match him fire for fire, passion for passion. He'd hunted the world over for the woman with the right amount of fire and spirit to fulfill his every desire and taste for bloodlust.

Beyond all that, she looked like his Dasoria with her onyx hair and sterling eyes. Dasoria who filled his dreams at night and tormented him with memories so aged they shouldn't have been fresh. But they were. Dasoria, who he watched die at the hands of humans more than a thousand years ago.

He closed his eyes and breathed deeply, fighting the horror of scalding memories that burned as much now as they did eons ago. He felt the shadows flow through his cold body. Every evil thought showed him the way to bring Erin into his fold and under his sexual power. Tonight may be the night she would taste him as he tasted her in his dreams. He'd waited far too long for her return to life, and he refused to lose her this time.

Moments later he saw the car drive into the library parking lot and her hesitation to leave the vehicle. Erin felt him. She may not understand what he represented, nor recognize her fear as a warning. Still, he would make sure she saw the heat and desire of his unrelenting passion. Then she would know that she belonged to him and *only* him. He would take the young woman, dominate her, and slake his lust on her mortal soul. He would teach her to please her master and enjoy it at the same time. Few women could be trained, but he knew one way was to enslave them to sex. Pleasure upon pleasure, pain upon pain.

He closed his eyes and imagined how her body would writhe against his and how his cock would slide deep inside her. Every jerk of her body, every moan from her lips would feed his fire and drive him to the ultimate goal. Her blood and eternal love.

For no mere human could satisfy him forever.

He'd enjoyed the nubile whore that had met him at the bar last night and eyed him from afar. She'd given him the eye long enough that he knew the signal. She wanted a hard, heavy fucking and he should be the one to give it to her. When he caught up with her on the street, she'd seemed pleased. Even when he'd made her powerless to resist him and had pulled her into the bushes to bite and ream her, she hadn't resisted.

But then she hadn't responded either.

Watching Erin from a distance, he anticipated the right moment to enter her life and introduce her to the dark fire.

Erin Greenway would learn to love his brand of sensuality, then she would die and be reborn as his beloved, undead Dasoria.

Chapter 1

"In the still of the night...."

Erin Greenway sang the last notes of the song as she pulled her Subaru Forester into the library parking lot. She surveyed the misty October evening and the empty area.

Empty.

No sign of Gilda's red Jag. Lights shown from the bottom floor windows and one solitary light illuminated a window on the second floor, so Gilda must be here. Erin glanced at the clock on the dash and the digital readout showed five thirty.

She glanced out the windshield at the tall, imposing building. Tendrils of fog drifted over the face of the Gothic Revival house now used as the public library. Soon the moon's silver illumination would give way to inky blackness and the old structure would look sinister.

Three stories of one hundred year-old stone bristling with old west history.

It sounded appealing on the local tourist brochure, but at night the structure became an eerie presence that made even Erin's steel nerves prickle with apprehension.

She shivered, grateful for her fleece hat pulled down over her ears, long coat, and thick mittens. At a frosty nine thousand feet altitude, the mountain town suffered under winter weather on a regular basis. A snowstorm should be here in another day or two and then she'd struggle through flurries. For now, though, the town appeared appropriately scary for the time of the year.

She shut off the ignition, she stared at the library. Her best friend, Elaine Panzer, grew up in Pine Forest, Colorado and warned Erin before she left Arizona that the town held an unusual sway over unsuspecting residents. Elaine claimed Pine

Forest was chock-full-o'-specters. Erin figured she could blame Elaine's ghost tales for making her feel as jumpy as a frog in a frying pan. Yet even if Elaine didn't talk about ghostly phenomena three-fourths of the time, Erin would have heard about them from the rest of the people living here. Everyone in town believed in ghosts, or so it seemed.

Yeah, right. Ghosts and goblins don't exist. A whole town couldn't be rife with boogiemen.

"Pfft!" Erin reached for her tote bag and unlocked the door. "As grandma would say…hogwash."

As she stepped into the night, the icy evening wrapped around her and she smiled. She could almost sense Halloween coming. The kids would love the spooky story time kickoff tonight. She hoped Gilda started on the decorations earlier in the day.

Just as she headed down the sidewalk, she heard the rustling in the bushes toward the back of the parking lot. Something big and heavy. Erin stopped, all her senses on alert. She sniffed. A musty, intrusive smell filled the air. Yesterday's headlines in the Pine Forest Sentinel sprang into her mind.

Woman Attacked In Park.

Person or persons unknown had assailed a young woman jogging at four in the morning in a secluded park and had bitten her on the neck.

The woman survived, but she now owned the biggest hickey this side of Texas.

While the article disturbed Erin, she believed the woman should have used common sense. Jogging alone at four in the morning before light touched the horizon didn't seem prudent to Erin.

She heard the sound again, this time closer. The huge ponderosa pines hovering near the library rustled, their needles moved by a soft wind. Everything within her came to attention, captured in an inertia that wouldn't allow her to twitch a muscle. Fear, primal and stark, slid through her like a serpent's touch. Utter dread, the kind that makes humans afraid of the dark, made her body tense. Her heart picked up a pounding pace. Suddenly, Halloween loomed out of the darkness like a monster, ready to swallow her with one enormous gulp.

A whisper touched her ears, shadowy and hot.

Want me. Need me. Erin.

A wave of dizziness filled her body and made her stagger. She put one hand out and found no support. As her vision started to go dark she wavered, her knees threatening total collapse. Her temples started to throb.

A picture formed, immediate and lucid. A bed, draped with blood-red satin sheets. A man lay in the center of the bed, his arms tied to the bedposts and his legs spread wide. Incredible musculature graced his tall, strong body. Her mouth opened in awe as she scanned, from his tumble of black hair, over his angel-of-darkness face, past a hairy and muscled chest. A stomach, hard with strength, next caught her gaze. She licked her lips and felt warmth intrude in her gut. Drawn exorability downward, her attention landed on his hips. His erection thrust upward, bold and without shame. Hard, long, and ready to service.

A new voice, deeper and tinged with heated seduction, filled her mind. A voice heavy with desperation. *Erin. Don't listen to the darkness.*

She snapped out of the visualization with a jolt.

Nausea filled her center and her vision blurred again. "What's happening?"

With both hands she reached out, her sense of reality boggled by this weird event. As her sight cleared she glanced around at the menacing night. Nothing moved, not even the wind. All around her the silent neighborhood seemed unearthly quiet. Tall trees lined the wide avenue. Their pine needles seemed to whisper messages even though there was no breeze to speak of. Darkness pressed close like a mantle, a blanket of evil she'd never experienced before. Shivers rippled through her body as she scanned the illuminated windows of houses across the street. A little piece of evidence that something lived gave her some comfort.

Why had she seen a naked man in her mind's eye? She'd never experienced a vision much less an intuition about anything in her life. At least she didn't think so. Sure, she'd fantasized about a handsome, well-hung lover on cold nights when it felt like she'd never have a date again. She even recalled inventing a scenario one night about a man with dark hair and haunting eyes. But imagination wasn't reality, and she doubted a man that devastatingly attractive would be interested in her anyway.

She put both hands to her cheeks and felt heat blazing under the skin.

I am going insane.

Once again the menacing voice spoke, as much in her mind as on the air. *You are mine, Erin. There is no escape.*

Fright jumped on the bandwagon as she stood in shocked silence. She shivered as new apprehension rolled up her spine in a wave. *Move, Erin. Move! Now! Now! Now!*

She didn't question instinct. She broke into a run and covered the few yards of concrete in swift strides. Erin hadn't won races in high school and college for nothing. She might be short, but her legs didn't care.

She scrambled up the few steps and reached for the right doorknob on the huge mahogany double doors. She twisted the knob. Nothing.

Erin heard the ruffling of the wind behind her like a voice. A whisper that called to her in strange tongues. Whirling, she peered across the street again to the other quiet old homes. She didn't see anything or anyone, but the urge to get inside the building came at her like a relentless chant.

Erin. Erin. Get inside the building. Now. The inky voice, rumbling and exotic with Scottish accent, overran the earlier voice that told her she couldn't escape. Two voices taunted her in the night, and if a psychiatrist had been there right now, they would have declared her insane on the spot.

She looked around again, wondering for the first time if maybe the neighborhood kids started Halloween early and decided to play a trick on her. Smiling at her own gullibility, she wrestled with panic. Strange visions not withstanding, she couldn't let her imagination play tricks on her. Ignoring the little creeps would be the best way to save her dignity. Maybe. If they saw her running like a scared rabbit, they accomplished what they set out to do.

Fumbling in her purse, Erin found her keys and jammed the correct one into the lock. Once inside, she slammed the door and locked it.

Glancing around the interior, she leaned against the door and felt the trembling that rolled through her body. She called out. "Gilda?"

Silence greeted her. Maybe Gilda had gone upstairs to finish decorating.

Good. At least Gilda wouldn't have witnessed her flight into the building. After that ridiculous reaction outside, she needed to put things in perspective and stop acting like a dumb heroine in a horror flick.

Then, maybe, she should make an appointment with a shrink. Shaking her head, she decided to put aside the weirdness for the moment and attend to business.

Erin checked her message slot behind the counter high desk but saw no messages. She took off her heavy wool cloak and hung it in the closet in the small break room.

She headed into the bathroom and took in her appearance in the mirror. Her short black hair floated around her head in out of control wisps that defied every styling product she'd tried. Bed-head was in style, so she supposed she should be happy. *Not!* She hated the wild and messy trend. She tried fluffing her hair with her fingers. Defiant tuffs continued to stick out. Growling with frustration, she smoothed her hands down the sides of her royal blue sweater dress.

Well, most little kids didn't give a rip what librarians looked like. A five feet three inch, twenty-nine year old librarian with a heart shaped face that made her look like a twelve year old rarely got respect. Erin couldn't recall the number of times people patted her on the head like she might be a cute, if precocious kid.

She blinked, and her large gray eyes seemed startled and insecure. Young and old alike assumed things about Erin, and she learned to live with their odd expectations.

Since she left Arizona more than a month ago and taken on this position, she hoped people in this town would treat her differently. For the most part, they did. People seemed friendlier around here than in her old town, and that made her more comfortable right away. Years of conditioning imprinted unwanted expectations on her mind; she thought people would dislike her more often then they would like her.

Her father and mother's desires once took up far too much of her life, and the awkwardness she experienced abated as time passed here in Pine Forest. Running from her family's expectations meant loneliness in a whole new way. With them she always felt different and unable to fit in to their down-to-earth, no-frills lifestyle. They made her believe for so long she couldn't get along in the big, bad world outside the little hamlet of Louis, Arizona. Now she resided in Pine Forest, she needed the promise of new friends to go with her new life.

Erin sighed and made a pledge to herself in that moment.

Each day is new. I can make a difference, and I can be happy here.

That is, if I'm not losing my ever-loving mind.

Still disturbed by the odd hallucination she'd had outside the library, Erin left the bathroom and entered the sprawling first floor area. She heard another rustling noise, this time distinct and unmistakable, like long skirts brushing against the stacks. Erin looked around as she walked, her pumps making clicks against the hardwood floor.

"Gilda? I swear if you're playing an early Halloween joke on me, I'll—"

A long, hollow groan, like metal or wood expanding, echoed throughout the entire building. Again Erin stayed glued to the spot. Waiting. Listening. The sound didn't come again.

A cold sensation slipped over her skin, almost as if she'd stepped outside and into the dark dampness of a crypt. She fought back the creeping trepidation she encountered earlier.

Treading cautiously, she went toward the stairway. The large chandelier hanging near the staircase spilled warm light over the entire first floor, softening the effect of night. She caught sight of the huge stained glass window gracing the area between the divided staircases. Although in the evening darkness she couldn't see the glass depiction of angels clashing with devils, she saw it every day in the light and thought it looked sinister. Taking a deep breath, she decided she wouldn't allow this situation to get out of hand. What on earth possessed her to worry this way? She headed upstairs, thankful for the threadbare stair runner masking her steps.

Before she reached the second landing, the odd echoing noise rammed through the building again. Erin gasped and almost took a step back. The sound became as much a feeling as a noise, vibrating the entire area, pulsating the wood under her fingers as she held on to the banister.

"What on earth?" she asked, keeping her voice to a whisper.

Unnerved, she continued upstairs. Seconds later the noise came again, reverberating like a drum of tremendous size. When she reached the second floor she saw light streaming from the east side of the room, beyond the children's stacks to the niche that served as the story time area. She reached for the switches near the entrance to the second floor and welcome light flooded the area.

"Hello?"

She started toward the alcove. A loud crash made her heart come to a standstill.

Instinct roared to life again. She took two steps back. Then three.

Another sound, this one more menacing and meaningful, dug into her hearing like a nightmare.

A soft snarl, almost like that from a small dog, came from the children's stacks.

Erin bolted.

She rushed toward the first floor without a clue what she'd do next other than to get the hell out of this building. When she reached the first floor, she heard steady and determined knocking on the front door. She placed her hand over her thumping heart and turned just enough to see if anyone or anything followed her. Nobody there.

Erin, get a grip. You don't believe in monsters.

Maybe some parents and their kids had arrived. The grandfather clock bonged out the hour. So they were thirty minutes ahead of schedule. *Let them in and have safety in numbers.* Besides, ghosts didn't knock on doors to ask permission to enter, did they?

Right that second her toe caught on a snag in the rug and she went face down with a grunt and a painful thud.

Damn it!

Her entire body throbbed as she lay immobile for a moment, embarrassed at her clumsiness. *Good going, Erin. If a monster had been behind you they would have eaten you by now.*

Hurrying on a spurt of adrenaline, she lurched to her feet and grabbed a letter opener from the front counter to use as a possible weapon.

The knock came again, this time more impatient.

"Okay, okay. Keep your panty hose on," she muttered.

Erin unlocked the heavy door and pulled it open.

Her breath stopped right along with her heart. She couldn't remember her name for a few seconds as she absorbed one startling fact.

The smiling vampire standing in front of her, sharp teeth and all, was the man in her vision.

Chapter 2

"Good evening," the vampire said in an abysmal imitation of Bella Lugosi's famous words of greeting.

Her mouth dropped open and she tried to speak but nothing came out.

Yep. It was the man she'd seen tied to a bed, ready and waiting just for her.

Holy son of a buckster.

Few women had a fantasy step right into their line of sight, attainable or unattainable. Having this delectable man appear from nowhere made her knees weaken and her heart quiver with an intoxicating cocktail of fear and excitement.

Lust rose inside her in an unexpected surge, and her entire mind and body went on high alert. Vampire or not, dangerous or not, the hunk in front of her inspired undiluted female appreciation that spread from her breasts down to her loins. Men this gorgeous were rarities. Even if he didn't look like her secret fantasy, she couldn't have denied his appeal.

Dark, delectable, and intriguing.

The man's stunning smile faded, and he removed the pointy teeth. Without the horrifying fangs, his handsome face overruled trepidation for a moment. He towered over her small frame, at least six feet tall. Whiskey brown eyes twinkled with a hot glow.

For a wild, frightening second, she thought that glow went yellow, like an unrelenting lion's gaze pinioned on a tasty meal.

Then he blinked and the illusion disappeared.

He stuffed his fingers through his hair, and the thick blue-black strands fell in a shiny, tousled wave just over his collar. His lips were carved with sin in mind, not too thin and not too thick. Along the right side of his neck were two small scars, visible enough to pique her interest. The man wore an ankle length black cape over a black turtleneck and black jeans. She glanced down and saw even his cowboy boots were black. A vampire in cowboy boots?

My God, he's the sexiest man I've ever seen. I wonder what he really looks like naked —

A wide, unrepentant grin touched his mouth, and that devastating smile made her insides feel warm. "What's the matter? Vampire got your tongue, lass?"

His voice held more than a smidgen of Scotland, and a rich, husky flavor that stirred warmth inside her. The unabashed smile on his mouth said he *knew* every lascivious thought running through her head at that minute. His voice also sounded like the second voice she'd heard outside—the one that urged her to escape the darkness and get into the library.

No. That can't be.

"If you're going to stake me with that, I hope it is silver," he said when she didn't speak.

Erin realized she held the letter opener in her fist as if she might skewer him any moment. She tightened her grip on the instrument. She cleared her throat. "Wooden stake."

"What?"

"You need a wooden stake to kill a vampire."

The smile that charmed her disappeared, his gaze turning serious. "That's what everyone thinks."

Sexy or not, she wouldn't give this man another inch until he explained himself. "Who are you and why are you lurking around outside in that...that costume?"

He bowed at the waist, a gallant gesture that spoke old world and appropriate for him. "Lachlan Tavish."

Lachlan. The name rolled off his lips with an unmistakable lilt.

"Well, Mr. Tavish, that doesn't explain why you're here."

"Didn't Gilda ring you up? She said she tried several times but didn't get an answer on your cell phone."

"No, I didn't get any calls on my phone."

He frowned. "She ran off to the hospital with her little boy and she called me at the last minute to fill in for her."

Caution still running in her veins, Erin asked, "Oh, my God, what happened to Mark?"

"Apparently he fell down at band practice and landed on his elbow and cracked it."

"Thank goodness it wasn't worse." An awkward silence flooded the area as an icy wind floated around the front steps, teasing the man's ankles and making his cape flutter about his body. "How do I know you're who you say you are?"

Reaching into the back pocket of his jeans, he extracted a wallet and handed it to her. "See for yourself. I'm on holiday visiting Gilda and her husband and searching for property."

Then she recalled Gilda saying something about a man visiting, an old friend they had met a couple of years ago in Scotland. Her trepidation eased the slightest bit.

She flipped open his wallet and located all the usual items, including an I.D. card for a company called Tavish International. The card identified him as Lachlan Tavish, CEO.

"Looking for property? Immigrating here?"

"On the hunt."

She handed the wallet back to him. "What?"

"For a good bed and breakfast. Do you know of any?"

His ability to change directions unnerved her, but she stepped back from the door and allowed him inside. He seemed harmless enough, but she kept the letter opener in hand.

As he walked by her, a sandalwood scent teased her nose, and she inhaled deeply. Down in her belly a primitive and uncontrollable reaction started. She clenched her muscles in a Kegel maneuver. Heat sluiced through her body, despite the coolness of the room. *God, he's sexy.*

"The Gunn Inn just closed temporarily," she said. "The owner died a few weeks back and the woman inheriting it hasn't moved into town yet. There's Jekyl's down on Hyde Street not far from here."

Without a smile he said, "Jekyl's on Hyde Street. You're joking."

She couldn't help but grin. "No. A little macabre, don't you think?"

He nodded. "A lot of that going on around here."

Once again she noted his assertion something odd plagued Pine Forest. "I've only been here a few weeks myself. So I couldn't tell you the best places in town to stay. Not like there's much choice in a place so small."

Small, but big enough for a resident vampire, she guessed.

Correction. A vampire wannabe.

Lachlan continued into the room, pausing near the front counter. He looked around the room as if appraising everything about the structure. "Magnificent place."

She agreed, staring at him without remorse as he turned his back on her. His lush, curling hair drew her appreciation; the sides had been trimmed shorter, though they still covered his ears. His sideburns were a bit long, but instead of looking strange, they gave his face definition and enhanced the dark and dangerous aura. As he turned back to her, he smiled again. A fresh wave of heat swept through her.

Disconcerted, she asked, "How do you know Gilda?"

"We met when Gilda and her husband taught at the university where I did research. In Edinburgh."

She nodded. "The teacher's exchange. I remember her telling me about it. You're originally from Edinburgh?"

"I had a home not far from there." He abandoned his intense survey of the room. He pinned her with those eyes, and her breath seized up for a second. "I'm here to take care of a little business. And you're right, I may move to the United States. It depends on several factors, actually."

She wanted to relax, but something about him kept her on alert, ready to flee if she caught the slightest hint of subterfuge. "Well, since Gilda's not here, I have to make sure upstairs is set up. And you won't mind if I call Gilda first and confirm you are who you say you are?"

"Of course not. Call away." Lachlan walked toward her, his shoulders wide and intimidating. The cape, with its blood red lining fluttering around and behind him, added to his vampire illusion. "She said she put up all the decorations before she got the call about her son. How can I help?"

She spied the big grandfather clock. "The kids should start coming in any time. If you could stay down here and greet them, I'd appreciate it. They should get a kick out of your costume."

Another loud, obnoxious groan radiated from the building. Lachlan frowned, crease lines showing between his thick dark brows. "What the bloody hell was that?"

Shrugging, Erin reached for the phone at the front counter and started dialing Gilda's home number. "I've heard it three times now this evening and your guess is as good as mine. I was investigating when you showed up." She almost blurted out about the snarling noise, then decided that Mr. Tavish would think she was one chess piece short of a set.

He took a couple of steps toward the staircase, his gaze narrowing. "Sounds like the whole building's about to collapse."

"Lovely thought." She paused as the phone rang and rang in her ear. Once she reached the answering machine she left her name and number. "They must not be home from the hospital yet."

"Then don't worry. I'll be right here and direct the kids up to your story time." When she gave him a skeptical look, he said, "You don't trust me."

Time to come straight out with it. "No, I don't. In case you haven't heard, a woman was attacked in the park."

He nodded, his eyes grave. "I heard. I don't blame you for being cautious. You're a smart woman." He moved a little closer, and she took a step back. He held his hands up as if she'd asked him to surrender. "It's all right. I won't come any closer."

Another knock sounded on the front door, and Erin realized she hadn't fixed the release on the door that would allow it to stay unlocked.

He headed toward the stairs again, "I'll go and see if I can figure out what's making that noise upstairs, and I'll be right back."

She murmured, "You do that, Dracula."

Erin couldn't help but stare as he walked, intrigued by his stride that screamed confidence, casualness, and sex. As if he could feel her attention, Lachlan glanced back. His grin, big and full of sensual promise, overflowed her center with heat. He winked.

Boy howdy.

She took one step toward the door when a bizarre feeling swept over her. In her mind's eye she saw that big cape flowing around Lachlan's aroused, one-hundred percent naked body.

The pounding on the door increased. She shook her head and tried to regain her control. *There you go again, Erin. Thinking about sex. Refrain for a moment and get the door.*

When she opened the door, two blonde girls stepped into the library and smiled. Behind them stood their mother, Jessie Huxley, an equally blonde, tall, and somewhat chesty woman with a round face and a bright smile. Divorced about a year ago, it appeared Jessie was already on the prowl for new meat.

"Hi, Miss Greenway." The oldest and tallest of the girls, Carrie, came toward Erin. "Where is everyone?"

"Should be here any moment."

"Where's Mrs. Jefferson?" The youngest girl, Patty, asked Erin.

Erin explained about Gilda's son while she took their coats. Carrie shivered and looked up at her mother. "This place gives me the creeps."

"It's just an old house, dear," her mother said, sounding unconvinced.

Once upstairs, Erin saw Gilda had decorated with paper pumpkins, black cats, bats, and scarecrows. Autumn touches of brown, gold and yellow graced the room and gave it a perfect festive feeling.

"Good evening," a powerful, deep voice said from the shadows. "I am here to drink your blood."

Lachlan stepped out from behind a bookshelf, fangs bared and hands held up in a position of mock attack. Patty and Carrie squealed in half fright and delight, backing up against Jessie for protection. Lachlan smiled and let out a booming laugh. The little girls giggled again and their mother joined in. Erin watched the display as he introduced himself to the two small females and their gaping mother. Amazing how he could change from serious to humor-filled in a few short seconds.

Jessie's long, artificially dark eyelashes blinked and blinked again. "Um...well, hello." Her gaze did a slow foray over his body. "That's a great costume. Where did you find it?"

Lachlan removed his fangs again and shook her hand. "Who says it's a costume?" Again he made the bow and put on a heavy Scottish accent. "Lachlan Tavish at your service. If you've got the blood, I've got the time, lass."

Jessie's giggle almost matched her daughter's on the silly scale. Amused, Erin joined in the fun. "Mr. Tavish is a friend of Gilda and Tom. He'll direct the kids up here for story time."

Jessie's eyes went wide and admiring. "Is the accent real?"

"Aye." Lachlan winked. "All of it."

"Were you born and bred in the Highlands?" Jessie asked with a hopeful tone.

Born and bred, eh? Erin pictured Lachlan running around a stable half-naked like an animal. She tried banning the picture from her consciousness before she started doing something ridiculous like slobbering.

Lachlan's chuckle, deep and husky, stirred new pleasure inside Erin. "I was born and raised in Edinburgh."

The single mother of two seemed a little disappointed around the edges. "Pity. I always wanted to meet a Highlander."

Erin sighed in mock sympathy. "Pity." She put her hands on hips. "But as vampires go, I think he'll do in a pinch."

I can do more than pinch.

Erin almost came out of her shoes as the voice filled her head. Heat flooded her face as the husky intonation continued. *Save me from this woman, will you, Erin?*

Shocked, Erin's mouth dropped open and she looked straight at Lachlan. He smiled, and the full-scale effect of his wide grin made her heart do a triple flip. As his gaze swept over her, she felt his appraisal like a touch.

Hot. Appreciative. Longing.

Wanting her with a serious heat.

Keep looking at me like that, Erin, and I'll have to do something about it later.

Without a doubt, she recognized the second voice as belonging to him.

Chapter 3

This is too ridiculous. Lachlan Tavish is not speaking to me telepathically.

Erin decided she would keep telling herself that until she got it through her head, and believed it.

"Looks like Mr. Vampire needs to go downstairs and watch for tasty children," Erin said with an evil lilt to her voice. She waggled her eyebrows at the kids and they laughed. "Have a seat, girls." The little ones scampered to find chairs. Erin smiled at Jessie. "That goes for you, too."

Jessie grinned and headed for an adult-sized chair.

"What do you say here in the U.S.?" Lachlan asked as he headed for the stairway. "I'm outta here." Before he started downward he added, "Can I have a moment of your time, Erin."

"Hurry back," Jessie said. "We can wait."

Jessie winked and Erin felt the blush in her face turn into an inferno. "I'll be right back."

Once downstairs, she asked, "What is it? I've got a couple of things to do before the kids start arriving in droves."

Clasping her right arm, he drew her between two rows of bookshelves and stepped close. Way too close for someone of short acquaintance. She would have been indignant, but a feathery feeling in her head invaded her common sense and wiped it away. It moved within her, this odd impression of something heady and mind-boggling and irrational invading her will.

She dared look into his eyes.

Big mistake.

Erin noticed, to her rising fascination, that once again his eyes seemed filled with dark gold fire at the center. Those highlights enveloped her within their embrace and captured her in a prison she didn't wish to escape. The dots formed a mesmerizing circle of light.

Drawn to the intriguing illumination, she leaned a little closer to him. She tore her gaze from his hypnotic eyes and pondered his mouth. Her eyelids felt heavy, drooping as a wave of uncontrollable desire rolled through her. Heaven help her, she *liked* being this close to him.

What would it be like to kiss him?

As if he could read her mind, he shifted closer. She stepped back and bumped into the bookcase behind her. His fingers came up and brushed under her chin, then passed over her throbbing right temple with a quick caress. She gasped as a slight tingling passed through her head, then the headache disappeared like a puff of smoke.

"How..." She couldn't believe what had just happened. Didn't want to believe it.

"Are you all right?" His eyebrows lowered, punctuating his frown. "You look a bit dazed."

"I think I am," she said. She swallowed hard and yanked out of the incomprehensible thrall. "I've never seen women drool over a man like that before. I mean, not in person. Could get a little messy."

His smile, gentle and wicked around the edges, made her breath catch again. "Drooling?"

She cleared her throat as embarrassment filled her face with heat. "The little girls loved you and Jessie about...uh...swallowed her tongue when she saw you. I thought I was going to have to look for bibs."

Lachlan smiled wryly. "Women usually run screaming from me in abject terror. The sight of my hideous face appalls them. It's the undead thing, you know."

She let out a soft laugh. "Right. Have you ever thought of taking this act on the road?"

He chuckled, and the sound ran over her skin like hot liquid. "Has anyone ever told you that you're funny?"

She shook her head. "Never."

"Well, that's a shame." He brushed his index finger over her nose in a light caress. "We're going to have to change that, now, aren't we?" His gaze turned intent and his voice dropped to a husky whisper. "Has anyone told you that you're pretty, lass? Your hair is like dark black silk, and your eyes are platinum gray."

Appreciation and surprise trickled over her. "Maybe once or twice guys told me I was pretty, but they were trying to get something from me. They didn't mean it."

"They may have tried to get something from you, but that doesn't mean they were lying." His gentle grin turned sultry as his gaze slipped down to her breasts for a second, then back to her face. "And you are pretty. Damned pretty."

She couldn't remember the last time she wanted to run from a man and at the same time wanted to be near him. After a compliment like that, she couldn't think straight. She'd always been suspicious of a man who could verbalize pretty words like black silk and platinum gray.

"Thank you." She could hardly say the words. "You're very kind."

He shook his head. "No. I'm very honest. I'd never lie to you, Erin."

If his appraisal came as honest as his words, Lachlan didn't only believe she looked good, he wanted her.

Panicking, Erin took a deep breath and tried to steady the odd thrum in her pulse and her heart. If she could eliminate the floating sensation in her head, she would be one happy camper. It wouldn't do to fall face forward onto the floor.

Lachlan surprised her by switching gears. "When you're done tonight, be very careful when you leave and make sure you're not alone in the parking lot."

"What? Why?" she said, startled at the sudden change. Old apprehension from earlier this evening crept up on her.

"Just take my word for it. It's dangerous for a woman to be on her own in Pine Forest."

For two seconds she wondered if he intended to frighten her with kooky assertions that she needed his protection. She wouldn't fall for that line, and she wouldn't tell a total stranger where she planned to go or where she lived.

She backed away a step. "I'm capable of taking care of myself. I refuse to be paranoid."

"Maybe you *should* be paranoid."

She planted her hands on her hips. "Are you trying to frighten me? Why should I trust you? We've just met."

"But I feel like I've known you forever."

Despite the teasing in his voice, she saw a change occur in his eyes and maybe his intent. His breath seemed to quicken, the only sound she could detect in this quiet place. Awareness thrummed between them, tightening the tension inside her. Tingles of desire danced in her stomach and reminded Erin that Lachlan was one eye-popping handsome man and she was very much a woman.

But looks told a part of the story, not the whole. Something else strange was happening here.

Like a flash fire, his expression went from teasing to dead serious. Before she could say anything or move away, Lachlan cupped her face with one hand. He leaned in and covered her mouth with his.

He swallowed her muffled sound of surprise. Minty and fresh, his taste held her immobile. If she expected ravenous, she didn't get it. Instead, he kissed her softly.

Feather light, his lips teased. Once. "Erin, this is crazy."

She gasped as his mouth brushed hers. "Try insane. What—"

Twice. His mouth took hers again, hot, drugging and unrelenting.

Three times. "Mr. Tavish, we've got to stop—"

Quick tastes of lips against lips. "Lachlan. My name is Lachlan."

On the fourth sweep of his mouth over hers, Erin moaned softly. Lachlan held the kiss, his lips coaxing and teasing with the most exquisite touches she could have imagined.

And she could imagine a lot.

Her last physical relationship fizzled so long ago she felt like a virgin again. Yet she knew one thing for certain.

She'd never tasted this type of kiss before.

Tentative and frightened by sexual feelings long ignored, she felt dazzled by his charisma. Six long years had passed since she'd had a man's lips upon hers or snuggled deep into his arms. Six years since she'd enjoyed the slide of a man's cock inside her. Until now she felt qualified for Nuns-R-Us.

Again his mouth took hers, twisting and moving in a dance that brooked no refusal. Seduction so complete and lighting quick terrified her and intrigued her.

Lachlan Tavish did possess a mouth made for sin.

For nothing but sin could generate the soul-searing, off-the-charts reaction she felt as he devoured her senses.

Dizziness made her body tremble. Her hands went in search of an anchor. She found his chest, hard with tight muscles and rippling with power. Her fingers delighted in the heat radiating from under the soft knit cloth over his body. His cape seemed to envelop them in a secret world, safe from intrusion and cocooning them against all enemies.

Lachlan's hands found her waist and held her there, strong fingers pressing. She heard the rustle of his cape as he moved against her.

Erin wanted more. She leaned into him, and suddenly his arms went around her and he pressed her against the heavy bookcase. His mouth slanted, forcing her lips apart at the same time he pressed his thigh between her legs.

Oh.

Roped with sinew, his thigh pressed and lifted her dress up her legs. His tongue entered her mouth and started a steady, pumping rhythm that suggested the deepest, most exciting sex she'd ever had.

No. *Never* had before this moment.

Dazed, part of Erin watched from the outside looking in, screaming at her to regain control of the situation before something bad happened. She'd lost her mind. Lost it and couldn't get it back.

She didn't want to.

His hands swept over her back and landed on her butt. He squeezed. She clenched around his thigh, and he groaned against her mouth.

He tore his mouth from hers and buried his face in her neck. His breath rushed in an out of his lungs and betrayed his arousal. He slid his fingers into her hair and held her face against his shoulder.

Against her ear he whispered in a tortured voice rough with Scottish tones, "Erin, we must stop, lass. I *dinna* know what's happening…"

She groaned. "Yes."

"Someone will find us here."

She gasped sharply inward as his hand left her hair and slid down toward her breast. "Yes."

Yes. She didn't know whether she meant the syllable as a request for him to touch her breast or as an acknowledgement that if they continued the craziness they would be exposed. The idea of discovery sent a tiny, forbidden thrill all through Erin.

Instead of following his own advice, Lachlan moved, his hand cupping one of her butt cheeks so he could grind his hips against her. The movement sent sparks of sharp pleasure through her. Inside her mind Erin could feel a torment begin, a shame mixed with a force so strong she felt as if her will had been torn from her.

"I want you, Erin," he said huskily against her ear.

Without roughness, the sensation of his big hand circling her breast made her shudder in wanton delight. She gasped again, and when his thumb and forefinger closed on the nipple, she writhed in his arms.

"Lachlan, oh, please."

She knew the words came out like a sob, and she didn't care. Didn't give a flying fuck if he invaded her mind and stole her will.

"I canna help myself, Erin. This sweet nipple feels so good against my fingers."

Lachlan kissed her earlobe, and his tongue slipped inside her ear, dancing against sensitive skin. Again his fingers gently plucked her nipple, brushing against the hard nub until she felt the deep, unmistakable moistening between her legs. She moaned softly, the multiple arousals almost more than Erin could stand.

He kissed her again, his tongue taking her mouth with deep caresses that poured more fuel on the fire. With burning excitement she gave it back to him, slipping her hands into his hair and feeling the soft strands tickling the pads of her fingers.

Erin. Erin, sweetheart, you are so wonderful.

The voice brushed against her mind, more erotic and exciting than any caress.

Didn't vampires seduce their helpless victims like this before draining their blood? She gave a mental shrug, not caring whether he wanted her blood or not. Not when she wanted his mouth on hers, his arms around her and—God forbid—his cock wedged inside her.

As her arms went around Lachlan's neck, Erin remembered where she was. In the library stacks with a man's tongue in her mouth, and his hand tormenting her breast. A slow, simmering burn pulsed inside her, and she knew if he reached inside her panties he'd find her wetter than she'd ever been in her life.

Wet because a man she'd known less than a couple of hours made her feel the most cherished, the most beloved woman he'd known.

Oh, God, oh, God, oh, God.

A tight throbbing started between her legs.

His fingers strummed her nipple.

Let it go, Erin.

She did.

Sweet throbs rolled through her as her clit tingled with sharp pleasure. The tiny, wonderful orgasm made her entire body quiver with mindless enjoyment. As the gentle orgasm reached a peak, he kept his fingers moving on her nipple, and his tongue in her mouth. She shivered, whimpered, and went limp in his arms.

Lachlan stopped kissing her and once again buried his face in her hair as he pulled her close.

"Erin," he rasped. "I don't know what happened—"

Disbelief and embarrassment that she'd just made out in the stacks with a stranger bolted through Erin. She shoved against him and he let her go.

Emotions battered her, caught up in the raging desire that seemed to leap upon her like a ravenous beast. Surprise and humiliation mixed together. Surprise at herself for allowing this man to almost take her up against a bookshelf. Humiliation for feeling like a slut of the first degree. A total stranger had made her come with little effort. Top that with the fact she'd experienced a strange hallucination and now she could hear voices in her head. She'd dumped her inhibitions and all her common sense in the heat of a reckless passion.

She put her hands to mouth and stared at Lachlan in bewilderment. Tears sprung to her eyes. Erin had never experienced anything this erotic, this amazing, this divergent to her normal behavior before tonight.

Contrary to what she expected, Lachlan did not seem smug or pleased. Instead he appeared as a man who'd enjoyed a mind-melting session of sexual exploration. He stood there, face flushed, and hands fisted at his sides as if restraining himself from pulling her into his arms and finishing the entire sex act. His eyelids drooped to half mast, giving him the lazy, contented satiation of a predator finishing a delicious snack. Mixed among his pleasure, his face showed amazement and shell-shock. Her gaze landed on the large bulge under the zipper of his black jeans. Still aroused and ready.

Almost against her will, Erin licked her lips. If they'd been anywhere but a public place, how far would they have gone? The possibility horrified her. She must control herself.

Erin, who never stepped wrong when it came to safe sex and relationships, had allowed this big, hungry looking Scotsman to give her a shuddering, sweet orgasm.

Unfortunately, she still throbbed between her legs, a sure indication that the climax had only taken the edge off what promised to be a bigger explosion.

Erin could be happy about it. Instead she started to cry.

She turned and made a beeline for the bathroom.

* * * * *

Erin took five minutes to stamp down her tears and take a deep breath. As she looked into the mirror she didn't recognize the face gazing back at her. Hell, no. This woman was wanton, satisfied, and not as distressed as she should be.

"I'm crazy. I'm losing it." She pressed her palms against her hot cheeks. "God, Erin, *what did you do?* Are you totally out of your mind?"

Part of her wanted more of the same. Another part of her said she'd stepped into a dangerous situation with her stupidity.

She knew little about Lachlan Tavish, even if he was friends with Gilda and her husband.

And how had he cured her damn headache?

No time to waste right now. You've got to get back upstairs with the kids.

She wiped her eyes with toilet paper and left the bathroom. To her chagrin, Lachlan stood near the same bookshelves where they'd engaged in their little tryst.

Lachlan approached, his stride confident. She stiffened in reaction. When he stopped near her, she wondered if he planned to kiss her again.

This time he kept his distance, looking worried. "Are you all right? Did I frighten you?"

"Yes. No."

His frown melted, replaced by a teasing grin. "Yes, you're all right, and no, I didn't frighten you?"

She took a huge breath. "Yes." She shook her head. "Look, Mr. Tavish, I don't know what happened a few moments ago."

He lifted one imperial eyebrow. "You don't? It seems clear to me. We got a little carried away. Nothing has ever happened to me like that before."

Erin couldn't repress a small snort of disbelief. "Right."

She saw the fire in the center of his eyes brighten at her challenge. "You think I go around *snogging* with women I've just met?"

His British expression for kissing would have amused her if she hadn't been the one he'd *snogged* between the book selves of a public library.

She shrugged. "You call that *just snogging?* We don't know each other well enough to do whatever...whatever that was."

Another irreverent grin crossed his mobile mouth. "Okay. We did more than kiss. It was hot and incredible. I may not understand it, but I won't deny how it felt." His voice dropped to a husky whisper, and he captured her eyes again. She felt that wave of dizziness again, and almost reached out to clasp his arm for support. "And I can't deny that I want to do it again, very soon."

Before Erin could form a reply, the front door of the library swung open and in stepped Kathleen Melville, the local gossip. Until she'd moved here Erin hadn't realized every small town possessed at least one woman or man who gossiped the way Kathleen did. The middle-aged woman's salt and pepper hair floated about her head in a static-induced panic. Her open coat showed a black turtleneck sweater with an orange pumpkin on it and blue jeans.

"Gawd, I'm late again." She towed her niece Debbie behind her. The ten year old looked bored. "Deb, honey, go on upstairs. Mrs. Greenway is probably—"

When she saw Erin and Lachlan standing not that far from each other, her mouth dropped open. Erin realized how the situation might appear, and she moved away from Lachlan and toward Kathleen and Debbie.

"Kathleen, it's great to see you. Glad you and Debbie could make it. Come this way," Erin said.

Before they could make it two steps, the door opened again and several kids and parents piled through in a noisy group. Laughing and talking, the gaggle greeted Erin and Kathleen. As soon as the kids noticed Lachlan, he entertained them with vampire antics. He made them laugh and they seemed to like him immediately. Their parents gathered around and asked him questions; his accent became a big topic of discussion.

As Erin and Kathleen started up the stairs, Kathleen looked back at Lachlan. It appeared the Scot was amusing a six-year-old boy with an explanation about his sharp teeth.

"How do you brush those things?" the kid asked.

Kathleen laughed and Erin didn't hear Lachlan's response.

Okay, clever guy. How do you answer that one?

"Who *is* that man?" Kathleen asked, her voice a tad breathless as she glanced back at him.

"Which one?"

Kathleen sighed. "Don't give me that. The only man in the room, ninny. The tall, dark, and supremely dangerous-looking fellow with the creature-from-the-graveyard get up and the killer smile."

With a breezy reply she hoped hid her thoughts, Erin said, "He's a friend of Gilda and Tom's in town on a short visit. He's helping out this evening."

"Uh-huh." Kathleen didn't sound convinced. "Think he'll stick around?"

"Don't know." Erin didn't want to sound peevish, but she also didn't want to contribute to Kathleen's gossip column or to get her hopes up. Kathleen spent three fourths of her time on the lookout for husband number three. "How's work at the Sentinel?"

"Oh, peachy," Kathleen said with a mocking tone. "My boss, Malcomb, thinks I should stop being a features columnist and start doing some investigative reporting on this serial throat-sucker."

Erin almost tripped on the stair, but clasped the banister. "Serial throat sucker? What's he think it is, El Chupacabra?"

"El Chupa- what?"

Erin knew she shouldn't have said anything. "You know, the creature sighted in places like Puerto Rico and Mexico. The one they call the goat sucker."

Kathleen nodded. "Oh, yeah, *that* thing. Way up here in Colorado? I don't think so."

"Well, you don't believe in stuff like that anyway, do you?"

"'Course I do. Always have. Good, Gawd, you have to if you live here." They reached the top of the stairs and Kathleen patted her on the shoulder. "You haven't been here long enough to be affected by this place. Just you wait, it'll happen."

Erin decided to ignore Kathleen's assurances. "But your boss wants you to write an article about this...this...sucker thing? Can't it just be a nut running around? I mean, the woman who was attacked didn't say anything about a monster."

Kathleen held up her hands. "You don't have to convince me. I might believe in ghosts, but I sure don't believe in vampires."

Vampires. Believe in vampires, Erin...

Erin scanned the area for anyone who might have whispered the words in her ear. Was it the strange voices she encountered outside the library? The evil voice she thought had called her name? Or could it be Lachlan's tender, husky voice urging her?

Flushing, she recalled Lachlan's voice urging her to come. Heat entered her stomach, arousal returning as a dim, but enticing memory of how Lachlan made her feel.

Kathleen said, "Malcomb believes the attacker will strike again."

Before Erin could comment, Kathleen joined the other kids and parents coming up the steps. Kathleen plopped down next to Jessie and they started talking.

Story hour went as planned, with several more families arriving in time to hear spine-tingling tales. Erin enjoyed watching the children's rapt expressions and the pleased smiles of the parents. She loved regaling them with stories, but in the back of her mind, she couldn't dislodge the thought of Lachlan. Had he left already? She drifted out of her story a couple of times and forced herself back.

More than once she wondered if the strange noises she heard earlier would reoccur, but nothing happened. How would she explain them to the parents and children? Tomorrow she'd tell head librarian, Fred Tyne, about the sounds. Maybe he would get the place inspected. If it turned out this creaky place harbored termites and might fall down around their heads at any moment, they needed to know about it.

After she finished the last ghost story, the parents and children thanked her and started to leave. It took less time for them to clear out than she expected. She followed Jessie and Kathleen downstairs and when she saw that Lachlan had left, Erin couldn't decide how she felt. Disappointment warred with relief. She didn't know if she could handle him right now.

Jessie left but Kathleen remained behind. "I think we should walk each other to our cars. With the weirdness going on lately it's not a bad idea."

"Sounds good. Let me get my stuff."

On the way out to the car, Erin made sure she glanced around at the property and house. She didn't see anyone lurking in the shadows, and she took her keys out and held them at the ready.

Kathleen's car sat next to Erin's, and before Kathleen and Debbie slid into her compact Kathleen said, "That man you were standing next to in the stacks tonight..."

Erin waited for her to finish, but she didn't. "Yes?"

"I know I said he looked delicious, but I'd be careful of him. He's a stranger and it pays to be cautious. Do you know when he first arrived in Pine Forest?"

Erin shrugged. "I'm not sure. He didn't say."

Skepticism crossed Kathleen's face. "I'll have him checked out. Danny would be interested in knowing a new guy is in town."

Kathleen's brother, Danny Fortesque, was a police officer for Pine Forest Police Department, and Kathleen tended to abuse his authority by getting him to do favors for her.

"I'm sure Lachlan is legit," Erin said, not sure why she defended him.

"You're on first name basis already?"

Kathleen's shocked tone yanked on Erin's strings. "I'm on first name basis with a lot of people here. This is a friendly town." She unlocked her car and opened the door. "This place is so affable even the ghosts come up on the first day and introduce themselves."

"They do?" Kathleen's niece asked.

Kathleen's chuckle sounded dubious. "No, honey, she's just teasing." She glared at Erin. "Be careful. He might be good-looking, but then so was Ted Bundy."

With that command, Kathleen rolled up her window and shot out of the parking lot. Erin slid into the driver's seat and made sure all the doors were locked. She stuck the key in the ignition.

A shadow passed over the top of the car. Huge, dark, and hovering.

Erin let out a startled squeak.

She tensed. The shade lingered over the car, turning the bleak night darker than before. Her fingers fumbled with the keys as she turned on the car. A sense of urgency and dread pursued her like a monster in a nightmare as she jammed the car into reverse, then roared forward out of the parking lot. As Erin barreled down the road, she couldn't shake the sensation that as she put distance between her and the library, that someone still watched her.

* * * * *

As the vampire observed Erin leave the parking lot, the car screeching as rubber spun on asphalt and rocks, he felt no regret. She knew something was wrong, but not with any true understanding. If she did she would leave this town and run as far and as fast as she could. He thought about initiating her tonight, but as in centuries past, he waited for the right woman to realize how much she craved sex. He preyed on that need like a hyena on carrion. He would build the fear and the need for sexual release until she gave into her most unholy desires.

He savored her fear. Adrenaline worked like steak sauce, tenderizing and making people taste so much better. He licked his lips.

How wonderful that he found his reincarnated love in this little town with its strange tendencies. He could hide among all the other unusual beings that roamed the night...those in search of mischief, those wandering without purpose, and those with evil on their minds. Even the high mountain forest creatures avoided town; the people never had trouble with cougars or bears as many places this isolated often did. For the animals felt specters and would avoid them at all costs.

He, on the other hand, enjoyed seeing entities in every corner of town.

He knew the darkness so well; dwelling here for a few days gave him the flavor of the area and the lay of the land. Now that he knew where the next taste would come from, he also felt new hunger. He could have taken her this evening and she couldn't have resisted. No woman resisted him if he wanted her with him.

He saw an old woman nearby the library, walking alone on the sidewalk. He made tracks in her direction. He didn't feel like working hard to get satisfaction and food. Tonight he would put an old coot out of her misery.

As he made his way toward the woman, he felt her sudden apprehension. She couldn't see him, and yet she perceived danger. So few understood how when the night came down and they felt that prickle on the back of their neck...well, the premonition was often correct.

The Hunter would come here soon and hope to change things, to keep even old ladies safe, but he would fail this time as he did all other times.

Yes, he would make a lair and defeat The Hunter and any pitiful human who sought his demise. Then, if things went as planned, he would dine with or perhaps *on* Erin Greenway.

Chapter 4

Somewhere in Morocco

Ronan Kieran sniffed the night air as he took swift steps down the dark alley between the two story buildings. Spicy scents, a combination of old leather, camel hair, and sweaty bodies filled his nose. Not so different from his birthplace near Limerick.

Minus the camel hair, of course.

Earlier, in his hotel room, he thought about going back to the old sod and staying for awhile. He needed the break and a return to the familiar scent of peat and the green landscape more emerald than any place on earth. Ten years had passed since he'd visited Eire's beloved shores, and he missed the ancient land with a fierceness that should have called him back long ago.

Instead, he continued the chase that had taken him around the world more times than he could count. Maybe this time he'd obtain the information he required to rid the earth of a hidden, vicious plague.

Noises the average human ear couldn't detect assaulted his hearing from all sides. The howl of a dog far in the countryside, the long, drawn-out breath of a woman in a room nearby, the screech of a cat in throes of mating.

Fuck me. This bleeding country has more distractions than Prince Hamad's harem.

He smiled as he remembered his last trip to this region about sixty years ago amid a war-torn time. Prince Hamad was long gone, and so was the harem. Hamad had been a bastard, but a good friend nonetheless, until the ancient one came to this land in search of blood and destroyed Hamad and his harem in a frenzy of hate.

Ronan shoved back the vicious memories. No time to think about the past or that era when things seemed more defined.

Not that it had been a simpler era, but a slower one when even a vampire couldn't go from one continent to the next with as much speed or destructive force.

Ronan heard the shuffle of feet from the alley and braced his body for attack. A leisurely smile spread over his face. The murmur of a language he hadn't heard in a while reached his ears. An old babble that people in this country didn't understand, but Ronan did. Seconds later Ronan found himself in the clutches of a skinny arm that had more power than it should. An Irish Gaelic greeting reached his sensitive ears.

"*Ronan Ciaran,*" the hoarse whisper spoke his Gaelic name rather than the anglicized version. "What a weird name for a big man. Little seal black. Makes no soddin' sense to me. Did your mother realize you'd grow up to be a big, ugly lurch?"

Ronan grinned wider. "My mother was a small, angry woman. She named all her children strange things. I won't even tell you what she named my brother's. I think it was revenge for having to push us out of the womb."

Ronan knew he sounded a little bitter, but his mother had been a cast iron banshee from the word go.

Ronan's bizarre explanation of his mother's odd naming techniques made his attacker pause. With one lunge and a twist, Ronan flipped the smaller man over his shoulder. The man landed with a thud and a grunt on his back on cold, hard cobblestone.

"Jesus, Mary, and Joseph," the man gasped, then groaned. "Are you feckin' crazy? You've been eatin' your Wheaties again, I take it?"

"*Somhairle Dubhe.*" Ronan said the man's Gaelic name.

The smaller Irishman clad in robes stood quickly and faced the man who'd bested him.

Ronan grinned when his friend of two hundred and fifty years said nothing. Sorley might also be a bastard, but his loyalty was unquestioned. His sentences sometimes came out sounding oddly backwards, but Ronan always knew what he meant. Although Sorley had only been a vampire for about three hundred years, the Irishman knew things much older vampires didn't. He also knew when to give Ronan space.

Sorley grinned back, his golden flecked blue eyes glowing like a cat's in the midnight darkness. "Aren't you going to tell me to take you to my leader?"

"Shit, no. You don't have a leader. Though maybe you should."

"Come on, then. Sure, and Yusuf is dyin' to meet you." The wiry Irishman kept his accent, even though he'd lived in Morocco for twenty years. "He wants you to say hello to his daughter Selima."

Ronan laughed, something he should do more often. His lungs felt rusty. *Came from too much time in dusty highways and byways.* "You're not serious."

"I bloody well am." Sorley walked ahead of Ronan, steering through the almost pitch blackness.

Not as if Ronan needed the direction, for this area hadn't changed in sixty years. He would have found the place nonetheless. "Is she pretty?"

Sorley snorted. "Pretty doesn't quite describe her, lad."

Lad. Right. I'm older than you.

Only by a hundred years. Sorley's mind whispered to Ronan's in the way of two vampires who'd known each other since the seventeen hundreds. *Now don't be starin' at her the way you do.*

What way is that?

That way. You know. All dreamy and romantic and like. Here's the thing, Ronan boy. The old man won't take kindly to it. And he knows enough about vampires to kill you twenty times over without so much as blinkin' a feckin' eye. Why, he told me last week about this one well-hung vampire that tried to romance his wife Atella. He cut the nuts off —

I get the picture, Sorley. You don't have to draw me a map.

Sorley laughed, the noise grating on Ronan's sensitive ears.

Another twist in the labyrinth alley, and they came to a small wooden door. Ronan would have to stoop to enter. The door swung open before Sorley could knock, swinging open on rusty, creaking hinges.

A little man, barely five feet tall, stood in the doorway. Ronan caught the power in the small man's personality right away and felt it down to the soles of his feet like an electric shock wave. *A blocking spell.* Ronan knew that old hunters like this one built up a resistance to a vampire's charms and power. This guy looked almost one hundred but was probably sixty. Still, the man's gaze held a sharpness that belied his used up and dry appearance. His wrinkled, almost flaky skin said the desert climate drained his reserves with each passing year.

"Come in. Don't just stand there. I can hardly see you, damn my old eyes." Yusuf pulled back from the doorway and they followed him.

Ronan knew that Yusuf lied through his yellowing teeth. Clear sight and intelligence shone in his eyes as he waited for Sorley and Ronan to enter his abode.

Ronan nodded and bent at the knees so he could enter without bashing his head. "Yusuf." He held his hand out in greeting. "I'm pleased to meet you. I've heard a lot about you."

Yusuf cracked a smile as he led them further into the nooks and crannies of the small, crowded home. They passed one room where several toddlers played with three young women. Ronan glanced at the dark-haired, olive-skinned women and saw their eyes widen into big circles. He smiled and proceeded, heeding Sorley's earlier warning about Yusuf.

He needed his balls and didn't plan to lose them any time soon.

Despite the fact he hadn't felt a woman's hot, wet channel around his cock in almost six months, he didn't seduce innocent girls with his extraordinary abilities. He could make it good for any one of the women in that room, but he didn't want the complications that could come with it just so he could indulge in pleasure. Finding a blood-thirsty vampire must be first priority.

As he passed the room, he heard the human women whispering among themselves.

"Vampires," a sultry female voice said. "How does Uncle dare bring them in here?"

A high voice answered. "Uncle said they are harmless."

"No vampire is harmless," a softer voice said.

"Did you see the tall, dark-haired one? His hair is rich with copper, yet shimmering like black fire. And those eyes. So dark you can't see the bottom," the first voice said. "How beautiful he is."

"He was delicious," the soft one said. "I wonder if Uncle Yusuf would allow — ?"

"Don't even think it. He intends Selima for the vampire."

The soft voice came again. "But will the beautiful one help her?"

Ronan stiffened his spine, winching at the thought. Damn Sorley. He bet the little weasel told Yusuf Ronan would fuck the newly made vampire and liberate her from pain. A maiden turned into a vampire must have a good humping to release her powers. Without that, she would eventually starve to death, unable to bite a human neck or drink blood, yet unable to consume human food. Even a newly made vampire woman who'd experienced pleasures of the flesh before would need sexual loving to prevent severe pain from immobilizing her.

Damn it, Sorley. If you've —

It was a condition of tellin' you how to slay the ancient one. Don't get your briefs in a wad.

Ronan wanted to clamp his hands around Sorley's lily-white, scrawny neck and choke the life out of him. Instead, he shook his head. He didn't relish initiating a virgin, but he might not have a choice.

Yusuf brought them into a larger room laced with the potent smell of incense. Around the room were shelves piled high with weapons — some of them stolen, no doubt. Yusuf might be honorable, but he wouldn't quibble on every principal when it came to keeping his family safe. A huge carpet, expensive for the abode, lay in the center of the room. Probably a payment for ridding a sheik of a vampire infestation. Piled high with the silken, overstuffed pillows, the area had the festive air of a place ready for a party. Containers of drink stood near a silver tray holding cups.

"Come." Yusuf gestured toward the pillows. "Make yourself comfortable. We'll talk and eat and drink."

Ronan's stomach growled. Since he'd stopped drinking human blood centuries ago, his stomach required human food. "Thank you."

They feasted in silence for some time, and then Ronan became a little impatient. "We must know how to kill the ancient one. What can you tell us?"

Yusuf popped a piece of spiced meat into his mouth. "Vampire, you grow impatient."

"Don't call me that." Ronan spoke without vehemence, but he didn't like being reminded of his eternal state. "My name is Ronan Kieran."

Yusuf's face, as wrinkled as a pug's, broke into a smile. "Ronan. A strong name for a warrior. There was a time, not so long ago, I would have hunted you rather than invited you into my home. You are blessed to have lasted so long."

Sorley held up his goblet and made a toasting motion. "Damn glad we are of that. By the way, this wine is almost better than ale. Got any more?"

Yusuf didn't flinch at the bold vampire's lack of manners. The old man poured Sorley another cup full of the red liquid.

"Would you rather it was blood?" Yusuf asked.

Sorley flinched. "No, indeed. You know better than that. Quit stallin' now, and tell my friend what he needs to know. It's urgent. What can he do to kill the ancient one?"

The old man seemed a little amazed, then covered his astonishment with anger. "Your lack of manners is abominable. Have you no shame? "

"None the feckin' at all," Sorley said as he smacked his lips.

Ronan gave his friend a hard, level glare. "Mind your behavior, Irishman. Yusuf might decide to stake you yet."

After slurping down another heavy draught of wine, Sorley's attention went to the steel-eyed expression on Yusuf. "Yeah. Yeah, you're right. Sorry. I forgot."

Soon after the wrinkled man told Ronan the bad news, Yusuf grinned widely and said, "A vampire will have to sacrifice himself to save a human from the ancient one."

Wary of this information, Ronan took a long time questioning. He sipped more wine. "Sacrifice how?"

Yusuf leaned back into his cushions. "A battle of wills. You are one of the strongest vampires on earth."

Ronan acknowledged he could kick most vampires into the next century without much effort, but the ancient one would be the exception. "Not strong enough to kill the ancient one. That's why I'm here. Are you saying I'd have to sacrifice *myself* in a fight to the death?"

"No one has the perfect answer on how to kill the ancient one, but there is talk that love might be the only thing strong enough to slay him."

"What?" Ronan and Sorley asked at the same time.

"Love," Yusuf said.

Ronan scoffed at the idea. "I love no one. Least of all a blood sucking killer."

"You don't love your friends?" Yusuf asked.

Ronan shifted on his cushions and propped up one knee. He rested his arm upon it and stared at the plain earthenware goblet in his hand. "My affection for my friends runs deep."

The man smiled, showing his crooked teeth again. He scratched at his white beard. "This will not be enough. The love of a woman must sustain you."

Sorley's narrow, pock-marked face twitched into a smile, and he laughed. "Weird idea, I say. You really expect us to believe that?"

Ronan slugged back the last of his drink, then stood and placed the goblet on a rickety wood table near the carpeted area. "And I think you're telling me this crap because you don't have a *real* answer for how to kill the ancient one."

With a smug smile that spoke of satisfaction, the vampire hunter said, "And why would I bother? What would be the point? If I angered you enough, you could just kill me. You are a very powerful vampire."

Sorley groaned. "Now he's tryin' to flatter you."

Yusuf's superior expression faded a bit. "Why would I do that?"

Ronan stood over the wrinkled man, careful not to move with preternatural speed and make the vampire slayer think he meant to attack. "You know my word is my honor and that I promised to come here to listen. You really wanted me to screw your daughter and couldn't think of another way to get me here."

At first the coot kept blank faced, but Ronan saw cunning flick through the white-robed man eyes. "Now that is a fine idea. I wish I'd actually thought of it. I say again, in the presence of one—nay two—strong vampires, it would be folly."

Ronan had enough. "More bullshit, Yusuf. You have a blocking spell in place. You invited us inside your home, but you put in place the spell first. Sorley and I could barely put a dent in your leathery hide. Now, unless you have more to tell us—"

"Wait." With a creaky groan the vampire hunter stood, walked past Sorley, then reached for the wine tankard. He poured more drink into his own goblet. "Your mind is shut against the worship of woman, but love can find you when you least want it. If it comes to you, it will give you the final strength you need to defeat the ancient one."

A fleeting memory of one elfin blonde pierced his memory. A thought so buried in the past it lived in the dust of time. "Love has eluded me." He shoved the painful thought back where it belonged. "It will never come again."

Yusuf gave a weary sigh and looked at Sorley. "Your friend has much to learn, despite his many years as a vampire."

Sorley snorted. "Tell me about it."

With a disgusted glance at Sorley, Ronan growled, "What would be the purpose in loving a woman?"

Yusfuf contemplated Ronan with serious, sorrowful eyes. "You must give the illusion of love in hope it will grow real if you cannot feel real love. Otherwise you will be defeated."

"So I just pick out some unwitting woman and pretend I love her?"

"That is the way of it." Before Ronan could refute the older man's statement, Yusuf continued. "Now you must pay for this information. Selima is in the next room. We will listen to make sure you don't deceive us."

"Us?" Ronan's eyebrows went up.

With a dry cackle, the old man slapped his knee. "Sorley, get out. My daughter and Ronan must copulate."

Copulate.

Ronan hated that word, despised the fact that human vampire hunters still taunted their vampire cohorts with that bestial description for a vampire mating.

"The shit one does for information, eh, Ronan?" Sorley chuckled. He stood and headed toward the door. "I'll be outside waitin'. Don't take too long."

Ronan almost threw his drink at Sorley. "Of all the vampires you know, you pick me to take her virginity?"

The old man shook his head, a solemn expression erasing all triumph. "You know this man's heart broke when the ancient one took my Selima across to the shadows."

Shadows. Over hundreds of years Ronan fought that evil place. He didn't want to copulate with Selima, but if he didn't he might sentence her to a withering death.

"She must be taken now or she will die. She will not even be undead if you do not take her virginity. She will wither to ashes and be truly dead once and for all." With trembling fingers Yusuf gripped Ronan's forearm. "She may be undead, but at least she will be alive to her family. Give her what she needs."

"I know how it works, Yusuf," Ronan said with a sense of inevitability. Ronan couldn't believe a man would rather his daughter be a vampire than to allow her to die in peace.

Ronan closed his eyes and sighed heavily. He couldn't refuse.

As Ronan headed toward the next room, he wondered if Selima would be beautiful or as plain as could be. In the end it wouldn't matter. He should feel sympathy for young Selima and knew her days would be fraught with misery for years as she learned her place in this eternal life of the undead.

Hardened to the facts, Ronan pulled back the curtain and joined Selima.

* * * * *

Erin tossed and turned, her night disturbed by dreams of a dark-haired man whose face she couldn't quite see. His hands floated over her body, tantalizing her with promises of sensual delights and long evenings filled with heart-stopping ecstasy.

You cannot resist me, Erin. I am the one.

She moaned as a fire built between her legs, promising a new climax.

Then, something unholy and disturbing intruded on the pleasure and a harsh voice screamed in her ear.

No!

Erin awoke and sat bolt upright in bed. Dull sunlight arrowed between the slats of the wooden shutters on her bedroom window. Her heart pounded as fear rolled in her gut. Another dull headache started at her temples, and she decided aspirin might be the only solution.

Her small digital alarm clock started playing country music and she started in surprise. She reached over to turn it off. As the chill air in the bedroom took hold, she flopped back against her pillows and burrowed under the covers. Desire left over from the dream thrummed through her body in glorious waves, and she closed her eyes and sighed. Erin supposed a person could be frightened and excited all at one time. The combination of fear and shattering desire left her weak.

How could something so decadent and unsavory feel so wonderful?

Decadent, unsavory? Since when had sex become dirty to her? She'd never been a prude, but maybe her wild sexual awakening experience last night with Lachlan generated guilty feelings. Stupidity had never been her game. She didn't play with men for pleasure. Two lovers in her entire life didn't qualify her for adventurous status. She certainly didn't do the wild thing without believing herself in love.

A picture of Mike Tottenham filtered into her thoughts. Her college best friend and supporter for three years was also her first lover. Mike was a virgin, too, the first time they slept with each other.

Then, years later, came Rick. Rick used and abused her love, and she didn't think about him much after six years. Maybe the drought in her love life sent her into a mating frenzy last night. In any case, she wouldn't be so stupid again, no matter how mesmerizing the intriguing Mr. Tavish seemed.

The phone rang and she jumped again, and she put her hand on her chest. Demanding a response, the phone continued to ring until on the third chime she picked it up. She snuggled under the covers again.

"Hi, darling."

"Mom?"

Her mother's gentle laugh came over the line. "Who else is brave enough to call you this early in the morning?"

"Only you."

"This seems to be the time to catch you. I tried calling last night and got your answering device."

Device sounded like something unforgivable, like breaking a commandment.

"Why didn't you leave a message on the machine?"

"You know how much I hate those things."

Erin restrained the urge to sigh. In fact, Marilyn Greenway rebelled against most new things, including e-mail, the Internet, and what she deemed loose morals. Somehow she managed to lump anything she didn't agree with into one giant cesspool called depravity.

"Darling," her mother started, "we haven't heard from you in a week. Dad and I were worried."

"Why?" Erin knew the answer, but decided to play dumb.

"We always worry about you in that town. I mean, you're hundreds of miles from home, and you don't know anyone there."

Damn you, mother. Don't start with that lame argument again.

"We talked about this before, Mom. This is a small town and generally very safe."

"But you don't know anyone there." A whining edge crept into her mother's voice.

Erin took a deep breath. "I've made several friends already."

Including a big, handsome, exciting Scotsman who makes me hot. How do you like them apples, Mom?

Somehow *friend* didn't quite describe her relationship with the mysterious man, but she wouldn't tell her mother that.

"We heard about those horrible attacks on those women. You can't tell me that town is safe with that going on," her mother said.

Erin glanced at the clock and saw that if she didn't get a move on, her mother's call would make her late for work. "I'm being sensible. There's no need to be overly concerned. You're going to give yourself an ulcer."

"At least give us a call more than once a week. We want to make sure everything is all right."

Erin asserted her boundaries. "I'll call as often as I can, Mom. Sometimes it gets busy at the library, and I've been working some overtime." Itching to end the conversation, she said, "I've got to go. I want to be at work early this morning before the library actually opens."

After her mother hung up some time later, clearly not pleased that Erin didn't plan to run home to Arizona, Erin set the receiver back into the cradle and stared at the phone in half triumph and a little disgust. She felt proud she hadn't allowed her mother to run over her, but fighting the woman in every phone conversation became tiresome.

Erin jumped into the shower. As she toweled off a short time later, she glanced in the mirror at her body. As every mirror was, it showed an unforgiving picture. She'd heard that you should love your body for what it was, but she found fault every time she looked. Then again, most women didn't like what they saw when they took a peek in the mirror. Not that her body held excess fat, but she didn't like her proportions. Her breasts were not exactly small or large, so she was satisfied with them. Her waist was small, but her hips flared more than she would like.

Her thighs never firmed up much, no matter how hard she exercised. Cellulite managed to find her.

Her narrow shoulders and collar bone looked delicate enough to snap. She traced her hands over her arms, then down over her chest as she did her breast exam. As she explored, she closed her eyes. It helped her concentrate.

A fog filled her thoughts, sudden and drugging. She swayed on her feet as she imagined Lachlan's hands in place of hers, warm and appreciative. He did a quick sweep over her breasts, then his fingers cupped over those rounded hips and warmed the outside of her thighs. He didn't care about cellulite.

Beautiful.

The word whispered in her mind, and the splendor of his appreciation made another longing tremor prickle in her body.

Up, up, his hands explored over her hips and then around to cup her butt cheeks. He squeezed and she felt that touch deep in her cunt. "Oh!"

Oh, my God. It felt like her womb contracted.

Deep, sexual desire blossomed with amazing quickness.

As Lachlan's fingers reached her nipples they tweaked with a gentle pluck that sent a lightning bolt sensation between her legs. She quivered and gasped in surprise. Soft, exciting desire slipped over her body, tingling like a mini fire in her blood. It almost tickled. Wandering hands circled and rotated all around her breasts until they came to her nipples again. Tender pressure built as he cupped her fully in each hand, then leaned forward and flicked one nipple with his tongue. She moaned softly and her eyes snapped open.

Gazing in the mirror, she trembled. Stunned by the realistic feelings, she couldn't look away. What she saw in the mirror didn't show the woman she'd known all these years. A hot flush covered her neck and then her face and unexpected trickling moisture started between her legs.

She inhaled deeply and tried to return to reality.

Did I imagine Lachlan's touch and voice?

Erin rubbed her hands over her cheeks in frustration. Now she'd let her imagination take complete control. Ridiculous. The next thing she knew, she'd picture him in full naked glory with his cock sunk deep inside her.

No. She shook her head and finished toweling her hair. Now she knew her brain had gone around the bend.

A man like Lachlan was knee-buckling powerful. Overtly sexual. Too *everything* for a woman like her.

"I'm better off with someone like Danny Fortesque, the cop."

She chuckled. Maybe not. Danny didn't exactly blow her skirt up.

Later, as she ate yogurt and coffee, she wondered why one gorgeous man could occupy so much of her thoughts.

She turned her musings away from Lachlan and back to her family. Despite their best effort to keep her from it, Erin wanted reality with a thirst and desire that nagged at her every day. Leaving Arizona had been one of the ways she'd asserted her independence, a long overdue move that she wished she'd accomplished years ago. She'd be damned if her mother would suck her back into total insecurity again.

No dwelling on the past. The future stands before me.

She turned on the radio and listen to local news as she finished puttering in the kitchen. She tossed the yogurt container into the trash when the announcer's words froze her to the spot.

"Late last night Mrs. Eliza Pickles was assaulted near the library. Police are withholding many details at this time, but it's suspected that robbery was not the motive since her purse wasn't stolen."

A dark, worrisome apprehension coursed through Erin. "Oh, my God."

She didn't have much use for Eliza Pickles. Erin went into the older woman's antique store once and learned she didn't care for the woman's I-know-more-than-you-about-anything attitude or her puritanical ideas. Yet she never would have wished something that horrible to happen to the old lady.

"Police say that as soon as more details become available there will be a press conference."

Erin stared at a spot on the floor, shocked as she acknowledged that maybe her own premonition of fear last night hadn't been so far off. Then another hideous thought came to mind. Lachlan Tavish knew it wasn't safe near the library. What if he was the culprit? Had she been kissing a madman?

Suddenly the illicit memory of his lips on hers no longer tantalized her. She stood without moving, her fear trying to rise over common sense. Perhaps she should tell the police about Lachlan's warning of danger.

She wanted to build her new future here in Pine Forest, seductive Scotsman not withstanding. If Lachlan showed up again, she'd be sure to contact the police with her suspicions.

With her feet planted firmly in reality, she left for work.

Chapter 5

From the quiet in the library, the vampire thought he heard a breath a hundred feet away. He watched the children playing, a few of them looking about as if they might feel his presence. He smiled.

Poor little tykes couldn't see him. He'd made sure his shields stayed too strong for detection. It wouldn't serve his purposes for sensitive children to notice him and run screaming down the stairs. Never mind the adults wouldn't believe the children, it still made a commotion and broke his serenity.

In silence, so the most inquisitive child wouldn't even imagine a whisper of his sound, he moved toward the main stairway. As he glided, he wondered how humans stood being so anemic with their weak hearing and weaker muscles. Before immortality his life had seemed pleasant enough, but the things he saw, knew, felt...ah, yes. Everything he could achieve now outweighed all regrets for a mortal life.

Blood.

He required blood like humans needed oxygen. Without blood he transformed to the dead, no longer the undead, but a rot in the bowels of the earth. He became nothing more than human.

In that moment he was more than thankful for the one who'd brought him over and transformed the end of his life. For, in his present state, he could do and be anything he wanted, any time he wished.

As he watched Erin from his hiding place between the pale rays of light illuminating the room, he wondered if he'd waited too long to possess her. He'd considered tantalizing her in her dreams, when she would be most defenseless. Instead he stayed in the shadows, in the quiet corners of this library and watched the comings and goings of the oblivious. Humans continued to disgust him more than ever.

Except for Erin.

She gave him a special light, a dawn appreciation for the humanity he'd never had, even before he became undead. Oh, he knew it. He realized his civilization fled long ago. Before Dasoria had been staked by humans and taken from him…before he became the undead himself.

He didn't care. Mortals abhorred all he stood for, and yet craved his darkness in the most rudimentary parts of their brains. In their most twisted dreams, they loved him and the mystery he brought to their lives. They envisioned him as a blood sucker much like fabled Dracula, yet they failed miserably in their assumptions. How awful, how terrified they'd become, if they knew his true form. He sighed, content for the moment to watch, to prey, to stalk.

With a smile he watched Erin and waited.

* * * * *

"Did you hear?" Gilda asked Erin as she greeted her in the library's small employee lounge. "About Mrs. Pickles?"

Erin hung her coat in the closet and reached for a mug. "Yes. Horrible news."

Gilda's long, red hair fell forward as she looked down to stir powered cream into her coffee. Freckles stood out on her long nose. Her soft voice, touched with nuances of her upbringing in Savannah, Georgia, made her sound gracious and refined no matter the situation. "It was in the Sentinel this morning that she was attacked late last night near this block of the street."

Erin almost dropped her mug, and hot coffee splashed onto the counter. "I know. It's very strange. Gives me the creeps, as you can see."

"I guess she was coming home from her bridge game over at Bethany Segal's house. Walking instead of driving, I understand. I don't know why any woman in this town would consider walking that late at night."

Erin thought back to when she'd left the library. "What time was the attack?"

"Ten-thirty." Gilda sighed. "Would *you* be out that late all by yourself?"

Discomfort ran through Erin. She'd left the library earlier than ten-thirty, but she recalled that unsettling feeling when she imagined a dark shadow hovering above her. "Probably not."

"You know that group of old ladies. They're like true party animals." Gilda poured the rest of her coffee into the small sink. "Apparently she's in Governor's Hospital."

Trying to calm the alarm in her mind, Erin took a sip of hot, black coffee. "How bad is she?"

"She's in a coma. Her daughter reported that she lost a lot of blood. In fact, they may move her to a larger hospital out of town."

Erin put her mug on the small lounge table and rubbed her temple. A headache started in her forehead already. "When I heard it on the radio this morning they didn't give details. Was she bitten on the neck like the other woman?"

Gilda's reddish brown eyebrows tilted up. "Bingo."

Erin sighed, her stomach lurching with a sickness that had nothing to do with black coffee. "That's sick."

"Well, there are a lot of sickos in the world."

Erin knew this, but it didn't make the reality any more palatable.

"I'm sorry I wasn't here to help you to reopen the library last night," Gilda said. "Was everything all right? With Mark's accident—"

Waving one hand in dismissal, Erin said, "It's no problem. I understand entirely. And thanks for sending Lachlan."

Maybe the initial stress of moving to Pine Forest had rotted her brain. Moving to a new place could do that to a person, and the stress might make them crack and do things they'd never think of doing any other time. She couldn't get the feeling of Lachlan's touch, real and imagined, out of her mind.

If he had behaved roughly or cruelly, she wouldn't be attracted to him. Instead he'd treated her like a goddess, one to be honored and loved. Even the words she'd heard whispered in her head had been tender and reverent. If she thought about it too long, she realized a caring feeling for him—potent and mind-boggling—rose up inside her.

No, she couldn't have feelings for a man she knew nothing about beyond a few minor details. She felt lust, but that didn't signal happiness came around the corner. *Yet there you have it, Erin. You're interested in him whether you like it or not.*

Still, it didn't mean she had to do anything about it. Especially not when she didn't know if she could trust him.

Sure, she'd become carried away with Lachlan, but if she saw him again she would pretend, with dignity intact, that she hadn't almost climbed his body and done the animal thing.

"He seems great with kids," Erin said with reluctant admiration.

Gilda's face turned sad. "He always talked about wanting a family, but he can't seem to find the right woman for him."

Erin made a disbelieving noise. "I find it hard to believe women aren't swarming all over him. You should have seen how the ladies reacted to him last night."

You should see how I reacted to him last night.

"He's a quiet sort of guy and not too gregarious with people he doesn't know. And you're right, women do flock to him."

"He seemed fairly talkative last night."

Gilda's grin held satisfaction. "I'm glad you had a chance to meet him."

Erin knew what her matchmaking friend planned, and as they headed out of the break-room and into the main room, Erin said, "Oh, no you don't. Remember the last time you tried to set me up?"

"Baker Kinsley. How could I forget him?"

Erin didn't want to even think about the pretentious guy Gilda's husband Tom had introduced her to at a dinner party three weeks ago. "What a disaster."

"You've only been in town about a month. We want you to feel welcome. You know Tom never would have introduced you to Baker if he'd realized the man was an octopus."

Well, Lachlan had been all over her. Yet, when he touched her, she felt no revulsion. Only startling, one-hundred percent fiery desire.

Erin nodded. "Every time I see Baker in town he gives me this greasy smile and I want to gag. Besides, I'm not interested in dating right now."

Gilda sighed. "You're certain?"

"I think I'm through with love for a long time."

"You're only twenty-nine. You've got plenty of time to find the man of your dreams."

"Maybe, but I'm not counting on it. I'm a realist."

"You mean a pessimist." Gilda started work behind the front desk. "Lachlan isn't like Baker, you know. Lachlan is a peach."

Erin chuckled. "He's the farthest thing from a peach I've ever seen. All hard angles and darkness and…"

With a twinkle in her eyes, Gilda grinned. "Yes? Go on."

Erin shrugged. "I don't know. He's just not a softie."

"The man works out religiously and is otherwise very active. But he has a gentle side."

He'd been gentle with her last night, even if his touch and actions had bordered on ravenous, intent, and determined to fuck her. Heat flamed in her face. He'd wanted her in no uncertain terms. Even she couldn't deny that.

Erin's throat went so tight she thought she'd choke. "He's imposing."

"Did he scare you?" Gilda asked Erin as she removed a few new hardbacks from a box and sat them on the front counter. "He's so unusually handsome that some women expect him to be conceited and shallow. They never give him a chance."

"No, of course he didn't scare me." Erin lied. Gilda wouldn't understand the strange hypnotic effect Lachlan produced in her. "I just didn't expect a vampire to attend story time. That and he told me I should be careful when I left the library last night."

"That means he cares."

Erin didn't want to offend Gilda by disparaging her friend, so she didn't tell her that she'd considered Lachlan a suspect in the attacks.

A patron interrupted, and Erin started other work. The library, with its vast, high ceilings and hundreds of books, looked peaceful and the slightest bit mysterious. Unlike last night, Erin didn't feel as if a boogie man might be hiding around the corner.

Not that you did last night, either. Ghosts don't exist in this library, nor do they exist anywhere else in Pine Forest.

People allowed tall tales and superstitions to get out of hand, and before they knew it, they created a mass hallucination. She reminded herself to keep focused on these thoughts and she wouldn't get caught up in the same fallacies.

She also wouldn't keep thinking about the crazy experiences she'd encountered last night, and the man who'd made her so wild and hot she'd combusted in his arms.

Erin. Erin, I'm here. The voice inside her head whispered softly. *You can't see me, but I see you.*

A chuckle followed, and she peered around in case someone might be on the other side of the counter, crouched down and having a joke at her expense. She peered over the counter. No one there.

Come to me, Erin, when the night deepens. Come to me.

The masculine voice rippled through her like a drug, making her feel sluggish and almost ill. *Lachlan?* No, it couldn't be. Besides, this voice sounded different. She scanned the room again. No one appeared to be paying attention to her. To say the voice gave her the willies would be an understatement. She steeled her determination not to allow her imagination too much freedom.

After Gilda finished with the patron, she turned back to Erin and lowered her voice. "Lachlan worked on his parents' estate in Scotland. He's quite rich, you know."

Erin didn't blink over the news. "Lots of people are rich. Am I supposed to be impressed?"

Gilda gave her a pained look. "Of course not. I just want you to understand him. About a year and a half ago the estate burned to the ground. All that's left is rubble. And that's not the worst of it. His parents were killed in the fire."

"Oh, my God." Erin's throat tightened as she imagined their horrific fate. Her headache intensified and her heart ached for Lachlan. She rubbed her temples. "That's terrible."

"We can tell it has changed him. You should have seen him before the fire when we first met him. You think he's dark and mysterious? He was full of life and good humor before his parents were killed. The dark edge you're talking about only happened after the fire."

After that, work became so busy Gilda didn't get an opportunity to tell her anything more about Lachlan. Erin didn't think she wanted to know.

Later that day, on her lunch break in the employee lounge, Erin told Fred about the creaking and groaning noises she'd heard the night before. Fred paced the room, his white hair sticking up like Alfred Einstein's hairdo.

He tapped his chin with his index finger and then adjusted his silver rimmed eyeglasses. If anyone fit the stereotype of the brainy but spacey librarian, this man did. "You don't say. That's weird."

She sighed. "I'm worried about the structural integrity of the place."

He stopped halfway across the floor and turned back to her. His skinny frame seemed to hunch, as if the weight of his thoughts burdened him. "It could be the ghosts."

Erin groaned. "Not more ghosts. What is it with this town? I've never heard anything so ludicrous—"

He held a hand up for silence. "I know, I know. There are a lot of people out there who claim to have a ghost in residence. They'd feel left out if they couldn't at least make believe. After all, Pine Forest has a reputation to uphold. We've been featured on that program, *Mysteries of the Supernatural,* and a half dozen fiction authors have written books with our town as a background."

"Well, that's the first time I've heard anyone admit that the ghosts are just a big publicity stunt."

"No, no." He shook his head and paced again. "Not a stunt. Many of the ghosts are real. Take this library, for instance. You know the history of the place and the two murders and three suicides that occurred here before the town converted it to a library. We've got the genuine article." He put his hands on his hips. "And the clanking you heard last night is something people have been complaining about for about...oh, I'd say...thirty-four years."

"Thirty-four years," she said in disbelief.

He sank into a chair at the little table near her. "Since about the time the place was turned in to a library. I think one of the ghosts is in a permanent snit over the whole thing."

As she chewed her last bite of roast beef sandwich, she closed her eyes. *Just great. The place could be structurally unsound and Fred is going to use ghosts as an excuse?*

As if he could read her mind, he said, "But not to worry. I'll get Bud to check it out. Talk to you later."

With that he left the room and Erin with her conflicted feelings.

Bud, a reclusive janitor, didn't often show his face except to clean up the library and do general grunt work. If he were qualified to check the building's safety, she'd eat her new winter boots.

She returned to work a short time later, but within fifteen minutes a different interruption occurred. Officer Danny Fortesque, his dull brown uniform military spit-shine pressed, strode into the library and headed straight for her. His rolling gate looked like a bad imitation of John Wayne's famous strut. Tall and lanky, he had to be at least six four. He kept his blond hair trimmed to crew cut length, and his small blond mustache sat on his upper lip like a bush that didn't quite fit with the rest of the shrubbery. If she'd been rude and tempted, she might have told him to trim off the mustache. His face tended toward leanness, and somehow the extra hair on his face narrowed his features even more.

"Hey, Erin," Danny said, a slight twang to his accent. Kathleen and Danny had grown up in Texas.

"Officer Fortesque," she said and nodded. "What can we do for you?"

His back straight as a poker, he gazed down on her. "Isn't it about time you called me Danny? We've known each other for a month."

Too tired to argue, she gave him a weak smile. "Danny. What can I do for you?"

His answering grin filled with triumph. "I checked out that Lachlan Tavish character."

Erin almost groaned. She'd forgotten about Kathleen's promise. "You didn't."

"He's clean. No criminal record either in this country or anywhere else that I can ascertain."

Relief gave her loose lips. "That's wonderful."

His green eyes narrowed and his mouth thinned. "That doesn't mean you shouldn't be careful around him."

Her cautious nature admitted he might be right. "Thanks, Danny. I appreciate you taking the time to stop by and let me know."

He glanced from right to left, then lowered his voice. "Say, I know this isn't exactly the time or the place, but since I've got my courage up..." For a moment she thought he'd stalled all together, but then he smiled. "I'm trying to ask you out and I'm messing it up."

Previous encounters with Danny didn't give her a warm fuzzy feeling, but she didn't know that much about him. Maybe she should give him another chance. At least with Danny there wouldn't be any danger of immediate sexual energy.

She smiled. "Where would you like to go out?"

A big grin stretched his mouth and he almost was handsome for a quick second. "Great!" He looked around. "Sorry. I didn't mean to speak so loud."

No one appeared to have noticed, but his sheepish expression charmed her. "No problem. Would you like to meet up at Betty's Café sometime for coffee?"

His face sobered at bit. Maybe he wanted a fancier, more complicated date, but she figured slower would be better. He shifted his feet, his gaze still assessing as any good officer of the law would. "Well, sure. How about tomorrow at noon?"

"That'll work."

"Great." He smiled again before turning serious. "I also have some questions to ask you."

She swallowed hard and thought about her determination this morning to speak to the police about Lachlan. She was acting wiggy about Lachlan, wavering back and forth from defending him to wanting to tattle like a kid. "Actually, do you have a few minutes right now? I have some information about the..."

She trailed off, her confidence in what she wanted to say drifting away.

Danny frowned, concern evident in his eyes. "Information about what?"

"Maybe this is a bad time."

"No, it's not. If it's something to do with a crime, I'm here to get the information now."

"You're right. Of course. Let me see if Gilda can cover for me a minute."

Nerves tightened her body and an ache started in her forehead. She located Gilda and told her she needed to speak with Danny right away. Looking puzzled, Gilda agreed to cover her position for a few moments. Erin felt guilty for asking, but if she didn't say something to Danny right now, she'd lose her nerve.

She took Danny to the employee break room, and he sat down at one of the small round tables. She paced the floor while he wrote in his notebook.

"Go ahead and sit down," Danny said.

"I can't. Let me just get this out, all right?"

He nodded and went silent.

She took a deep, shaky breath. "I'm not even sure if I'm doing the right thing."

"Just relax and tell me."

Easy for him to say. She felt like she was betraying a lifelong friend, which was idiotic. She didn't know Lachlan, so why did this feel so wrong?

She stopped pacing and rubbed her throbbing temples. "Lachlan Tavish was here at the library last night."

He nodded. "I know. My sister said she'd seen him here."

"Oh."

He smiled gently. "Yeah, oh." He shrugged. "Kathleen is a reporter, so you can't blame her for being a gossip sometimes."

Erin decided she wouldn't tell him he'd better not repeat his generalized belief about reporters to Kathleen. "When I heard the report about Mrs. Pickles tonight it got me to thinking about something Lachlan said last night." She took another deep breath to try and dispel the nervous flutter in her stomach. "He told me that there was someone dangerous wandering Pine Forest and that I should be careful when leaving."

Danny scribbled in his small notebook, frown lines starting to form between his eyebrows. "And that made you afraid of him?"

"No, not exactly." She shook her head, not wanting Danny to get the wrong idea. "I just wondered if maybe he knows more about what is happening. Maybe he could tell you more."

Danny looked at her sharply. "So you're not saying you suspect *him* of being the attacker?"

She hesitated, and a steady throbbing began in her temples. She couldn't remember the last time she experienced a headache that evolved so fast. "Not necessarily. Innocent until proven guilty, you know."

Danny nodded, but suspicion showed in his eyes. He kept her pinned with his gaze. "So you think I should question him?"

She shrugged, and the movement hurt. Feeling a bit nauseated, she walked to the small table and sank down in a chair across from him. "I don't know. I figured after I spoke to you that you'd do whatever necessary." She smiled to ease the tension. "You know. Do the cop thing."

His frown eased, and a smile tilted one corner of his mouth for a moment. "Thanks for giving me this lead."

"I thought it might be useful."

He sighed. "I'm hoping so. We got some angry citizens out there demanding answers."

"I've heard about the uproar from the reports in the papers. They want vengeance right now." She shook her head. "Don't they understand that sometimes these investigations take time?"

"No, they don't understand. For example, one of Mrs. Pickle's nephews is coming in to town late this week. He's been on the phone with us several times."

"Interfering with the investigation?"

"We're trying to accommodate him because he's a cop, but they can be the worst kind when it comes to their own kin. Then there's the general public. They're scared out of their wits. But I suppose that's a good thing. Keeps them on their toes and alert instead of stumbling around like witless cows." He stood up and started toward the door. "Thanks again, and I'll take it from here."

The slight touch of overconfidence in his tone amused her. "I'm sure you will."

With a quick salute, he said, "I'll see you later."

After he left, she sighed. *Okay, Erin, let's hope you did the right thing.* She wanted to feel relieved, but instead the tattling hadn't eased her conscience one bit.

She returned to work a moment later, drained. Her head continued to throb, and she wished she'd stopped to grab an aspirin. Instead she pushed forward with work, chastising herself for being a wimp.

Later that morning the voice started up while she worked at the front counter.

Erin, darling, I'm here.

She wished she wore a thicker sweater. Drafts in this old place assured plenty of chills. Shivers radiated up and down her spine as she waited for more words to fill her mind. It didn't take long.

Erin, don't you know who I am? I was with you last night.

When Erin looked for Gilda, she saw that she stood at a computerized card catalog station helping a teenager. Gilda didn't seem to notice a thing. The voice mixed with a bizarre sensation that something else had changed in the huge library. An encroaching darkness weighed down along the back of her neck and shoulders. She stopped working and waited, hoping the sensation would leave.

The air felt dark and thick. Blackness hovered at the end of each aisle. She tried taking a deep breath, but couldn't. The pain in her head increased and she touched her temples again. Rubbing did nothing to give her relief.

Then the front door creaked open, and in walked Lachlan.

Chapter 6

Lachlan approached her with that fluid motion that spoke of power and danger. Fear danced along her spine, insistent and unwilling to give an inch. The sight of Lachlan didn't ease the feeling that something dark hovered nearby. Still, the darkness had come just as he arrived, as well as the strange voice. Suspicion rose inside her.

No. No way. Mind to mind communication isn't possible. And the shadows are from clouds throwing gloom over the windows high above, not some sinister entity. I can't let this crazy town get to me.

As soon as she considered the thought, the dark shadows floated away like a bad dream. Inching and crawling, the shades receded to the back of her mind. She couldn't allow recent events to creep her out, or she'd be seeing the boogieman at every corner.

Lachlan strode toward the paranormal section not far from her. *Figures.* He stopped at the edge of one shelf, his back to her, and perused the vampire section. Erin's gaze snagged on his dark red sweater, and she noted how it fit along his broad shoulders to perfection and covered his narrow waist. His casual dark blue pants hugged his sculpted butt. Not too tight, not too loose.

Mama mia. She swallowed hard as her mouth literally watered.

He turned and caught her staring at him. A blush spread over her face, hot and sure. A huge grin parted his lips. Warmth filled her stomach as she absorbed once again how damnably rugged and intriguing he looked. When he came toward her, book in hand, she almost held her breath. Every stride brought her nearer to feeling an insane attraction that had no basis in reality.

Warning, warning, Lachlan is nothing but walking heart-break. Avoid, avoid.

She must maintain her composure or this man would walk all over her. She should have tame and comfortable like Danny, not a man with who should come with a highly-flammable warning label.

"Hi, Erin." His liquid velvet voice cut through her defenses with a soft and seductive tone. "I'll bet after last night you thought you'd seen the last of me."

His golden-brown eyes melted with uncertainty. This big, handsome man was tentative? Did he think she'd slap him in the chops as an afterthought or accuse him of sexual assault?

Her throat felt parched. Suddenly, even though the library harbored dozens of people, she felt as if she stood with him in a private oasis.

Before she could speak he said, "Or perhaps you hoped that would be the last you'd see of me."

She summoned a weak smile. "I thought you were gone until next Halloween. Doesn't every good vampire go back to his coffin?"

"Halloween is in three weeks. I'm here for at least that much longer."

Another good reason not to get interested in this man; he'll be gone soon.

Lachlan looked at her sharply, and for a moment, she almost thought she'd spoken out loud.

Before she could say another word, Erin heard the front door open and then Jessie Huxley sauntered into the library. Jessie's extra sassy distinctive walk seemed designed for male enjoyment. Today she wore a red mini dress that rode high on her slim, beautiful legs. The turtleneck design looked warm, but Erin also realized the short hemline would cause men to drool at fifty paces. Encased in black hose, her legs ate up the floor. She headed straight for the checkout counter, her gaze pinned on

Lachlan with voracious intent. Erin knew right away that Jessie wanted to start something with the tall, handsome Scot.

Jealousy did a spike inside Erin, and she took a surprised breath. Where had that come from? She'd better get a grip on reality. She had no claim on this man.

"Why, hello." Jessie's voice held a purr as smooth and soft as a baby's butt without the layer of innocence. She placed her hand on Lachlan's forearm. A mere brush of her fingers, just intimate enough to put her intent across. "Great seeing you here. What are you doing in a library?"

Lachlan smiled. "Hallo." His British way of saying hello gave the word a sexy nuance. "Jessie, isn't it?"

Damn. The man remembered her name, too?

Jessie's smile showed even, pristine white teeth. Her blue eyes sparkled with interest and mischief. She didn't even greet Erin. "Jessie Huxley." She removed her hand from his arm and placed her hand on her hip. "That's me. The kids loved your Halloween program the other night."

He nodded and smiled graciously. "Thank you." Turning his gaze to Erin, his grin went wider. "It was Erin's program. I just filled in for Gilda in an emergency."

One of Jessie's blonde eyebrows twitched upwards as she allowed her hip to tilt even more. Her sizable breasts heaved in a sigh. "Erin is talented with kids, isn't she?"

To Erin, the compliment sounded flat and unauthentic, but she kept her mouth shut and observed how Lachlan would handle this *hot mama*. "That she is."

As he slanted a hot glance Erin's direction, she felt his words all the way down to the soles of her feet. Embarrassment made her face turn red. Jessie's gaze landed on Erin and filled with a derision she'd never seen in the woman's face before.

Jessie put her hand on his shoulder this time. "Wow, you must work out."

Lachlan kept his smile, and even though Erin didn't think he could mistake Jessie's flirtation for anything else, he kept his cool. "Five times a week."

"Do you use the gym over at the community center?" Jessie's fingers did a no-nonsense assessment of his shoulder then landed on his chest for a moment. "You have great musculature. You must use the weight machine."

"And the treadmill, too. It's a little hard to walk or run around here in the winter weather."

"Oh." Jessie's breathy sound came out soft and seductive. "I do, too. Maybe we could meet up there sometime. They have that great little juice bar nearby."

Did Jessie's eyelids just flutter? Give me a break.

Lachlan smiled at Erin before turning his attention back to Jessie's preening attention, and for a second Erin could have sworn she heard a rumbling male laugh echo in her head.

"I'll keep that in mind." Lachlan gave a small, noble nod.

Lachlan kept his gaze pinned on Jessie, and Erin felt that twinge of unwarranted jealousy once again. She almost gritted her teeth trying to hold back a comment. Surprise danced through her. Since when had she become a catty woman with a desire to rip another woman's hair out?

Since Jessie started moving in on him with all the subtlety of a freight train, that's when. I wish she would just go away and stay away.

Not to worry, lass. I'm not the least interested in her.

Erin's mouth dropped open. There was that damnable voice again. It sounded like Lachlan's, but how could it be?

Before Jessie could say another word, her kids ran up and greeted Erin and Lachlan. Erin wondered how two such nice kids could come from such a woman. The children started asking Lachlan more questions about vampires.

Jessie grabbed the kids before he could comment. "Come on, kids. Let Mr. Tavish get on with his business." She threw another smile filled with suggestions that couldn't be denied. "Hope to see you again soon, Lachlan. Call me and we'll get together at the gym."

She turned away and herded the children back upstairs toward the kids section.

Lachlan's irreverent expression said he either liked the encounter with the overblown blonde, or that he found her humorous. Maybe both.

He leaned on the counter. "Wow. She's an interesting one."

"Think so?" Erin cringed inside at the spite in her voice. "I mean, she's always been nice to me." As an afterthought she mumbled, "She seems like she's really interested in you."

Without a hint of denial in his voice, he said, "Does seem like that. Do you mind?"

Erin's mouth opened again without a word coming out. She tried to think of something to say, but it wouldn't materialize.

Lachlan saved her. "You seemed a bit annoyed around the edges. As if you cared that she was coming on to me."

Damn him for being so honest and perceptive. She kept her voice mild. "Why should I?"

Gilda walked into their area and startled Erin. "There you are, Lachlan. Still coming to dinner tonight?"

"Wouldn't miss it," he said. "I'll bring the wine."

Gilda grinned. "Sounds wonderful. Why don't you come over, too, Erin? You haven't eaten with us in a long time."

"Um…" Erin hated sounding like a dunce, but awkwardness crept into her psyche. "Sure? What time?"

"Six-thirty."

"I'll pick you up." Lachlan's matter-of-fact statement surprised Erin.

"Wonderful idea," Gilda said as she went off to help another patron.

"You didn't have to offer." Erin wanted to scream because she knew Gilda had set her up again. "I can drive over myself."

He stepped closer to the counter, and the world around her receded again, leaving the two of them alone. His masculine, delicious scent sent shivers of pure female appreciation straight through her system. Her pulse went off the charts and into the stratosphere.

"Wouldn't you rather have company?" he asked softly.

"I like being alone." At least she spoke the truth this time. "After working with a lot of people every day, it's great to have private time."

His gaze locked on hers. Dark fire sparked in his eye eyes again, and the golden glow at the center made her breath hitch in her throat. "I agree. In Scotland, my company keeps me very busy. This has been like an exploration for me."

"Vacation?"

"Not exactly, but I try and fit in a bit of private time."

"What is your company, by the way?" Maybe if she led him away from talking about her, she could feel more comfortable.

His gaze turned thoughtful. "My father founded the business when I was a boy. We restored old castles and estates and sometimes helped the owners start bed and breakfast schemes."

"Schemes?"

His grin added to a teasing light in his eyes. "Scheme means something a little different in Britain than it does in the United States. It doesn't have a bad connotation. It just means a plan."

"Oh. Did your family have a bed and breakfast?"

"They did." He looked uncomfortable for a moment. "My home had been in the family about six hundred years."

"Wow."

Good going, Erin. He'll think you're a complete dunce. But then, if he does, maybe he won't want to date you. Then again, maybe he doesn't want to anyway. Gilda is the one pressing this issue.

She didn't know him well enough to probe into hurtful territory. She thought she saw pain flicker in his eyes. Perhaps he thought about his parents and the fire.

"When do you get off work?" he asked.

"Five-thirty. Why?"

"I can pick you up here rather than at your house."

Lachlan's switch in plans took her off guard. She glanced down at her denim skirt. "I'm not dressed for a party. I need to go home and change."

He twisted his mouth into a show of disbelief. "It's not a fancy ball. You're beautiful."

Beautiful. His gently spoken word hung in the air and made her feel every inch gorgeous, if just for a moment in time. "Thank you. I can go home and get changed. I don't need a bodyguard."

"You might. You heard about that older woman who was attacked last night?"

"I heard."

"That's why you should have someone leave with you."

"You weren't here last night when I left." *Shut up, shut up, shut up, Erin. He's going to think you wanted him to stay.*

"Were you frightened?" His brows dipped downward with his frown. "If I'd known—"

"No…I….no."

"That doesn't sound certain."

She made an impatient noise. "Kathleen left the library with me. I wasn't exactly by myself."

Again, Lachlan's eyes spoke of secrets she couldn't comprehend. Yet, she wanted to understand him with everything she possessed, and the feeling disturbed her. He drew her at the same time her cautious side screamed for her to run as far and fast as she could.

"Oh, I was watching you," he said.

"What?" Surprise and a little alarm skipped through her veins. "You were watching me? I didn't see you."

"I was there." He gave her a patient expression, as if he waited for her to explode any second and knew how he would handle the situation.

"Lurking in the bushes? That's a bit odd, don't you think?"

As he shook his head, hair dipped onto his forehead. "From my car down the street."

"You could see me that far away?"

"I've got excellent night vision."

A mingling of fear and a bizarre excitement made her wary. She felt caged in and protected by his attention all at the same time. She glanced at that fall of hair over his forehead and impulsively reached over the counter to brush it back. Soft, the tendril of hair caught around her index finger and brushed with an incredibly sensual texture against her skin. She sucked in a breath and snatched her hand back. It was almost…almost as if the hair had clasped her finger on purpose.

His gaze caught and held hers. Melting gold flared to life in his eyes, and the heat she saw in that look made her want to kiss him so badly, she almost went around the counter and did it in front of God, country, and anyone else who might be in proximity.

"You're in danger," he said. "All the women in this town are potential victims."

"You mentioned that already. In fact," she swallowed hard around her fear, "How did you know Mrs. Pickles was going to be attacked near the library last night?"

"I didn't. I simply know that women alone are targets. It doesn't take a rocket scientist, lass, to know that."

While a bit of relief flowed through her, she still didn't trust him one hundred percent. She'd keep her guard up until she knew more about this mysterious man. She wished now, though, that she hadn't said anything to Danny. What if she caused trouble for Lachlan and he had nothing to do with what happened to those women?

A dull stab of pain in her temples made her wince, and she narrowed her eyes.

Lachlan's gaze went intense as he searched her face. "Are you in pain?"

"How did you know?"

Without saying a word, he came around the counter and stood near her. He reached up and touched both her temples. "Easy."

She didn't have time to protest or worry what people would think if they saw him touching her like this. Instead, she gazed up at him. He snagged her stare and held it. That strange golden glow caught her attention and wouldn't let her go.

He rubbed very gently, just under her hair. "Breathe deep and listen to my voice." Seductive and throbbing low with heat, his tone sounded whisper soft. "Nasty headache, lass. Where did you pick it up?"

"Pick it up?"

"Is it this place? This building or this town? Do they worry you?"

"What? No."

He continued the gentle movement of his fingers. "Do the ghosts press in on you and create darkness?"

She couldn't even be alarmed by his strange question as dizziness took hold of her. "What do you mean?"

"I think the headaches might be from overload of psychic energy."

She made a very unladylike snorting noise. "Uh-huh. Sure."

He laughed softly, a whisper of sound she barely heard. "You're very sensitive and you need a way to release the build up, or a way to block it out. I can teach you how to do both things."

Now she knew this disgustingly gorgeous man was nuts.

When she wavered on her feet, he stopped his massage and gripped her shoulders. "Steady. Come on, now. Breathe deeper. That's it."

Erin did as commanded, unable to move and grateful for his support. She realized that her eyes had closed, and she opened them with a snap.

Her headache disappeared, replaced only by a slight unsteadiness on her feet. "What happened? How did you do that?"

He smiled. "I'll tell you about it some time. Feel better?"

She nodded. "Oh, yes. Much better. I feel a little weak, though."

He slid his hands down to her elbows, and she felt the heat and strength of his support. "That'll pass in a few moments. If it doesn't stop, lie down for awhile and that should take care of the problem."

With a care and reverence she never experienced before, Lachlan let go of her. He still stood so near she could see those golden flecks in his eyes, but now they didn't seem as intense. All she saw there was warmth and concern.

"Thank you," she said a bit breathlessly. "That was incredible."

Oh, lass, I could show you some more incredible things.

She blinked in astonishment at the voice in her head.

Before she could say a word, he reached for her book cart and picked up *The Sentinel*. She hadn't looked at the paper that morning. Now the main headline screamed at her as he held it up.

El Chupacabra Menacing Pine Forest?

81

"I can't believe Kathleen would write up such garbage." Erin read the byline. "Wonderful."

She realized she sounded sarcastic, but she didn't want to hear anymore tabloid speculation.

"I'll pick you up tonight then?" he asked, switching gears as he put the newspaper back and picked up a book still on the cart. He looked at the title. "Ah, just what I was looking for. Very fortuitous."

He smiled and looked up at her, and as their gazes locked, curiosity and intense scrutiny flamed in his eyes. Then she realized she hadn't answered his question.

"All right. Fine. Pick me up at five-thirty. But I'm going home to change." She looked down at the book he held. "Are you going to check that out or hold it all day?"

Lachlan's gentle chuckle made a small ripple in the silence. He handed her the book. *Vampires: Historical Fact or Fiction?*

"Of course. I should have guessed," she said with a tinge of mockery. "You don't believe in this stuff, do you? Are you trying to say a vampire is attacking women in Pine Forest?"

"Actually, yes." He winked. "It's far more likely than El Chupacabra."

She made a noise, disgust and incredulity wrapped into one tight package. Lachlan Tavish, seducer extraordinaire, doubtless belonged in the funny farm with half the other people in this town.

"Check the book out to me," he said. "Have dinner with me tomorrow night, and I'll tell you everything I know about vampires and curing headaches."

"Uh-huh. Next you'll tell me that *you're* a vampire."

She didn't wait for him to answer. Once she reached the front desk, she handed him a temporary library card application. He signed the last line with a flourish.

Erin penned her authorizing signature on the application and got the card ready to laminate. "You didn't answer my question."

"And you didn't say you'd have dinner with me tomorrow night. How does Ricardo's sound?"

Surprise slipped through her. Ricardo's was an exclusive, expensive restaurant connected to a country club and golf course thirty miles outside of Pine Forest. "Ricardo's is—"

"Expensive. Dinner is on me."

Erin didn't know what to say for a moment. She wanted to have dinner alone with him, and that disturbed her more than anything. She couldn't recall the last time she'd experienced a fancy meal with all the trimmings. A gourmet meal *and* a handsome man sounded like too much heaven.

"Erin?" His expression, sincere and non-threatening, made her agree.

"All right. Dinner with you tomorrow night."

"Brilliant."

Good God. How would she survive having dinner with him two nights in a row? As his eyes glowed with that amazing fire, hot and all-consuming, she almost thought he wanted to seal the agreement with a kiss. As he stood so close, smelling so good she could eat him alive, Lachlan Tavish did strange things to her hormones. Her gonads went on high alert every time she saw him.

"I need to take my car home tonight," she said.

"I'll follow you home and make sure you get there safely." His voice offered no options for refusal. "Then we'll take my car to Gilda and Tom's."

She wanted to say no, but instead his physical proximity scattered her senses.

Again he searched her gaze. A new wave of lightheadedness hit her, and she closed her eyes for a moment. She felt a brush of hot skin against hers as he took her hand between both of his and raised it to his mouth. There, in full view of any patron who would care to look, Lachlan planted a heated kiss on the back of her hand. Passion-touched lips brushed over her skin, feather-soft and promising.

Her eyes opened, and as he did so many times before, he caught and held her gaze.

"You must trust me." His voice floated over her senses like an aphrodisiac, encouraging her to surrender. "I would never hurt you."

She leaned closer to him. "How can I be sure?"

He grinned and released her hand. "Nothing is ever for certain, lass. But I'm a descent man. I try and live by that golden rule everyone is so fond of talking about."

Erin wanted to groan. *What's happening to me?* She felt almost drugged, unable to ignore the quick-paced acceleration of her attraction to him. Erin never admitted when she liked a man, because too many times she'd been teased about it as a teen. She didn't like the implication she might be one chess piece short of a set, or even worse, out of control.

How long have I been staring at him like a blithering idiot?

She shook her head. "I don't know you."

"Get to know me." He frowned. "I'll leave you to your work."

As Lachlan turned away, she felt a cord between them tighten and then snap, as if he'd held her prisoner. Shaking her head, Erin reached up and brushed hair away from her face.

He left her standing behind the counter, her heart thumping like crazy and her mind a confused whirl.

Right then and there Erin decided she'd lost her ever lovin' mind.

And what if he found out that she'd told Danny her suspicions about him?

You're safe with me, Erin, lass.

She heard the deep voice and knew this time she couldn't mistake that rich voice. Lachlan.

Chapter 7

Pine Forest oozed with the paranormal, and as the vampire glanced around him, he saw the evidence. *Ah, what an excellent place to hide.*

Night came down around him as he left the neglected tomb in the graveyard near the old inn. He would prowl the streets tonight for sustenance, for the water of his life. He walked among the people as they tarried downtown. Wrapped in warm clothing, frost on their breaths, they didn't notice him.

But why should they see him? Much like the ghosts lingering in every building, he kept the minds around him clouded. Some entities wanted living people to see them, to give any sign they understood the torment of being between worlds. He preferred the anonymity of cloaking. To some he would be a whiff of breeze on this cold night. To others he represented a shadow against a building or along the sidewalk.

He could see and feel ghosts as they went about their ethereal lives. Some of the haunts were enduring energies and not true entities, but most people didn't perceive the difference between a ghost and haunting. The lingering stain of death touched every historical place, like the blood he tasted whenever he could. Few people sensed the stain, and those that noticed didn't often understand what they felt. *Really, they are rather stupid creatures.* So few things interested them other than their little, insubstantial worlds.

Reality, as they defined it, stuck to the solid. Formless entities with either good or bad intentions dwelt in this town, thick on the ground and causing havoc. The entities that needed assistance getting to the other side sought out the perceptive, but sometimes the ghost's entreaties continued to be ignored. After all, the form-filled world possessed more than enough distraction.

As distracted as the public was, he took no chances. He dwelled in the shadows almost all the time. Even perceptive people who caught glimpses of him would think they imagined far too much. He'd spent centuries laughing at humans and their ability to conceal their real feelings and thoughts.

As he sniffed, his advanced sense of smell took in the delicious scent of fresh baked apple pie and maybe a hamburger and fries. He enjoyed the smell of human meals, even if he could no longer consume food. No, he would never give up blood for solid food. He couldn't, and he wouldn't.

A young woman walked past him, and he caught her essence with one sniff. She'd just had sex. His blood ran hot. *Ah, yes. Women who'd recently been fucked gave off a hormone he could detect a half-mile away.* As he turned and followed her, he remembered that he loved the taste of freshly fucked woman.

But no one will have Erin but me. She will be mine, and I will be the first to screw her.

No. He wouldn't allow her to escape with evasion tactics or dating other men.

All through the day he'd watched and followed her. Though he'd observed her for weeks, she didn't know how long he'd wished to be near her. He needed to be closer than transitory glimpses of her shiny hair and seductive smile.

That weakling police officer, with the equally idiotic name like *Danny*, wouldn't save her when the time came. Danny held no sway over her; she didn't find him interesting. No answering spark came into her gut when she saw him.

Soon The Hunter, Ronan Kieran, would find him again, intent on killing him as he had tried so many times before. Kieran searched by day and night, fitting his relentless wanderings into the fiber of every twenty-four hours. The vampire always kept several steps ahead of The Hunter, and this realization flooded the vampire's immortal soul with satisfaction that almost replaced the thirst for blood.

Almost.

But not quite.

* * * * *

"What on earth am I going to wear?" Erin asked as she rummaged in her bedroom closet that evening.

Lachlan waited patiently for her in the living room.

I was with you last night. You're safe with me. She continued to wonder if Lachlan had whispered these things in her mind.

She rummaged through her deep, walk-in closet hoping to find the answers. Her relationship with Lachlan was crazy and impossible, but not necessarily in that order. If she didn't get a grip soon, she would need an appointment with a specialist who dealt with hallucinations.

A short time later she dressed in a black soft stretch blend turtleneck and lower leg length skirt. It clung to her curves with gentle attention without being too revealing. It was vital she have courage for what she planned to say to Lachlan in a few minutes, and maybe if she dressed like a confident woman, the courage would come with the garment. *Right, Erin. Sure.*

Part of her wanted to run from the situation. The other part of her knew she couldn't hide from a man like this Scot in the next room. Relentless and certain, he knew the where, how, and what of just about everything. She'd never run into a man with this heady presence, this overwhelming sense of taking her on a whirlwind ride.

When she walked into the living room and Lachlan saw her, his lips parted into a big smile and his soul-deep eyes widened before he spoke the words.

"You're stunning."

Heat flamed in her face and as she snatched her coat off the couch. "Thanks."

Erin decided the strain couldn't last. She would explode if she didn't set the rules right now. She moved closer to him, careful to avoid his curious stare. She looked everywhere but him, intensely aware that he wouldn't like what she said next.

"Lachlan, before we go, I have to make several things clear."

He stayed silent, his calm a balm on her worries.

She put her hands out in a plea. "We can't do what we did last night. I don't indulge in casual sex. I lost control with you once, but I don't have to do it again." Erin felt sweat break out on the back of her neck. Nerves made her stomach roll. "We just…can't."

He crossed his arms with a slow casualness. His gaze dropped to half-mast, mysterious and maybe even a bit uncertain. "Can't? Or won't?"

Relieved she didn't need to spell it out in explicit terms, she nodded. "Both."

Before she could walk passed him, he tilted her chin up so she looked into his eyes.

Oh, no, oh, no. Mistake. Mistake.

As his gaze encompassed her, Erin felt the pull of his desire. "You're not playing fair." She couldn't move, her limbs heavy and her senses riot with sudden arousal. How did he do this to her? "Please don't."

"You feel it again, don't you?" His eyes glittered with new progress. His hand slipped to the back of her neck, big fingers caressing. "You're feeling this pull between us. It's damn powerful, Erin. I canna resist it."

Whenever he seemed on the verge of ardor, he slipped into a deeper accent, thick with his craving. Her interest in him surged, attracted by the blatant sexuality in his whisky-rich voice.

The room, the soft light, all of it dimmed. Nothing but her heart, thumping an eager new beat, seemed real. Only his wonderful, passion-thick scent mattered.

His gaze searched her, growing more intense by the second. She felt like fingers were pressing against her skin, searching out new and delicious places for pleasure.

"You feel this attraction we have, lass. Why are you fighting it? What are you afraid of?" he asked.

"You."

As his fingers caressed her neck, she reached up and clasped his forearm. Hard muscle, vigorously masculine, flexed under her touch and promised satisfaction if she would take it. She closed her eyes against the probe of his curiosity. Erin felt as if Lachlan knew everything inside her. Maybe he *could* read minds. But how?

If she expected him to answer her telepathically, he didn't. Instead, he kept her gaze pinned with his.

Before she could blink, his mouth came down on hers. Heat ran through Erin like a flash fire, bursting rampant in her body. Lachlan's arms slipped around her and pulled her against his body. Hot and demanding, his mouth slanted over hers and his tongue plunged deep into her mouth. He swallowed her gasping moan of surprise and exhilaration. His kiss didn't ask this time—it demanded.

As Lachlan's kiss intensified, she responded with answering caresses of her tongue. Wild with sudden, staggering passion, she tore her mouth from his and came in at another angle. His low, deep groan of satisfaction fired her into sweet frenzy. Her panties dampened, and she felt the throb and ache as she responded to his overwhelming sexual intensity.

Oh, God, I'm so wet.

How could this man turn her on so fast, before she could resist or think about consequences? Erin decided she would fall off the edge of the world, and her arms went around his neck in desperation. Dizziness swamped her for a moment, as if confirming something she already knew.

Lachlan Tavish held sway over her in a way no man should or ever had. Somewhere in the back of her mind, she struggled for control. Instead, soft moans of pleasure left her. Her nipples tightened into nubs and a burgeoning necessity for completion throbbed low in her belly. She arched against his hold, her fingers sliding through the thick silk of his hair. He took over the kiss, thrusting his tongue repeatedly into her mouth.

Textures became all—the continual, relentless movement of his mouth and tongue, the searching of his hands as he rubbed and palmed and brushed. The rough soft combination of his sweater, the fabric of his pants as her hands dropped to his hips. His warm, musk scent teased her, and the soft seduction of the smell made her desire more.

More kisses, more of his eager fingers touching her nipples. More of everything including sliding his cock inside her.

Oh, yes. She wanted his cock inside her with an overwhelming and sudden desire. Her vagina clenched and released. *Yes. Yes.* She would writhe upon him, slide herself up and down as she rode him like he'd never been ridden before. She would fuck him until he gave her another one of those animalistic groans of male excitement.

Erin tried to think, tried to reason her way out of this frantic call for completion. Her brain refused to cooperate, centering on the way Lachlan plied her with his determined kiss and roaming hands. With any other man, she might have fought his advances and his sexual penetration of her senses.

Penetration. Oh, yes.

His hands cupped her ass and squeezed, kneading and stroking as he pulled her up so he could nestle his hard cock between her legs. He would make her come at this rate, even if he didn't touch naked skin. She moaned like a madwoman without shame, rubbing her clit against his clothed cock to take pleasure in the sensation.

His palms slid up and down her back, testing the shape of her body. His movement sent tingling pleasure into new, unexplored places. Her breasts screamed for his attention, but he seemed determined to keep her hanging on a precipice, strung tight with desire. As if he knew she needed something, Lachlan reached around and cupped one breast. He didn't stroke it or reach for her nipple. He simply kept it in hand.

Hot jolts of pleasure filled her stomach and she almost tore her mouth from his and demanded satisfaction. Any satisfaction.

Her body felt light, as if lifted above the ground, swirling high into the night and to the heavens. Fanciful feelings danced inside her. Enclosed in Lachlan's embrace, Erin's world turned into a star-filled night, replete with love that couldn't happen in short acquaintance. No, she couldn't love this man, no matter what crazy sexual draw she felt.

She flushed at the thought, and the heat rocketed into her face. She *wanted* to experience extraordinary sex. Somehow she knew Lachlan would give her a ride she would never forget. Her inhibitions flew away in eagerness to know him. She wanted to whisper decadent, racy, nasty words that expressed every measure of her wishes.

Cock. Dick. Hump. Fuck.

Ah, yes. Crazy, forbidden, bad words whispered when lovers want to excite each other. Nonsensical and yet meaning one thing with a raging desire that knew no bounds.

Beyond that, she wanted him speak those unmentionable words to her, whisper them in her ear so that she'd fire up on the mere idea.

Fuck. That is the ultimate word. She repeated it in her mind, savoring the deliciousness and the way it made her cream just thinking the word.

Fuck.

Fuck me.

Not yet, sweetheart. You're not ready for that.

Not ready?

Erin jerked back, tearing out of his arms and stumbling into the couch. She sat down hard on cushions, her breath rasping in and out like bellows. Erin knew she shouldn't be surprised that Lachlan delved into her mind again.

Or had he?

Maybe she'd lost her mind and that explained her willingness to have sex with him without blinking an eye. It clarified why she thought he could read her thoughts. What woman could resist golden-fired brown eyes, heated touches, and a sizzling combustion that swelled higher and hotter than she'd ever known before?

Shamed again by lack of control, she shivered from cold. The room felt freezing without his arms around her.

She gazed at him in amazement and chagrin. "Why did you do that?" Erin flapped her hands in a dismissing gesture. "Why did you back off?"

"Because you didn't want it."

"You are..." She sputtered. "You are the world's biggest tease. You kiss me, then fondle me, and put your...your cock between my legs, then you say I'm not ready?"

Words spilled from Erin that didn't even sound like her. She never used words like cock, but this man made her so angry she wanted to scream. When she stood and poked her finger in his chest, he watched with a patience she found laissez-faire in the extreme, especially for a man who'd been as hard as a rail-spike a moment ago. She glanced down and saw that rail spike still described his state. He looked so wonderfully hard and able to satisfy. Another rush of liquid spilled from her, and that dampness between her legs made her want to squirm.

With a quiet huskiness in his deep voice, he reached down and took her right hand. "Your body was ready, but your mind wasn't. You wouldn't have enjoyed it. We must take this one step at a time."

She wanted to scream. *Not enjoy it? Right.*

"And I only want you," he said, "when your body and mind are both willing. When you and I have sex, it'll be one of the greatest things that happened to us both. But it won't work unless it's mutually exciting."

Amazed by his sudden patience and willingness to wait for her, she stood there in shock, her mouth slightly open. "You sound like one of those television talk show psychiatrists."

She didn't mean it as an insult, but he frowned and she knew he'd taken it that way.

"I'm sorry," she said hastily. "I didn't mean that the way it sounded."

"I know."

Lachlan moved around her and sat on the couch. When she followed, he touched her hair, caressing the back of her head with a gesture so comforting and cherishing, tears came to her eyes. Confusion reigned in her system.

"I was...ready." Her voice, so soft she could hardly hear it herself, sounded a little petulant. Right away she wanted to take back the tone, if not the words.

"You weren't. I could sense a small part of you that thinks making love with me would be wrong." His gaze returned to hers for a small second. "You're afraid of many things, Erin, including getting close to a man. I understand that. We're virtual strangers." He slid his palm over her back, rubbing with a gentle gesture that spoke of comfort and not copulation. "We've connected, but you aren't certain it's what you want. I won't take you until you're completely comfortable with the idea."

Words of wisdom. Erin inhaled to calm the continued pounding of her heart and regain her breath. She'd turned wild and feral in his arms, but she still couldn't give him that final sexual commitment.

Screw the man. He was right.

She slipped her hands through her hair, flustered and wanting answers to the uncertainty. "You could have just taken me up on the offer and had sex with me anyway. Many men would have."

With tenderness in his eyes that removed much of her discomfort, he said, "I'm not like most men, lass. Far from it."

He stood again and held a hand out to her. "Shall we go to the dinner party?"

"Excuse me a moment."

She went to her bedroom and put on a new pair of panties. No way would she go to Gilda's house with the scent of sexual excitement lingering around her.

Several minutes later, as they cruised in his rented gold Lexus, she waited for him to speak. Silence this deep and profound sometimes bothered her. Her last boyfriend back in Arizona started the silent treatment not long before he dumped her. Amazing how the mind could make connections where there shouldn't be any.

Or was there? Would Lachlan also separate himself if they had sex?

"Did the janitor discover where the noises were coming from in the library?" Lachlan asked, breaking her out of morose thoughts.

"No, but Fred said I shouldn't worry." She explained about the so-called ghosts. "At this point, I'd almost like to believe it. I could stop worrying about the building being unstable."

As they pulled up to Gilda and Tom's two story Victorian reproduction home, he smiled. "He's right. It's ghosts."

She sniffed. "Sure. And I'm Gandhi."

He turned off the car and unbuckled his seatbelt, and turned toward her. "Are you always such a wee, stubborn lass?" He added extra burr to his voice, and the rolling, husky sound thrilled her in a way she didn't want to think about. She'd have to watch out or she would start salivating like Jessie did the other night. "Or are you afraid of something else in the library?"

Just afraid of you.

Don't be afraid of me. I'd protect you with my life. Lachlan's voice came into her head again.

"Oh...my...God," she whispered.

Lachlan reached for the driver's door handle. "What's wrong?"

"You just—" She clamped her mouth shut.

What if the voice in her head was a delusion? She didn't want him to think she'd popped her cork.

His frown stayed fixed. "Yes?"

Erin shook her head. "Nothing. I'll get the wine."

Chapter 8

Erin reached back for the bottle and then slipped from the car. As she walked toward the house, she felt an icy sensation on the back of her neck. As if someone breathed on it and stirred the fine hairs. She paused as the shadowy sensation slid right over the top of her—cloaking and smothering. She gasped.

She stopped in her tracks and Lachlan bumped into her. "God, what is that?"

His arms came around her waist, and he held her back against him. "What do you hear?"

"It's not what I hear, it's..." Realizing that she'd started to confess she saw formless darkness around them, she clamped her lips shut and closed her eyes. "Nothing."

His hands slipped from her waist and he turned her around. She held the wine bottle between them like a shield. "I know it wasn't 'nothing', Erin. Will you explain later?"

Shivering, she hunched into her long wool cloak and tugged her scarf closer about her neck. Erin moved out from under his touch, despite the heat and strength of his body. "Yes."

She upped the pace of her stride, eager to enter the house and chase away half-imagined sensations and worries.

They rang the doorbell, and Tom answered right away.

As Tom let them into the foyer, he said, "Saw you drive up." Tom hugged her with his short, slightly plump body. "Welcome. It's been awhile since you had dinner with us, Erin." Without waiting for her to comment, he turned to Lachlan and they shook hands. "Why don't you bring her around more often?"

Erin's eyebrows went up. "We just met the other day."

Tom winked and shoved his hand through his sandy, short blond hair. "What have you done with *her* sense of humor, Lachlan? Her frown is hanging down around her ankles right about now."

Lachlan played along, giving his friend a good-humored grin. "I think she left it back at the library."

She glared at him with mock fierceness, half serious. "My sense of humor is perfectly intact, thank you."

Lachlan slid his arm around her shoulders, but whether to placate her or warn her to keep her lips shut, she couldn't say. "She's a right prickly one, at that. I dinna think the wee lass knows what she's about. The library is old and musty anyway. Has to affect a body's ability to stay cheerful."

She sniffed.

Right, bud. That's where we almost did the deed right between the stacks. It's pretty difficult not to think about the library without remembering that wild encounter.

She thought she heard soft laughter in her head, deep and masculine.

Tom grunted. "Ugh. That library is about as comfortable as a porcupine quill up the ass. No wonder she's looking as thrilled as a dead fish."

Lachlan's hardy laugh superceded Erin's gasp of mock outrage.

"Ever the king of colloquialisms," Lachlan said when he stopped chuckling.

Erin waved her hand in a shooing motion. "Get outta here, Tom. That library is a fine institution."

Tom shrugged as he put their coats in a hall closet. "That place is creepy beyond belief. I hope you're not planning on doing any more late night kid parties there. I doubt the adults would bring the children and if they don't want to be out at night with some weirdo running around attacking people. "

Erin gave him a conciliatory smile. "No one has evening events planned until Christmas. Besides, the head librarian is the one who decides that, not me."

Tom grunted. "I know, but you and Gilda shouldn't be working late at night in that big mausoleum anyway."

"I promise we'll try our best to be the exception, not the rule."

As Tom led the way toward the big living and dining area, Erin glanced around. Mediterranean and Spanish influences graced the closed floor plan of the Victorian house, giving it a snug aspect. Finely decorated, but with understated colors of blue and green, the house felt comfortable, lived in and yet elegant.

Maybe someday she'd have a home like this with her husband.

Husband. Marriage wasn't inevitable for her. Some day she might step into matrimony, but at this juncture, she didn't expect a husband or a home like this one.

Gilda found paradise with the man she loved. Erin couldn't blame Tom for being worried about his wife. She also knew that, although Pine Forest had its ghostly image to uphold, the recent attacks on women made the entire situation grimmer. Tom didn't often grouse about anything, and that made his concern all the more realistic. He didn't scare and he didn't suffer fools; his warm personality always made her feel right at home.

By the enthusiasm he showed for Lachlan, Erin could tell Tom respected the Scot great deal. While Lachlan seemed to have this dark and mysterious side, the relaxation in his eyes showed how much he trusted and liked Tom.

Part of Erin wanted to use Tom's opinion of Lachlan as a measuring stick. What if they were wrong, though? Lachlan could have fooled them. Then she had to wonder when she'd become such a cynic.

Gilda walked into the living room, her fluffy blue sweater and long denim skirt made for cold winter nights. "There you guys are. I was rummaging around in the basement for the Halloween candelabra. I almost forgot it."

Tom rolled his gaze to the ceiling and sighed. "She insisted on having it lit and on the dinner table."

Gilda beamed, her smile indulgent and mysterious. "So get in there and light it before I peel your head."

Lachlan's eyebrows shot up. "Peel your head?"

Gilda wiggled her eyebrows. "My favorite high school teacher in Savannah always used to say that when she thought someone wasn't doing what they were supposed to. You think I have an accent, you should have heard Miss Glover."

After everyone had drinks in hand, Erin followed Gilda into the kitchen. Once inside the cozy, oven-warmed atmosphere of the kitchen, Erin felt safe from the strange shadow that lurked outside the house. Maybe the shadow wasn't the same as the one she'd sensed in the library, but Erin had about run out of scientific excuses for the edgy darkness. Maybe, if she could summon the courage, she'd ask Gilda if she knew about the shadowy presences.

God, Erin. You always said there are no such things as ghosts. Are you finally letting this nutty town turn you into a superstitious twit that attributes every inexplicable event to the supernatural? The litany of condemnations from her psyche continued.

Erin inhaled and allowed the scent of Gilda's marinara sauce to soothe her senses and her growling stomach.

"So?" Gilda asked as she stirred penne pasta into a stockpot.

"So what?"

"It seems like you and Lachlan are getting along well." Gilda's pleased smile said it all. "He really likes you."

"You put him up to this, didn't you?" Indignation meant her voice went higher than she intended. "I mean, put him up to being my escort."

"Shhhhh." Gilda placed a pot holder encased finger to own mouth. "I did not put him up to this. He'd mentioned the other night that he'd like to ask you out."

"Really?" Erin's voice squeaked and she swallowed in embarrassment.

"Really."

Erin sliced French bread in preparation to make it garlic bread, her motion with the knife automatic. "Well, I don't think it'll work."

Gilda stopped stirring. "Why not?"

Words burst from her before she could think much about how they'd sound. "He's from Scotland."

"You don't like men from Scotland?" With a puzzled frown, Gilda put the glass top back on the stockpot so the bubble and spatter of the fragrant sauce wouldn't muck up the stove and counter. "Half the women I know would give their right arm to meet a man from Scotland."

Erin grinned. "Ridiculous. Why?"

Gilda turned toward her and answered Erin's smile with one of her own. "Because they have it in their head that every Scottish man on the planet has the lovely brogue and sexy presence of a man like Lachlan."

Erin almost snorted. "As if. I've never seen a man as sexy —" Erin choked off her words with a cough. "I mean, men as handsome as Lachlan are a rarity anywhere. He's extraordinary looking. And being a Scotsman has nothing to do with that."

Gilda held up one hand. "Hey, you don't have to convince me. I think some women have the idea that every man in Scotland wears a kilt and has the sex appeal of a Liam Neeson in *Rob Roy* or Mel Gibson in *Braveheart*."

Glad to see that at least Gilda had common sense, Erin nodded. "Simply not true, as we all know. Otherwise there would be wholesale emigration of American women to Scotland."

Gilda laughed. "Okay, since Lachlan is extraordinary, why are you keeping him at arms length? We already vouched for him, and he's nice as any man could be."

"I realize that, but he'll be going back to his own country soon. Why start something I can't finish?"

Gilda chuckled softly. "Honey, you can't guarantee you'll finish any relationship, whether they're American or Scot or from Timbuktu. There's nothing certain."

"There you go, then. You answered your own question. I don't need to get involved with anyone now or in the distant future." Erin put the bread on a cookie sheet and spread butter on each piece. "Especially not a man who could up in leave in a few days."

Gilda looked a cross between exasperated and amused. She went to the refrigerator and searched for salad makings. "So, you want to set yourself up to be unhappy." She put the bag of pre-made salad on the gray-toned countertop. "I don't understand why people do that."

Growing a bit tired of Gilda's interference, she sprinkled garlic powder onto the bread and took it toward the oven. "And I don't understand what you're talking about. I'm not trying to be unhappy."

With a sigh of total resignation, Gilda opened the oven door for Erin. Erin slid the bread into the oven. "You're setting yourself up for failure in relationships. You're saying that if you could be hurt, which we all can, that any relationship between a man and woman is a mistake. Pretty all inclusive, don't you think?"

Erin stared into the lighted wall oven, her eyes focusing on the bread. "Maybe." Although she knew her answer came across limp as a spent dick, she pressed onward with her point. "Think about the divorce rate. So many people aren't willing to try. They give up long before the party is over. And still others are truly irreconcilable."

Gilda peered at her friend with an intensity that saw right through the veneer. "And what does that have to do with getting to know Lachlan?"

"He's unpredictable."

Gilda's nose wrinkled up, confusion clear on her face. "Unpredictable how?"

Erin put her pot holders on the counter. "If you're like me you want consistency and security. You can't get those with a man who might take a hike. If I was going to make it with a guy, it would be someone I know is here for the long haul."

"Make it with?" Gilda smiled. "You're jumping straight from dating to bed?"

A flush filled Erin's face. "No. No, of course not."

Gilda started rinsing tomatoes for the salad, then stopped. She looked at Erin with a knowing expression. "Wait a minute. I see that pink in your face. You're embarrassed about something."

Damn it. How does she know?

"I'm not," Erin said.

"You are."

"I'm not."

Gilda laughed softly. "Okay, have it your way. If I didn't know better, I'd say you were already half in love with Lachlan. I saw the looks you've been giving him."

"You've seen us together for less than an hour, and you think we've got something going?"

"There's certainly something going on between you. The heat is palpable."

Denial seemed the proper escape route. "It's all in your imagination, Gilda."

Gilda sprinkled a bit of cheese on the salads. "Switching gears, then. Did you see that crazy article Malcomb wrote about an El Chupa — El Chupa — ?"

"El Chupacabra."

"That's it."

"I didn't waste my time reading it."

As if on cue, a series of footsteps paced over their heads. Erin had heard these steps on the first visit to their old cottage, but hadn't heard it the last couple of times she came over.

"Is Mark up and about?"

Gilda picked up two salads and headed for the dining room. "Oh, he's doing well. He's in the library reading a book. His elbow wasn't actually cracked, just severely bruised."

Erin trailed after her friend with two more salad bowls. "Then who is upstairs?"

"Rudy. He's been active lately. I guess something is bothering him."

Of course. Rudy the ghost.

Erin didn't pursue the subject, tired of ghost-permeated conversation. Moments later, Gilda called the others into the dining room.

Once everyone settled down to eat, Mark talked about school and the Halloween party coming up at the old house next to the Gunn Inn.

Mark, sitting to the right of his mother, seemed eager to talk about anything and everything. Tom sat at one head of the rectangular table, while Gilda sat at the other. Lachlan sat across from Erin and next to Mark.

Good. At least he's not sitting next to me. I don't know if I could have taken that luscious scent of his. When she glanced up at the big, dark-haired man, his smile melted her into her shoes. She smiled back, feeling delirious and dangerous. She wanted to rush right out of the house and make love with him until the sun came up. Instead, she'd restrain her overactive hormones.

Mark laughed at something Lachlan said, and the young boy's freckled face, red hair and green eyes made him look a little like Howdy Doodie. Cute as a button, the young extrovert preferred talking over eating everything on his plate.

"I'm on the ghost committee." Mark smiled and a piece of spice from the marinara sauce stuck in his teeth. "Jackie Cohen and I are making this really gross skeleton with missing teeth and blood running out of its eye sockets."

"Charming," Erin said as she looked down at her plate of blood-red marinara.

"Like there *needs* to be make-believe ghosts set up for the party?" Tom asked.

With the nonchalance of youth, Mark shrugged. "Yeah, but it should be fun. I think I can make some really disgusting special effects."

"Lovely," Gilda said, throwing a glance at her husband. "My son is becoming a special effects artist for Wes Craven movies at the age of eight."

"Hey, that sounds cool." Mark brightened up. "I love that movie *Halloween*."

Everyone chuckle, even if Gilda did look chagrinned with the idea.

Seconds later the conversation veered to the attacks on women.

"I told Gilda she isn't going home alone from the library." Tom poured more wine. "It's way too dangerous out there right now with a nut running loose."

Lachlan glanced at Erin. "A very wise idea. I'll be picking Erin up from the library from now on."

Erin felt anger boil up, but she kept her voice modulated. "That won't be necessary, thank you."

Gilda put down her fork. "I wish you and I could carpool, but since our schedules are a little different on certain days..." Gilda shrugged.

Erin wanted to wipe the worried look off her friend's face and prevent Lachlan from trying to take over her life at the same time. "I can go directly from the library to my house without any worries, I think. Unlike the two women who've been attacked, I'm not out walking or jogging early in the morning."

Lachlan took a swallow of wine and said, "Then at least give me your schedule. I'll follow you from home to work and back."

She looked him dead in the eye. *You hardly know me.*

I still care about you. *The masculine voice, undeniably Lachlan's, came into her head.* I want to protect you.

Amazing. Mind-to-mind communication sounded like a neat concept, but how could it be?

"I think it's a good idea," Tom said. "You never can be too careful when it comes to things like this."

Gilda patted Lachlan on the arm. "You're such a sweetie to do that for her."

Erin wouldn't be pushed. "I'll be fine. I don't need a bodyguard."

But I'd love to guard your body.

Her gaze snapped to his, and Lachlan's smile said he knew the outcome his thought would have on her. She couldn't retaliate, unfortunately, with the family sitting here.

Contrary emotions bounced inside of her like rubber balls. She'd never met a man that caused multiple odd feelings within her all at once. She liked him far too much; obviously her hormones had been deprived long enough that any great looking guy with lethal magnetism could throw her off kilter. Erin glanced away, determined to not spend any more time ogling him. Besides, what if Danny had already discovered something unsavory about Lachlan? What would she do then?

Gilda gave a visible shudder. "I can't imagine who could be attacking people and biting their necks. I mean, how sick."

"A nasty bugger with no soul and no remorse," Lachlan said.

"A monster?" Mark asked.

Erin smiled and took a sip of her wine. "Of course not, Mark. There are no such things as monsters."

Mark frowned. "What about the Loch Ness monster?"

"Son, no one has proved the Loch Ness monster exists," Tom said as he reached for another helping of salad. "Maybe someday, but there's no proof right now."

Yikes. So Tom is like Gilda. They really do believe in all this hokum about things that go bump in the night. It was difficult to fight the odds when everyone but you believed in ghoulish creatures roaming Pine Forest.

"Bigfoot," Mark said. "Now there's a monster."

Lachlan wiped his mouth with a napkin. "I'm not so sure I believe in Bigfoot."

Erin lifted her eyebrows. "You?"

Lachlan grinned. "I think Nessie is a better possibility. After all, she has a fair amount of water to hide in. The loch is deeper than the Atlantic Ocean in some spots, and over twenty miles long. Plenty of room for a wee beastie to hide."

Mark's grin went as wide as the aforementioned loch. "Thanks."

"Humph." Erin decided to egg on the big, bad vampire wanna be. With a huge smile designed to blind, she said, "And with thousands of miles of forest, poor ole Bigfoot gets dissed?"

Lachlan reached for the pasta bowl. "At the present time...yes."

"Do you have ESP, Erin?" Mark asked.

She smiled, amused by the boy's lightning change in direction. "Not that I know of."

"Do you believe in it?" Lachlan sprinkled parmesan on his pasta and didn't look at her.

She touched the sterling silver heart necklace she'd slipped on before leaving the house. "I'm not sure that I do. Anything the slightest bit strange I can usually pass off as coincidences."

Lachlan's skeptical expression and searching gaze unnerved her. "I don't believe there are any coincidences. Things happen for a reason."

"Things happen," Erin said, "because people make choices."

Lachlan grinned. "That, too."

His agreement threw her, and she paused with her fork halfway to her mouth as she stared at him.

Tom leaned on the table, his gaze singling out Erin and Lachlan. "Live in this town awhile longer, Erin, and I'll bet you'll change your mind. Gilda and I were pretty unconvinced about ghosts and weird stuff until we moved here. Of course, Rudy the ghost had something to do with that."

Erin started to feel like a woman trapped with ladies in a luncheon designed to convert her to a card-carrying quilt maker.

Before she could respond Mark said, "I still say it's that Mexican or Puerto Rican goat sucker thing."

"Why?" Lachlan asked.

Mark took a swig of his milk and came up with a white mustache. As he wiped his mouth he said, "'Cause I've been reading about it on the Internet."

"Oh, that's great. A wonderful source of truth and information. The Internet," Gilda said as she glanced at the ceiling in apparent disgust.

Amused by Gilda's prejudice, Erin decided to tease her friend. "Now, Gilda, you know as well as I do the Internet has some valuable information."

Gilda's frown grew deeper. "It also has a lot of misinformation."

"No more than anywhere else," Lachlan said as he finished his pasta.

"I still think it's that Mexican goat sucker creature," Mark said with conviction.

Tired of the supposition, Erin said, "Not only is El Chupacabra unlikely to be stalking people in Colorado, the entire idea is stupid."

Her strident response slipped out before she gave full consideration to how it might sound. Mark frowned, and Lachlan looked at her sideways. Right away she knew she shouldn't have been so hard on the boy.

"I'm sorry, Mark." Erin pushed her plate away. "Anything is possible in this town." When he smiled she continued. "At least that's what I keep hearing."

"It's okay." Mark bit into more bread. "Mom and dad said the same thing earlier."

Lachlan reached for his water glass.

"Next thing people will say is that it's a vampire," Erin said.

Lachlan's glass slipped from his fingers.

Erin saw it all like a slow motion cartoon. Mark's mouth opened, Gilda let out a small "oh-oh" and Erin gasped. Time slowed, sticking like honey to the air around it. A moment that should take a fraction crawled as if stuck in the goop.

Lachlan's hand flashed out.

And caught the glass.

Time snapped back into place.

With a grin Lachlan placed the glass back on the table. "Whew. That was close."

"Wow," Mark said, holding his fork halfway to his mouth.

"Didn't spill a drop," Tom said as he put down his utensils and stared at the undamaged water glass. "How did you do that?"

The big Scot took a sip of his water. "Quick reflexes."

Erin saw the exchange in her mind again, and realized time seemed to stop awhile as Lachlan caught the glass. She knew she must have been blinking like an idiot.

Time didn't stand still, Erin.

His voice again, in her head, made Erin glance up at him. Sure enough, he watched her.

Then why did everything seem to slow down?

I really do have extraordinary reflexes.

Astounded and speechless for the second time that evening, she looked away and concentrated on the remainder of her dinner. He was—they were—communicating with their minds. She didn't want to think about how demented that sounded.

After coffee and apple pie for desert, they started home. As they cruised along in his car, Erin decided now would be a good time to ask him about their mind connection. She gazed into the night, catching the diamond-point reflection of the stars against the black velvet sky. Crisp and bracing, the evening felt like a good one to go home and curl up in bed. Even one glass of wine made her drowsy, so she knew she'd fall asleep fast. Unless, of course, this crazy mind-reading business didn't keep her awake. She shifted on her seat and sighed.

God, the lass has beautiful legs.

Her head snapped up. Sure enough, his gaze flickered over her nylon clad legs for a millimeter of time. Heat spread over her entire body. Unused to men appreciating her body, she admitted it felt good to know he liked what he saw.

"I heard you," she said before she could stop herself.

His mouth twitched in amusement or embarrassment. "Sorry. I couldn't keep that thought to myself."

He'd said it and confirmed the one thing that couldn't and shouldn't happen in her ordered world.

Erin searched for words to describe how she felt. "This is…is incredible. Is this really happening? Are we reading each other's minds?"

Seconds later he pulled into her driveway and shut off the ignition. "We're reading each other's minds."

She shook her head and remained stunned. "You're not even surprised by this?"

"When I first realized I could do this, it freaked me out as well. But because it has happened to me before, I'm not one hundred percent surprised."

"Eight-five percent surprised?"

He laughed softly and turned towards her. "It's cold out here. Let's go inside and talk about this."

Erin lifted one eyebrow. "You're assuming that I'm inviting you in?"

"Inviting me in is the only way you're going to hear about mind-to-mind communication."

While he'd been in her home once before, in the back of her mind she wondered if inviting him into her home this time might be one of the biggest mistakes of her life.

Chapter 9

Once inside the house, Erin offered Lachlan something to drink, but he refused. She took her time making some chamomile tea, nervous about allowing him in and wary of learning about this so-called mind reading.

Why him? Why now?

She paused as she poured boiling water over the teabag, half waiting to see if Lachlan would answer in her mind. When not a whisper came to mind, she sighed in relief.

She came back into the living room. Lachlan sprawled over the center of the couch, his big body taking up most of the room. She headed for the chair.

"Wait," he said. "Sit by me."

She hesitated. "Why?"

His grin went seductive and his gaze searching. "I want to be near you."

She placed her drink on the coffee table and eased onto the couch. When he made no effort to move over, but snuggled her into the corner of the couch and pressed nearer, she almost protested.

He turned towards her. "You're still afraid of me. Why?"

She jammed her fingers through her hair. "Look at it from my point of view. You came into town like gangbusters, kissed the stuffing out of me, made me feel things..."

Again that dark, carnal gaze drifted over her. "Yes? How could *I* make you feel things? Aren't *you* responsible for your feelings? You just said at dinner that people make choices."

"Yes, of course." Exasperation made her want to smack him. "What I mean is there's something about you. I've never been like this with another man. On short-term acquaintance, that's frightening."

"Don't be frightened. You're safe with me. I'd never do anything to you or with you that you didn't want."

Yes, but what if my will is not my own? She allowed the thought to flow whether or not he could read her mind. *What if you have some strange, otherworldly power over me?* When Lachlan smiled, Erin wondered if he'd heard her last mental statement.

"Tell me about your family." His request sounded velvet soft and raw with a need that didn't match the words.

God, he could be talking about cumquats and still turn her on. "What about them?"

"You're from Arizona?"

"Yes."

"Where in Arizona?"

She reached for her tea, taking a sip to stall. "Near Flagstaff and the Grand Canyon. My parents have a ranch there. They wanted me to stay in my comfortable little job, but I felt hemmed in. Living with them in the big ranch house didn't help."

"You didn't feel as if you had a place to call your own."

She saw deep sympathy in his eyes. "Exactly."

"So you had to leave and find your own way."

"I should have done it a long time ago."

He shook his head. "Would have, should have. Humans are strange creatures. They spend far too much time trying to analyze what might have worked rather than doing what works today."

When he slipped his hands through her hair, drawing his fingers through the short strands, Erin put her cup down on the table again to escape that disturbing touch.

"It's the only way we learn from our mistakes," she said. "We have to learn what we did wrong and not to do it the next time."

He looked doubtful. "Not if it means we punish ourselves with eternal guilt for events beyond our control. And there is much beyond our power."

"But I thought you believe in taking responsibility for ourselves?"

He closed his eyes a moment. "Yes, lass. But dwelling on what might have been can do harm to you and those around you. Call it negative thought forms, or bad attitude. You can't change anything about what happened yesterday. You can only live today."

Erin knew he spoke the truth, but she felt an urge to challenge him at almost every turn, almost as if she could find a way to discredit him. If she could discredit him, then she could escape his sexual prowess.

She crossed her arms. "I know that I can't afford to shirk my responsibilities to others, if that's what you mean."

Used to men who became irate when they didn't get their way, she waited. Her father always sputtered and bellowed when people defied him. Intellectually, she knew Lachlan wasn't like her father, but emotionally she reacted by rote.

"Now you're putting words into my mouth, Erin. Of course that isn't what I mean."

"I'm sorry."

Again those tantalizing fingers speared into her hair and caressed the back of her head. "Apology accepted. Now that we have that out of the way, why are you drawing away from me? When we first kissed I felt something powerful, and I think you did, too."

"Yes, but—" His passion made her crazy, throwing her pulse into a wild, ragged thing she couldn't control. "You're unlike any man I've known before. I'm used to a bully of a father and a passive-aggressive mother. I'm better off away from them, but sometimes I react like Pavlov's dog to certain situations. I'm not used to the kind of acceptance you've shown me." *Go ahead, blurt it out.* "Hell, I feel like a passion virgin."

114

His eyebrows tilted up a bit. "Are you a physical virgin, lass?"

His voice came soft, caring and not the least bit derogatory. With a tone like that, she couldn't become livid with him.

She smiled sardonically. "I could tell you it's none of your business."

Arrogance, albeit mild, touched Lachlan's expression. "I'll only find out anyway."

His calm and perceptive acceptance of her emotions gave her some relief. Leaning back against fluffy pillows, she tried to put distance between them so she could breathe and think. Lachlan turned sideways until he could hitch his knee up onto the couch. His position told her he remained open to talking with her, but he gave her distance.

Claiming her control meant she would have to jump right into the deepest part of the lake and hope she could swim. "Do you know what I'm thinking all the time?"

"No, not always." He leaned forward slightly, and she pushed back against the pillows. "Only random thoughts."

"Then I'm also picking up your random thoughts?"

"I can project my thoughts into a receptive mind." His gaze swept down her body in a sweeping perusal that felt like a caress. "I've projected several thoughts into your mind, others you've picked up from me on your own."

Unease rippled through her. "I'm not sure I like the idea of you projecting thoughts into me. What if I don't want you to?"

"We have to have a bond for me to be able to project those thoughts."

"We've just met. How could I have a bond with you?"

He leaned forward and his scent, musky and masculine, filled her senses. "It's very complex, Erin. I told you'd explain at dinner tomorrow night."

"You said you'd explain about vampires. What's that got to do with our so-called telepathic connection?"

Lachlan ruffled his hair with one hand. "Actually, more than you might think."

Confusion rolled within Erin, and she wanted to smack the truth out of him then and there. "Tell me now. Not that I'll believe a word of it."

He swung his feet to the floor. "Back at Tom's and Gilda's you protested when Mark spoke about El Chupacabra."

Exasperated, she said, "Again, I want to know what does that have to do with us having a...a bond and reading minds and vampires?"

He looked worried. "Ah, lass, it's very intricate."

She put her hands up. "I have all the time in the world. Spill it."

With another grin, this one full of mischief, he asked, "You American's have an interesting way of saying things."

Amused, she returned his smile. "And the Scots don't?"

"Oh, aye." He deepened his voice and his brogue. "We do. In fact, I think we invented odd sayings. I'd like to tell you about it sometime. I dinna have the time now."

"Back to mind reading, buster. The night I first met you at the library, I heard you in my mind."

"That's right." She saw the edgy, hot restraint burning in his eyes, his gaze lambent and full of desire. "And I wanted you from the first moment I saw you."

His surprising words, combined with his intent assessment, about unraveled her defenses. She was afraid. Plain and simple.

"Don't be afraid of me. When I said I'd protect you with my life," he said, his words deep with a sensual quality that scattered her wits, "I meant it."

Trembling started in her stomach, then turned to a blaze that incinerated all her reasons for refusing Lachlan and ordering him out of her life.

"You wanted me to know what you thought of my legs?" she asked.

His eyes sparkled. "That thought got away from me. You're the only woman I've met who can make me project a thought. When it's powerful enough of an emotion, I can't hold back with you. I've never felt this out of control with a woman."

As she pondered on the incredible admission, she marveled at how wonderful his fingers felt against her. Big, masculine fingers caressed her neck with sweet attention. Erin imagined those long fingers stroking between her thighs until she felt wet and swollen. Instantly, a rush of moisture touched her panties. She clenched her thighs together. She visualized him slipping two fingers deep inside her, pressing upward to hit her G-spot, sliding and dipping until the ache became unbearable. Consistent throbbing started deep inside her belly and between her legs.

With an out-of-this-world gorgeous smile, he said, "I'm glad you like my touch." His voice deepened to a husky whisper. "And yes, I will touch you there, if that's what you want."

A blush flamed her face. "You're reading my mind again."

He tilted his head to the side, and she fell into that dark fire once again. "Yes."

When he didn't apologize, Erin tried to dredge up some indignation and found she couldn't. Instead she wished to tease him, tempt him into doing what she'd imagined. She wanted to bathe in the admiration she saw in his incredible eyes.

"Thank you," he said as cupped her face with his other hand.

She couldn't think, only feel. "For what?"

"For believing I have incredible eyes."

She made an exasperated sound. "Damn it, Lachlan, do you plan to read *all* my embarrassing thoughts?"

He shrugged, a twinkle of amusement mingling with the heavy duty desire she saw in his eyes. "Well, you heard my thoughts about your legs. Turnabout is fair, don't you think?"

"Humph."

"I take it that's the closest to yes I'm going to get?"

Unwilling to allow the conversation to deteriorate into a discussion on mutually attractive body parts, she said, "You hardly know me, yet you want to protect me?"

Erin thought she detected a modicum of irritation in his face. "Why do you think no man could ever care about you?" His voice went quiet. "Who made you believe such rubbish?"

Disturbed by his easy evaluation, she remained silent. She ducked her head and looked at her hands in a moment of weakness.

Her father's strident voice seemed to materialize in her head, as real as the day he'd muttered the words two months ago. *You think you'll find any friends better'n the ones you got here? You sure won't find a man a better man in some Podunk town like Pine Forest.*

Lachlan's touch brushed over her cheek, possessive and protective. He tipped up her chin. "When I first saw you, I thought you were pretty and gentle and honest. I need a touch of that in my life, and there you were." He paused, daring her to look away from his fathoms-deep eyes. "I want your body, but I also want to know you as a person."

I want your body.

No man had ever said those words to her, blunt and without remorse. Yet his qualification, that he wanted her as a person, also fueled the fire building inside her.

His words settled in her heart and took up residence, daring Erin to refute him. Other men said sweet words, in fact a few once promised her similar things during short acquaintance. She soon discovered they didn't mean a word of it. Wariness held back appreciation.

Her chin tingled from his touch, and she reached up to touch his fingers. Those crystal lights seemed to glow in his eyes again, and as Lachlan held her gaze, he gathered her hand in his and kissed the back of it.

"You think I should get protection from El Chupacabra?" she asked.

"I know Tom and Gilda are concerned about you, too. I told them I'd keep an eye on you."

Overprotection. Her parents did enough of that when she was young. Could she allow a man to do the same, no matter what his intentions?

There it was—that creeping doubt, the kind she encountered often. Despite his assurances, despite Gilda and Tom vouching for him, she couldn't accept a virtual stranger's protection. She slipped from his grasp and stood, looking down at him as she positioned herself near the coffee table.

"Thank you for your kindness and concern, but I can't. I don't know you well enough."

"You still won't trust me." His matter-of-fact statement sounded flat but it went with his calm demeanor as he stood.

He shrugged, and his big shoulders looked broad enough to take on the world. Everything about the Scot was solid, dependable and sincere. So what held her back?

"I can't, Lachlan. Not until I know you better."

"So there's hope." He nodded as he if he understood her rejection and possessed infinite patience.

She knew she must confess one thing to get his reaction. "There's something I have to tell you."

"About what?"

"I told Danny Fortesque about what you told me the night Mrs. Pickles was attacked."

Lachlan didn't look the least confused. "I know. You told him your suspicions because you were concerned I had something to do with her death. I don't blame you. You were being sensible. He stopped by the bed and breakfast last night to question me."

Surprised, only one word came to her mind. "Oh."

A smile flickered over his lips, then vanished. "You expected me to be angry?"

"Frankly, yes."

"Get used to me understanding things, lass. Life is too short to be angry all the time." His gaze narrowed. "Is that what your parents used to do? Yell at you?"

Disconcerted by the depth of his comprehension, she sighed. "Dad yelled a lot when he was frustrated. Mom was the strong, silent type when it came to being mad." Guilt ran through her, and she stepped toward him, eager to remedy any gap between them. "Did my statement to Danny harm you in any way?"

"No." Lachlan put up one hand. "I told Fortesque everything I knew. He seemed satisfied to some extent."

"Some extent?"

"He didn't say he was going to arrest me, if that's what you're worried about. But he said he would be watching my every move."

Erin groaned. "Oh, Lord."

Lachlan chuckled. "Now that we've got that out in the open, does this mean you'll still have dinner with me tomorrow night?"

"What time?"

"I can pick you up at six-thirty." He started for the door, retrieving his brown leather jacket along the way.

"No picking me up from work."

He slipped into his jacket and zipped the front. "Okay. I won't suggest it again, unless you ask me."

Before she could say a word more, he slipped his arms around her and brought her close. As his mouth came down on hers, she knew she'd lost the battle again.

Chapter 10

Erin didn't try to resist Lachlan's kiss, but she didn't expect what happened next. His one sweet, tender kiss dissolved, and he stepped back. Surprised that he didn't take the kiss further, she felt a twinge of disappointment.

With an assessment that spelled sizzling heat, he let his stare drift with slow precision from her breasts straight down her body to her shoes. Fire blazed a path wherever his gaze touched. "If you want more, you have to take it, lass. You know what I want."

How could she miss it? His eyes burning for her, he appeared every inch the muscular, skilled lover she knew he must be.

More than sex, she found her desire for him came as much for attraction to what she knew about him. His bravery, his kindness, and his mysterious allure gave strength to her need for him. Affection followed, even though it was too soon to say love.

Lachlan stood like a defiant soldier, and she hesitated. He started to turn toward the door, and her commonsense left her, swept away by a renewed hunger that tingled in her breasts, her nipples, and high up in her vagina. Again she clenched her muscles and felt a response, the trickle of moisture.

Without a word, she clasped his forearm and turned him back to her. She reached up and cupped his face between her hands. "One more kiss."

She dared to look into his eyes again, mesmerized by the sheer power of his intensity. He slipped his arms around her waist and kissed her, his mouth searching with a ravenous intensity. She groaned, welcoming his tongue. She met his foray with her own, half mad with keen desire.

As the kiss lingered, Erin moved against him, a shimmy that said she intended to give him what he wanted. Rubbing her entire body against his like a slinky cat, she pressed her breasts against his chest. She clasped at his leather-covered arms, wanting to tear the coat off. She wished to rip off the shirt underneath and see if hair sprinkled his chest and if his pecs looked as hard as they felt. She wanted that hot skin under her fingers, brushing against her with heated caress.

As he took her mouth with his tongue, she imagined his cock there instead. He would slide it between her lips, giving her it all and she would love it. She would lick and suck and show Lachlan how much she wanted him in her mouth. She would even allow him to climax in her mouth if he desired.

Heaven help me. Shocked by the thought, because she'd never allowed a man to climax into her mouth, a forbidden thrill launched her desire to new levels. With Lachlan she wanted his cum. In her mouth and inside her body, shooting hot and fast.

She shivered with an illicit pleasure.

He pulled back, a moan on his lips. "God, sweet Erin, feel what you do to me." He pressed his hips against her, and she felt the hardness of his cock against her belly. "I want to sink inside you and never leave."

With quick, precise moves, he removed his coat and flung it away. His carefree attitude, full of confidence and potent sexuality, said he didn't care where the expensive garment landed. To him it mattered far more to keep engaged with her. He pulled her into his arms again. Satisfaction shot through her.

"But we aren't going to have sex tonight," he said softly.

"We're not?" she asked in a half-daze.

With a wildness she never recalled feeling before, she arched against him. He kissed her, his hands urging her toward the couch. They sat down, and he leaned over her, pressing her into the cushions. She drowned in his attention. An erotic magic encompassed her, sweeping her senses to an exotic place she'd never experienced.

They seemed to kiss forever, until her mind twisted and twirled and took flight into the darkness just beyond the door. Within her psyche she realized something extraordinary happened between them, and with all her heart she wanted it to continue.

Lachlan retreated from the kiss again. "I must have a little of your sweetness."

Sweetness?

His words whispered into her mind, as light as snow. *I will show you.*

He reached down for her pumps and slipped them off. "Don't move."

Shivering with a raging desire, she nodded. "All right."

As he caressed her calf, she felt the exciting touch straight through her hose, and another shudder skipped through her body. He worked up her leg, touching with slow deliberation until he reached her thigh. He cupped and caressed and palmed the inside of her thigh.

She stopped his hand as it slid up her thigh. "Take them off. My hose. Take them off."

For a moment she wished she'd worn thigh high stockings and garters.

Next time, lass.

As he slipped the hose down her legs, the arousal built, promising a sweet, hot detour into the wildest sexual experience she'd experienced.

Lachlan didn't fumble and stumble as some of the men she'd dated once did. And although she hadn't taken many lovers, she couldn't believe the extraordinary heat racing through her at his mere touch.

Her nipples pulsed with the need to be touched. They pressed against her bra, causing hot desire to jolt through her lower stomach. As if reading her mind once again, he kissed her and cupped her breasts at the same time.

Is this what you want?

Yes.

Each movement felt gossamer-soft as his big hands clasped her breasts and manipulated them, charting over untouched territory, never rushing, always giving.

"Erin, darling, these are beautiful."

His eyes blazed, appreciating her as he cupped and rubbed and tormented until she wanted to beg him to touch her nipples. Instead he brushed around and around the outer edges for what seemed an eternity before he lifted her sweater. A tiny panic rolled through her as he gazed at her white, utilitarian front clasp bra. Nothing sexy about it, nothing to entice a hot-blooded male.

Yes, Erin. You alone are enough enticement.

His caring voice inside her head, raw with sex, eased some of her fears. As if realizing Erin didn't feel one hundred percent comfortable with baring herself, Lachlan cupped her cotton-clad breasts. Heat gathered in her skin, warmed by his fingers and palms and by the excitement of his intimate touch. As the sensation built, her nipples felt hard, tight, and desperate for caresses.

She grasped his hands and stilled his movements. At his pause, she heard the breath rasping in and out of his lungs and the quickness of her own breath. She dared look into his eyes and saw the golden fire she longed for glimmering in his gaze. Erin knew Lachlan wanted her with an ache she could feel clear down to her soul.

She thought about everything she'd be leaving behind if she allowed this mysterious, incredible hunk of a man to make love to her.

She barely knew him. Lachlan would soon leave her. Love had nothing to do with the uncontrollable urges that drove her to couple with him.

Since when had she become one hundred percent fucking certifiably irresponsible?

Erin didn't know and didn't care.

Her will seemed sucked from her as she stared into the amber deep pull of his eyes.

"Erin?" He kissed her forehead, his voice full of worry. "Are you all right?"

"Yes." She shoved aside her previous worries.

"I don't have protection for us, lass. That's another reason we won't make love tonight." Again his voice roughened with brogue. "But we will." He whispered to her, his voice a comfort. "You have me under your power. I'll do anything you want. Touch and suck your nipples, stick my fingers deep up inside that sweet, slick channel. *Anything but take you tonight.*"

Such blunt, blatantly sexual words might once have seemed rude to her. Now they made her hot. Her face flushed, then heat ran down through her torso and into her middle.

"When we make love, it'll be right," he said.

Make love.

He hadn't said fuck, as men had said to her before. They seemed loathed to speak tender words, and those associated with emotion. Not Lachlan.

I will say both to you, Erin. I want to fuck you. I want to make love to you. I want you every way I can get you. I will say any words you need to arouse you and make you come.

Erin gasped in surprise and gratification.

She dared look into his eyes and all resistance fled without a gasp of protest. "Yes."

She ached so much for him, Erin almost ripped open his pants, jumped on him and impaled herself on his cock. The breathtaking idea made her belly tighten with anticipation.

He clasped her nipples through the material and even through her bra she could feel the tug as he gently began to strum. "Oh, my God, Lachlan."

He smiled. "More?"

"Please."

With deliberation, he plucked her nipples non-stop, giving her no safe place to retreat. Erin realized he would show her the measure of her passion and make her acknowledge it. He worked her breasts, tormenting until her nipples stung with longing. She rubbed her thighs together to alleviate the awful tension building to relentless life deep between her legs. She wanted him there, pounding hard until she had the most extreme sexual experience of her life.

Lachlan released one breast and kissed her. As he tongue plunged inside, he reached for her bra clasp and snapped it open. His big, warm hand cupped her naked skin, and she shivered with delight.

To show how much she wanted him, she worked at the buttons on his jeans, popping them open one by one. His hand closed over her fingers and stilled her mad rush to release his hardness from its confines.

His restraint drove her mad and aroused her even more. She decided then and there she must be into torture.

Suddenly his thumb passed over her nipple. The jolt of pleasure and surprise, the feel of his hot flesh against hers, made her gasp into his mouth. His fingers started a relentless, maddening massage over her entire breast, sweeping across her nipples with enough pressure to create excruciating bliss.

He released her mouth, and she closed her eyes against the sexual hunger. Lachlan's hands cupped both breasts and he lavished attention on each globe, his fingers tracing her nipples.

"Please, Lachlan."

This was it. If he didn't do something to alleviate the throb inside her she would simply die on the spot.

"Tell me what you want," he whispered against her nipple, tasting it with tiny flicks of his tongue.

"More."

Obliging, he massaged one nipple with the very tip of his tongue. Heat radiated from the captured bud and spread outward to the rest of her body. She'd never felt this hot, this unable to control her sexual needs.

"More." She moaned again.

He rubbed the nipple, stroking over it with repeated, long laps that included a circling motion. "We're going to do this until you come."

Come? Yes, she'd moved upon his muscled thigh and almost came in her panties, but she tried to imagine a climax caused by Lachlan sucking her breast—

His mouth sealed over the tip, sucking deep and hard. Erin almost came unglued as she moaned and arched against his body. His index finger barely brushed over her other nipple. The contrast of hard suction and soft touch about drove her insane.

"Oh, God. Lachlan that feels so good. Don't stop."

Her own hands fluttered over him as she searched out hard muscle, testing the contours of a body she wanted naked and on top of her. Powerful biceps shifted as she gripped them, muscles in his back bunched as she traced her fingers over them. She parted her legs and shifted so she could arch her hips into his rigid cock. He groaned and pressed downward, pinning her still. His movement pressed her clit and she gasped.

Lachlan continued his torture, and she heard his breath coming rapidly hot against his skin. He closed his mouth over the other nipple and suckled in time with the continual swirling motion of his fingers over her other breast.

He stopped for a moment and gazed into her eyes, his molten expression enough to tell her that he wanted her very much. "Erin, sweet, you have the most beautiful breasts I ever seen."

As his lips brushed over her flesh, her nipples hardened even more. His fingers tugged and rolled and she cried out.

Arching her back, she groaned as he played with brushes of his thumbs, then tender plucks between thumb and forefinger. Again he suckled, alternating long slow licks with deep pulls. A fire built by steps and degrees between her legs, urged onward by the hard press of his cock. A new rush of moisture dampened the curls between her legs, and the sensation made her ache.

"Lachlan, I'm begging you."

His hot mouth encompassed one nipple, then released it long enough to take it between his teeth. Spikes of staggering arousal hit her as he swirled and darted against the captured nipple with his tongue. He gently pinched her other nipple.

"Come on, lass. Come for me." His voice, heavy with fire and husky with demand, sounded sexy as hell. "Come."

With lightning quick intensity, she felt the heat gather inside her. Her breathing quickened, her heart raced. She arched into his body and begged. "Please, please, yes."

On and on he sucked and licked and strummed her nipples until she thought she'd go insane.

Fire sparked low in her belly, sweeping downward until it ignited in her hot channel. Heat spilled through her clit in glorious waves. She cried out in surprised delight, amazed at the incredible sensations streaking through her body. As she shuddered, he pressed reverent kisses between her breasts.

"Lachlan," she gasped, looking up into his eyes as he gave her nipples one last brush of his fingers. "That was wonderful."

Unrepentant and full of mischief, his smile said he loved what he'd done to her. "It was."

With a sigh, he levered off of her. "It will be even better when I'm inside you."

Even better. Wow.

His gaze went raw with barely suppressed desire and raged with a hunger that looked almost animal. "Are you afraid?"

She moved into sitting position and pulled her bra back together, latching the front clasp. She shoved her sweater back down. "Sometimes I am. This is all so quick. I need the evening to get my head on straight and think."

Maybe I require the entire century.

His gaze pinned hers. *I will give you an eternity if that's what you want, lass.*

"You fear what you don't understand," he said. He ran his hands through the tangled mess of his hair. "But I told you I willna' hurt you, and I meant it." He leaned in a little closer to her, his hot breath puffing across her mouth, and the heat in his eyes continuing to blaze. "I'm at your command. We'll make love when you ask for it, and not before." A new pride slipped into his tone, one filled with primal male assurance. "And you will ask me to take you, Erin."

As he picked his jacket up off the floor, he gave her a gentle, though predatory smile. "I'll leave you for now, sweet lass." He reached for her hand and kissed the back quickly. "Night."

Long after he left, she double-checked the locks on her doors. At some point she remembered he hadn't explained a thing about vampires or how he'd cured her headache.

* * * * *

The vampire watched from his high tree perch as she closed the shudders on her windows, wondering if Erin believed the shading would stave off the attentions of someone like him. Did she even realize the implications of what she did? He doubted it.

She didn't seem vulnerable, at least not in the way Gilda would be. Ah, yes. Gilda. Soon he would taste the warm, creamy flesh of the woman and know temporary surfeit. Nothing in the night, no mortal flesh, could ever fulfill him the way Erin would. But at least Gilda would seal the void rolling within him and give respite from the piercing hunger the sight of Erin produced.

She would soon know her soul-mate stood near. Watching. Waiting for the right time to bring her to his eternal bed.

Nothing, and no one, could stop him.

Gritting his teeth against overwhelming lust, he flew into the night and searched for one who would give him surcease.

He wanted someone who knew passion and fire and appreciated a hot union with everything in her whore's heart.

He felt her unreleased passion calling to him, like a soft message on the cold night wind. She needed a man, wanted one to take away the heavy ache that pulsed through her clit and demanded satisfaction. He sensed she would turn to her own finger if he didn't satisfy her soon. What a pity to waste a lovely orgasm on her own touch.

He drifted in the night for some time before he found another woman's house. He laughed, keeping his voice low so no one would hear. He would enter her bedroom and take the woman without remorse. With a smile and full lust in his groin, he prepared to enter her room and show the woman the excitement only a vampire's touch could bring. Then, if her loyalty was true, she would be a willing slave and servant to him all her undead eternity.

* * * * *

Ronan's slumber broke as the phone next to his hotel bed rang. He snapped bolt upright, a cry halfway out of his mouth before he stifled it. Pissed, his heart pounding and his reserves depleted from a day in the sun, he reached for the phone with an attitude. He squinted as a strip of sun from under the too short drapes pierced his eyes.

"What?" he growled into the phone.

"Ronan Kieran."

Deep and full, the voice sounded almost familiar, but not enough to penetrate his perturbation. "Yeah?"

"You've forgotten a good friend after all these years?" The man's tone rang with mock astonishment.

The hearty voice on the other side felt like home, though they'd been born on two different continents at different times. Ronan grinned. "You bastard. You wake me up after a couple hours sleep—"

"Sorry, sorry. I forgot you fang types need your daily beauty sleep."

Ronan groaned and propped up against the headboard. He looked down at the sheet that covered his nakedness and remembered he'd been dreaming of Selima and the sweet curves of her new vampire skin. "Daily is right. And I haven't had much sleep since I got to this country. How the hell did you find me?"

"I've got my sources. I would have come in person but something's up. We need your help in Pine Forest, Colorado. The ancient one is here."

The hair on Ronan's neck prickled. "Colorado? What the hell is he doing there?"

"He's found his mate. A woman he wants to make into a vampire and take with him on his hellish life. Help me, Ronan. You're the only one who can stop him."

Ronan's throat tightened. "Bullshit. But you knew I'd want to be there to see him die."

"Yes."

Ronan jammed his hand through his hair, then swung his feet out of bed. He frowned when he saw an insect run from one corner of the room to another. One of the best hotels in Morocco and they had bugs. "We may not be able to kill him."

"I thought you said that old man in Morocco could tell you how to kill the ancient one."

Ronan grunted. "You wouldn't believe what he told me. He said I'll have to be in love, or at least pretending it, to kill the vampire."

"Ridiculous."

"Exactly. We don't have time for me to find a woman who'd even be willing to fake love."

The deep voice on the line laughed. "From what I've heard, just about any woman would fake it if you asked them to. Couldn't you put them under your thrall—"

"You know I won't do that."

"Then come here and we'll think of a solution together. I'm disappointed that Yusuf gave you useless information."

"You're disappointed?" Ronan knew he sounded like a wounded boy, and he covered his eyes with his hand for a moment, revolted. "Look, we'll think of something. It'll take me awhile to get there."

"He'll have all the women in the town for lunch before too long."

Ronan realized, with that one statement, that maybe the time for true battle had arrived. He'd chased this hell-demon clear across the globe. Maybe now he could settle the score once and for all. Even if it meant seducing a woman to do it.

Chapter 11

"Did you see the headlines?" Gilda asked Erin as she stepped up to the library counter. "We didn't get the paper this morning, but I heard someone saying something about Mrs. Pickles and Jessie Huxley."

"Unfortunately, yes." Erin slipped the Sentinel across the counter toward Gilda. "This is horrible news."

Woman Dies From Injuries Inflicted In Attack. Second Woman Attacked And Killed.

Gilda gasped as she read the article. "Oh, God. Poor Mrs. Pickles. And Jessie. My God."

"And to think she was here yesterday flirting with Lachlan like there was no tomorrow and now she's—" Erin couldn't finish the sentence, leaving the horrible facts to speak for themselves. "Her children are alone now."

Gilda looked up from the paper, her expression grim. "Honey, they have their father. He'll come from California to get them."

Erin shuddered, a relentless chill sweeping over her skin like a tidal wave. "She was so full of vitality and alive when I saw her last."

Gilda frowned and put the paper aside as she came around the side of the counter. "Something else is going on here. What is it?"

Erin clutched her own arms to her body, her blue fleece top and long gray pants didn't seem warm enough in the echoing, huge room. "Jessie was flirting outrageously with Lachlan the other day, and I was thinking what a—" Erin surveyed the room. "I wished that she'd just disappear out of his life."

Ashamed, Erin said a silent apologetic note to the dead Jessie's soul.

Gilda's frown looked worse than a gangster who'd just been told he wouldn't get paid. "Now don't blame yourself for this. You didn't make some creep attack her."

"I know, but it's so strange that it would happen to her when I wanted her out of Lachlan's life."

Gilda smiled grimly. "I'm happy you're finally realizing how you feel about Lachlan, but the killer attacking Jessie was a coincidence."

"I'm surprised you think anything is coincidence in this town."

Gilda folded the paper in half, then folded it again so that Jessie's picture wasn't in full view. She shoved the paper aside. "This town rates twenty on a one to ten scale of weirdness, but I don't attribute every weird event to the supernatural."

"Jessie was a pain in the butt and a flirt, but she didn't deserve this. Neither did Mrs. Pickles."

Before Gilda could respond, Danny came in the front door and headed their direction.

"Ladies." He tipped his cowboy-type hat, his face a mask of determination.

Gilda held the paper out to him. "What are the police doing about this?"

Danny's face turned dour, and she couldn't blame him. Most of the police officers in town worked hard. No doubt this was one of the biggest crime sprees they'd seen, though, and it must be taking its toll.

He nodded and his big hands settled on his hips. "We're putting on extra patrols tonight. We also want women to take extra precautions going home at night until we figure out who is doing this. Erin, are we still on for lunch?"

Gilda's grin said she approved, but Erin tried to ignore Gilda's satisfied look. "Noon it is."

"I'll pick you up."

Erin kept her resolve. "I'll meet you there. None of these attacks occurred during the day. The perpetrator isn't likely to change his pattern, is he?"

Danny shook his head. "Doubtful."

"Who do you think attacked these women?" Gilda asked as she ran both her hands through her hair in a show of nervousness.

"Any leads we have at this time are confidential," Danny said. "I'd like to tell you but—"

"But then he'd have to kill you," Erin said with a grin. She wanted to lighten up the thick tension hovering in the room. Palpable and frightening, the apprehension seemed to cling to the very walls.

Gilda and Danny joined in her soft laugh, and relief settled the tight sensation in her stomach.

"Say, did the library have that structural engineer come in and check this place out?" Danny asked. "You know, because of the noises you heard the other night."

Gilda nodded. "Earlier this morning before the library opened. Apparently there's nothing wrong with the place."

Danny shrugged, appearing unconcerned. "Well, that does it then. Nothing more to worry about." He glanced at Erin and gave a wide grin, as if his reassurance would make her feel safe. "Maybe Erin imagined the noises."

Erin's defenses came up, but she kept her response cool and calm. "I wasn't the only one who heard it. Lachlan Tavish did, too."

Danny sniffed and tucked his thumbs in his gun belt. The leather creaked. "Maybe he's been living in drafty castles for too long. Doesn't know what he's hearing."

The unusual put-down grated against her like saw against bone. She felt her shoulders go back. She lifted her chin. "I'm sure he knows what he heard, just as I know what I heard."

With his smile fading by degrees, Danny took a step back. The sparkle of amusement disappeared in his smile. Now his grin seemed plastered on like a clown's.

Gilda cleared her throat. "Well, we should get back to work."

Relieved at the escape hatch, Erin turned away from Gilda and Danny and began to work. Her progress was impeded several times by her traitorous thoughts. She'd known Danny longer than she had Lachlan, and yet she still felt compelled to defend Lachlan against Danny's not-so-subtle insults.

Gilda said nothing about Erin's coffee date with Danny, or his statement about Lachlan. Erin couldn't help being relieved. She didn't feel like deflecting conjecture about dating. Not when she'd told Gilda she didn't want to get involved with anyone right now.

Yet she was involved with Lachlan whether she wanted to be or not. In less than a couple of days the man had turned her inside out with his scorching looks and passionate caresses.

Her face flamed as she remembered the sexual heat that flared between them last night as he'd seduced her with the steady, intoxicating touch of his hands and mouth. She shuddered and her nipples peaked against her bra, almost as if in protest of the confinement.

Seduced, my ass.

She would be fooling herself if she didn't admit she'd wanted him every bit as much as he'd wanted her. Yet something still held her back.

The eerie voice that spilled into her head at weird moments? The dark influence seemed tinged with peculiar nuances, scary and unreal. Yet that voice didn't sound like Lachlan's. Or did it? Confusion made her frown. She couldn't separate the loving, calming sound of Lachlan's voice from the slithering, unusual voice she heard at other times. Could they be one in the same?

No. It didn't make sense.

Still, one last little piece of her didn't trust him.

Erin, you are freaking loosing it.

A soft touch on her shoulder made her jump. Gilda stood there, concern in her eyes. "Something wrong?"

Erin smiled and gave a laugh to cover her state of mind. "I'm a little tired. I didn't sleep well last night."

Gilda nodded. "Me either. It's just starting to get too spooky for words around here."

A few minutes later the lethargy hadn't left, so Erin headed for the water cooler. After she took a long, cool drink of water, she went into the bathroom. Florescent lights flickered, their buzzing becoming a sputtering before one blew out. She stopped cold, a bit startled.

Well, with ghostly goings on, why should that surprise me?

Another voice slipped into her mind, this one cloaked with a dark side she couldn't deny. *Erin, my sweet. It shouldn't.*

She jerked, startled. Pain filled her temples and she reached up to clasp her head. She gasped as pain spiked once again.

When the pain subsided, she glanced around, almost as if the voice had come from a verbalization rather than an intrusion into her mind. "Who's there?"

She glanced under the stalls. No one appeared to be there. Then she remembered a scene from the movie *Scream* when the young heroine realized someone did lurk in the bathroom with her.

Erin's breathing accelerated, her heart pounding with new alarm. She stared at the bathroom stalls. Heaviness settled over her, bleak and draining. Her knees weakened and her stomach rolled. Putting her hand on her stomach, Erin fought nausea. When that didn't work, she gritted her teeth. She didn't understand the origin of the sudden fear and sense of evil or why it assailed her now.

Panic attack?

She'd never had one in her life, though she'd heard of the symptoms. Unless something else had gone desperately wrong with her, a panic attack might explain why she felt so disoriented.

A cold wind passed over her and ruffled her hair.

Her eyes snapped open. She saw a dark shape forming in one corner, opaque but almost obscuring the dull gray wall. As it grew denser, the blackness also came closer. Closer.

Dread.

Sickness.

Darkness.

Fear.

New throbbing started in her sore temples.

Erin whimpered as the ache took her off guard. She reached up and tried to rub the pain out of her head. *Not again. No more. Please.*

She knew only one person could assist her. *Lachlan.*

Lachlan, please help.

She ran. When she pushed against the door it swung open so fast she almost bumped into a woman stepping inside. She apologized, half worried about the other woman as the lady smiled and went into the bathroom. Erin stood near the door, tempted to grab the lady and drag her out of the abysmal place.

As fear continued to send waves of tremors through her body, Erin knew she could no longer deny that something dark haunted her.

* * * * *

Erin noticed that few patrons utilized the library that morning. Those that did seemed more inclined to chat about Mrs. Pickles and Jessie. The talked about the criminal that lurked somewhere *out there*, more than they checked out books. Erin saw real trepidation in some of their eyes, and ghoulish inquisitiveness in others. Rumor upon rumor flew. El Chupacabra continued to be the main culprit.

No one said a thing about ghosts for a change, now that a new monster invaded town.

Despite the creepy conversations going on all around her, she managed to keep her strange experience in the rest room from obsessing her thoughts. She'd decided that she must have suffered a small panic attack and nothing more.

Before noon, clouds puffed up in the west and came up over the mountains with a vengeance, chilling the air with snow flurries. As a bizarre afterthought, thunder rumbled. Odd weather, to be sure, but not unheard of. Once in a long while, thunder would mix with snow in this high altitude climate.

Thunder sounded again as the door opened and Lachlan walked inside.

His gaze immediately landed on Erin, and her breath caught. His expression flickered from pleasure at seeing her, to a frown of deep concern. As it always did, his presence seemed to take in the whole room, as if no one and nothing else mattered. Suspended in his thrall, she allowed her gaze to tangle with his as he walked toward her. Golden fire lit his eyes for a second, then flickered out so fast she thought sure she'd imagined it.

Two women sitting at nearby tables gawked at him. When he passed by, they smiled and whispered. They looked enthralled, just as she, by the mere sight of gut-wrenching good looks and staggering masculinity.

Movie star gorgeous, he gave the gossiping women a genuine smile before turning his full attention back to Erin. A strange, almost possessive feeling came over her, and she didn't like it one bit. She couldn't blame the other women for going gaga over the man. Lachlan's leather jacket hung open in the front. Underneath he wore a cobalt blue sweater and expensive black wool slacks. He possessed the refined air of cosmopolitan European male, with all the athletic rawness of the American man. She allowed an admiring sigh to leave her lungs.

Yep, hunk didn't begin to describe his sheer magnetism. Testosterone rolled off of him in waves, and any female within sight could see it.

Face it. The man is walking, breathing, absolute sex.

"Erin." His voice rumbled deep as he leaned on the counter. His gaze moved over her with an enduring assessment filled with heat and genuine longing. "Your jealousy is showing."

"What?" she gasped, mortified.

"You're a mite jealous." His deep voice came so softly, no one else could hear. "There's no reason for you to be worried. I dinna' want any other woman but you."

"Damn it, Lachlan, are you reading my—?"

He placed one finger over her mouth for a second. "Shhh...you wouldn't want anyone to think we were having a fight, would you?"

One of his brows lifted as he grinned and gazed at the other patrons. Thank goodness no one appeared to be paying any attention to them.

Exasperation mingled with sheer heat as his finger brushed her lower lip. "I wouldn't think you would care what anyone thought."

He nodded. "I don't. But you do." As his gaze swept downward and paused for a moment on her breasts, she felt the combustibility factor launch into force ten magnitudes. "You'd love to be free of what other's think, wouldn't you?"

How true. "Yes."

"Then let it go. Just let it go. You're a beautiful, wonderful woman who has everything and every opportunity open to her."

His ability to see not only into her heart, but her mind, disturbed her deep down at the same time it comforted her. "What about you? What if I'm worried what you'll think?"

His smile held a stunning gentleness. "Are you?"

She couldn't speak, astounded by the strange conversation. How did he do this? How did he bring her into these exceedingly intimate conversations with so little effort?

You know I think you are the most exciting woman I've ever met.

You do?

His gaze held hers, relentless and filled with hot desire. *Yes, lass. By all the saints, yes.*

She shivered with fine awareness and inhaled his heady, warm scent. *Heaven help me, we're speaking entirely in our minds.*

Yes, and just remember, no matter what happens, you're the only woman I want. His potent voice filled her head. *There's no one else for me but you.*

Once again her senses homed into his frequency, thrumming with a strange, continuing yearning deep inside her. She decided to ignore all talk of jealousy and concern about other people's perceptions of her.

Shaken, she finally spoke. "I didn't think I'd see you until dinner tonight."

"I couldn't wait to see you."

Erin's heart almost triple timed. "You're irrepressible, Lachlan."

He placed one hand over his chest. "She wounds me deeply. " His frown came back, his gaze narrowing. "I also felt something was wrong. I almost stopped by earlier."

"Wrong?"

"Something dark and worrisome came over this place." His attention wandered to the room, skimming and searching. Like a radar he seemed to home in on everything at once, glancing at the rafters high above, then back to her. "It felt...dangerous. I thought I heard you calling me, but I wasn't sure."

She saw the question in his eyes and at first didn't know whether to confirm or deny his belief. "Lachlan..."

"I like that way may name sounds coming from your lips." He closed his eyes for a moment and then opened them. "A sound from heaven."

She licked her lips and his gaze followed the movement. "Something weird happened in the ladies room earlier. I...you were the one I thought could help me."

He nodded, his gaze holding a mixture of worry and satisfaction. "So, I did hear you call out for me. Does your head hurt again?"

"No. It went away." She looked around, again aware they spoke of strange things and anyone might hear them. She lowered her voice. "I've had a headache every time something strange happened. The first time being the night we met. So I'm thinking these headaches either mean there is something medically wrong and I'd better see a doctor, or they have something to do with you."

"No, lass. They don't have anything to do with me. And physically you're all right. You remember when I mentioned that you are picking up vibrations from the library?"

"I remember, but I didn't believe it."

"You believe it now?"

"I'm not sure. Too many bizarre things have happened."

"Well, it's not all from the library, but from something else."

"What?"

As if waiting for a drum roll, he hesitated before he said, "An evil force."

She opened her mouth to tell Lachlan he must have stopped at the Blarney stone on the way to the United States, but Danny abruptly stomped toward the counter.

Absorbed in Lachlan, she hadn't seen Danny arrive. Lachlan's magnetism and his superior physical power showed up in his broader shoulders and more muscular arms. Although Danny stood quite a bit taller than Lachlan, when it came to sheer good looks, Lachlan would win the prize. Chagrinned that she even bothered comparing the men, she smiled at them both.

Lachlan turned toward Danny. "Good afternoon."

Danny's gaze appraised Lachlan with a standard-issue police overview. Mistrust came over Danny's face. "Afternoon." Danny's shoulders went back. "You spend a lot of time in the library?"

At Danny's strange question, Lachlan didn't blink an eye. "I'm afraid so. Erin's caught my attention."

His blatant statement caught Erin off guard, and heat filled her face.

"Attention, how?" Danny asked, his face hardening into undeniable challenge.

Oh, oh. Now, boys…

Lachlan winked at her, and that slow, sultry blink held her as his husky voice flowed on the air. "She's beautiful, of course. That's enough to keep any man coming back for more."

Danny's lips twisted in apparent displeasure, but he didn't speak. Erin noticed that his fists clenched at his sides, as if he wanted to punch Lachlan or maybe throttle him. Fine tension stretched between the men, and Erin almost believed they might be green-eyed. *Surely not. That would be incredible if two men showed interest in me at the same time.* She gave Lachlan points for being blunt rather than rising to Danny's challenge with a show of machismo.

"So you're Scotch?" Danny said, an edge in his voice that kept his question a hair short of friendliness.

Lachlan's mild grin showed no malice. "Scot. Yes."

"Visiting a short time?" Danny's question sounded almost hopeful.

Lachlan jammed his hands in his coat pocket, and his gaze swung to Erin. "Maybe. I haven't decided yet."

"Here on business?"

"Business and..." Lachlan's gaze drifted to Erin a second time, and he gave her a slow smile. "And pleasure."

Erin felt rather than saw Danny bristle.

Danny and Lachlan stared at each other for so long, like two rams ready to fight, that she cleared her throat. "Ready to go, Danny?"

His gaze snapped back to her. "Ready."

"I'll see you tonight, lass," Lachlan said.

Erin could feel Lachlan's gaze on her all the way out the door.

Chapter 12

Danny and Erin traveled in separate cars, and on the short distance to the café she wondered if her imagination worked overtime. Did Danny and Lachlan see each other as rivals for her affection? In a secret, forbidden way, she liked the idea of them fighting over her. Such wishes might be childish, but the primal feelings existed nevertheless.

Absolutely incredible. I've gone cave woman.

And she knew exactly who would win the fight for her if it came down to the two of them.

Lachlan.

She sighed. Damn it. This situation became more alien by the minute. Somehow she must maintain control and not allow her feral sexual feelings for Lachlan overrule common sense. She'd already ventured beyond reasonable limits with him. Between now and her date with him at Ricardo's, she would think of a way to keep him at arm's length. She contented herself with a reminder that everyone made relationship mistakes, and she was allowed her fair share of bloopers.

Lachlan was one gigantic blooper waiting to happen. She wouldn't and couldn't allow herself to fall in love with him and be hurt.

Fall in love?

No. No. A hundred times no. I will not fall in love with him.

Once inside the café nestled with a cup of coffee and a steaming bowl of chili, she noticed the subdued nature of the crowd. About six people occupied the restaurant besides her and Danny, a low turnout considering the lunch hour.

To her surprise, Danny stayed quiet through the first part of lunch. A disgruntled expression remained on his face. "How long have you known that Tavish fellow?"

She forgot her chili. "We've gone over this ground before. I've known him about a week."

His expression turned a smidgen sour. "He's kind of out of place in a town like this, don't you think?"

A little irritated, she said, "Well, you're from Texas, Danny. Some people in Colorado think that's foreign. You know how playful Texans and Coloradoans are about each other." She grinned to take some of the frustration out of her voice. "He's not American, he's Scottish. He dresses a bit differently."

"Kind of fancy."

Rather than go for an acerbic reply, Erin kept her tone even. "Apparently he likes more formal clothes. He was wearing black jeans the night I met him, though."

"When did you say you first met him?"

She'd mentioned this before, but Danny had switched into high-gear police mode.

"Story night at the library." She put down her spoon. "Lachlan told me you went to the bed and breakfast where he was staying and questioned him."

"I'm surprised he told you." Danny sipped his steaming black coffee, then winced and put the cream ceramic cup back on the table. He spooned a couple of cubes of ice from his water glass into his cup. "Did he also tell you I caught him in a lie?"

A little taken aback, she took a moment to answer. "No. What lie?"

"He said he wasn't anywhere near the area where Mrs. Pickles was attacked." He grinned sarcastically. "But then he did admit that he was watching you that night."

Erin remembered that Lachlan had admitted the same to her. "How is that a lie?"

"In order for him to be near you, he had to be within the vicinity of Mrs. Pickles."

She stared at her coffee cup and frowned as she thought. When she looked up at him she said, "So you think he does have something to do with the attacks? But I was in the area, too. I could have been the one, in that case, to have attacked the women."

With a huffing noise he leaned back in the booth. "No way. You couldn't have overpowered those women. Besides, I know you. You wouldn't do something like that."

"You haven't known me that long. How can you be sure?"

He paused, and she knew she'd made him think about the flaws in his logic. "Why are you defending him? You were the one who told me you were suspicious of him."

"Because I've revised my thinking a little. Maybe he was watching me that night because he was worried about my safety."

The thrill of that possibility wasn't lost on her. She *liked* the idea that Lachlan cared about her. Just the possibility of Lachlan having feelings for her sent her stomach into cartwheels of exhilaration.

Danny grunted softly, as if not wanting to refute her statement in full. He rolled his shoulders as if to release tight muscles. "Things are crazy around here lately. I'm lucky I can have lunch with you, darlin'. The chief wants us patrolling extra hours."

His endearment didn't get passed her. She supposed he called every woman he knew darling. Erin smiled to ease his apprehension. "This El Chupacabra nonsense has people nervous right now." She glanced out the window to her left. "There are less people on the street."

He finished a bite of his chili before he spoke. "Shops are closing up before it gets dark."

"Probably not a bad idea."

"What about the library?"

"I doubt it. Our boss may be a kind enough soul, but he's a workaholic and he expects the rest of us to stay at our regular hours no matter what the crisis."

"I'll talk to Fred and maybe we can work something out."

"Good luck."

Danny's displeasure showed his eyes. He sipped his coffee. "Seems this Tavish bubba has quite a hold on the ladies around town."

"Bubba? I'd hardly call him a bubba. Every time someone uses that word, I see one of those stereotyped redneck dudes with a gun rack on their pickup and their ass crack showing because their pants won't stay up around their waist."

Danny seemed scandalized, but she didn't know if her blatant word choice did the trick, or the clear derision in her tone. "Whatever you want to call him, women are whispering about him at the station, and every time I turn around someone is talking about him."

Mistrustful of his statement, she took her time answering. "He's new in town. People were gossiping about me when I first arrived here, right?"

He smiled. "Well, yeah."

She shrugged and let that be her statement.

"What about you?" he asked.

"What about me?"

He pushed his bowl away. "You like this Lachlan guy?"

How could she answer that without giving away her conflicting feelings? "Just because I think he isn't a murderer doesn't mean I've fallen madly in love with him. I'm reserving judgment until I know him better. Why are you asking?"

Danny fiddled with the extra paper napkin on the table. "Because I want to know if I should consider him competition."

Her mouth opened, but she didn't know what to say.

"I mean," he said, "I've liked you from the moment I saw first saw you. I want to go out with you on a real date some time."

She saw her moment to escape his earlier question. "I'd like that, too."

Total relief flashed over his face. "Great. Maybe we could take in a movie this weekend?"

Immediate doubts formed in her mind. Danny might be a nice enough man, but she didn't feel attracted to him. Still, she couldn't say she knew him well enough to dismiss him out of hand, and she wouldn't become one of those women who judged on looks alone. Depth of character meant more than a tight ass and a handsome face. She compared Lachlan's amazing good looks with Danny's ordinariness, and wondered if she'd allowed Lachlan's sexual prowess to overrule consideration of Danny as a date.

Tired of speculating about the mysterious Scot, she said, "Mrs. Pickles' and Jessie's murders are the first Pine Forest has had in years, right?"

"Twenty years, to be exact."

"That's amazing."

"Yeah. The chief of police barely remembers that crime." When the waitress came by to fill their cups, they both refused more brew. When she left, Danny continued. "Now there's talk around the department about a vampire or that El Chupacabra thing being the culprit."

"The police department doesn't take that seriously, do they?"

He took a deep breath and let it out slowly. "No, but you never can tell in this town. When you've been here longer you'll understand. Pretty weird things happen around here. Gilda was telling me about the strange noises you heard at the library the night you met Lachlan."

"You don't connect the noises with him, I hope?"

"Who knows? A guy as strange as that might have a lot of tricks up his sleeve." Danny's carefree shrug didn't convince her. He might pretend he didn't care about Lachlan's presence in town, but Danny's comments and insinuations said otherwise.

"You think the noises in the library have something to do with the women who were attacked?" she asked.

"No. I was using that as an example of how strange this town is."

On a roll, she said, "Just because the women had bite marks on their necks does not mean it's a vampire or some monster. I can't believe anyone would believe that in this day and age."

He leaned forward and spoke low. "Mrs. Pickles died of unknown causes. They thought at first the loss of blood did it, but they'd given her transfusions and that should have taken care of the problem."

"Shock."

"They'd gotten that under control, too. Jessie Huxley didn't make it that far. Her body was almost drained of blood. She didn't have enough left in her to fill a teacup the medical examiner said."

Exasperated, Erin rolled her gaze to the ceiling, then stared at Danny. "So just because the poor woman dies, somehow she's been killed by a vampire? That's the most incredibly ridiculous thing I've heard yet."

Her argument rang in her ears for what seemed the hundredth time in a week. Despite the fact that her and Lachlan seemed to have formed a mutual mind link, she found the idea a monster roaming Pine Forest to be inconceivable. Telepathy remained more believable than vampires.

Danny's eyes widened at her strident tone. "I'm not personally saying that's what happened, but it's the biggest mystery we've faced in some time. And this town has been haunted for so long, anything is possible."

So even the police in this town believe in boogie men. She sighed. Maybe coming to Pine Forest *had* been a mistake.

"And Lachlan Tavish arrived here not long before the attacks started." Danny leaned back and crossed his arms as if he expected her to deny his statement. "That makes a person wonder."

"You're convinced Lachlan Tavish attacked these women?"

"We have no evidence, but you can bet he's in line for more questioning."

Her reply came tinged with anger. "Why are you telling me this? Wouldn't it be police business and therefore none of *my* business?"

"Normally I'd say yes, but since this Lachlan character is obviously interested in you I thought—"

"Thanks." She held up one hand. "But I'm doing a pretty good job of taking care of myself. What is it with this town and overprotective men?"

He sniffed. "Well, I'd think a woman would like having a man to protect her with some stalker prowling the area."

Somehow she couldn't see Danny shielding her.

No one can protect you against me, Erin.

Shadowy, filled with malicious intent, the voice hovered in her mind. It couldn't be Lachlan's voice. It just couldn't be. Her insides trembled, her stomach clenching with renewed fear and confusion. She looked out on the afternoon, trying to distract her thoughts from menacing creatures of the night. Snow lay in a thin blanket on the area, no longer drifting from the heavy white clouds shrouding the area. That dull, relentless throb started in her head again.

"Let's talk about something else, all right?" She didn't add a smile to her request, unhappy about the returning headache, the conversation centering on Lachlan, the attacks, and her so-called need for protection.

After lunch, he followed her back to the library, leaving in a rush when he received a call on his police radio. She took a deep breath and drew her gaze over the forbidding façade of the library. Suddenly she didn't feel so anxious to go back into the dreary structure. Although the headache lingered, it didn't pound with the relentless force it had on other occasions. She had no excuse not to go back to work. She took a step toward the library.

Erin.

The whispery voice made her stop, and she turned. No one in sight.

Lachlan, is that you?

Maybe it is.

What do you want?

You.

The word filled her mind like an icicle, pinpointed and painful. The throb entered her head with more force, and she gasped. Again she reached up for her temples and rubbed. If the voice didn't belong to Lachlan, could he be right in saying the pain was an indicator of evil close at hand? Or did she suffer from a migraine? >From descriptions others had given her, this headache didn't carry all the indicators of migraine, but what did she know?

She searched for any sign that Lachlan might be nearby. Other than cars driving down the lane and teenagers crossing the street at an intersection, she saw no one. She turned her attention back to the cold façade of the library. With a resolute deep breath, she demanded the headache to recede and wished that Lachlan had already shown her how to get rid of the pain.

A cold wind wafted over her, and without dithering, she headed into the library with fear close on her heels.

* * * * *

As Erin drove home later that day, the sky deepened into full night, and a niggling of apprehension made her wish she'd never agreed to go out with Lachlan tonight. She felt grateful for the headlights of the car behind her, illuminating the darkness of the street as she turned into her driveway. The car behind her continued, and soon the night surrounded her. She allowed her car to creep down the short driveway until she parked as close to the house as possible.

Bushes surrounding the small Queen Anne style home formed a thick wall, and it came to mind for her to call her landlord and ask if the vegetation shouldn't be trimmed back. It might be a fire hazard and also could hide any number of crawlies and undesirables. She didn't want to think about what might be hiding in there or she'd soon have a case of the creeps.

After turning off the ignition, she looked up and down the street in both directions. Three streetlamps provided dim illumination in the immediate area, but since the town didn't like blazing neon signs or billboards, it followed they didn't care for brilliant lighting on the street at night. Right now, she would have appreciated a stadium full of lights pointing right at her house. Taking a deep breath, she grasped her keys in a defensive position and stepped out of the car. She pushed the auto lock feature on her car and started toward the front door. She hesitated a second, a feeling of apprehension coming out of nowhere.

Something was wrong.

She'd left the porch light on that morning, but now darkness surrounded the porch. Had she really forgotten to leave a light on inside the upstairs bedroom window?

Erin heard a rush of air, like the sudden suction of a tornado, and her breath seemed pulled from her lungs. It happened so fast she didn't have time to think or flee. She gasped and whirled to face the menace.

A huge figure loomed in front of her and she opened her mouth to scream.

Chapter 13

"Easy, sweetheart," Lachlan said as he appeared from around the side of the house. He clasped Erin's arms, his concern evident in his deep frown. "Are you all right?"

She jerked out of his grip, anger making her snappish. "I was until you jumped out of the bushes like Jack the Ripper."

His eyes seemed to glow in the semi-darkness, and a weird shiver of trepidation brought goose bumps to her skin. "What's wrong? Why are you acting afraid of me?"

"I'm...I'm not." She went up the porch stairs and quickly unlatched the door. "Maybe it's not a good idea for us to go out tonight."

"Why?" He didn't sound angry, only confused.

She opened the door in a rush and then stood in the opening without any indication of letting him enter. "Because we aren't—we don't have anything in common."

He laughed.

Whatever she expected him to do, laughing wasn't it. "Go ahead, laugh it up."

She stepped inside the door and began to close it. She felt a second's resistance against the door, but then it slammed closed. Relief flooded through her. She didn't have it in her to discuss love, sex, or rock and roll with Lachlan right now and didn't care about being rude, either.

She turned around and gasped.

Lachlan stood not far from her.

"What?" she mumbled the question, her lips feeling numb, and her mind suddenly overwhelmed. "How?"

He sighed. "That's a very long story."

She planted her hands on her hips. "You seem to owe me several long stories, Lachlan Tavish."

"I know, lass. Now, why don't we go to Ricardo's and discuss it. We can have some wine, dinner, do some dancing..." His gaze swept over her like a hot tide, filling her center with that overwhelming attraction she always experienced when he came near. "Then we can come back here for...dessert."

Dessert. Uh-huh. His suggestion sounded decadent. Like warm custard slathered on chocolate mousse, or maybe whipped cream dipped strawberries, or hot fudge dribbled over —

Oh, yes, lass. I want that, too.

He moved almost too quickly for her to see. His arms slid around her, drawing her against his body with enough force to startle her. Lachlan's mouth came down on hers with hunger, twisting to find a tight fit as his tongue took immediate command. The continual rub of his tongue over hers made her moan with instant exhilaration. A sigh left her throat as red-hot longing flared in her stomach and traveled downward with a rush. Her center tightened as she imagined his cock doing the same thing, stroking in and out of her wet sex with forceful thrusts.

Ah, sweet Erin, stop thinking about making love. You're torturing me.

Erin pulled her mouth away from his and sucked in a breath. "Lachlan, what is happening? How did you do that?"

A slumberous daze came into his eyes, as if he could do nothing else but show her his desire. "What? Make you wet with longing?"

She gasped again, then in regretted it. God, she sounded like an outraged virgin. "No. Come into the house without me — I mean I couldn't see you do it —"

"Don't worry. I'll explain more later. Right now you should change into something sexy and slinky for dinner."

Oh, shit. I forgot how ritzy that place is. "I shouldn't have agreed to go to dinner at Ricardo's. I don't have anything sexy and slinky for a place like that. I'm sorry, it was stupid of me to agree to have dinner there."

He released her, and for a moment she thought the anger on his face meant he thought she was dumb as well. He brushed his fingers with a light touch across her cheek. "You're not stupid, lass. Don't ever put yourself down like that." He looked at his watch. "We still have plenty of time for you to get a new dress." Lachlan's expression twinkled with dawning awareness. "In fact, I know just the place. There's that shop over on Main. I walked by there the other day and saw this blood red dress that would be beautiful on you." As his gaze did another hungry assessment of her body, Erin felt amazement mix with the arousal he inspired inside her. "It's long and there's a slit up to the thigh." He licked his lips.

Imagine my hand sliding up your leg, Erin. Touching you between the thighs. Imagine me slipping your panties off. Think of how good it will feel to have my cock inside you.

Lachlan, now who is thinking of making love?

She closed her eyes, and with a swiftness that staggered her, she saw him pressing her against the wall, his big body trapping her as his demanding touch roamed her thigh.

Lachlan, don't. I can't think when you do that.

Then don't think. Just feel.

She opened her eyes and her gaze clashed with his. *We'll never get to the dress shop if you keep this up.*

A slow, carnal grin parted his lips. *We could spend the entire night having hot sex, then.*

The ravenous sexual potency of his voice in her head made her thoughts reel with excitement. Images of them tumbling onto her bed, him on top of her, his thick sex thrusting into her hot center, made everything inside her tighten with full-blown wish for sexual release.

"No!" Erin put one hand to her trembling lips, and stared at his flushed face.

Lachlan's hands clenched and unclenched. He looked almost unsteady, a bizarre weakness passing over his rough-hewn features. "Sweet lass, if we keep this up —"

"If *we* keep this up?" she asked, coming closer until she could poke him in the chest. "Why are you projecting those sex scenes into my mind? How did you get in the doorway without me seeing you?"

He clasped her hand and held it against his chest. Erin felt the strong, quick beat of his heart. She saw the arousal fading from his face, replaced by regret. "I was desperate. I shouldn't have played that trick on you."

"Which one?"

"When I came into the room without you being able to see me."

"Tell me, were you really a magician in Scotland?"

"No. Like I said, I'll explain later. After we've bought you the dress and had dinner."

"Lachlan, I really can't afford the dress."

"No, lass. I didn't mean for you to pay for it. It'll be my gift to you." She shook her head, but when she would have spoken, he leaned in close. "Please. No obligations. I know I said we could stay here all night and have sex. But that would only be if you're ready. Remember, I said when we did make love it would be under your terms." He cupped her face and leaned in to kiss her nose. "And to answer your question about the images of us having sex together…that isn't my doing. I can see the images in your head, but I didn't put them there." A smile broke over the carnal line of his lips. "Anytime you think about sex is because you want to. I have no control over your thoughts."

When she didn't speak or move, astounded by what continued to happen between them, he said, "Let's get you that dress."

* * * * *

"Are you sure you want to do this?" Erin asked as Lachlan followed her into *All That Glitters*. "This place is expensive."

"Don't worry, Erin. It's a gift."

The quiet place held a myriad of gowns, all luxurious. Satins, silks, taffetas, velvets. You name it, this store had it. Erin always wondered how the fancy shop made it in a town this size. When she stopped by one dress and spotted the price tag, she winced. All of this went beyond her budget. As they wandered forward, she marveled at the Victorian motif overlaid with a hint of baroque. In some respects, the glitter of gold, silver and sparkling fabrics might have overwhelmed the eye. Instead it enchanted.

The backroom door opened and a twenty-something woman with long, jet-black hair and wearing a stylish royal blue suit, stepped into the room.

The woman's smile came easy and genuine when she saw them. "Hello. I thought I heard the bell." The girl swept her hair away from her face and stepped forward to greet them. "I'm Janna Billingsgate." She shook their hands as they introduced themselves. "Oh, Lachlan Tavish. You're the vampire."

Erin's eyes went wide, and Lachlan laughed but didn't deny it.

Janna blushed as she took in his tall form. "Sorry. My niece told me that you were the vampire at the Halloween story hour." She nodded at Erin. "And you're the librarian who does the story hour, right?"

"Most of the time," Erin said.

Janna's gaze continued to rest upon Lachlan, her interest in him blatant. Erin felt a twinge of jealousy and tried to hold it back. For all she knew, Lachlan would be able to sense it. Knowing the rascally Scot, he'd probably get a huge kick out of either her jealousy, or Janna's interest.

Lachlan slipped his arm around Erin and tucked her into his side. "I saw a blood-red velvet dress in the window the other day. Do you still have it? I don't see it on display any longer."

Janna smiled. "Of course. We sold that one, but there is stock in the back. I have three sizes left." Jana turned her gaze on Erin. "What size are you? Petite?"

"No, actually, I just fit into a regular misses size...seven, I think."

"I think I might have something that will fit." Janna headed into the back room.

Erin remained quiet, disconcerted.

Lachlan snuggled closer to her, and she inhaled his masculine scent. It sent her senses into a new riot of attraction. "What's wrong, Erin?"

"I still don't know about this. When a man buys something for a woman, things get complicated. I had a guy once promise me a beautiful amethyst ring. I believed he cared for me more than he did. He didn't end up getting the ring because he couldn't afford it. He shouldn't have committed to something he didn't have the funds for."

She realized she sounded bitter, and her attitude made her blush. *God, you sound like a petulant child.*

Lachlan stared deep into her eyes, and there she saw the golden flecks deepen with understanding. "No. You sound like a woman who's been hurt." He slipped his index finger under her chin. "He shouldn't have promised you anything he couldn't honor. Since I don't know the man, I can't say what motivated him. But I do know one thing; if I get you this dress, it doesn't mean I expect anything of you." When she didn't speak, her mind still full of doubts, he continued. "I don't pay women for sex, Erin. I never have. Did the man who promised you the ring try and buy your sexual favors with gifts?"

She shook her head. "Maybe. I don't know. He seemed like a good enough guy, but I think he was confused. I think he fell in lust hard and then when he'd gotten what he wanted, didn't feel compelled anymore." Remembered pain, as fresh as yesterday, gnawed at her heart. She took a deep breath and tried to lighten the moment. She shrugged. "Well, he was a Libra."

Instead of taking the joke, Lachlan's gaze turned inquisitive and darkened. "Erin, I'm sorry."

She shrugged. "It was a long time ago. I'm over it."

"You may be over it, but you carry a wound. You wouldn't be suspicious of me if you didn't."

Erin moved away from him, slipped off her coat, and put it on a pink velvet covered chair. "I'm suspicious because I've learned my lesson. I won't be manipulated by a promise that won't be kept."

He nodded, his gaze glowing with new understanding. "And you see receiving gifts as a promise?"

Confusion built in her psyche, and suddenly she had the feeling she'd screwed something up big time. "No, no. I don't expect anything from you."

He stuffed his hands in his coat pocket. "When I make a commitment, I follow through. I was engaged once a few years back. I was ready to marry her, but she decided she couldn't marry me and it didn't work out. If it will make you feel any better, I'll tell you all about it at dinner."

"Only if you wish to."

Lachlan nodded. After a small pause, he said, "I know what you're thinking."

"Of course you do. What else is new?"

He chuckled. "I'm not like any man you've known. It's impossible for me to hurt you." He pulled her near and looked deep into her eyes. Keeping his voice low, he said, "You're going to be the death of me."

"Oh?"

Lachlan shifted even closer, and the hard press of rock-solid muscle and power made her feel feminine and desired. "You're driving me daft." He nuzzled her hair aside and whispered in her ear. "I'm walking around with a hard-on half the day."

She inhaled sharply, surprised and yet turned on by his blatant statement. "Lachlan."

"When we go to *Ricardo's* anything that happens tonight will be at your discretion. If you want me, you'll have me. If you don't want to make love, we won't. It's as simple as that."

Before she could reply, Janna came back with the dress cradled in both arms. "Here it is." She handed it to Erin. "Why don't you try it on in the dressing room in back?"

Erin hesitated for a second, then decided it didn't hurt anything to see if the dress fit. As she walked to the back, she heard Janna striking up conversation with Lachlan, and a new spike of jealousy attacked.

Drop it, Erin. This isn't going to work if every time he talks to another woman you get nutty. It's not healthy.

Resolved, she stepped into a dressing room and put on the long sheath. The low cut v-neck and thin straps accentuated her shoulders and neck. She would have to go braless in this dress because the cut didn't allow for any visible means of support. Quickly she took off the bra, then slipped the dress straps up over her shoulders again. When she smoothed the dress down over her hips, she saw that it looked damn good on her. The brilliant coloring enhanced everything — including her hair. The way the material cupped her breasts was beyond daring. She turned to the side and noted the material cupped her butt without appearing too tight. An audacious slit ran up the left leg and ended in the middle of her thigh.

Erin grinned when she noticed her ankle strap shoes added to the daring illusion and added length to her legs. She turned and presented her leg so that it slipped out of the slit entirely. Her hosiery clad limb seemed long and sexy.

All together the dress screamed two words.

Fuck me.

Red-hot desire slid into her belly when she thought about what Lachlan's expression would be when he saw her in this dress. A silly grin parted her lips, and when she glanced in the mirror again her smile said she couldn't wait. What the hell? She'd go for it and see where this entire experience led her. She could call the shots; he promised her he expected nothing for the dress. Why not take the gift?

She stuffed her bra in her purse and took a huge breath. Now or never. She gathered up her top and skirt and stepped out of the dressing room.

Lachlan stood nearby a dress rack staring into space. When he glanced at Erin, his reaction far surpassed her expectations. His eyes widened, glowed with instant heat, and he came toward her with a big smile. He stopped a couple of feet away, his attention dancing from her face and then making a languorous sweep to her breasts. His mouth opened, lust clearly written on his face as he seemed to fixate there. Then his attention drifted down over the rest of her, landing on the slit that rode her leg.

"God." His accent went thick and rough. "Look at you. I've never seen anything more delicious in my life."

A wild rush filled Erin, and her entire body felt like it heated with fire. Of all the times he'd looked at her with clear admiration, she couldn't remember feeling such intense awe coming from him before. This man made her feel like royalty in every way.

Lachlan reached for her hands and held them, his grin one of total satisfaction, and full-throttle desire. The heat of his skin against hers made her shiver with pleasant warmth. "You're so damned sexy and beautiful, I want to strip this off you and love you here and now."

Heat filled her face, and Erin's gaze darted to Janna and the other customer.

"I'm not talking that loud." His grin teased her, and he placed a tender kiss on her forehead. "If you keep looking at me like that, we're not going to make it to the restaurant."

His voice held an unbearably sexy nuance, filled with primitive response.

To break the sensual spell, she said, "Thank you. You'll be happy to know that I didn't even look at the price tag."

"Good." He winked and went to the register to pay for the dress.

Erin looked away, not wanting to know if he paid cash or credit card, or produced play money out of thin air. Guilty pleasure edged out her earlier fears, almost erasing her worry that this dress didn't mean anything. In truth, she couldn't say what it meant, other than he wanted to give her a gift. Why couldn't she enjoy and take it at that?

Before she could ruminate any longer, Lachlan came back to her, helped her on with her coat and they left.

As they drove to the outskirts of town toward Ricardo's, she smiled with contentment. She decided she would enjoy their date and stop worrying about the whys and wherefores. Right now she would savor the moment.

"Thank you, Lachlan. The dress is beautiful."

"You're welcome." Soft and deep, his voice sent liquid longing straight into her loins.

The damned man can turn me on with one word.

One word? His voice questioned in her mind.

She smiled and watched as the town receded and they headed into the countryside. Vulnerability slammed into her. *One word.*

I think I know one word that makes you excited.

Oh?

Fuck.

Her skin flamed at the raw and unexpected word. Her nipples hardened, and she ached deep between her legs.

Even in her head his voice sent swirls of burning hot arousal all over her body. *I know it sounds forbidden to you. I think you've had sex, Erin, but I don't think you've ever experienced a good, hard, nothing-held-back fuck.*

Embarrassment warred with arousal. *What's the difference?*

He laughed softly, the sound lingering on the air as his mind talked to hers. *I'll show you, when you're ready. Sex that comes hard and fast and long. Sex that blows the top of your head off and lasts in your memory forever. The kind of fuck that promises to kill you if it doesn't make you come.*

"Lachlan." She cleared her throat, but her voice rasped anyway. "Lachlan, you are a very naughty boy."

"I aim to please." A wicked smile flirted with his lips. "Does talking dirty bother you? I'll stop if you want."

This elegant and yet rough-hewn man confused and delighted her. One moment he looked stately, a man of the manor. The next he could whisper torrid love language in her ear and it didn't sound crass. Excitement filled Erin with delicious desires. She had a feeling this night would be one she would never forget.

Chapter 14

Lachlan and Erin reached the restaurant without additional mind games. As they pulled into a parking space, she noticed their car was the only one at the restaurant. The entire place, though lit up in each window, seemed quiet and deserted.

Ricardo's, much like the rest of Pine Forest, had an otherworldly presentation. Although it resided a few miles outside town, it seemed linked by the Queen Anne structuring, and the haunting glow of lamplight that streamed from the windows.

"Is anyone here?" she asked.

"Of course."

"You didn't do something like reserve the entire restaurant for us, did you?"

His grin teased her. "No, although I like the sound of that."

Like a gentleman he leapt out of the car and opened the passenger door for her, even though she didn't expect it. She grinned as she slipped from the vehicle. "You didn't have to open the door."

"No, I didn't have to." He took her hand and his warm, big palm squeezed her gently as they walked toward the entrance. "I wanted to."

Seemed like this man never did anything but what he wanted. She didn't know if she liked that. Didn't life's complications affect him any way? Didn't he ever have obstacles to endure?

As they stepped into the restaurant, she put aside speculation and admired the beautiful antique furniture and the delicate glow of muted lighting.

"Mr. Tavish," the host said with obvious pleasure. "Welcome back." Tuxedoed like something from the nineteenth century, the host led them to their table in a secluded small room off the main dining room. "The wine list and your menus. Cedric will be with you shortly."

With an old-world bow and a toothy smile, the man closed the door to their room. She glanced around the room, impressed by the opulent decoration of red velvet and brocade. A huge chandelier sparkled with subdued light in the high-ceiling room, sending diamond points over the white china, gold utensils, and expensive blue table linen. A delicate rose scent lingered on the air, and she inhaled. Soft classical music was piped in from somewhere, adding to the romantic allure. A large fireplace sparked with a gas lit glow, cozy enough to appear the real thing.

"Like the room?" he asked.

Erin smiled. "I didn't even know this room was back here. It's like an enchanted fairytale."

"I found out about it the first night I came to town. I was tired and didn't want a crowd around me. This place gets noisy later in the evening."

She glanced at her watch. "It's almost six. Maybe we're a little early for the crowd."

He put down his menu. "Are you afraid to be alone with me?"

"No. Why should I be?"

"Because you're still acting skeptical and suspicious."

She sighed and looked at him over the glow of candlelight in the middle of the table. "Sorry. Give me some time, Lachlan. You have to admit we've been..." She struggled for the right words to describe their relationship. "We've been hot and heavy right from the start."

"I know." His voice held a masculine huskiness that threatened to keep her on the edge of arousal every minute she stayed near him. "It took me by surprise, too."

"Could have fooled me." She gave him a weak grin and reached for her water glass, her voice dry with nerves and anticipation.

He reached over and rubbed his fingers over her hand in a light caress. "Believe me, Erin. I would never lie to you."

Deciding she should stop being mistrustful of him, she nodded. "All right. I'm sorry. This is all new to me." She waggled her eyebrows. "Being courted like a queen."

Cedric, their waiter, entered the room after his knock received an acknowledgment from Lachlan. He took their wine order, then handed a small envelope to Lachlan. "I'm so sorry, sir. We forgot to leave this on the table earlier."

With a broad and knowing smile, Cedric exited the room and closed the door.

Erin peered at the small parchment-colored envelope Lachlan placed on the table. "What's that?"

Lachlan's expression held pure mischief. He nodded to another door not far from the fireplace. "There's a room beyond this one. I've reserved it for the night in case it gets late and you'd rather not return home."

"A bedroom?"

He slipped the envelope across the table toward her. "I'm giving you the key right now. We'll only use the room if and when you want tonight. It's all in your hands."

Although his voice reassured her, she saw the desire simmering with molten intensity in his eyes. His nostrils flared the slightest bit, and his gaze dropped to breasts. Mesmerized by his attention, she closed her eyes for a second. The brush of soft material against the sensitive flesh made her nipples ache. A fantasy popped into her head, and she knew right away he might read the decadent thoughts in her head. Lachlan's tongue dancing with flicks over her nipples, pulling them into his mouth and sucking, his fingers stroking her other nipple until she burned with uncontrollable craving to have his cock deep inside her.

Her eyes popped open, and he stared at her. He licked his lips, and she wanted that carnal mouth over every inch of her body he could reach.

She touched the envelope, then left it on the table near her hand.

Another knock on the door breached the tension-thick air, and when Cedric brought in the bottle of merlot and presented it to Lachlan, she felt relief. If the waiter hadn't arrived, she had a feeling she would have been in the big Scot's arms in seconds.

Cedric left the room with a promise their dinner would arrive soon.

Lachlan held up his wine glass. "A toast, lass. To the most beautiful, intelligent, and loving woman I know. Erin Greenway."

He touched his glass to hers, and tears filled her eyes. "Damn it, Lachlan, you're going to make me cry."

He sipped his wine. "Sweetheart, the only thing I want to do is make you weep with pleasure."

The low growl in his tone made her toes curl. *Holy tamales*, if he kept his up, she would come right here and now without another ounce of stimulation.

"What *I* want right now," she paused to take a sip of her merlot, "is some answers."

"All right."

"Tell me about your fiancée. The woman you didn't marry."

Sadness crossed his face. "We were childhood friends. We thought we were destined to be together, but then something tragic happened. When she discovered that I wasn't the man I used to be, she broke off the engagement."

Erin tilted her head to the side in question. "Not the man you used to be?"

He swept a hand through his hair, and her gaze lingered on the blue-black sheen in his hair. The man extruded masculinity in every move, no matter how innocent. Her stomach fluttered with pleasure again.

His gaze fixated somewhere beyond her. "It's complicated. It's wrapped up in how I can read your thoughts."

"Curioser and curioser. Go on."

"All right." He looked reluctant. "When my parents were killed in the fire at our castle a few years back, I was injured."

"Your fiancée left you because of the injury?" She wanted to hate the woman right away. "But if she loved you, how could she?"

"It's complicated."

Her breath hitched, almost as if his pain became hers. "Gilda told me about the fire, but not in detail."

When his gaze caught hers she saw genuine grief. "When the fire started I was away from the castle at a party. I came home and the place was already smoking. I called the police on my cell phone and rushed in to find my parents upstairs in their bedroom, overcome by smoke and bleeding from what looked to be small puncture wounds in their neck. I managed to drag them out one by one. As I was pulling my father out of the house, I slipped on the stairs. A stupid thing. I hit my head and almost didn't make it before the fire reached my location. By that time, neighbors had seen the smoke and pulled me the rest of the way out of the castle. When I awoke in the hospital I could...do certain things I couldn't before."

"Read minds?" Her heart beat with a slow, painful reaction to his tale. "That's why your fiancée left you?"

"Yes. Among other things."

She saw evasion in his eyes, and knew right then the story held more facets than he'd revealed. "Lachlan, this isn't going to work if you hold anything back."

He nodded, regret lining his handsome features. "Things happened you wouldn't believe."

She summoned a smile. "After living in Pine Forest a month, I'm about ready to believe anything. Try me."

Before he could tell her, Cedric again knocked and brought in their dinner. Salmon for her and a prime rib for Lachlan. Lachlan asked that they not be disturbed for next hour. Cedric assured him they wouldn't be interrupted unless they rang the small bell pull near the door.

After eating their dinner for a quiet minute or two, Lachlan spoke as he poured more wine for them. "Can we leave explanations for later? I want our meal to be pleasant, and talking about murder isn't exactly my idea of a good time."

Contrite, she realized she shouldn't push him into talking about his parent's death or his fiancée leaving. A year may have passed, but that didn't mean his heartache left him entirely.

"Of course." She smiled. "Let's enjoy dinner."

After taking their time with the succulent dishes, they rang for Cedric and he brought a dessert cart. She decided she didn't have room for a sweet, but Lachlan grinned wolfishly and picked a piece of cake called *Death by Chocolate*. Lachlan ate the dessert with obvious enjoyment, and she teased him about where he could have room for all that food.

"I have a very high metabolism." His lashes lowered slowly with one of those lazy, all-knowing looks that made her stomach flutter with excitement. "I work it off."

She imagined too well what he might do to burn those calories. An image flashed into her mind of him on top of her, pumping his lusty way between her thighs, his cock rasping against her sensitive walls. Desire resurged almost painfully. She wanted him inside her.

Now.

"Erin?" His whispered question made her eyes pop open. "If you don't stop visualizing, I'm going to have a difficult time keeping my hands off you."

Damn, she'd drifted away on another wild daydream. "Sorry."

One corner of his mouth twitched in a cocky, knowing grin. "No apology needed. I liked what I saw in your mind. I liked it very much."

Heat traveled straight from her face down to her breasts.

"Would you like to dance?" She couldn't believe she'd asked, but it popped out of her mouth. The soft music held the right sway for a close dance, and she craved nearness with him. "Please."

He went to the door and locked it, and when he turned back, he walked toward Erin with a stride that showed his assurance. Lachlan held his hand out to her and she took it. As he drew her toward the center of the room and slipped his arms about her, she slid her hands up to his shoulders. They didn't keep distance; his hands tucked her closer and soon they nestled together like long-time lovers. Their bodies touched, chest to breasts. As they turned his hips and thighs brushed against her, and she felt his full-blown erection.

Realizing this man could be this turned on by her this fast gave her a heady sense of power. She urged him nearer, and they pressed cheek to cheek. Flowing into his arms and swaying to the music seemed the most natural thing in the world.

Soon his hands explored, drifting with possessive, yet gentle caresses over her shoulders and down her back. The first brush of his palm against the bare skin of her neck caused her to shiver.

"All right?" he asked huskily into her ear. He touched the lobe with his tongue, then kissed it.

"God, yes. It feels good. You feel good."

"Mmm..." The low, deep sound almost sounded like a male predator's longing growl for his mate.

He continued the cadence of the dance, and his leg slipped between hers as he swung her around. As they moved with a smooth turn, one of his hands slipped down and cupped her ass. She gasped, startled and yet desiring the touch. Erin reached up and pushed her fingers through the thick hair at the back of

Lachlan's neck and kneaded him. Brushing his hands over her ass, he cupped and squeezed and played over her until she moaned.

She squealed when he dipped her. He laughed and when he brought her up, their lips almost brushed.

Kiss me. Please kiss me. She whispered the words in her mind.

He stared into her eyes and a strange weakness overtook her limbs. Erin clung to him, expecting the kiss any time. When he hesitated, she took the decision away from him, once and for all. She cupped his face and hoped he could see hunger and determination. No more pretending.

Lachlan said it would be up to her.

She could no longer deny she ached in every place a woman could ache. She throbbed with an overwhelming and consuming desire to make deep, hard love with him and appease the burning inside her that had built from the day she met him. Over the short time she'd known, him she'd learned very few things about him, and yet she felt as if she knew Lachlan down deep where it counted.

He would never harm her, and he wanted to protect her with his life. His soul felt pure and his heart golden. Her senses told Erin that Lachlan Tavish was the most exciting man she'd met. Learning fresh things about him every day would change her world and expand it until she would never be soul-deep alone again.

She wanted everything with him.

Mental. Physical.

And, oh, yes…Erin wanted the incredible fuck he'd talked about.

Reaching up for his arrogant, gorgeous head, she pulled his head down and kissed him.

He groaned, and she took advantage of his parted lips to plunge her tongue into his mouth. The taste of his tongue tangling with hers, brushing and challenging, made her want him hard and hot between her legs.

She pulled back from him, breathless. His gaze held more fire than she'd ever seen in his expression before. Without a word she took his hand and walked to the table. She grabbed the envelope and went for the closed room. When she reached the door, she hesitated before ripping open the envelope and taking out the key.

"I'm yours to take, Erin," he said, his voice rough with passion. "If you want me."

She shoved the key in the lock and opened the door. "I want you, Lachlan. I want all of you."

Chapter 15

Once inside the bedroom, Lachlan flicked on the light. The large room boosted an opulent setting much like the rest of the establishment. Swags of extravagant velvet drapery covered the windows as well as the deep couch. An opulent matching comforter covered the king-sized bed.

"Wow," Erin whispered as she took in the room and the bed.

I'll say. We could do some serious fucking on that bed.

With a gasp and a laugh, she verbalized her thoughts. "You are too much, Lachlan Tavish."

He stripped off his suit jacket and tossed it on a chair.

He locked the door and reached for her. He brought her against his body, his grip enveloping her in safety and warmth. If ever a man's protection felt sincere and without a desire to take more than to give, Lachlan Travis's arms proved it.

"Tell me if you want me. Now," he said with a husky nuance in his voice.

Again, she cherished his assurance. "I want you, Lachlan, *now.*"

A confident smile swept his face. "I can't wait to get inside you." He whispered against her ear as he brought her close, his powerful arms cradling her with tenderness. "We'll do everything you need, and more."

"More?"

"Anything you desire, any way you want it. I'll slide into you and move deep and hard and fast, so fast you'll come apart in my arms. God, I want to see you come. I want to fuck you until you scream."

An idea flashed into her mind, and a heated flush spread from her neck to her face. "Talk dirty to me. That's what I want."

With a husky groan he said, "Oh, lass, you got it."

He licked her earlobe, then caught it between his lips and sucked. "You want me to lick your pussy?"

"Oh, God, yes."

"Flick your clit with my tongue?"

She shivered. Arousal spiked inside her, and she felt a telltale trickle of moisture between her thighs. "Please."

"Stick my tongue deep inside you?"

"Yes." Her breathing came rapid, and she clutched at his shoulders and writhed in his arms as he pulled her dress up in back. "Yes."

With one smooth move, he slid inside her panty hose and her panties to cup one butt cheek in each hand. "You have the sweetest ass."

Lachlan's husky, lust-thickened voice sent deep, uncontrollable need straight into her center. He massaged her butt with a continual squeezing motion. He kissed her, his tongue making love to her mouth with lush movements that teased and demanded.

When he pulled back he slid one hand out of her panties so he could tilt her chin upwards. "I'm going to do some things to you that you may not have experienced, Erin. But if you don't like what I'm doing at any time, tell me and I'll stop."

Just the idea of him committing forbidden and exciting sex acts with her made her excitement more urgent. "Yes. Anything."

With a nod, he slid the strap down until the top of her breast was reveled. Her body trembled with anticipation as he gazed down at her breast like it might be a precious jewel. He cupped her, holding her breast high as his mouth dipped.

Lachlan's warm breath gusted over her. "So damned sweet. Do you want me to suck it, Erin? Lick it?"

His dirty talk, no-holds-barred, sent her libido into high gear. "Yes."

As he slipped the fabric of her bodice completely down and bared both her breasts, he said, "These are as pretty as I remember."

With a moan he indulged. His tongue and lips became a firestorm across her skin, white hot as he nibbled all around her nipples until at last he suckled and licked. The exquisite sensation of his fingers tugging one nipple while he sucked and laved the other, made her cream her panties in a wild rush.

She cried out, half mad with screaming desire. He broke contact with her breasts.

Lachlan's hands wandered down to her waist and then to her hips, caressing as he traveled. As Erin's excitement built to frantic proportions, she decided nothing mattered but finding that all-consuming orgasm. She wanted him any way she could get him. He slowly unzipped the back of the dress then slid her dress upwards over her head. With a hurried movement he tossed the garment on a chair.

For one earth-shaking moment she felt vulnerable. With naked breasts and only panty hose, panties, and screw-me shoes, she veered from a wild desire to shove him on the bed and give him the ride of his life, to a terrifying sensation of panic.

He seemed to sense her fear, and with a smile that promised pleasure like she'd never known, Lachlan said, "Erin, lass, you're in control. Remember that."

He waited, and seconds later she nodded her consent.

Lachlan went down on his knees. With quick deliberation, he unhooked her shoes. As he cupped the length of her leg, he allowed his fingers to travel up to her thigh. His big, gentle fingers felt hot on her nylon-clad skin. To keep her balance, she kept her hands on his shoulders, enjoying the sensation of hard muscle at the same time.

She shuddered and closed her eyes as he removed the high heels one by one. He tossed the shoes aside. Working with deliberation, he carefully stripped her hose and panties down her legs. Silky nylon glided down her skin and the slow brush of garment against skin heightened her arousal.

Naked, she stood vulnerable to his heated gaze and ravenous touch.

When he rose back up, he gathered Erin close again. This time, as he kissed her, he kept his tongue deep in her mouth, moving and exploring.

Every ounce of shyness she might have had, disappeared as his fingers slid down her backside and found their way to her wet and aching folds. He touched her labia and drew her moisture up, passing it over her anus with gentle glides.

She jerked and shivered in his grip at the unaccustomed sensation. Each moan of pleasure escalated as he made certain her puckered rear entry was lubricated.

Erin moaned against his mouth, excited by this forbidden love play. She'd never indulged in this type of sex before.

Do you want this, Erin?

Yes. Please.

She knew he wouldn't hurt her.

With a light touch, he gently inserted the middle finger of his left hand a small way into that tight entrance.

She gasped and broke the kiss.

Worry overlaid his smoldering gaze. He slipped his finger out of her. "Does that hurt?"

Shivering with the most powerful stimulation she'd ever felt, she shook her head. "Don't stop."

With a grin of satisfaction, he maneuvered so he stood slightly to the side of her. She kept her right arm looped over his shoulder, a steadying grip and a desire to bring him closer.

"Mmm…wet…hot." He licked her nipple just as his fingers slipped and slid across her folds. With a super slow touch, he slid two fingers deep inside her cunt.

She arched against his fingers as pleasure rocketed through her. As he slid his fingers in and out in a soft, excruciatingly slow pace, the sensations made her move in torment. He kept his fingers embedded, his thumb sliding up to part the hood protecting her clit.

One swift pass over Erin's clit, and she gasped and moaned.

"Oh, yeah," he breathed. "That's it. Cream up for me. You're going to be so hot and wet when I take you."

She wanted that all right, and the potent, husky flavor of his voice stirred her into a frenzy of excitement.

"You want me inside you don't you?" His combination of pleading and deep sexual arousal added to the fuel.

Again he moved his fingers and he touched something inside her that brought exquisite pleasure. She moved, tormented. "Yes, yes."

He slid his finger, slow and sure, back into her rear entry. The gentle pressure, barely inserted, drove her nuts. She moved on his fingers, enjoying the double penetration. When he leaned down and sucked a nipple into his mouth, moved his finger in her ass, and flicked her clit with his thumb, she almost screamed with excitement.

"Oh, please, please, please, please," she gasped with pleasure.

She didn't care what she sounded like, what she looked like. Erin had gone animal. Gone wild with a sexual desire so profound it sent doubts straight out of her head.

"I want you so much, Erin." His voice rasped against her ear as he started a verbal assault on her defenses. "I want to suck your clit. I want to stick my tongue inside you. I want to hear you beg me to take you."

Erin almost reared out of his arms and demanded a quick fornication to remove the pounding ache. He slid his thumb upward and rotated, a light brush right over her clit.

She moaned and chanted her feelings. "Lachlan. Oh, God, oh, God, oh —"

Erin's breathing went into high gear as she reached for orgasm. Ripples of pleasure built as his fingers caressed inside her, and his thumb brushed teasing flicks designed to drive her insane. His finger moved in her ass again.

"That's it," he groaned into her mouth. "Come. Come."

Pressure built with lightning speed, roaring into her. Erin stifled her scream as a climax ripped from her, taking her by surprise with sweet bliss. Her fingers dug into him and held on for dear life. She shook as her breath squealed out of her, high and sobbing. She panted, trying to catch her breath and half out of her mind.

Instead of releasing her flesh, he continued to ply her clit, keeping up the pressure with relentless attention.

Oversensitive from the blasting climax, she moved her hips and whimpered. She felt wet, slick and swollen, ready to hold Lachlan's cock deep inside her.

As another wave of pleasure hit, her vagina rippled and tightened around his deeply imbedded fingers and his stimulation of her anus. He stopped as her muscles clamped on him, but then he inched his fingers in and out, in and out, forcing the tight muscles to throb and burn with renewed need. Pumping his fingers with a rhythm that mimicked sex, he dipped and slid inside her.

With a moan of male satisfaction, Lachlan slipped his fingers from her. Erin whimpered in protest. Her body wanted his with a ferocity she couldn't contain. She felt like she could come dozens of times in this man's arms.

Oh, Lachlan, that felt fantastic.

Mmm…that's good.

As she shuddered and quaked, he held her. "That's it, lass." He kissed her forehead and then gently led her over to the huge bed. "Sit down." His demand came husky and with a hint of a smile. "Lay back." Before she could catch her breath, he went to his knees in front of her. "Spread your legs, sweetheart."

179

Eager, she did as told and lay back. She knew what he would do, and the idea made a new heat build between her legs, slick, hot and full of wanting.

Lachlan held open the folds over her clitoris, and leaning down, licked her wet labia. She quaked as each long, slow lap of his tongue brushed over but didn't concentrate on her clit. Soon after he started licking Erin, her tissues cried out for a new orgasm. His tongue reached her slick, swollen clit, flicking and tapping against her over and over again. Her hips thrashed, and he held her down. Lachlan drove his tongue inside her and with his other hand he brushed over her clit. She gasped.

Building anew, the pressure in her cunt reached brand-new heights. She could feel it throbbing, the walls tightening and clamping, aching to hold him deep inside. As his tongue made another pass over her clit, she almost screamed. Then he enveloped her clit in his mouth and sucked. Pleasure exploded and another high-test climax ripped through her. She almost screamed, then held back the wild exclamation.

As her orgasm faded, she panted her next plea. "Lachlan, now."

Lachlan went for his coat and grabbed the packet of several condoms from an inside pocket and put them on the bedside stand. With rushed movements he removed his crisp white shirt, hurrying and throwing it aside. He pulled off his boots and tossed them away. He yanked his pants open, stripping them and black briefs down over his long, muscular thighs and then throwing the garments aside.

He stood there for a long time, looking down on her with a smile that reassured and yet held the slightest touch of arrogance. She wanted him all the more for his confidence, because even though she was independent, his undeniable male strength turned her on.

"You're the most gorgeous man I've ever seen," she said, and meant it.

She'd seen naked pictures of male models and actors, as curious and entertained as most other red-blooded women. None of them approached the magnificence of this male animal.

Lachlan's expression held a voracious hunger. As he smiled his eyes seemed to turn golden, lit by a red fire that disappeared in a flash.

Erin couldn't help but catalogue his attributes. His broad, muscled shoulders and molded arms showed that he worked out on a regular basis, and so did the hard chest sprinkled with a generous amount of hair. Her hungry gaze trailed down to his flat stomach. Beyond that lay the most the most delicious item of all, and she licked her lips in anticipation.

Long and thick, his cock rose erect from a bush of dark hair, hard and ready for serious love making.

No doubt about it. Lachlan Tavish pushed a fifteen on a scale of one to ten.

Without thinking, she sat up, reached out and gripped him, holding his sturdy length and breadth in her palm and admiring the hardness and the smooth-velvet-over- steel sensation. "You're beautiful."

He inhaled sharply as she slid her fingers from the tip to the base. A wide grin sparked around the blazing desire in his eyes. "No woman has ever called my cock beautiful."

"It is," she whispered, almost groaning the words. "Long and thick and just right."

"Made to take you deep."

At his erotic words, she almost grabbed him and threw him down on the bed. Her breathing seemed to rasp in her lungs, her desire running higher and faster than anything she'd experienced in memory or in fantasy.

Stroke me deep. Oh, please.

With excruciating slowness, he slid on a condom. She watched his fingers move down his cock, a touch that seemed casual and yet loving. As if he appreciated his own body for the pleasure it gave him. A man confident in his sexuality and his desires. That touch of haughtiness fired her like nothing else could.

Another flood of hot juice flooded her cunt, and she groaned. "Lachlan, I can't stand it."

With a tender expression, his dark eyes softened and the naturally hard line to his lips warmed with a sweet smile. To her surprise he reached for her hand and brought her up to standing position. "I'm yours."

His gaze flicked from her breasts to her pubic hair, resting on the glistening wetness she felt there. She'd drowned in his sexual attention until this moment and now her worries stretched forward, those concerns that said she was about to slip into something terrifying and beyond comprehension.

"Put your hands on my shoulders." He drew her closer, then clasped her waist and lifted her up. "Wrap your legs around my waist. This first time is going to be fast."

She did as he asked, and then the big head of his dick slipped inside her.

Erin gasped. *Oh. My. God.*

Yes, lass. That's it.

Incredible. She knew he was very strong, but oh, holy shit—

He inched inward, pushing, pushing, pushing.

Erin had never felt anything like it. Rock hard man wedged upwards and with one powerful thrust, he plunged balls deep. Lachlan growled.

She whimpered, and her head dropped back as she clung to him, filled to the womb with solid, heavy cock. Hard, hot, and impossibly deep, he stretched her. Out of instinct she rotated her hips.

He gasped. "Oh, sweet lass."

With his arms tight around her, he turned her and propped her against one wall. With excruciating slowness, he drew out and then shoved forward.

She cried out. Erin's fingers clawed at his shoulders as she wriggled her hips in torment, dancing on him with tiny gyrations. She'd never been able to feel a man's cock moving inside her as keenly as she did now. He continued a steady, incremental thrust, enough to rasp inside her cunt and yet not enough to hit her high and deep where she needed it the most.

God, save me. This is pure torture.

Yes, sweetheart. Yes.

"Erin." His voice, ragged with desire, sounded as if he loved her and couldn't bear the idea of ever leaving her body. "Erin. Tell me. How do you want it? Do you want it hard and fast?"

"Yes." She wanted to scream at him. "Please, do it. God, please do it."

He pulled out with excruciating slowness. She whimpered.

He took her mouth, his kiss ravenous and demanding entrance. As he plunged his tongue between her lips, he thrust hard into her center. Erin gasped into his mouth, the heady, enveloping ecstasy of his body wedged deep inside caused her entire body to shudder.

Without missing a beat he began to rut, each thrust forceful. His cock plunged and retreated, then hit something deep inside her that caused her to clamp down and then release in a rhythm that matched the plunging motion of his hips.

Yes, Erin, lass. Yes! More, sweet God, more! Come! Come!

She did as commanded, stirring her hips into an undulating motion as he kept her pinned against the wall. His tremendous strength never wavered, his arms tight and sure as he hammered over and over inside her. Swollen and wet, she felt her channel widen and lengthen to accommodate his fiery, powerful lunges.

He'd stopped kissing her, and now his breathing rasped in and out of his lungs, his grunts and gasps exciting her wildly. Her body ran through a gambit of escalating rapture. Her mouth felt sensitive and his chest hair brushed again and again over her tight nipples, making them burn. Deep inside her, an orgasm started to build. An out-of-control tightening started in her lower belly.

Just as she always wanted, just as she'd needed her entire adult life, she now understood the meaning of being fucked out of her mind.

She loved it.

As he thrust with increasing power, she keened in uncontrollable pleasure.

She thought she would die, and when she reached heaven she would never require another thing but the memory of this man inside her body and mind.

She couldn't stand the torture any longer. *I'm coming. I'm coming.*

One tremendous thrust hit high and deep.

Detonation.

Her orgasm splintered, causing her to shake, her lungs gasping for air as she let out a whimper that ended in a long, drawn-out moan. Her body squeezed his cock, pulsating and tingling with a mind-splitting excitement she couldn't contain. He kept up his pounding movements, groaning as he worked to give her more pleasure.

Erin's body shook and continual moans parted her lips.

As his cock rammed between her legs, she felt another climax building with lightning fast approach. She wasn't prepared when it slammed her, and she shrieked at the same time he thrust one last time. Lachlan's entire body quaked as he bellowed like a triumphant male animal.

Chapter 16

Lachlan held Erin against the wall, his body shivering as his wild climax eased. Erin's senses felt scattered as she took in the hot feeling of his body against hers, the tremendous power required to keep her pinned against the wall.

"Lachlan."

"Ah, lass." He lifted her off his cock, and as she slid down his body, she felt the wetness of her release trickle down her thighs.

He held her tight, his face nuzzling her hair, his hands moving over her back and butt as if he'd never explored her skin before. With her face buried against his hard shoulder, she steadied her breathing. Her mind felt adrift, replete. She couldn't seem to form one reasonable thought. He released her, and she realized he had broken away from her to discard the condom.

Erin watched his shoulders ripple with muscle as he turned away from her, and her gaze traveled with hungry insistence down his back until she reached his incredible tight butt. He looked up and caught her gaze in the mirror. With deliberation she walked toward him. When she reached Lachlan, Erin allowed her fingers to slide up and over his shoulders, palming the hot, smooth texture of skin over steel-hard musculature. Did any man deserve to be so damned gorgeous? Her mouth watered with the desire to show him how much she admired him and his sexy body.

She allowed Lachlan to turn around. Erin slid her hands around his slim waist and touched the muscle-ripped texture of his stomach. He sucked in a breath and kept her gaze pinned with his. His hands covered hers as she traveled, exploring up and up until she rested on his chest. She felt the rounded, powerful structure of his pectorals and savored the strength she found. With deliberation she trailed down, down, down until her hands almost touched the hair at his groin. Now that the first blush of sex was appeased, she had time to share new pleasures and explore. Erin reached down and fisted his cock with her left hand. Her other hand went back up to his pec and her fingers latched onto his nipple. She squeezed his cock and nipple at the same time.

"Erin." He gasped as she started a sure fire stroking over his long length. "Sweet lass, you're gonna kill me."

"Ah," she said with a breathy sigh. "But won't it be a wonderful death?"

He groaned. "Yes."

She'd given blow jobs before, but never with this grinding desire to take a man down her throat and feel his excitement spurt into her mouth. Without another hesitation, she knelt in front of him and gripped his cock at the base. Then she slid her lips down over him.

"Ah." He jerked in her grip, but she kept her hand fastened to the base of his cock while she tasted him with her tongue and the warm heat of her mouth. "Erin, darlin', I canna."

Satisfaction and a sense of power engulfed her. When his accent got this thick, she knew she had him.

"More." Rough with accent, his voice demanded. "I've got to have more. I dinna think I stand it if I canna be inside you again."

Lachlan grew harder inside her mouth. Driven beyond any control, she drew his cock into her mouth over and over, sucking and licking as she encompassed him.

He gripped her head in both hands and groaned as his head fell back. "No, lass. Please, God." He chanted, his voice hoarse with emotion and lust. "I need to be inside you."

She would give him something she'd never given another man. A safe haven right here in her mouth where he knew nothing but divine pleasure, and where she could have the satisfaction of giving.

As she pumped him with one hand and sucked him with the other, he pleaded. "That's it. Take me all."

She smiled with triumph. A fierce expression of harsh pleasure etched into his features. Raw excitement made his face seem wild and somehow animal. His fingers fisted in her hair, but not tight enough to hurt. His breath rasped in and out, his chest rising and falling quickly. Tender, considerate Lachlan had turned primal, in full view for her enjoyment. The sensation of taking him in her mouth added to her arousal and the slickness between her legs grew hotter. Oh, how she wanted him between her legs again.

As she sucked him harder and faster, his eyes closed and his head fell back. She decided she'd add to his torture with a few exploratory touches. She massaged his balls gently, then probed the area between his balls and anus. He sucked in a breath.

A groan echoed from his throat. "Yeah. Oh, yeah."

She kept up the torture as she fucked him with her mouth, and that seemed to be all he needed to launch into the stratosphere. His gasps turned to a guttural sound as Lachlan's hips twitched and then his fingers tightened in her hair. For a few seconds he took the movement away from Erin as he moved back and forth in her mouth.

Then he stiffened and a low growl of completion left his throat. He came with a quick explosion, and she continued to suck, taking his hot, liquid essence down her throat. She swallowed as he shuddered, and another spurt, then another filled her mouth as he exhaled on another growl.

She released him, leaning her head against his thigh as she panted. With a sense of wonder she realized it felt almost as if she'd enjoyed an orgasm; her heart thumped and her breath came fast. The taste of him in her mouth, she stood and slipped into his waiting arms.

His expression said it all. A tender smile parted his lips, then transformed into ready to devour her. "Lass, that was incredible."

And he kissed her.

Lachlan plied Erin with a tender, exploring kiss that tantalized even as it kept her from total fulfillment. His lips swept from her top lip to her bottom, teasing caresses that made her appetite for him surge higher and higher.

Lachlan lifted her in his arms and walked with her to the bed. He released her long enough to flick the covers down to the bottom of the bed, then he lifted her again and placed her on the crisp, white sheets.

"Are we really here?" she asked softly as he slid onto the bed beside her.

"Yes." He smiled and leaned over her, brushing his lips across her forehead. "We're really here."

Her throat tightened, and unexpected tears moistened her eyes. "Lachlan, what we just did...it was everything. It was wonderful."

He frowned and brushed away a tear. "Why are you crying?"

"With happiness. Only with happiness."

With a groan he leaned in and took her mouth voraciously. As his mouth and tongue learned her anew, she rolled with him across the big bed. He landed on top of her, and she felt his cock harden again.

She knew Lachlan must see the startled, totally amazed expression in her eyes.

I've never wanted a woman the way I want you.

His voice in her head reassured her as he reached to the bedside table and found another condom. She half expected their loving to go slow and sweet this time, but their hunger felt too new and insatiable. He slipped on the condom, but before he could settle between her legs, she turned the tables on him and rolled onto her stomach. The sheets felt smooth and cool against Erin's heated skin, and she savored the touch of his hands on her butt as he helped her kneel. He palmed her, exploring like a new map as he traced his fingers over her skin. She shivered. Hands flat to the bed, her legs wide apart and her hips tilted high, she waited in a special agony that belongs to lovers who want each other more than anything else on earth.

Without hesitation he parted the lips of her sex with his cock and inched his way inside with inexorable but gentle thrusts. His iron-hard, furnace hot cock spread her walls.

Oh, yes, yes, yes, yes, he feels so good. So hot. So hard. So big. As he reached around and cupped one breast, then began plucking and stroking one nipple, she shivered with delight. *Mmm. Good.*

Yes, lass. It's wonderful.

A delirium tossed her up, brought her to a new place she never expected again so quickly. How could this man, any man, turn her on with a single look, touch, sound? With one pass of his fingers over her breast she couldn't wait to spread her legs for him and accept all he had to give her.

With one last push he sank deep inside her. With a wiggle of her hips she tightened around him.

Lachlan twisted his hips and touched something high inside her that made her body tighten in mind-melting bliss. With an animal sound, he commenced a steady, powerful thrusting that brooked no denial. Each hammering motion made her want to scream and beg, and seconds later she succumbed. A low moaning left her throat, something she couldn't and didn't want to stop.

Deep excitement spilled free in his voice as he pounded into Erin, his new words more potent and earthy than the last time he'd been inside her. "That's it sweetheart. Come on. Fuck me. Fuck me harder."

His words were spoken in a throaty Scottish pitch that said he'd gone over the edge, and it fired her libido into hyper drive. She moved her hips faster, rearing back against him at his command. He hunched over her, his body learning and venturing and driving her to within an inch of screaming madness. His persistent, demanding fingers danced on her nipples with electrifying caresses, manipulating until all she could feel was his cock drilling her and his fingers playing. Her arousal seemed to climb higher as she allowed herself to feel everything, experience each sensation and sound.

She clamped her lips shut but the chanting came from her anyway. "Yes. Yes!" The rhythm and friction became too much to endure. She demanded with her body, with the relentless tempo that matched his movements.

She lost all control, all inhibition and let the words spring free. "God, yes! Fuck me! Fuck me! Oh, yes, yes, yes, yes!"

She knew she was almost screaming, and she didn't' care. She whimpered as that first hint of orgasm tightened her stomach.

Lachlan, please, oh, please.

He gave one last thrust.

With a skyrocketing sensation that stirred first in her belly, made her walls clench in burning pleasure, and then sparked in her clit, she came with a screech. Erin's passion seemed to set him loose, and Lachlan came right after, his shout of completion echoing in the room as he shuddered against her, his arms tightening about her.

It took them a long time to come down, lying side by side without saying a word. Her contentment echoed his quietness, and she wondered if anything could surpass the happiness she knew this moment. With a sweeping sensation that transformed all her thoughts into mush and made her body ignite, she realized she wanted more than anything to share all her nights with this man deep inside her. Loving her. Showing her his world and sharing all the time she had to give.

Later, after they agreed the restaurant would close soon and they didn't have this room for the entire night, they dressed.

Erin felt shy and yet free as she kept her eyes averted from him while she slipped on her underwear. Not because she didn't desire each glance she could at his incredible body, but because she didn't think she could watch him without wanting to fuck him again.

"I'll pay out front and we can slip out the back if you want." He slipped her coat over her shoulders. His palms slid down to her waist, and he brought her against him. As his hot breath teased her earlobe, she quivered with delight. "Unless you don't mind running the gambit of all the people in the dining room."

As reality returned, so did her apprehensions. She'd performed what some people would qualify as screaming monkey sex with this man. For one irrational second she thought the evidence would show on her face.

He sighed and kissed her neck. "I know what you're thinking."

Feeling like a broken record, she said, "What am I thinking?"

"That we don't know each other well and here we are in each other's arms."

"Yes."

"And I canna tell you how wonderful it felt to be inside you." His accent went rough with strong emotion. "Of course, I know you're also thinking that we canna possibly be doing this — what did you call it — wild monkey sex."

So much for him not reading her mind.

She sighed and turned toward Lachlan. "If we go out there right now, in front of the world, everyone in that dining room might look at us and read something in our faces, right? Maybe I didn't comb my hair well enough, so I have bed head, and if my lipstick is smeared the smallest bit they'll know we've been kissing." She kissed him for good measure, accepting the arousing massage of his tongue with pure delight. "And there's this other part of me that rejoices because there will also be women out there who will be envious because I have this incredibly gorgeous hunk on my arm. And they'll realize I've fallen in lo—"

Erin clamped her mouth shut, but she could see he knew what she almost said. Of course he did, damn him.

He cupped her face in both hands. "Lass, I heard you the first time." The twinkle of laughter in his eyes turned to heated, undeniable desire. When he took her home tonight she half expected they'd land in bed without a whimper of resistance. "You broadcasted it loud and clear while we were making love."

He touched his lips to her forehead. "Do you know what it does to me to know you care about me?"

"I more than care, I…" Her throat threatened to close up as tears came to her eyes. She tried to remember a time when she'd been so happy.

He put his finger over her mouth. "Don't say it now. Not if you don't want to."

Apprehensive, she caught that dark fire and kindness in his eyes all mixed into one stunning package. "Is this the part where you tell me not to get involved with you? Not to care so much?"

Care? Yes, that was a meager word to describe it. Cupid has fired one sure arrow into my heart. She knew whatever happened next, she would have to live with his decision, even if she didn't like it.

Lachlan's good looking face seemed more precious, more handsome than ever as a guarded air filled his eyes.

Before he could answer her in full, the phone near the bed rang. She started. "Whoa. I didn't even know that was there."

He laughed as he released her and walked toward it. "I think time is up."

Sure enough, the "wake up call" let them know the restaurant would be closing in thirty minutes. After they collected their coats and walked out their private abode, she knew she wanted every woman out there to see her with Lachlan. For once she would be carefree and flaunt her condition; the ridiculous state of tumbling one hundred percent, amazingly, out-of-her-mind, in love with a man.

As it went, they didn't see anyone they knew in the crowded main dining room, and no one seemed to pay special attention to them.

"I still can't believe we did that," she said in a hushed voice.

He slipped his arm around her and pushed open the door to leave the restaurant. His voice rumbled against her ear. "Believe it. And I want to do it again soon."

Her stomach did a little jump of anticipation. "That room is something else. Why haven't I ever heard of it before? Wouldn't you think it would be illegal or something? It's so…so…incredibly hedonistic —"

He laughed. "Are you complaining?"

"No, no." She snuggled into his warmth, grateful for his strength and the security on a cold night. She chuckled. "Hell, no."

"I don't know why you've never heard of it. I learned of it through…um…"

"Yes, come on, fess up."

"Through the grapevine."

"That's not an answer."

He cleared his throat. "Tom told me about it."

"I'm scandalized," she said with a deadpan tone.

"I thought you would be." The dry tenor in his voice made her smile.

"Now, Gilda…I could believe her telling you about the room." She laughed.

Just before they reached the car, Erin heard a strange whisper nearby, almost as if the night came alive.

A clinging, awful darkness wafted around her like wind and wrapped her senses. Her throat tightened and instant sickness assaulted her stomach. She stopped and Lachlan ran into her back, his arms going around her waist.

"Do you feel that?" she asked, her voice shaking, her body following with one wrenching shudder of revulsion. "What is that?"

"Don't move." His grip tightened, and in the semi-darkness of the parking area, she searched for the source of the bizarre hate.

Her head filled with a swimming sickness, then pain. The night dissolved around her.

Chapter 17

"Erin? Sweetheart, open your eyes. Come on, talk to me."

"Is she all right?" The voice belonged to Cedric.

"I don't know." Lachlan sounded bleak. "Please, open your eyes, Erin."

At his rough demand, desperate and full of heart-wrenching anxiety, she surfaced from the fog enshrouding her mind. She blinked open her eyes and looked up into the concerned expression of Cedric and two other patrons that hovered alongside. She lay half on the ground, Lachlan holding her in his arms.

"Thank you, God." He brushed his fingers through her hair, then reached down to take her pulse. "How do you feel?"

"Should we call an ambulance?" An elderly woman, dripping in diamonds, asked.

"No," Erin said, eager to go home and get away from prying eyes. "I'm — it's all right. I'm fine."

Lachlan shifted her in his arms. He stood up, and she gasped as he heaved her up as if she weighed nothing. "Thank you everyone. I think she'll be fine now."

He marched with her to the car and sat her down on her feet gently as if he thought she was as fragile as glass. He cupped her face in his warm hands. The concern hadn't left his eyes. "How do you feel?"

"Perfect now. Maybe a little weak. I don't know what happened. There was that horrible feeling again."

"Like hate?"

"Yes, that's it. It was hate. Or like a miserable, endless winter." She couldn't stay quiet, afraid if she didn't explain this dire sensation, it would somehow eat her alive. "Like I've felt at the library several times and outside my home earlier tonight. It always gives me this headache."

He inhaled deeply, as if by his calm he could vanquish whatever plagued her. "It can't harm you, no matter how it feels. Just remember that."

Without another word, Lachlan opened the car and tucked her inside. The odd experience of moments before made her wonder if she'd imagined things again.

He started the car. "No, you didn't imagine it."

He pulled the car out of the lot, and then drove a little faster toward town, perhaps eager to take shelter in the number of people who might venture out tonight. Perhaps he wanted to escape the perilous sense of impending doom as much as she did.

Night rushed passed them, hedge-rows whished by in the deep, moonless darkness. Like hulking monsters the trees alongside the road hovered over them, and the lines on the road went on forever. As silence stretched, Erin decided the quiet interior of the car felt almost as creepy as what happened outside the restaurant.

She couldn't take the silence. "What is it? Or should I say, *what* was that?"

"I can't tell you. Not without you believing I've gone raving mad."

She sniffed with derision. "Oh, come on. With this crazy mind reading thing, and this weird town, you don't think I'll believe you?"

"That's about the size of it."

"Is this some undercover thing? Something where you'd have to kill me if you told me the truth?" Half joking, she gave him full attention.

The dash glow gave his skin a pale cast, and his face seemed carved into the hardest and most unforgiving granite. He shook his head. "No. And yes."

And as he turned his head to glance her way, she realized Lachlan's whiskey eyes grew bright with a glow that shined in the meager light like a cat or another midnight creature. The light flickered out.

She sank back against the car seat, her heart pounding with fear of the unknown. "Lachlan. Please tell me I didn't just see what I thought I saw?"

Worry wrinkled the skin between his brows, but he turned his full attention back to the winding road. "What did you see?"

"Your eyes…they are…"

"They glow a bit sometimes in the darkness. Yes, I know." He said it so matter-of-factly she felt a hollow, disbelieving sensation in her stomach.

"Your eyes just glow. For no reason at all." Even her own voice sounded incredulous to her ears.

"I don't let many people see me in this kind of light. I figure when I have to start explaining why my eyes can glow, it'll send them screaming into the night."

"Or buying a one way ticket to a rubber room." Erin felt bone cold, and she rubbed her mittens together. A shudder rippled her body. "So you're telling me you know something extraordinary about that weird happening back at the restaurant, but you won't explain what it is." She swallowed hard. "And then there's this little problem that you read my mind and your eyes glow." She heard sarcasm in her voice, but didn't try to stop it. "If you told me everything you knew you'd have to kill me—maybe? Gee, I guess I'm supposed to conveniently ignore that?"

"Of course not." Impatience laced each syllable. "I didn't want this to hit you at once. We need to take it a little at a time."

"You're spoonfeeding me the truth?"

"In essence."

Blow your essence, Lachlan.

Erin, this isn't how I wanted to discuss this —

Then what way were you going to discuss it? If I didn't find out that something odd and horrible is going on in this town? Were you going to conveniently forget it then? Were you going to hope I wouldn't ask any more questions about why your fiancée dumped you when she learned you could read minds, or how your eyes glow for no earthly reason?

Yes. Maybe.

Her heart dropped straight into her shoes, along with the hope she'd gained at the restaurant that her budding feelings for him wouldn't be dashed among the rocks.

Does it have something to do with the murders in town, Lachlan?

"How did you know that?" His voice came thick and hard with allegation.

"I don't. I'm giving an educated guess."

"Leave the murders to the police, Erin. I don't want you hurt."

His words, sincere and meaningful, warmed her heart a little. But the frost didn't go away. "Will you tell me everything?"

"Erin, I don't think it would be wise."

She tried not to anger, but found it impossible. "Before we made love you promised you would."

When he stayed silent, watching the road with single-minded intent, she heaved a deep breath. So that's the way it would be. She rubbed her temples as they came into the outskirts of town. Not long now and she'd be home. She could close the door on him and do some sober thinking about where their relationship went from here.

Resentment mixed with hurt. They'd had such a wonderful, beautiful evening. Until the darkness had leapt out at them like a ghost intent on scaring the hell out of them and destroying her peace of mind about Lachlan.

With purpose she tried to keep her mind free of incriminating thoughts. If he could read her wishes, dreams, and fears, she didn't know if she could live with that. The situation bordered on too intrusive for her to accept. Even if the hunk reading her mind was the most incredible, wonderful man she'd ever laid eyes upon.

When they reached Erin's home, and he walked her to the door, she stepped inside but didn't invite him to follow. "Lachlan, I must think. Please give me this time." She smiled, lessening the blow and hoping to hell he wouldn't hate her for this. "I don't know if being with you is right. After these additional revelations tonight, I'm not sure I can be with you."

She shook her head, unsure what else to say and feeling empty.

For a moment Erin allowed Lachlan's deep, hypnotic gaze to gather her close. Before she could protest, he slipped his hands into her hair and his mouth came down on hers. As his mouth devoured, his tongue taking instant possession, she leaned against his powerful body. Her arms slipped around his neck, and the cool texture of his coat against her skin made her bury her fingers in his hair. He broke the kiss. His gaze, lacking that strange glow she'd seen earlier, but still hot and needing, almost made her change her mind. She could tell he wanted her, and dear God, she wanted him regardless.

"Remember this moment, lass. And remember I'm a phone call away if you need me. If you ever are frightened, don't hesitate to contact me. I'll be watching."

With another swift, mild brush of his mouth against hers, he turned away. As she closed and locked the door, she knew without a doubt the pain in her chest was her heart breaking.

* * * * *

The dream came to Erin late at night, and it swept her into a nightmare world. *Lachlan danced with her once again at Ricardo's, his hands on her body possessive and hurtful. His eyes glowed down at her with cruel intentions. She struggled against his grip, and his fingers pressed into her upper arms so hard she cried out in pain.*

"No! No!" She shoved at his chest, her heart pounding and fear growing higher. Why was he doing this to her? "Let me go!"

How could he do this to her? How could he betray her with such awful brutality?

"You are mine now," his voice said, thick with that same lust she'd heard in his syllables when they'd made love. "And I'm never letting you go. Ever. You are bound to me and no other will take you."

"No!"

She broke from the dream and sat up. The cold night wrapped around her like an entity, unforgiving and desolate. Her heart pounded wildly in her chest, and she stared into the darkness of her bedroom. She glanced around, half afraid Lachlan might be in the room with her in reality. After all, he'd done some odd things on their date that he couldn't explain. Correction, wouldn't explain. Soul-deep hurt reminded her that she couldn't be with Lachlan, no matter how much she wanted it. If he wouldn't tell her the truth, she refused to remain his lover.

Maybe she'd never realized how important honesty in a relationship was to her until Lachlan wouldn't come clean with her. Fresh pain splintered her world as she huddled under the covers and tried to become warm once again. After a few moments, she realized she couldn't regenerate heat. Shivering, she slid out of bed and switched on the bedside lamp. She grabbed her robe and slipped into the warmth. Grabbing some thick socks from her dresser, she put them on her freezing feet. After going into the hall she did a quick check of the thermostat. It showed the house temperature much warmer than what she felt. Could she be coming down with a bug? That would explain the weird dream, perhaps, and maybe why she'd fainted at the restaurant.

Erin got under the covers again and tried to visualize the pleasure she'd experienced with Lachlan not so many hours ago. She didn't want to forget that ecstasy right away.

Obviously the disagreement they had intruded on her sleep, and that brought on the horrible dream. She cringed when she remembered the malice she'd seen in his eyes in the nightmare and the meanness in his touch.

Would Lachlan treat her that way?

No. *No, he wouldn't do that.*

Or would he?

She deliberately tore her thoughts away from making love to him and concentrated on imagining a pond with lily pads on the crystal surface. She drifted on a huge pad, content to drift upon the water downstream.

This image worked often, but not tonight. After an hour of her mind running in circles, and the lily pad visualization going nowhere, she gave up. She peeled open one eye and spied the digital clock on her bedside table. Three a.m. Maybe she should read.

She'd left her latest book in the living room, so she headed in that direction, flipping on lights as she went. After retrieving the hardback mystery from the coffee table, she stopped in her tracks.

She was being watched.

She whirled around.

Scanning the hallway, she didn't see a thing. Erin wondered if the dream's effects continued to linger in her psyche. She rubbed her arms, well aware that nightmares could keep fear heightened for some time after waking up.

Look outside, Erin.

The whispery voice, thick with sinister tones, called to her in her mind as it had done so many times. She shivered again; the robe and heavy socks didn't seem to keep her warm.

Instant fear gripped Erin in a primitive area of her soul. Doubts made her afraid, as well as the trepidation that happened to anyone exploring the unknown.

Could Lachlan be the owner of this mysterious voice and the strange cloaking apprehension that assaulted her lately? Who else could it be if not him?

If he was the perpetrator, why didn't she feel afraid of him all the time? How could she have fallen in love with him?

Perhaps she didn't love him as much as she thought.

Look outside in the front yard, Erin.

As if directed by an outside power, she switched off the living room light and went to the window to the right side of the door. Anxiety wracked her, and she gripped the thick curtain with tense fingers. With agonizing slowness she drew back the curtain.

A dark shape stood near the old tree outside her apartment. Fascinated, yet frightened, she tried to see if she recognized the shadow silhouetted against the small amount of light.

She blinked. The figure disappeared.

She jerked back, pulling the thick blue covering back over the window.

Tempted to call Danny, she then thought how it would sound if she mentioned the peculiar things that happened lately. Strange voices and lovers with otherworldly light in their eyes? Shadows that lurked in bushes and the sensation of being watched? Odd apprehensions that something forbidding and evil skulked in the shadows? Danny would think she'd popped a cork.

Erin backed up until she sat down on the couch. She waited in fearful silence for the voice to talk to her again. She recalled Lachlan's entreaty that she could call him if she was frightened. But Erin couldn't rely on him if she didn't know if she could trust him.

When no solution came to mind after several minutes, she grabbed her book and drifted back to the bedroom.

Somehow she had a feeling she wouldn't sleep again tonight.

* * * * *

The vampire watched Erin peer his way. Anger, lust, and hatred filled his heart. He knew her dread with an untamed intensity he experienced deep in his immortal heart. A heart that stopped beating centuries ago, but that remembered human pain and suffering. Perhaps he didn't feel that distress in the same way, but it tickled at his brain with relentless memories. As his greed once blossomed for her weeks ago, it now it mixed with stirrings of loathing for her stubbornness and pride.

She *would* obey him. She *would* learn that she was Dasoria and therefore his.

Because he could not have her yet, he turned into the night and hurried to taste easy prey.

Chapter 18

"It's happened again," Gilda said as she tossed the newspaper on the library check out counter. "Another woman has been hurt by some sick bastard."

The empty feeling Erin had fought all morning increased as she read the headline and then the article beneath. "Margie Willensky was attacked and brutalized on Hyde Street not far from Jekyl's."

Right where Lachlan was staying.

That's right, Erin.

The disturbing, whispery voice filled her head in an instant, and she looked up, startled. Fright invaded her, replacing the barrenness she'd endured since her disagreement with Lachlan last night.

"Blood drained." Gilda came around the counter and lowered her voice, even though the library hadn't opened yet. "This is getting beyond scary. I'm so glad Lachlan is around to look after you. I doubt a Sherman tank could get through that guy."

The memory of Lachlan's inhuman strength as he held her against the wall and fucked her ran rampant in Erin's mind. Irritation ran over Erin's exciting memory of his embrace. "Lachlan's not my keeper."

"Well, of course not," Gilda said. "But I thought after last night—"

"What about it?" Immediately Erin realized that she sounded snappy. "I'm sorry it's just that Lachlan and I aren't together."

A conspiratorial smile lit Gilda's face. "That's not what Diane Lucas said."

"What? Who is Diane Lucas?"

"She's an old acquaintance I saw on the way to work today. She saw you at Ricardo's."

So much for keeping a low profile. "Yes, we had dinner there, but we aren't going out again."

Gilda's face fell. "Wow. Diane said you two really were going—" Gilda cut herself off, her cheeks turning pink, and her gaze suddenly evading Erin's. "I mean—"

"Gilda?" Erin crossed her arms and frowned.

"Diane was in the ladies room last night, and she though she heard…uh…something that would indicate you two were together. In a big way." Gilda's face turned even redder.

Comprehension dawned on Erin. "Are you saying she could hear us—oh, God. I thought that room was soundproofed."

Gilda patted her arm. "Well, it's not *that* soundproof."

Mortified, Erin covered her face with her hands. Then anger replaced embarrassment, and she glared at her friend. "First of all, that woman has no business gossiping about what she thought she heard or didn't hear. It's none of her business. And I'm mad at you for even listening to her gossip."

Gilda had the decency to look contrite. "Honey, I'm sorry, but she just started talking to me about it. Blurted it out, really. She's got a mouth on her like a bull horn when it comes to hearsay." Looking more than unsettled, Gilda sighed. "She'll have it all over town by the end of the day. If people didn't know that you and Lachlan are in a physical relationship already, they will by…" She looked at her watch. "By no later than five o'clock."

Erin sputtered. "We aren't in a physical relationship."

With a smile Gilda said, "Right."

"We aren't. At least, not any more. Not after what I thought I saw last night." Erin winced.

Good going, girl. Now she's going to want to know more, and you don't know what you saw for certain.

Gilda's expression turned curious, and she leaned back against the counter. As if she thought someone might overhear, Gilda glanced around the room. "What did you see?"

Erin waved one hand in dismissal. "Nothing. I didn't see anything."

Before Gilda could question her, Fred Tyne entered the main area and headed straight for the counter. When he reached the desk, his gaze took on an accusing glower Erin had never seen in his expression before.

"Ladies, I have some worrisome news, but I think it's for the best." His lips were tight and particularly grim. "Did you hear the announcement on the radio that the police want everyone to close up by at least five o'clock?"

"No," Erin and Gilda said at the same time.

"I got a call from Chief Donaldson and he confirmed it. They aren't going to institute a curfew, but if businesses close early, there won't be as many people out." Fred picked up an eraser on the counter and tossed it up and down. "The weather report said it's going to snow harder this afternoon, so it's probably just as well. I've also got some serious questions for you, and I wanted to get them out of the way before we open. Last night I heard those weird noises you complained about, Erin."

All the hair on the back of Erin's neck prickled. "You mean that bizarre sound like the ceiling was going to collapse on your head?"

"Yes. But that's not all. I thoroughly investigated and didn't come up with an explanation."

"Was anyone else with you?" Erin asked.

He shook his head and put the eraser back on the counter. His face held a pale, frightened tinge. "No. So I can't prove that I heard it."

"You don't need to prove anything to me," Erin said. "I heard it first, remember?"

"What can we help you with?" Gilda asked.

"Actually, it's Erin that may be able to help me. When I left the library, I saw that boyfriend of yours. The tall, dark, creepy-looking fellow."

Erin shivered, and she wondered for a moment if perhaps Fred meant someone other than Lachlan. "Who?"

Fred sniffed. "Lachlan Tavish, of course."

"We're not…he's not my boyfriend, Fred."

The man said, "That's not what I gathered from my sources."

"Sources?" Erin almost squeaked the question, starting to get ticked. "First Gilda, now you."

His eyebrows went up as he eyed Gilda. "Oh?"

Gilda waved one hand. "It's personal."

"I don't care what you do in your personal life," Fred said as he lowered his voice. "But I think you ought to watch out for that man. He's a stranger and you haven't known him more than a few days. With the bizarre things going on with that El Chupacabra, you never know."

Erin wanted to protest that whatever attacked women in Pine Forest, it couldn't be an El Chupacabra. She refrained because she knew an argument wouldn't solve the problem.

"Then how can I help you?" Erin asked.

"Maybe you can chat with Danny about Tavish. He would love to keep a watch on that fellow, I'm sure."

Oh, yeah, I'll bet he would.

"Danny has better things to do than stalk Lachlan," Gilda said.

"I second that notion." The words came from Erin before she could think, and she wondered at her own motivations. She decided she wouldn't tell him that she'd already spoken with Danny about Lachlan. "I'm sure Danny is too busy."

Fred nodded. "I suppose. But it's not like there's a lot of crime other than these attacks."

Looking more than incredulous, Gilda said, "Lachlan has nothing to do with these murders. Tom and I have known him a long time. He's a credible man."

"People change." Fred didn't give either one of them time to respond. He turned away and headed into the stacks.

Erin loathed acknowledging that what Fred said about Lachlan made common sense. She'd sped down a fast, furious road with the Scot, and she hadn't known him a week. Since when did a responsible, sane woman have sex with and fall in love with a man in that short a time?

Only the ones looking for inevitable heartbreak.

"He's right." Erin determined she'd have a good, strong cup of coffee. "I don't know Lachlan very well. And I don't plan on getting to know him any better."

Ignoring Gilda's chagrined expression, Erin left for the break room and a bracing cup of caffeine. Before she could reach the room, though, she heard Danny's voice and turned about. Danny said hello to Gilda, then caught sight of Erin. He headed her direction.

She couldn't avoid a man of the law, and Danny's uniform said business mission, not pleasure. "Hi."

He smiled, but his face showed worry. "On the way to get coffee?"

"Yes. Want some?"

He followed her into the lounge, and she wondered when people would start gossiping about her and Danny since they kept disappearing into this small room together. Danny closed the door, so that made it worse. She almost told him to open it again, then remembered Lachlan's assurances that she shouldn't care what anyone thought. When would she get that message through her head?

When you believe it yourself.

After pouring them a cup of coffee, she sat down at the small table once again. "I take it this is official business?"

He tasted the coffee, then winced as if it was bitter or too hot, or maybe both. "Make sure when you get home tonight to lock your doors and don't open them to anyone you don't know."

She smiled. "Danny, I'm not a child. The police are scared spitless and can't figure out who is doing this yet. They figure if all the law-abiding citizens are off the street two things will happen. Innocent people will be out of harm's way. And any bad guys lurking about will stick out like a sore thumb, right?"

He didn't seem amused by her light presentation of the situation. "Yes, and no. This is personal to me. My sister is following my advice."

"Kathleen?"

He didn't even smile at her amazed tone. "Yeah. I know. Surprising, isn't it? But it's more than that, darlin'."

His earnest expression, almost puppy like in its sincerity, made her long for Lachlan's more assured, powerful presence. Like it or not, Danny didn't inspire either romantic feelings or a sense of being protected.

She stood up and retrieved a plastic spoon and creamer, deciding she needed something to reduce the sludge texture of the coffee. Once she'd settled down again, Erin waited for an explanation that didn't come.

"More than what?" she asked.

His chest heaved in a sigh. "I like you a lot, and I want to be more than friends. I care about you."

That's all I need. More complications. She wanted to feel appreciation, but exasperation overflowed instead. "Why don't we take this slower?"

"You aren't taking things slow with Lachlan."

Exasperation turned to anger, and she took a deep breath to hold back a nasty retort. She couldn't remember when she'd been so primed to snap at people. "First of all, whether or not I'm taking it slow with *anyone* is none of your business, Danny. Second, I can't be more than platonic friends with you."

He didn't look away as she half expected, and she realized she'd underestimated Danny Fortesque's resolve. "I'm not asking for an exclusive relationship. I thought if you and I could get to know each other it would be nice."

"I thought that's what we were doing."

"Yeah, but not like you've been getting to know Tavish."

With a thump she put down her mug and liquid sloshed over the edge. "What is that supposed to mean?"

Danny seemed to have abandoned his beverage altogether. Doubt touched his eyes. He scrubbed one hand over his chin. "Look, I'm not doing this very well."

"No, you're not. If you're referring to the various rumors swimming around about Lachlan and I going to dinner, well, the gossip is true. Lachlan and I did spend time at Ricardo's."

He nodded. "I know. I followed you."

"What?" She sat up straighter, resentment bolting through her like lightning.

"Police surveillance."

She reached for a napkin on the table and dabbed at the mess she'd made, half tempted to leave the room without another word. "I can't believe this. You're spying on us?"

"In an official capacity. I had orders from the Chief."

"Right." She stood up and took her mug with her. She tossed the napkin in the trash can on the way to the sink.

"You think I'm investigating Lachlan because I want to date you?"

Erin dumped the rest of her coffee in the sink, her annoyance unabated. "Aren't you?"

"I told the Chief my suspicions and he sanctioned the surveillance."

"And that was convenient for you, wasn't it?"

Danny stood, his gaze intent as he walked toward her. He moved so fast she didn't think much of it until he stopped right in front of her. "This is why I'm worried about you. You used to be such a steady person."

"I may not be the same person you met, but that isn't necessarily a bad thing," she said. "If people don't grow and change they go stagnant."

He nodded, his face going stiffer but with determination remaining in his expression. "All right. But that doesn't change the fact that I'm worried about you being around this guy, darlin'."

"Please don't call me that."

"What? Darlin'?"

He stepped even closer. His closeness inspired none of the hot, forbidden feelings Lachlan's nearness would have. Instead, she felt nothing, not even mild attraction. "Exactly. Don't call me anything but Erin, please."

"Fine. Now getting back to Tavish. Even if Gilda and Tom have known him for ages, he could still have them thinking he's a great guy when he isn't. People's instincts can be wrong."

Again she took a deep breath to maintain what she could of her temper. He pushed her buttons like she couldn't believe. She crossed her arms. "Again, my relationship with Lachlan is none of your business. And I'm not willing to buckle under and think its okay that you're spying on me."

"I'm investigating Lachlan Tavish. He's the only suspect we have."

A mild panic tickled at her brain. She allowed her arms to drop to her sides. "You're saying the entire police department thinks he's involved in these murders?"

He nodded.

She closed her eyes for a moment and tried to formulate her next question. "So you aren't just trailing us because you want to date me and you have a personal dislike of Lachlan?"

He put his hands on his hips and his leather belt creaked. "Even if he wasn't a suspect, I'd still watch out for you."

Erin could see she wouldn't change Danny's mind about Lachlan any time soon. Maybe she shouldn't try. Since she continued to have her own suspicions about Lachlan, she couldn't be a hypocrite.

"Lachlan isn't a murderer," she said.

"Don't be so sure about that." He stepped that last inch until they almost touched.

Before she could blink Danny pressed her back against sink, and his hands went into her hair. He swallowed her protest with his mouth.

Surprised, she put her hands to his chest and realized Danny wasn't as skinny as she thought. Strong, hot muscle bulged in his chest. Panic surged up as he tasted her lips with a thorough kiss. Aggravated and shocked, she pushed against his chest and squirmed to get away, but his grip wouldn't budge. His kiss owned none of the fire and passion she'd experienced with Lachlan. She tried wrenching away again.

A second later she heard a sound at the door, then a shadow moving quickly into the room. "Let her go, Fortesque."

Lachlan.

Danny released her, springing away from her like a kid caught searching in a closet for Christmas presents. Lachlan darkened the doorway, his leather coat, black jeans and blood red sweater a strong contrast. Thunder appeared in the tight line of his mouth and the blazing anger in his eyes. For a moment she imagined him leaping across the room and fastening his hands about Danny's throat.

"Tavish," Danny said, his voice hoarse and his hands clenched at his side. "What are you doing here?"

"Checking out a book. Doesn't look like that's what you had in mind, Fortesque." Lachlan's voice reverberated with strong dislike.

"I'm here conduction official police investigation."

Oh, please, Danny. That is the lamest. Erin wanted to slap him.

Lachlan stepped into the room, closing the door behind him. "Erin isn't enjoying your *official* police investigation."

With a smirk on his face that she never would have imagined seeing on Danny, the police officer stepped forward until perhaps three feet separated him and Lachlan. "That's for her to say."

Lachlan's gaze centered on her, and she saw that golden glow hovering in his eyes like sparks from a conflagration. He didn't smile. "Damn right it is."

Erin felt her stomach flop. Were these men going to fight over her?

"This isn't necessary," Erin said as she walked toward them. "I don't want to see either of you in this lounge again. Both of you seem intent on getting me fired, which is exactly what might happen if you keep coming in here and staying for long periods of time." She swallowed her disappointment in them as she pointed toward the door. "Get out and let me enjoy the rest of my break."

Danny glanced away from his adversary long enough to pin her with an intent, almost apologetic look, "Erin, this isn't over."

"The hell it isn't. If you come near me again, Danny Fortesque, I'm calling your supervisor and pressing sexual harassment charges."

His mouth popped open. "Sexual harassment?"

"That's right. I thought you were here to investigate these murders. Instead I find out all you want is to—to—never mind. Just get out."

Danny's expression hardened into granite before he moved with swift strides past Lachlan. After the door closed behind him, Erin watched Lachlan standing in the middle of the room. Silence ran deep between them.

Unable to keep up a pretense of cool collection and feeling like her knees might wobble any minute, she leaned against the sink again. "Thank you. I think."

A gentle smile teased his mouth, but then it disappeared as he stalked toward her. She clasped the sink behind her, realizing for the first time that her heart still pounded from the bizarre encounter with Danny and Lachlan's sudden appearance. As the uncompromising Scot made tracks toward her, she saw the intent in his eyes. Predatory male was written all over him, and in the golden flash that sparked in his eyes for a few seconds, then winked out.

That flash of fire reminded her of why she couldn't have anything more to do with him. At least not romantically.

He stopped in front of her, his nearness sending her senses into instant riot. She inhaled the warm musk of his masculine scent and felt the heat of his body. Even now the damned man made her belly clench with sudden desire.

He reached up to brush his thumb over her cheek. "Are you going to tell me what that was all about, or are you angry with me?"

"I'm still angry."

When she wouldn't meet his eyes, he tilted her chin up and held it in his gentle grip. "Unhappy that I interrupted that kiss?"

"Of course not. You know I didn't want him to kiss me."

"That's what it looked like. But I wanted to hear it from your lips. After what we did last night…"

"I'd never be sexually involved with two men at the same time."

If she thought her reassurance might take the underlying flame from his eyes, she discovered differently.

Again he touched her face, cupping it in one hand. Tantalizing and hot, the feeling of his big hand cradling her tenderly almost undid all her defenses. How could she afford to trust him with so many questions unanswered?

"Erin, don't pull away from me. I came here to apologize for last night and for not telling you everything. I was afraid if I did you'd turn away from me like my fiancée did."

Unwilling to give in to his apology, she said, "Well, I did anyway, didn't I?"

He nodded. "I also came here to make sure when you left tonight that you were safe."

"I don't want your help, Lachlan." She trembled deep inside. "I need to think about all of this awhile and understand what I'm feeling. There's too much happening."

His gaze, filled with male hunger, captured her as his fingers caressed her face. "Let me keep you safe, Erin. It's torturing me. If anything happened to you—" He choked off the words, and she saw anguish touch his features. "I lost my parents to this damned vampire, and I'm not going to lose you."

Vampire?

"Lachlan, did you just say vampire?"

"I did, but let's talk about one thing at a time, please."

Passionate and consuming, his entreaty made her heart soften the tiniest bit. "All right."

"You still care for me. You love me," he said huskily, desperation touching his voice with a plea.

There. He'd said it out loud, the words she hadn't said the night before despite a deep longing in her heart to scream the words to the heavens. Part of her felt overjoyed, and yet the other part stayed cautious and couldn't yet believe his declaration.

She dared look into his eyes, which was a mistake, of course. Longing stirred her heart when she detected the desire inside him. But she also saw something dangerous and rough, and she didn't know if he directed it at Danny or her. Gently she put her hand over his and drew it away from her face. When he touched her she couldn't think straight.

"You're not the man I thought you were. I'm confused. Please give me this much."

He frowned. "Take all the time you need. Erin—?"

"I can't do this right now." Tears threatened her eyes and it angered her. She sniffed and held them back as best she could. She scrubbed a hand through her hair, weariness catching up with her. "Thank you for telling Danny to leave me alone."

"I would have dragged him away if he hadn't released you."

She saw the animal inside him come to life. As he leaned closer she knew if she didn't do something he would forget all convention, all worries and kiss her right here in the employee lounge. She didn't know, in one second's space, if she could resist that intimate touch. The heat in his eyes said it all. Lachlan knew she loved him, and part of her hated him for stating it and using that intimate feeling against her.

She put a hand on is chest to hold him away, but that was a mistake, too. All she could feel beneath the sweater was hot, hard muscle.

"How did you know I was in here?" Her question came out scratchy and dry.

"Gilda said you were in here with Fortesque. I had to know what was going on." His smile held disgust for the man. "Do you know what I wanted to do to him when I saw him restraining and kissing you?"

She thought she knew, but she asked anyway. "What did you want to do?"

"I wanted to kick his bloody arse," he whispered harshly.

"I'm glad you didn't. He would have arrested you for assaulting an officer."

"If he hurt you I wouldn't have cared."

"Yes, you would have." Her voice squeaked the slightest bit as she held back a strange anguish tearing at her heart. "And I wouldn't have bailed your Scot's butt out of jail, either."

A tear trembled on her lower lash, and Erin blinked hard. Unfortunately, the tear escaped and Lachlan leaned forward to kiss it from her cheek. His hot breath branded her with excitement. Swirls of electricity filled her stomach, and as he tilted even closer, she knew she was a goner. Her breath hitched in her throat as he pressed the most tender, exquisite kiss to her mouth.

"Erin, please, let's talk later. I'll explain—"

"No."

His mouth closed over hers again. This time he lingered, challenging her to resist the caress of his lips and the searing temperature that rose between them.

He tasted of cinnamon, and the deliciousness made her dizzy. God, she wanted to touch him everywhere. Wanted him inside her body and soul. She almost clutched him close and responded. Almost threw away caution all together.

Instead, she pushed against his chest with both hands, and he backed away.

"You're no better than Danny," she said. "And you didn't explain the other night about that glow in your eyes."

"Damn it, Erin, you know I'm not like Fortesque. Have I ever forced a kiss on you?"

She shook her head. "It doesn't matter. Look, I can't do this here, Lachlan. I've got a job to do, and I don't think Fred is going to appreciate me causing a fight between you and a police officer. And I should be working—"

"Gilda said she'd hold the fort and Fred off until we sorted things out between us." He kept close, despite the fact that her gentle shove had sent him a step away. Renewed anger, this time directed at her, filled his dark eyes. "But I can see it's going to take more than a few kisses to convince you I'm not a sod."

"There isn't anything..." She felt the tears well again. Ashamed of her lack of restraint and inability to hold back her feelings, she allowed more tears to rain down. She felt them leave a trail down her face, and she rubbed them away with her palms. "It's too complicated."

Her fear they'd be caught in an intimate embrace made her retreat when she wanted to fall into his arms and sob like a ninny. She moved away from Lachlan, wiping away the tears as she left him in the lounge alone.

Chapter 19

The vampire waited until last rays of sun swept across the winter landscape and disappeared behind the mountains before he left his hideaway. Already the nip in the air turned icy, and snow flurries touched the night sky.

By the time he reached the library and slipped inside, most cautious patrons straggled into the frost gathering darkness outside. People stayed in groups these days, as if worried the bogie man would take them otherwise. A few individuals, most men, occupied study cubicles or looked through books on the numerous shelves. They wore an unusual nonchalant attitude that said they didn't believe goblins or ghouls awaited them somewhere in the cover of evening.

He admired their misguided bravery.

People like them made easy prey because they didn't listen to their gut when it said evil hovered nearby in the gloom. And oh, how he loved shadows. So cold, so solid, so very baneful these dark sections between shafts of light. He could huddle here forever if blood didn't call to him. If Erin's sweet possibility didn't torment him every step of the way.

From his quiet observation area between two bookshelves, he cloaked himself so that none could see him. It wouldn't do for Erin to see who he was until he put her under his complete thrall.

A lone woman passed by him, and he savored the shiver she gave as she walked onward. Perhaps she thought the draft belonged to the building and not his soulless body.

He observed Gilda striding up the stairs toward the children's section, and he considered tasting her blood. He could glide upstairs, pin her in a dark and secluded corner and suck her life force. Oh, he would make it pleasurable for her. He didn't like giving women unneeded pain unless they asked for it. He might touch her nipples, stroke her clit, and sink his fangs into her neck as he slid his fingers into her cunt. As he drained her almost to death, he would give her the biggest, best, most earth-shattering orgasm of her life. What woman wouldn't want to leave this life with an ecstasy most men couldn't give them? He relished his inhuman sexual prowess and savored the next opportunity to bring a woman to soul-shaking climax.

Then again, he'd taken women who possessed strong will. They did not tame easily. The last woman he'd tasted resisted his seduction, and he'd subdued her with force rather than loving.

Yes, giving a woman a hard, bone-rattling come was an even trade for her blood.

Of course, the bliss he gave the women made the blood taste better.

Sometimes his hunger grew too fierce and then he took an older woman like that Pickles bitch. Her taste, as dried up and used as a prune, had given him life force but little enjoyment. She'd fainted. Not that he'd bothered to give her an orgasm. He knew she'd never had one in all her days.

No. He liked the younger ones. Ripe. Subtle. Their eagerness fueled his feeding frenzy and sometimes, after their orgasm, they died on the spot.

He sighed. Ah, the hazards of being the undead.

His attention snapped back to Gilda, and he almost went upstairs. Almost.

Then he saw a spindly, older man talking to Erin and it drew his awareness back to the woman he wanted more than anything. After the man went away, Erin organized the front area. The huge grandfather clock at one side of the room bonged four thirty. People started to leave the library, and he recalled that the town closed down early these days because of El Chupacabra.

He laughed at the ridiculousness of it all. Poor El Chupacabra, being blamed for something it didn't do.

His bloodlust revived, hardened by a few long hours without nourishment. Deciding that Gilda might taste nice anyway, he decided perhaps he would take her after all.

Still, Erin drew his attention a little longer. As he watched her, Erin seemed nervous. He knew why and relished that she could feel his presence. His intimate touch into her mind said she didn't care for everything that happened to her of late. And although he wished to possess her in body, mind, and soul, he didn't want her sexual blossoming to diminish. No, the heady energy gave him life, and he consumed it and suckled it like a babe at a mother's breast. Food for his immortality, warm and as sweet, came in the form of her sexual vigor. Erin's awakening held wonderful and terrible consequences she couldn't yet envision.

He laughed, and Erin's attention jerked toward his area. She gazed right at him. At first he felt a bizarre apprehension. Could she see him?

But, no. Her gaze went right through him.

Suddenly, he didn't know if he liked that, or not.

* * * * *

"Fred's been giving us weird glances all day," Gilda said as she scanned the room. "Not to mention Candice and Greg."

"I'm trying not to notice," Erin said.

Both Candice and Greg worked the second kid's area as well as the research rooms upstairs. They'd come downstairs at various times of the day for one thing or another and their attitude held a strange coolness Erin didn't try to decipher. She supposed the town gossips managed to spread the word that she'd done the nasty with Lachlan last night and somehow that made her a pariah.

"Besides," Erin said, "I don't think Fred is looking at you. It's me he's watching and it's making me nervous."

Gilda lowered her voice. "Don't worry. All he saw was Lachlan going into the lounge and then Danny storming out."

Erin made a soft huffing noise. "That's *all*?"

"I distracted him with some questions after that." Gilda's eyes twinkled with mischief. "You'll have to tell me later what happened. Both men came out of that room with their eyes blazing. I half expected to hear sounds of a knock-down, drag-out fight happening in there."

"That's not funny."

Gilda sobered a little. "No, sweetie, it isn't."

Erin smiled weakly. "And I always wondered what it would be like for two men to want me at once."

The phone at the front counter rang stridently, and Erin wished the day didn't seem so damned long. She wanted the peace and quiet of a good book and maybe hot chocolate. She needed something to remove the anxiety that seemed to have gripped her since the strange encounter with Lachlan and Danny earlier in the day.

Fred came up to the desk, and Erin's anxiety rose at the displeased stare on Fred's face.

"Erin, do you have a few moments?" Fred asked. "Come into my office, please."

Erin followed him back toward the small office area near the restrooms and lounge. Back here Fred reigned supreme with Arlene, an elderly woman that worked part time in the mornings assisting him with secretarial duties. Arlene hadn't come in today so they had the office area to themselves. He gestured toward the chair in front of his desk, and she sank onto the hard, cold wood. Her muscles felt tight as boards and her nerves rattled. Taking a few glances around the room of his utilitarian office, she wondered why he didn't have any family photos around. She tried a deep breath to eliminate apprehension, but it didn't seem to make a difference.

Fred sat down in his plusher chair. After adjusting his glasses on his nose, he spoke. "I wanted to ask you if everything was all right."

Oh, oh. Here it comes. "Yes, of course."

"Danny Fortesque called me."

Renewed irritation flashed inside her. "Oh?"

Fred leaned back in his chair a little, his position casual and relaxed. "He's very concerned about your safety because of this Scotch fellow."

"Why would Danny call you about that?"

Fred shrugged, and the harsh florescent lighting bounced off his wispy white hair. "He asked me if I wouldn't watch out for you while you were at work. And if Tavish showed up and harassed you again, I'm to call the law."

Erin shifted in her chair, her fingers clutching the chair arms. "Lachlan didn't harass me. He came in because he was...because we had something personal to discuss." She swallowed, her throat dry as crackers. "I'm sorry if that was inappropriate."

To her surprise, Fred's narrow face creased in a smile and one dimple dented his left cheek. The older man's eyes sparkled with amusement. "Personal, eh? Well, don't worry about that. I wasn't angry with you, if that's what you were thinking."

Relief loosened her grip on the chair arms. "I thought for sure you were going to reprimand me."

"Heck, no. Whatever would give you that idea?"

She shook her head. "It's just that so much has happened and with the murders, I guess I'm a little on edge."

"You should be. Lots of mighty strange things going on right now. I told my wife she wasn't going out shopping even in the daytime unless she was with someone else. It just isn't safe until they catch this killer." He stood up and walked to the single big window overlooking the parking lot at the front of the building. Snow now drifted down steadily. He kept his gaze on the weather. "I know what I said about Tavish earlier, and I don't know the guy from Adam. But if you think he's all right, then I'll take your judgment."

"Thank you." Erin wondered about her motivations, deciding she needed once and for all to decide whether she trusted Lachlan one hundred percent, or not. "I know Lachlan isn't a murderer." She felt the truth of it down in her soul. "I think Danny is suspicious of any stranger in town and Lachlan is new to the area. So it's natural, I suppose, that Danny wants to investigate him."

"Well, do me a favor, just try and keep them from having fisticuffs in the library, will you?"

* * * * *

After Erin left Fred's office and headed back to the front counter, she thought she heard something. A deep, malevolent laugh.

As she glanced around the area, she wondered what difference it made. All patrons had left as the hour grew closer to closing time. Other than the laugh Erin thought she heard, the old building had a graveyard quiet that made all the hair on her body prickle.

Determined not to let nerves or atmosphere take control, she turned her attention to the storm continuing outside. Grayish clouds and swirling white snow assured a darkening gloom. Just watching the fluffy white stuff fall made her glad she'd worn silk thermals under her sweater and pants.

Gilda had gone upstairs, Erin figured, to make sure the area cleared out. Although she should have been relieved the day ended soon, she couldn't help but feel icky.

Icky because the library seemed shrouded by that same cold, awful blackness she'd felt last night outside Ricardo's and several other times since these attacks started. She also felt terrible because she couldn't decide if she feared Lachlan's hold on her or loved him so much she couldn't see straight.

That must be it. You're so bewildered you don't know what you're doing. She could absolve herself from guilt and worry if she could blame her deeds on confusion. But she never blamed anything or anyone else for her actions. She'd lost her heart, and yet a tiny piece of her didn't trust him with her heart. Not when he wouldn't explain how he could read minds and why his eyes glowed. She shivered as she imagined him wandering the streets of Pine Forest, enjoying attacking the women of the town like a cat's nocturnal wanderings for prey.

"No," she said and shook her head. "No."

No matter what she thought of him, he couldn't be a murderer. She'd told Fred so with complete confidence.

Disturbed, Erin concentrated on clearing her work away. As she gazed around at the numerous bookshelves and the nook-and-cranny effect of the entire library, she realized if a strange attacker wanted somewhere to hide, this would certainly be an excellent place. For a short while she enjoyed the quiet, her nerves soothed by the pedantic nature of her work.

Silence became unnerving when Gilda didn't return to the first floor. Nerves prickled along Erin's skin as the haunting quality of the room brought her unease. Seconds later she heard the laugh again, this time fainter. She froze, each muscle tight as she waited for it to return. When the sound didn't echo, she decided the acoustics in the cavernous area must have been playing tricks on her. Fear did a dance up her spine despite self-assurances.

I know what this place is like. I've been here late in the evening.

Damn her conscience for comforting her, then deciding to scare her with spooky thoughts. She left the counter and headed into the bookshelves, scanning the corridors in between. When she saw no one lingering in the stacks, she figured she'd imagined the laugh.

Her low-heeled boots made small clicks on the hardwood floor. She took even breaths to quiet the uneasiness trying to surface. Each step brought her past one row, then another. As she stopped at the last row, near huge windows, she took another look outside at the weather. Fading sun couldn't make it through the clouds, and she knew the slick roads would require caution.

A shadow moved somewhere by the trees near the windows. She gasped and stepped straight back into something solid.

A startled squeak came out of her throat as she wheeled around. Her hands went out, as if to hold back an attack.

No one was there.

Her breath came in gasps, her heart thumping. "Shit, shit, shit." She *had* bumped into someone. Where were they now? "Who's there?"

Quiet.

A dull ache started behind her eyes, but she didn't dare close them. Trembling a little, she started back toward the front counter. She'd find Gilda and they'd get the hell out of this place before the willies drove her to within an inch of screaming.

She'd become a wimp after today's encounters with two stubborn men. That was all. No ghosts lingered in the rows of books waiting to assault her. She'd imagined the feeling of someone behind her.

Yet the sensation of being watched skulked behind her like a monster in an old movie. She tried to smile at her silliness, but she couldn't. She headed toward the restrooms, determined not to care that shadows grew long in the hallway.

Instead, skin on the back of her neck prickled. If she'd been the religious type she might start now, whispering the Lord's Prayer or some other chant. Instead, she stopped at the entrance to the women's restroom and waited. No sounds, no footfalls.

Seconds later she heard it, the shifting of footstep on flooring.

She whirled around.

No one.

"Hello?"

She hoped a friendly, *human* voice would greet her.

Human. Of course it would be human. Why did she feel like one of the converted, those who let Pine Forest transform them into something they despised? Those that feared and those that worried dwelled in this place called suspicion. She didn't want every old building in town to haunt her. She put one foot in front of the other, resolute.

She pushed aside fear and went into the bathroom. Once she finished there, she figured she'd find Gilda. When she left the restroom, though, Gilda hadn't returned to the counter.

Concern built inside Erin, so she headed upstairs. As she ascended the steps, she remembered the first night she'd met Lachlan and the incredible things that happened. Yet they lost so much when he wouldn't tell her the truth about his glowing eyes or his assertions about vampires.

When she reached the landing she attempted to ignore the persistent feeling of someone behind her. She glanced down the stairs.

Nothing but silence.

Maybe the creepiness of the light in this old building made everything seem more insecure. She glanced at the high ceilings and imagined that a winged creature could hide in the darkness near the top of the enormous ceiling. No matter that chandeliers threw sparkling illumination, the light never seemed to reach the top. Then she spotted something along one towering wall she'd never noted before, and her eyes widened.

A faded gargoyle drawing, its face grinning evil, looked down upon her position.

It blinked.

Chapter 20

Erin jerked in surprise and gasped. She blinked and when she looked back, the grinning gargoyle had disappeared. She laughed, the sound self-deprecating. How idiotic. She'd allowed this place to influence her into having horrifying hallucinations.

The persistent ache behind her eyes now turned into a full-fledged headache in the temples. Cold seemed to penetrate her bones.

Shivering, she rubbed her sweater-clad arms and searched the children's area. "Gilda?"

Seconds later she heard an almost inaudible whimper. Her heartbeat quickened. Seconds seemed to crawl into minutes as she listened. Could she have imagined the pitiful human sound as she had the laugh downstairs?

What if Gilda had been hurt?

"Gilda? Gilda, where are you?"

Again, the barest sound, terrified and pleading, sent a terrifying sensation of being stalked into her system. Fear threatened at the door, and she thought about calling for the police.

Another cry, this one stronger, came from the storage area where they stored supplies and some older periodicals that needed archiving. She hated venturing into the vicinity where light never seemed to reach. She stepped into the dim recesses, girding her courage.

A shadow moved into the dim light with such swiftness, Erin flinched but couldn't move fast enough to run.

Hands caught her by the back of the neck and pulled her forward against a granite hard chest. Her breath felt frozen in her chest and dizziness filled her head. She couldn't see anything but a dark shadow.

She couldn't breathe.

Panic touched Erin as her vision wavered and blackness threatened.

"No, little one, you won't die." The voice whispered, this time in full volume. She pushed against the man's chest, unable to see his face in the murky light. Terror made her thrash, and she tried reaching up to rake her nails over her captor's face, but she could barely move. "You will be mine."

"No," she rasped, as her limbs weakened. "No."

Cold breath filtered over her face. Chilling and yet blazing hot, the man's terrific strength held her like iron bars in a prison. She struggled, flailing against the powerful body. She refused to allow death so close, to surrender to whatever or whoever held her.

"You will be mine for eternity. Surrender, and I will shower you with riches beyond your wildest dreams. We will travel the world and the planet shall be our feast."

Butter-soft tones, deep and filled with insistence, demanded her compliance. Panic danced through her body, and she wavered between coherence and fading consciousness. *Why can't I see him?*

She knew the voice and yet she didn't, and terror hovered, waiting to attack. His grip tightened on the back of her neck. His icy breath passed over her face in a beastly touch.

"Let...me...go." She forced words past her lips, the pain in her throat starting to become overwhelming.

"Hush, Dasoria. Hush, Erin. Hush, wee one."

Erin struggled again, but her muscles wouldn't obey. The pressure on the back of her neck increased and her consciousness ebbed. She coughed as she fought for oxygen.

"I'm not your enemy, Erin. Not if you obey me. I will be yours to command in our night of love. I'll teach you things and show you things you never dreamed. When I take your blood you will die, then return to me as Dasoria."

With a relentless and smooth cadence, his voice seduced her, slowing down the pandemonium within her and giving her hope that maybe he didn't mean to kill her. Erin sagged against him.

Her throat felt tight and dry, and she struggled to speak. "Please...no."

Then, with slow deliberation, her heart seemed to slow, each beat drumming in her ears, thumping to a new rhythm that fit with her captor's.

Erin wondered why she feared him so much. His body felt solid next to hers, his arms tight but sheltering. A woman could get lost in his embrace and never return.

"Feel me," he whispered, his breath now hot against her ear. "Feel what you do to me and know I am your slave."

Her mind struggled to stay focused on surviving this strange lethargy. One small part of her realized if she didn't fight him, she might end up like the other women who'd been attacked by this creature. She must fight. *Fight!*

She tried commanding her muscles to move, but weakness now spread through her entire body.

The strangling sensation eased as she ceased all struggle.

His lips touched her nose, and the touch of chill flesh made her shudder.

Erin.

At first she thought he now read her mind as Lachlan did.

Then it hit her.

Maybe the man who held her now *was* Lachlan.

She strained to see in the darkness and couldn't make out his features. He wasn't even a shape in the shadows anymore.

God, no. I can't see anything. He's invisible.

New panic welled up, and she tried to scream, but her throat refused to issue a sound.

He's done something to me.

Erin! A new voice blasted into her sore head and demanded attention. *Erin, listen to me. Just hang on. Resist him. Don't listen to him. I'm almost there. Do you hear me? Don't listen to his voice. Think of something else. Think of me.*

Lachlan?

Yes, love. It's me. I'm coming for you.

Lachlan, please hurry.

Think of us together by a warm fire. I'm holding you and you're safe.

"I am yours to command, Erin," the man holding her said. "You are the birth, the death, and the life. No one can save you but me."

Seconds later she felt a hard jerk as she was released from the man's grip and her legs buckled. She fell to her right side, her body jarred by the impact. Everything wavered, and the impressions she received floated disjointed in her head.

Cursing. Sounds of struggle. A loud groan. A punch.

The beat of great wings fluttered above her head.

Wings?

What seemed minutes later, hard masculine hands touched her head, and she fought. She flayed out with her arms and legs, intent on escape. Powerful hands gripped her arms and held her still.

"Erin, it is Lachlan. You're all right. You're safe. Please stay still until I can make sure you're not hurt, lass."

Despite wanting Lachlan and the safety he promised, fear still rolled inside her. How could she trust him?

Her eyes popped open, and for one moment in the darkness of the hallway, she saw his gaze glowing with that unmistakable aura. She blinked, then blinked again, but the radiance lingered. Lachlan leaned over her and brushed back her hair.

He pulled her hair away from her neck and looked closely. "Thank God. I wasn't too late."

Too late for what?

He didn't answer her telepathically or verbally. His stricken face and gentle touch told her everything. Lachlan's hands, so much more tender than the madman's grip, made her long to wrap her arms around the Scot and never let him go.

Before she could reach for him, a dark haze clouded her mind, and she slipped into blessed unconsciousness.

* * * * *

More hands touched her, and Erin wanted them to leave her alone. Confusing noises filled her head. People talking, whispering.

Her body ached like one overused muscle, her head fuzzy and her thought process confused. Could she be thankful she lived, or did more horror wait once she opened her eyes?

Lachlan?

I'm just outside the room, lass. Don't worry, I won't leave you for long.

"Lachlan?" Her throat hurt. She reached out with one hand. "Lachlan?"

"It's all right," a young woman's voice said. "We have to examine you now."

She tried to peel open her eyes, but they wouldn't cooperate. She heard a man's gravelly voice. "I'm Doctor Majors. Can you open your eyes?"

She thought she heard angry voices outside in the hallway. Danny Fortesque? Lachlan's voice sounded aggravated, then Tom's calming voice entered the conversation.

The strange fog in her brain lifted. She opened her eyes and the harsh, glaring light of an examining room greeted her. "The hospital."

She realized she was lying on an examining table. A young, auburn-haired nurse smiled down on her. "You'll be all right. Just rest now. Let's get this top off so we can take more vitals."

The doctor, an older man with a pleasant smile, asked her questions as he started his examination.

Erin tried to piece together scattered impressions of what happened at the library. Images rushed through her memory, and she realized the entire experience seemed surreal and no one would believe her.

El Chupacabra?

Lachlan's voice came into her mind. *No, lass. There is no El Chupacabra here in Pine Forest. Rest easy now and let the medical people do their job.*

Lachlan's voice echoed in her head, and the warm rush of heat filling her body comforted her more than a soft blanket. She reached out with her mind.

Lachlan, I'm scared.

It's all right. I'm just outside the room. I won't let anyone harm you again.

Cherishing the mental communication that a few days ago would have seemed ludicrous, she relaxed.

"What time is it?" she asked the doctor.

"Almost six-thirty. Did you hit your head?"

"No. I think I just fainted." With a rush she remembered Gilda. "Gilda? Where is she? Is she all right?"

The doctor smiled, and she got a little relief from the sincerity in his eyes. "She'll be fine. We're keeping her overnight for observation."

Relief warred with doubt inside her. "I want to see her."

He patted her arm. "Easy now. Let's get you taken care of and we'll see about visiting with her later. All right?"

She took a deep breath and released it. "Yes."

Erin tried to relax, reminding herself that Lachlan was nearby. As the examination went on, she realized that other than feeling very tired and that dull headache, she felt fine.

After the exam, Doctor Majors said, "It looks like other than some bruises, you're all right. I want to run a few more tests, though. We're going to keep you overnight for observation."

Immediate alarm made her flinch. "No." She didn't know why she didn't feel safe in the hospital, but she knew she shouldn't be alone here. "I'd be more comfortable at home."

The doctor glanced at the nurse as if to say he didn't cherish arguing with Erin. "I can't force you to stay, but I advise against it. You've been through a substantial trauma." He started toward the door, then smiled at Erin. "You've got some very worried friends that wish to see you, but it's going to have to be after we finish with tests."

After ordering the nurse to arrange for the tests, the doctor left. She heard an urgent rush of questions, all of them in Lachlan's brogue. Then the voices faded down the hallway and mild panic slipped into her.

Lachlan!

It's all right. I won't be far away.

The assurance in his strong voice comforted her, and she realized, despite all the doubts she'd experienced before, she trusted him. She could get through more medical poking and prodding as long as she could see him and visit with Gilda soon.

Her heart twisted, wishing she'd been more forceful and demanding to know Gilda's condition in full. Guilt rushed through her. Tears stung her eyes as sharply as remorse filled her heart.

If she'd gone upstairs earlier could she have saved Gilda from harm?

* * * * *

Redressed and sitting on the exam table, Erin gave the Dr. Majors a firm look and keep her voice determined. "If there's nothing wrong with me, I'd like to see Gilda and then home."

He nodded. "We can't find anything serious, so yes, you're free to go. We'll check on your friend and get back with you in a minute."

After he left the door swung open again almost immediately and Danny and Lachlan stepped into the room. Concern showed on their faces; Lachlan's strong features showed strain and unhappiness. Danny's gaze was determined, critical, and somehow possessive.

Feeling teary, Erin smiled as best she could at them. "Hey, cheer up, guys. I'm almost good as new."

Lachlan's features eased into a genuine smile, relief stark on his face. "Are you really all right?" He reached for her right hand and brought it up to his mouth. The touch of his lips against her fingers comforted her. "I know what the doctor said, but I'm worried."

"I'm fine." She squeezed his fingers in appreciation. "And I want to go home. How is Gilda?"

Danny spoke up. "She's all right, but she's very quiet and they're worried about her mental state."

Erin frowned. "What do you mean?"

Lachlan and Danny stayed silent long enough, their grave expressions sending worry straight through her like a dagger. "What's wrong with her?"

Lachlan shrugged, but he kept his grip on her hand. "She's acting as if nothing really happened."

Erin pulled her hand from Lachlan's and covered her eyes. "I knew something happened to her."

Danny cleared his throat. "Like you she doesn't have any serious injuries. A few small bruises they say."

Grateful for at least that much, Erin dropped her hands away, knowing she couldn't hide behind a barrier forever.

Had Gilda been raped? The horrible thought ripped through Erin like lightning. Her stomach lurched and her heart pounded with renewed dread. She felt a darkness lurking, even here in the glaring lights of the hospital. Nowhere felt safe anymore. The throbbing started in her head again. She winced.

Danny placed a proprietary hand on her left shoulder. "We were very worried when we got the 911 call." He gestured to Lachlan. "He called it in and we rushed the ambulance over. I've got some questions for you about what happened. Do you feel up to it?"

"I think she should rest first," Lachlan said, his voice rough around the edges.

She noticed for the first time the small bruise on the left side of Lachlan's jaw. "Lachlan, what happened to you?"

"Came in contact with the bastard trying to hurt you." His brogue emerged, thick with emotion. "He took a swing at me and connected."

"Got away, too," Danny said in an accusatory tone.

"If Lachlan hadn't of showed up, I don't know what would have happened." Tears threatened, but she forced them back. She took a shuddering breath. "Let's not start a blame game."

Danny wasn't ready to back down one hundred percent from his obvious dislike for Lachlan.

Erin saw Lachlan's eyes narrow. "I'll be with her from now on."

"That's up to her." Danny's tone held reason and calm seasoned with a coolness Erin found disconcerting.

Erin held up her hands. "I'm not staying with *anyone*. I wish you'd stop talking about me like I wasn't here. I'm going home." When they spoke at once, she put up her hands again. "I really appreciate your concern." Tears spilled over and fell on her cheeks despite her efforts to keep them inside. "I don't want you to think I don't appreciate it."

Danny squeezed her shoulder. "Erin, we can put you in protective custody—"

"I can protect her."

Erin tensed when she saw the muscle twitching in Lachlan's jaw and the anger building in his intense eyes.

Danny bristled. "She needs police protection, not some foreign—"

"I swear to God, Fortesque—" Lachlan started.

"Stop it," Erin said. "Both of you stop it."

Danny kept his intense stare pinned to Lachlan. "I ought to have you arrested for obstruction."

Lachlan's voice came out a harsh whisper. "You could try."

Tense silence filled the room, and the stress of the last day built inside Erin. She couldn't believe how weepy she felt and how much she wanted to sleep. "Cut it out. I don't need two testosterone overloaded males playing games over me."

"I must question you about the attack." Danny glared at Lachlan once again, and Lachlan's returning glower seemed to say he would rumble anytime Danny wanted a fight. "Without anyone else in the room."

"Erin?" Lachlan's voice rumbled over her ears. "I'll stay if you wish."

His protectiveness made her feel safe and, if she admitted it, loved. She attempted a weak smile. "I'm fine."

Lachlan headed for the door. "I'll be outside if you need me."

"She'll be fine with me, Tavish." Danny's sour expression disappeared once Lachlan stepped out the door. "How are you really, Erin?"

"If one more person asks me, I'll probably scream." She tossed a half-ticked look his way. "I'm not porcelain you know."

He frowned and shifted from one foot to the other. "I know. I just don't want that man near you any more than necessary."

Anger poured into her, and she almost left the room right then. "That man? You mean Lachlan?"

"Right." He slipped into a horrible attempt at a Scottish accent. "My poor wee lass and all." He went back to his normal voice. "He wouldn't be separated from you even when the paramedics asked him not to get in the ambulance. I thought I was going to have to arrest him. He said something about having to be with you to protect you. Maybe it's him you require shielding from."

"Lachlan wouldn't hurt me. I know that much."

"How can you be sure?" Danny's perturbed expression extended to her and not just the Scot he loved to hate. "Could you see who attacked you?"

Uncomfortable with this fact, she cleared her throat. "No."

"Then do me a favor, darlin', and consider the possibility that until this investigation is over, you should stay safe somewhere. Maybe you should get out of town. Go back to Arizona for awhile."

She shook her head. "No way. I'm not going back to Arizona any time soon. My family would drive me bonkers."

'But you'd be safe."

"At this point I'd rather be in danger than put up with my parent's anxiety. My mother already called me and asked why I hadn't come home yet after these murders. If she hears about this, she'll pop a cork."

Danny stepped closer, and she tensed. "All right. Then at least stay with Gilda and Tom until we catch this bastard."

She sighed. "You just don't get it, do you? You think the answer is for all women to alter their lifestyles and cloister away?"

"No. Look, Erin, about this morning when I kissed you —"

"Let's not talk about that now. Stick with the investigation. I meant what I said about reporting you, Danny. I don't want that kind of relationship with you."

His gaze possessed equal parts longing and exasperation as he picked up a notebook he'd put on a table earlier. "I know this is difficult, but I have to know what happened in detail. As long as it takes, I need to know."

Erin couldn't tell him what she'd felt and heard when she couldn't be certain herself. She scraped her hair back from her face, wishing she had a comb right now. The repetitive motion of smoothing her tangled hair would have soothed her nerves. In this impersonal examining room, she didn't feel comfortable. It felt as though a million eyes watched her.

"Erin?"

"There's a lot I don't remember." In halting sentences she gave details without alerting him to the *odd* things that occurred.

He sighed and the piss and vinegar drained from him for the moment. "Erin, can you do me a favor?"

His request surprised her, but the sincere sadness in his eyes made her realize that whatever he asked he didn't do it lightly. "All right."

"Gilda isn't saying much about her attack, but I think she's been..." He inhaled deeply. "That the madman raped her."

Erin went still, her mind attempting to wrap around the horrible concept. "Oh, God."

"Yeah. Did..." He swallowed hard and perused the floor as if it held answers to the universe. "Did the attacker rape you? If he did, I swear to God I'll hunt him down and —"

"No." She stood, her legs steady. "No."

Danny's frown went harsh. "Tell me the truth, Erin. Did Lachlan Tavish have anything to do with this? If you're protecting him —"

"How dare you? How dare you even think that if he had hurt Gilda or me that I'd shelter him from arrest?" When he simply stared at her, she decided to say the one thing she couldn't have admitted before tonight. "Whoever it was...wasn't human."

"What?"

"I couldn't see him, Danny. Whoever had me in his grip was almost invisible. At first he was a shadow, then he faded until I couldn't see him. All I could feel was his grip. He was so strong."

Danny's officious demeanor dissolved a bit as he came a little closer. He let his pencil and pad hang at his side. "The Chief believes in the supernatural, if you can believe that. But I don't know if he's going to believe in the invisible man."

She shrugged. "Then what will you tell him? That I've lost my mind?"

"Of course not."

Silence covered the room for a minute before she spoke. "What about the other women? Were they raped?"

"Neither the jogger or Mrs. Pickles showed signs of sexual assault or rape." He lowered his voice, then took a glance at the closed door. "Jessie Huxley is another story. The medical examiner said she'd had sex not long before the murder. Consensual sex."

"Where did they find her again?"

"In the bushes near her home." Silence hovered in the room like a beast until Danny spoke again. "Tell me the rest of what you recall."

"I heard a man's laugh a couple of times while I was still downstairs, but I never saw anyone."

Danny studied his notepad, then pulled up a stool. As he sank onto the stool he scribbled notes with a pen. "Like a ghost."

"I'm not saying it was a ghost I heard or a ghost that attacked me. But the laugh was the only sound I heard that indicated someone else might be in the building besides Gilda and I. I knew it wasn't Fred because he was in his office. By the way, is Fred all right?"

Danny's mouth quirked to one side. "Yes. He never heard a thing because he had his classical music turned up in his office." As he scrawled new notes, the cop's tone implied something undesirable about a man listening to classical music in the first place. "A lot of good it did you and Gilda having him there."

"You can't blame Fred for what happened. He had no way of knowing."

No one could have guessed at the strangeness of this evening or the invisible entity that attacked Gilda and her.

Then she remembered that Danny called the attacker "whatever." "Danny, are you saying you think whoever attacked me and Gilda was otherworldly?"

He laughed, the sound unforgiving and not the least convinced. "I think your attacker was the man who jumped that jogger and murdered Mrs. Pickles and Jessie Huxley. You were damned lucky he didn't accomplish what he set out to do."

Once he finished his questioning, he clasped her shoulder in a gentle hold. His voice held more of that icy edge she'd heard moments ago. Danny allowed his hand to slip down her arm until he clasped her hand in a proprietary gesture. "You aren't going to let that Tavish guy bully you into staying with him, are you?"

"I'm going to see Gilda and then go home." She headed for the door with him following close behind. "And no one is going to argue with me anymore about it."

Danny hooked his thumbs in his wide leather holster belt as he followed her out the door. "You need protection. You don't know when the bastard might try something again."

Before she thought much about what she said, the words blurted. "You can't protect me."

"What? Why not?"

Could he handle the truth? "Maybe there is something strange going on in Pine Forest. Something evil and new. And if that's the case, how could you protect me from something supernatural?" He held his thoughts in check, and she waited. When he continued his silence, she spoke. "You can't keep me safe from something you can't see."

Before Danny could ask any further questions, Lachlan walked toward them. Lachlan's gaze locked with hers as he approached. *He wants you, lass, but I want you more. And you desire me.*

His thoughts whispered into her mind like flowing water, smooth and cool. Tension eased in her mind for the moment, calmed by Lachlan's presence and the soothing quality of his mind communication.

Time seemed to slow, just as Lachlan's approach crawled. The air around her thickened, her thoughts and feelings captured for a microsecond that stretched into infinity. Captured in his gaze, she couldn't move. Didn't want to move.

Then the lengthy languor snapped, and time lurched back into normalcy.

When he arrived in front of them Lachlan said, "Fortesque was right earlier. You need protection."

"Glad you're seeing things my way, Tavish."

Lachlan formed a sarcastic smile, but said nothing. Danny stuffed his thumbs in his belt again and puffed out his chest.

Erin stepped between them. "I won't have you overgrown boys fighting over who is going to be my bodyguard."

Lachlan's sense of humor resurfaced as he smiled and backed away one step. "All I want is for you to be safe, Erin. If that means under police protection, so be it."

His attitude surprised her, but Lachlan's acquiesce melted a little of Danny's bluster.

"I want to see Gilda," she said.

"They've given her a sedative and said she'll sleep through the night. Tom's with her and they said no more visitors tonight," Lachlan said.

Erin decided maybe it was for the best. If she could go home and be alone to think over the strange events of the evening, maybe she could find some peace in her heart. Her belief system had taken a serious beating. *Time to regroup.* Then her gaze meshed with Lachlan's, and she knew she wouldn't feel safe unless he stayed with her. Her worry about his possible deceptions vanished under the wave of protection she felt coming from him.

Trust me. His voice whispered to her with concern and a seduction she couldn't resist.

She allowed her mind to reach out to his. *I think I do.* "I'm going home, but Lachlan is staying with me."

Danny's chagrinned expression didn't bother Erin. "If you think that's the wise thing to do."

She nodded and ignored his dismay. "Yes. It is."

Without another word, Danny turned and left.

Lachlan watched the cop for a few seconds before saying, "He's like a dog panting at your heels, lass. It's disgusting."

The amused tone overlaying his annoyance made Erin smile. Tears threatening her eyes moments before abated. "And what would you call your relentless attention?"

His gaze searched hers. "Can we talk about this somewhere else? After I've taken you home?" He pressed her shoulder with gentle comfort. "You've been hurt, you're exhausted, and it'll drive me insane if I can't keep you safe."

"All right." Profound sadness welled anew inside her. "Are you reading my mind this time?"

"Lucky guess."

She took a big breath and tried to resurrect her courage. "Danny suspects Gilda's been raped." Lachlan slipped his arm around her, and warmth bathed and comforted her frazzled senses. "If he thinks she was sexually assaulted or raped, why doesn't he think that about me?"

He pulled her closer to his side. "You weren't alone with the attacker long, and apparently Gilda said something during his questioning that makes him believe she was raped." Silence hung between them a moment before he spoke again. "I know who attacked her."

She pulled back from him. "And you haven't told Danny?"

Lachlan's hands went up in entreaty. "Wait until we've left the hospital and I have time to explain."

She crossed her arms and felt a cold shiver start at her back and work its way up. "Just the way you promised to explain your glowing eyes?"

Although she kept her tone low, he appeared afraid others would hear. "This time, I will explain." He reached up and brushed a piece of her hair from her cheek and that tiny touch sent new lightning into her system. "For your safety."

Lachlan kept his arm around her waist as they exited the hospital, as if afraid she might fall over any moment. Fatigue threatened her, and her body started to feel a little sore. The relentless throb in her head had disappeared.

You're weary, lass. We'll be home soon.

Home?

To your house.

Snow nipped at their ankles as they hailed a cab. As they settled into the cab, Erin continued her mind communication. *We must talk.*

Only after you've rested. There is plenty of time tomorrow. Don't be afraid. I'll be with you all night. I'll hold you and soothe you in any way you need.

As his arm slipped around her shoulders, and he tucked her close, she half expected him to kiss her.

Is that what you want, Erin?

No. I want to know what's going on.

He didn't answer.

She leaned her head on his shoulder. Heat from his body seeped into her, taking away some of the tension from her coiled muscles. She felt like she would never unwind again, never walk into that library without seeing that hideous gargoyle grinning down on her from the high ceiling. How could she forget that other voice in her head, the one she understood now wasn't Lachlan?

As another shiver slipped through her body, Lachlan's voice came again. *It can't hurt you, lass, if I am with you.*

It?

Evil.

What is it? Did I really see it? Did I see a gargoyle face?

Yes, you did.

Oh, sweet God. It's a real gargoyle?

Not exactly.

When she looked up at him, more relentless tears in her eyes, he kissed her nose. *There. A small token of how I feel.*

How do you feel?

Later, lass. I'll show you later.

They asked the cabbie to stop at his room at the guesthouse to pick up his things. At the checkout desk, the proprietor, Mrs. Drummond, looked at them with keen curiosity.

"Sorry I have to check out early," Lachlan said to Mrs. Drummond.

Mrs. Drummond, a rickety, sometimes rough-around-the-edges sort, said, "You're leavin' town?"

He glanced at Erin and then winked at Mrs. Drummond. The older woman blushed. "No. I just have other accommodations for the rest of the time I'm here."

Mrs. Drummond's thick eyebrows shot up. She pushed back her waist-length gray hair. "Hope it wasn't our service that drove you out."

"Not at all. Everyone here has been great."

Mrs. Drummond eyed Erin, and Erin wanted to tell the lady to mind her own business. "Stayin' with Miss Greenway?"

Lachlan's smile turned to a sly grin. He slipped his arm around Erin's shoulders and said, "Now, that's a secret."

Mrs. Drummond didn't seem too eager for them to leave. Her gaze darted around the small lobby as if she expected the boogey man to jump out. "Sounds like the Gunn place is going to have a new innkeeper before Halloween."

"Really?" Erin asked.

"Yeah. A lady named Micky Gunn. Guess she's the niece of Carl Gunn who died a couple of months ago," Mrs. Drummond said. Lachlan didn't seem interested, but the woman continued. "Sounds like she's got some idea of making the old place into a high class bed and breakfast." Mrs. Drummond's words thickened with a scarcely concealed scorn. "Can't see any reason for a place like that around here, can you?"

Not wanting to get into a snipping contest with the woman, Erin smiled. "Guess there's room enough in town for everyone."

Mrs. Drummond sniffed and gave them a distinct glare. "Well, there'll be trouble if that woman tries to mess with the old pile. God only knows what's in the place. It's probably infested wall to wall with demons by now."

Wonderful. Erin wanted to get out of here, but either Lachlan didn't seem to feel urgency, or he hid it well.

He gave Mrs. Drummond one of those grins that usually made Erin's knees weaken. "More likely it's infested with rats. See you around, Mrs. Drummond." Lachlan turned his smile on Erin. "Come on, lass, let's get my clothes."

As they trudged upstairs in the small Victorian establishment, Erin whispered, "Was that really necessary?"

"What?" he asked as he unlocked the first door on the right at the top of the stairs.

They went into the room, and she noted right away how tidy it appeared. He closed the door with a click.

"Calling me lass," Erin said. "Mrs. Drummond has loose lips. She'll have the whole town thinking there's something going on between us."

"There *is* something going on between us." His voice caressed her like the softest velvet against her ears. "Why are you denying something you know is true?"

He twitched one eyebrow, and the predatory male flickered to life in his stance and his gaze. He stalked toward her, but Erin backed up a step and bumped into the small desk. Lachlan bristled with a tension in his expression that said everything without a word.

If they didn't have a cab waiting, they'd be making love right now. The force of his need and hers would obliterate everything else in the world. Nothing would matter but here and now and their feelings.

She blushed and almost said something. Nothing came out. Instead, her gaze ate up the sight of him. Fierce man, clad in a form-fitting red Italian-made sweater and ass-hugging jeans, stood before her with a wild, unstoppable desire to keep her safe.

Her heart contracted with fierce love.

Everything inside her wanted him near her. In her heart and in her body.

Lachlan took that last step and his hands came up to cup her face. He took her gaze and held it, and again she saw the dark fire come alive in his eyes. He leaned in and traced her lips with an exquisitely soft kiss that sent fire into her veins, wiping out anxiety, fear, and mistrust with one flame. And the inferno licked higher, consuming her. Aching body aside, she shifted nearer until his arms went around her and drew her tight against every inch of his hard body. As she felt his arousal grow hard against her, she plunged her fingers into his hair, greedy to have everything and anything she could in a moment.

His tongue took her, relearning the heat of her mouth and stimulating deep passions and longings as if he hadn't touched her in a thousand years. When the kiss threatened to lose control, he pulled back gently.

As Erin stared at him and he stared at her, she felt the connection between them broaden and grow. Tonight she would discover the truth, once and for all, so she could bathe her soul in this glorious excitement that couldn't be denied. She wanted his love and desire.

As he moved away from her, he spoke with a voice that had gone hoarse with desire. "We need to get you home."

He gathered his clothing and other items and packed them quickly.

"Lachlan, so much has happened. What are we going to do about this...this thing or whatever it is?"

"Don't worry about it now. You've been through too much tonight."

She paced the room. "How can I take it easy? First I learn that you and I can read each other's minds. Then some man—if he can be called that—attacks me in my workplace. Then, somehow you're there—wait a minute. How did you know I needed help?"

"I'll clarify when we get to your house."

Exasperated with the mystery surrounding Lachlan, she tried to stay patient. An image crept into her head, scary and unrelenting in force. "Then there was that gargoyle. A nasty gargoyle."

He continued packing. "Let it go for a moment, sweetheart. And when we reach your house, I'll tell you all about the gargoyle."

Chapter 21

Hot chocolate seemed right, mixed with a little brandy, to remove the edge on Erin's fears and calm her mind. As she sipped the hot liquid, Lachlan settled on the couch next to her. With him beside her the fears that had lingered subsided.

"Tell me about the gargoyle," she said. "Tell me everything you know about these assaults around town." She took a big breath and forced the next words. "Tell me now, or I'll ask you to leave and not come back."

For a few seconds she saw reluctance marked in his eyes. At the same time, she knew he didn't want her to banish him. "Lass, even if you sent me away, I'd still watch over you. Forever."

Forever. He whispered again in her mind.

His husky promise excited her in a way more primitive and uncontrollable than any emotion she'd experienced before. She resisted a temptation to lean over and kiss him. She wanted his touch so much, and at the same time she knew control was a must.

"Don't try clouding my mind, Lachlan. Just tell me what I want to know. It's important to me."

You thought the attacker was me at first, didn't you?

Shame ran through her. *Yes.*

She chose to speak out loud. "I know now you wouldn't hurt me." Without thinking about it, she touched his arm and felt the muscle move beneath her fingers. "How can I thank you for saving my life?"

With a gentle grin, he put his hand over hers, holding her fingers to his hard forearm. His touch heated her palm with a pleasant tingle. "Repay me with a kiss."

She returned his smile, hard-pressed not to comply with his seductive request. "Later. I need my thoughts clear. Why didn't the man kill me or Gilda like he did Mrs. Pickles and Jessie?"

"I think he only kills women who resist him."

"But I did resist him."

He nodded. "One piece of the puzzle I don't understand, other than the fact he seems to treasure you. As I said before, he wants you for his own, beyond all other women."

"He said something very strange at one point. That he would drain my blood, and I would die and return as the vampire Dasoria."

Lachlan's eyebrows twitched up, his brow furrowing as he tried to understand this new development. "I'm not sure what that means."

A horrifying thought made it through her mind. "What about Gilda? You think she didn't resist him?"

"His persuasive methods sometimes seduce women so they'll do what he wants. But you're a very strong woman, Erin."

She kept her grip on his arm. She allowed her gaze to tangle with his and saw warmth, concern and something hot flare inside his eyes. He cupped her chin as he surveyed her with an intensity that seared her right down into her soul. A heady, strange feeling narrowed her world to his gaze. He tilted her chin up and gave her a quick, sweet peck on the lips.

Heat poured through her stomach when he brushed his lips over hers. In a million years she never would have imagined a swift brushing of lips would cause her heart to jackhammer and her pulse to throb. Then there was the strange, floating sensation that wrapped around her when he looked into her eyes right before he kissed her. The man was so damned delicious and dangerous all at one time.

She thought back to when she'd made hot chocolate. Lachlan had gone into the guest bedroom to dump his luggage, then he'd started checking the window locks around the house.

When she'd stood in the kitchen with its warm dark oak cabinets, glass fronts showing her collection of milky white plates and cups, she realized she felt safe. She never could have imagined a stranger coming into her life that could have made her feel secure in every way.

Correction…not in every way. I feel out of control and crazed with a strange hunger whenever I'm in his proximity. Nothing safe about that.

"Life isn't safe," he said, bringing her back to the present.

A blush burned her face, and she gave him a nervous smile. "Can't a girl get any privacy in her own mind?"

"Can't help it. It comes and goes with you. I can't control when I hear your thoughts. I don't even have to be near you."

She gave him a mock glare. "Okay, buster, what is this expression telling you?"

Lachlan chuckled. "That I'm driving you out of your mind and you want to hit me?"

Enjoying the lightness of their banter, she didn't want to think about the bad things that prowled in the night and the creature wanting to possess her for his own. "Good guess. Now stop stalling and explain what's going on."

Lachlan's long legs sprawled out in typical male fashion. He commanded a big section of the furniture, his body and sheer presence of personality enveloping all around him. She imagined lying in bed with him, relaxing in the residual fever of mating. Despite her need to understand the bizarre events happening in Pine Forest, she wanted his arms cuddling her tight and his hairy, muscular legs entwined around hers. His next words broke her from the fantasy.

"I'm worried, Erin."

Lachlan Tavish? It didn't seem possible. He possessed more confidence than any man she knew. "About what?"

"You may turn away from me if I tell you everything that happened the night my parents were murdered, and the reason my fiancé decided she didn't wish to marry me."

A chill raced along her arms. "Why?"

"It's beyond the norm. Beyond what most people in their right mind would believe. If it hadn't happened to me, I wouldn't believe it either. The gargoyle you saw isn't a gargoyle in a true sense. It is one form this beast can take."

"Beast?"

"Let me start at the beginning." He sighed. "The night my parents were murdered they were alone in the castle. All the servants were gone and because the place was in renovation, we had no guests. The creature you saw, the gargoyle, stalks Pine Forest this minute. That bastard killed those women and harmed Gilda and you. That thing murdered my parents."

"You're saying he followed you from Scotland?" She heard her voice go up and recognized anger edging into her tone.

"No. I followed him from Scotland to the United States. He's an illusive force. He isn't entirely of this world." Lachlan reached for her left hand and tucked it within both of his. "He's a night visitor and needs blood to survive."

His words didn't make sense at first, too astonishing to believe. "What are you saying?"

"He's a vampire, Erin. A vampire."

"That's even more insane than El Chupacabra."

Lachlan's expression turned grim and determined. "I know that it seems impossible, but there are vampires among living humans. Pine Forest is host to but one of these beings."

Stunned into silence, she felt his warm hands engulfing hers. *How can it be? This is insane.*

Believe me, sweet Erin. As I said, I would never lie to you.

I'm sorry. It's just that this doesn't seem real. I know telepathy is real now that I have experienced it first hand. Yet the rest of this is too incredible.

She snapped into the realization they conversed in their minds once again. "I've been fighting with the idea of ghosts and now this? I know there are people who are wannabe vampires. In fact, when we first met, I thought maybe that was the case with you."

"I knew this would be difficult for you to believe." He smiled weakly, as if trying to hide his disappointment. "I have two things to apologize for. I could have told you about the vampire when we were at *Ricardo's*, or even better, when I first met you."

She sniffed. "Like I would have believed you then."

He managed a smile at her light tone. Then his face went back to serious. "When I came to Pine Forest, I was on the trail of an elusive killer. I've traveled the world trying to find this bloodsucker."

Her eyes widened. "Are you a cop?"

He smiled. "I wish I was at this point. It would have given me some contacts and authority. No, I'm simply a businessman." He put his mug down on the big dark chest that served as a coffee table. "I also must apologize for not realizing his plan. My guess is that he either wants to spirit you away, or he wishes to make you his and stay right here in Pine Forest where he can feed off the psychic and spiritual energies. You are the one he needs." He leaned forward and balanced his forearms on his legs. The pose said casual and alert all at one time. "The other women were to amuse him and for sustenance. He believes you are an ideal mate."

Simultaneous emotions battled inside her for supremacy. Horror, skepticism, amazement. She recalled the words of her attacker. *I am yours to command, Erin. You are the birth, the death, and the life.*

"That's what he said?" Lachlan asked, moving closer to her.

"Yes. He seemed capable of controlling my breathing. I was so weak around him and couldn't move even before he clasped me tight. Why would he want me?"

Lachlan remained silent long enough that Erin almost screamed in frustration. Before she demanded answers he continued. "Because he sees you as capable of sustaining a life with him in eternity as a vampire. He wants to make you a vampire, lass. He wants to feed not only on your blood, but on the extra energy inside you."

Disbelief continued to reign supreme inside her. "How do you know he thinks this way about me?"

His drink forgotten, his attention riveted on her. "I sometimes hear his thoughts, just as I do yours. Not enough to tell me where he is or how I might stop him, only enough to know his evil intent." His hands soothed over hers, staving off the chill that seemed to have taken up permanent residence in her bones. "He doesn't just *think* he's a vampire. He *is* a vampire."

"So this vampire is mixed right in with the so-called ghosts here."

"Right again. This place has the biggest infestation of ghosts per square mile that I've encountered in my travels. One side effect of being in contact with this vampire is that I can now see ghosts, just as I can sometimes hear his thoughts."

Feeling dazed by this crazy information, she groaned. "Great, now you're telling me you can see ghosts, too?"

"I'd never seen a ghost in my entire life until after I came in contact with the vampire." Exasperation crossed his face. "What reasons do you have for finding this so hard to believe now?"

She pulled her hands from his because the feeling of his palm sliding over hers was starting to distract her. "I only need one reason, Lachlan. Sure, I think there are probably some weird vibes here. But I think that most of it is hallucination and fabrication. What else does this little place have? Tourist trade and those passing through to other more exotic places on the trail. It's an old mining town just like a lot of places in Colorado. Urban legends grow up around these areas. That doesn't make them true, no matter how many times you tell them."

He shrugged. "Many falsehoods are mixed with the truth. When the reality does come out, people don't always recognize it."

"Okay, I'll admit again this mind reading is the most incredible thing I've experienced."

"It happens when people have been attacked by this vampire and survive. They retain many of his powers without becoming a creature of the night. Seeing ghosts and reading minds are two of the things I can do."

She smiled, uneasy with his explanation. "You're starting to sound like that doctor in Bram Stoker's Dracula. Very creepy, Lachlan."

His brows pinched together a little, and the corners of his sensuous mouth turned down. "I wish this were a novel, lass. But it is serious business." He considered her like a man buying a fine car, his gaze perceptive and concluding. "This is coming at you a little fast, isn't it?"

"You could say that." She shifted and his hard thigh brushed against hers. "Okay, let's back up a bit. What else are you saying?"

"I've been trying to find a way to stop him."

She stood and wandered to the fireplace, then touched the small pumpkins she'd arranged on the fireplace mantle to give the house Halloween spirit. Since she moved in a short time ago, she hadn't decorated with the flair she would have liked. Right now, in the scheme of things, it seemed unimportant.

Shivering, she rubbed her arms.

"I'll start a fire," he said.

"Reading my mind again?"

He smiled. "No. Clear observation. You're either scared or you're cold."

She sat on the couch and watched him prepare the fire.

Erin never saw a man so capable of blending human grace with animal prowess. He stirred the wood and turned the tiny flame into wondrous heat. As Lachlan looked back at her, electricity sizzled and danced with each glance. She felt it in her skin and in her soul. Fire blazed in the hearth, and a new conflagration started in her body. She drew in a breath and tried to maintain her composure.

"Whatever it is about this place, he knows he can draw energy from it as other entities have. He is feeding on strong electromagnetic and spiritual energies in Pine Forest and on the blood of innocent people," he said as he returned to the couch.

She shook her head, not believe she was saying this. "I heard that some hauntings may be caused by high electromagnetic energy field."

He swept a warm, determined gaze over her. "Many entities and spirits use that energy to come forth and show they are here. Some are pure haunting, the impressions of past events embossed on the place where an event happened or where an entity lived out their life."

Erin startled, a long-forgotten thought came to her. "I used to make all kinds of equipment fail. I'd forgotten about that. Microwaves, you name it. My brother's lap top would go wiggy every time I got near it." She smiled. "Pretty soon he wouldn't let me in the same room with it."

"Since you're the skeptical sort, what did you think was happening?"

"Coincidence."

Lachlan looked at his watch and made a face. "Damn it, this thing isn't working."

She grabbed his wrist and peered at the timepiece. The second hand continued to go around.

She smacked his arm playfully. "Jerk."

He chuckled.

She sighed. "But none of those types of things have happened to me since I moved here."

"Perhaps because you're in a place that already has so much energy, you belong here." While she absorbed the idea he continued. "Artistic people often have this power whether they know it or not and they are drawn to people and places that are similar in power. When you experienced those headaches, I felt them. Your pain is my pain."

She saw the conviction in his eyes and heard it in the strong bass of his voice. Lachlan Tavish meant each word down to the bottom of his Scot's soul.

"When you get the headache, it's a sign of psyche drain," he said. "Your body is feeling the evil around you and you're fighting it. I'll have to teach you how to block the pain so that it doesn't overwhelm you."

"I'd like to get rid of it forever."

"I doubt you can do that. Besides, it could be a good tool. It would let you know danger or spirit is near."

Amazed, she shook her head. "How do you know all this stuff?"

He smiled. "I learned from an old man named Dominic. He taught me everything I wanted to know about this *stuff* as you call it. He also explained that the pain I felt could be my own, caused by the presence of the supernatural. Or the ache could be caused by a connection with another human." Lachlan's gaze held hers. "A person I had deep feelings for."

He didn't reach for her, but if he had, Erin knew she couldn't have resisted him. Instead she let more inhibitions fly out the window. "All this is so outside my understanding. I still have a difficult time believing it. But after what I experienced tonight, I'm not sure." She pushed her hands through her hair, staying there for a minute, as if she might have to hold her head on her shoulders. "You and Danny almost fought over me in the hospital."

"Okay, I'll admit it," he said with a light, unconcerned tone. "I get jealous every time I see how territorial he is with you."

"Jealous?" His admission sent gratification rippling inside her.

"Not a very admirable emotion, I'll admit. I'll get back to this attraction between us in a moment," he said with a matter-of-factness that surprised her. "What is important right now is that you understand who and what this fiend is. He can dissolve and reappear by turning into different animals. He can transform into a bat, a hare, a bird and a wolf. The gargoyle form is his most hideous shape, but not the only one."

Humor edged into her voice. "So now every time I see a bunny rabbit I should run in terror?"

A husky, deep rumbling laugh came from his chest. "Not exactly."

"Are the other legends about vampires true?"

"Much of the folklore is real. They must be invited into your house in order to enter."

"Then someone must have invited him into the library?"

"At some time, yes. A stake through the heart is the most effective way to release their tortured spirit. Romanians have a good name for these creatures. *Strogoi.*"

"*Strogoi,*" she whispered. "Even the word sounds evil."

"These undead inhabit every country on earth and there are thousands of them. No one knows their exact numbers, but they account for many of the missing persons you hear about."

Pondering, she reached for her hot chocolate and tasted it. It had gone cold, but she drank it anyway. "You mean missing children cases?"

"Some children have been taken and killed, or made into young vampires bound to the one who sired them."

"Sired?"

"Made them *strogoi.*"

She put down her mug again, her fingers and the rest of her body going cold. "And other people who go missing?"

"Some of them as well. There are other monsters in the night, Erin. Most of them are human."

"Of course."

"I consulted experts on vampirism when I was still in Scotland. They explained this vampire has traveled the world attacking innocents, but he never stays long enough in one place for hunters to track him and destroy him."

"So you've become a vampire hunter?"

"Yes. But there are others. There are good vampires who work side by side with humans to protect others from the evil ones."

Erin rested her head on the back of the couch and closed her eyes. "This gets stranger every minute."

"It is that. A friend of mine is tracking this fiend. He's also a vampire."

Erin opened her eyes and stared at him in alarm. "What?"

"Like I said, there are good vampires as well as bad. My friend is a master at catching up with the evil spirits of the night. He's so good at it, he's called The Hunter. His real name is Ronan Kieran."

"Does the evil vampire have a name?"

"No one knows either his name or where he was originally born. Perhaps when I encounter him for the final time, I'll discover the truth."

The final time.

Fear danced over her as she thought of him in a battle again with the unnamed vampire. "I don't like the idea of you fighting him. Can't you ask this Kieran for help?"

He picked up her hand and kissed it. "Ronan is in Morocco consulting with some tribal elders who've had experience tracking this type of vampire. I've already spoken with him, and he's on his way."

"This type of vampire?" she asked warily. "There are types?"

He chuckled. "Sorry, lass. There's something else you don't know. The vampires come in different levels depending on how old they are. The one we face now is one of the strongest."

"Of course." She sighed as she sat up straight. "How old is this evil vampire?"

"A thousand years."

"Oh, God."

"Ronan is at a disadvantage. He was born in Ireland in 1300."

She saw the humor in the conversation, even though a terrible sense of inevitable battle simmered inside her. "Only in 1300. And that's a disadvantage?"

"His strength is not as great as this vampire. He's trained for some time, as well, to learn how to fight with weapons and poisons and other methods. He's lived in so many places around the world, but he immigrated to the United States during the American Revolution. It was around that time Ronan began hunting the other vampire."

"Why?"

"I don't know. He's closed-mouth about it."

After a quiet pause where she thought about how insane this would have sounded a week ago, she asked, "So you could see this creature when he was attacking me?"

"I saw only shadows and not his true face. Shadows where you couldn't see him at all." She shivered, and without notice he drew her close. She sank into the comfort his powerful arms gave her. "They are beings of the night. Sunlight will not kill them, but it can drain their power completely after a time. This vampire hides in the shadows and can become invisible at will."

"I heard a man's laugh, very evil and predatory in the library."

"Most likely it was him you heard."

Another thought occurred to her. "Have some of them tried to turn themselves back into human by staying in the light?"

His fingers rubbed her upper arm, and the tender caressing almost distracted her entirely. "Some have tried, but most fail. It may or may not work. They may still crave blood. Also, if they are out they must cover themselves in dark clothing from head to toe so there is little sun exposure, and this makes their presence obvious. Because of that, they rarely go out during the day."

Curiosity made her press onward. "What else can you tell me?"

"They can be wounded but not killed with a silver bullet. Ronan is bringing special ammunition with him."

She giggled at the insanity of what she'd heard in the last few minutes. "I'm sorry, I'm sorry. But I thought that was for werewolves."

Lachlan smiled. "No, actually, there are no such things as werewolves."

She sighed in relief. "Good. I was hoping at least some fairy tales weren't true. I still have to wrap my mind around this vampire concept and it isn't easy."

"You must try. It's the only way you'll survive. This is not a game, lass. My family ignored his legend and it cost them their lives."

"Do you have a gun with a silver bullet?"

"I do. I would have tried to shoot him with it tonight, but you were too near. I couldn't risk it."

She'd never liked guns, never wanted to touch one. But what if she needed to use one to kill them monster that stalked this town?

I'll get it. His voice rippled, low and soft in her mind. "I'll show you how to use it. But there is one thing you must know. This vampire is so powerful that we aren't sure if the silver bullet will even slow him down. It may only sicken him. Most can't get near enough to harm him in any way."

A new fear invaded her heart. "So you're saying he's invincible."

Lachlan lifted her hand and kissed the back of it again. "Not invincible. We just haven't found the right way to destroy him yet."

A curious thought came to her mind. "What made him so evil?"

"No one knows. Legend says the older a vampire gets, the more jaded his soul becomes. Not everyone believes this, but it's a theory." He squeezed her hand gently, then stood. "Wait here."

She waited on the couch while he went back to the bedroom. When he came back, he held a sleek, modern weapon that gleamed in the low light like pewter. As he showed it to her, she wondered when and where he'd obtained it.

I had it made. Before I came to Pine Forest. I got it from Amadeus Creed.

Another vampire hunter?

A man retiring from vampire hunting. He wanted me to have it. He's hoping, as I do, that I can kill the ancient one with this weapon.

He showed her the clip, and she wanted to laugh again. This seemed too beyond, to odd to be true, yet she knew once and for all she couldn't deny the reality in front of her. When he placed the heavy weapon in her hand and showed her how to fire it, her hands and arms began to tremble.

His fathomless, compelling eyes reassured her. "You'll only need to fire it if something goes wrong when you're with me. I told you I could protect you, and the vampire knows that. With Ronan coming here, though, the vampire will be angry and will attack again. That's why you've got to stay with me from now on until we kill this bastard."

"If he is so all-powerful, then why can't he just thrust you aside and...and assault me?"

"Because I've been watching you all the time."

"But you're human with a few vampire traits. How can that make any difference to him?"

"Because of your bond with me and your feelings for me. This vampire craves all the horrible emotions in the world, lass. He thrives on war, destruction, murder, and all forms of evil. It's his life-blood. Women are most vulnerable when they have no hope left. No love within them."

Erin was shocked at the thought of Lachlan killing someone.

Lachlan's gaze turned from the gun to her. *Not killing someone. Killing a thing, lass. I've got no choice. The carnage won't end until someone eliminates him.*

Again she shuddered. He put the gun down on the coffee table and slipped his arms back around her.

"If he's been slaughtering people for hundreds of years, what makes you think you can stop him now?" she asked.

With the confidence of a man who'd determined his course in life long ago, he said, "With Ronan's help, I think we can combine our strength to put him at a disadvantage. It may not be enough, but it has to be tried. We can't let this go on."

"Isn't there some other way? So that you won't have to go near him?"

"No, lass. There's no other way."

She didn't like the answer, but she would live with it for now.

"So you heard of him before your parents were killed?" she asked.

"There are many legends about him that have been around for centuries. I lived outside Edinburgh, and the village I lived in has long spoken of his dark influence. I heard the tales growing up, but my parents didn't believe the stories and told me not too, either. It was their downfall. I couldn't bear it if you were hurt again."

She wrapped her arms around his neck and hugged him close. When she pulled back and looked at him, the hunger and tenderness she saw in his eyes thrilled her.

"You canna know what it felt like to realize I couldn't save my mum and dad from that bastard," he whispered into her hair, his accent turning thicker. "So you see, lass, I've felt the madman's grip. I know how you felt when you tried to get away. I'm a strong man, but there was little I could do against him. He bit me on the neck."

She pulled back from his embrace a little and glanced at his neck. "The scar."

"Yes, lass. When I woke up, the emergency technicians were loading me into the ambulance. I lapsed into a coma for two days, and when I awoke again, I could do and see and hear things I never could before. I thought I'd turned into a vampire, but as the days passed, I didn't crave blood, nor did I have other symptoms."

"How did you escape becoming a vampire?"

"I think because the emergency personnel came to the fire quickly and the vampire couldn't afford to linger."

"Thank God."

She felt his bicep and the incredible muscle structure. "Are you stronger than normal? And that reflex thing you did with the glass. I wasn't imagining that time slowed down, was I?"

"I worked out before the vampire attack, but some of the vampire strength transferred to me. I also possess extraordinarily reflexes. The glow you saw in my eyes the other night is an indicator of sensitivity to danger or desire. I felt the vampire's presence, just as you did outside *Ricardo's*." His palms caressed her back. "Even after the vampire is found and destroyed, it'll be a good long time before I forget the bastard." He kissed her forehead. "But I'll know you're safe."

Erin's heart triple-timed and they stayed in their close embrace for what seemed forever before she managed to speak. "You said the glow in your eyes is also from desire?"

"It can be, yes," he said.

She snuggled deeper into his arms, her love mingling with wild longing. "This thing between us is unusual, whatever it is."

"This thing?" One corner of his mouth turned up in a half smile. "You mean the fact that since the night I met you, I can barely stand to be away from you?"

She dared to gaze into his eyes and saw nothing but the truth. His words warmed her deep down, excited her in every membrane and brain cell. He leaned closer and demanded she notice him with his sheer size and nearness. Desire gathered in his eyes and built force. He reached up to cup her face, his thumb tender as he touched her cheek. Feelings stood on the surface, tingling like a burn, waiting to ignite.

"I've never felt like this with a woman before," he said.

Feathery sensations moved all along her body, and she knew he generated that sweet, wild feeling in her belly. He flattened his hand against her stomach and as his fingers caressed her, she felt her body moisten as it prepared for mating.

"Feel that, lass?" His voice went deeper, clearly changed by desire. "That's real. It's you and me, and every second longer that I go without kissing you, I think I'm going to die."

She parted her lips to tell him to kiss her, to beg him to taste her, but he must have read her mind again and he beat her to it.

Chapter 22

Lachlan's mouth captured Erin's and everything within her filled with pleasure. A heavy throb started between her legs, and reminded her of sexual needs she couldn't deny.

The slow, seductive persuasion of his mouth lulled her into a languorous response. Opening to him, she shivered with a fine thread of desire as he pressed tender kisses to her mouth. Each brush of heated skin drew her arousal higher, her burning desire into a raging thing that would be appeased.

"Lachlan."

He swept his tongue over her lips, begging for entrance. When Erin gave it, he sank into her mouth with a deep plunge that said he possessed her here and now. Each rhythmic, famished taste sent tremors of unprecedented longing into her body. She couldn't hold back soft moans, and she moved in his arms with eager anticipation. She reached for every inch of him she could touch. Her palms brushed across his back, testing the groups of muscles. Strength radiated from him — in the curve of his shoulders, in the power of his rock-hard biceps and forearms. He could have broken her in half, but he used that authority to cradle and protect. A woman could drown in Lachlan's care, in the very lifeblood of his concern. She could sink to the bottom of this ocean and never want for another thing so long as she lived.

With a groan, he pulled away and yanked his sweater over his head. As he tossed it aside carelessly, he paused as if he knew she would feast upon the sight. Erin savored this man, no longer caring that a vampire gave him powers in exchange for blood and life. He was here now, and she would love him.

He looked like a god awaiting her consent. *Her approval.*

Admiration burst to the fore as Erin devoured the glorious sight of incredible muscles in his shoulders, arms, chest, and the rippling sinew of his stomach. It didn't matter that she'd seen Lachlan naked before. Right now it seemed new, different, and inconceivable. Never in all her years could she have imagined this man before her. A banquet of fantasy and imagination she would enjoy for as long as she could.

His eyes blazed, male animal and primitive. His chest expanded as he drew a deep breath into his large body.

Oh, yes.

His whispered thought drifted into her mind, and she captured it and held it to her heart. He wanted this.

A long shudder ran through his body, and for a moment he closed those magnetic eyes. He leaned back his head, and inhaled again. Fists clenching, he resembled a sacrifice awaiting torture. Her special brand of intimate torment.

As he opened his eyes, that glittering glow illuminated them, this time hotter, wilder than before. "Touch me, lass. I want to feel your hands all over me."

His request, filled with desperation, turned her on. She complied, wanting more than life itself to give him as much pleasure as she could. Lack of control snared her in a fiery, free exploration. The craving for more pumped through her veins — more touching, more fire.

The force to create.

As Lachlan devoured her with kisses, her hands explored the contours of his brawny, hair-covered chest. Heat poured from him, generated by the pure screaming longing to make love.

Yes, lass. Nothing else will do.

He lay back on the couch, drawing her on top of him and cupping her ass in each hand. He squeezed gently, and Erin couldn't deny the way her body tightened and released with a forceful need to have him deep inside her as he pounded out his lust. He arched upward, nestling her against the hard evidence of his cock. She gasped into his mouth, and he tilted his hips upward again, instigating a primal rhythm that simulated sexual joining.

God, I want him!

Lachlan heard her thought and the pleasure rushed through him. He'd worried about her, desperate to keep her from harm. Now that he had her in his arms, he never wanted to let her go. He sent a thought back to her. *I want you, too.*

Lachlan saw the flush spread over Erin's face. This overwhelming attraction and affection he felt transformed into a starvation for her that was far more powerful. Once he'd endured Erin's mistrust, but now she realized he wasn't the ancient one. She was safe in his arms. He wanted her lips parted in ecstasy as he showed how he needed her and how she burned him with desire. Now, the truth came out, and she realized he was her protector, he could worship Erin until she cried out for orgasm.

Ronan would be here soon, and together they would fight the ancient one and keep Erin safe. That solidifying thought pushed all worries out of Lachlan's mind so he could love Erin the way she deserved to be loved.

Whatever force brought them together, he would keep her near and show her how much she meant to him every time he sank deep into her wet heat. His cock tightened and hardened more, and he died a little each minute he didn't thrust inside her sweet, hot body. He thought he'd once loved his fiancé, but now he realized what he felt for Erin far surpassed the desire he'd experienced for Sharon.

Lachlan drew Erin against him, his hands moving over her in a restless search—her arms, her back, her neck, her face, sliding down to her hips. Again he tilted his hips against her, a ravaging drive for her nakedness against him.

"I need you," he managed to choke out.

Erin loved that he felt so intensely for her. But she had to know one thing. "Are you...is this a part of your powers? Can you make a woman want you against her will?"

He drew back and the sexual haze in his eyes transformed into a frown. "God, lass, is that what you think? That I'd force you to have sex with me?"

Shame made her flush. "No. No, of course not. It's just that, when we first met, the sexual pull for me was staggering. When we were between the bookshelves and you made me so crazy with desire..."

"Yes?"

"That wasn't normal. I don't do things like that."

A feral grin curved his mouth, sensuous and damn right sexy. "That's something else I have to apologize for. I can influence a woman to allow me near her. And I was desperate to touch you and kiss you. I can't automatically control it. The vampire uses his power to attract victims. My power is not nearly that strong. "

Doubt made her wary. She pushed out of his arms and started to climb off of him. "Lachlan Tavish—"

"Wait, wait." He grasped her arms, his fingers gentle, and as he sat up he said, "Hear me out, please." He leaned near and whispered into her ear. "Please listen."

His tender words, whispered velvet in her ear, made Erin's entire body shudder in delighted response. She subsided and took a deep breath.

Lachlan's eyes went tender, and Erin couldn't think straight when he did that. "That's how the vampire held you captive beyond his physical strength. I do not have the power he does to hold you against your will." His deep voice lowered even more, made husky by a gentleness that melted her bones. "You could look away from me and leave at any time." He nibbled on her jaw. "I want what is between us to be real and because we want to be near each other." His hands caressed her shoulders. "What we feel when we're together is something special, Erin. Not vile and controlling. That first night in the library, maybe my power drew you to me quickly. But once I had you in my arms, what we felt was real."

His gaze pleaded with her, and she believed him. "I was attracted to you from the moment I saw you, goofy teeth and all."

Lachlan grinned and kissed her again, softly and quickly. "Do you realize how many times I was dying to kiss you when I couldn't? It was all I could do to keep my hands off you when others were around. That night in the library, when I first met you, I would have taken you against the bookshelves if no one had been in the building." He winked. "Maybe we could try that one night."

Just the idea of him taking her in a public place, a chance they might be caught, sent a wild fission through her. "I'd like that." She put her arms around his neck again. She knew that this time there would be no going back. "Here we are, though I can hardly believe it. It's been so quick, Lachlan—"

Another mind-numbing kiss held her captive for a minute before he released her. He waited, and Erin could tell he wanted her to make the next move, to show she believed him.

So she gave Lachlan the answer. She pulled him off the couch and toward her bedroom. He stopped along the way to pull her top over her head. Before she could think about how quickly this was all happening, he backed her up against the wall.

He leaned close and said with a husky tone, "I adore you." His arms slid around her waist and drew her tight against a body gone rock-hard. "I want to feel those hot walls around me again and feel them tighten around my cock as you come."

Lachlan's raw words, rough with arousal, made her body moisten. She was already sopping wet, and shaking with desire.

She took a deep breath and ventured to ask him one question she must know. "Your fiancée. You said she left you?"

He nodded. "When I tried to explain about the vampire and my new abilities as a result of the bite on the neck, she thought I was insane." He swallowed hard. His hand slipped through her hair, caressing the back of her neck. "And when she saw the glow in my eyes, it frightened her so much she left England for Australia. I never heard from her again."

"She was crazy for leaving you." The words left her mouth before she could stop them, and now they were out, she felt better for it. "Do you still love her?"

"No." He leaned in and kissed her forehead. "No, lass. I stopped loving her as soon as I realized she didn't trust me enough to believe me."

There it was. The truth of her predicament. If she loved him, Erin knew she must accept his assertions. He told her the truth, and she felt it with soul-stirring conviction. She loved him with a wild passion that went so deep she couldn't pretend her emotions were fleeting or that this love wasn't a real, intense worship that would last a lifetime and beyond.

His hands went to her slacks and made quick work of the button and zipper. As the tweed fabric brushed against her skin and slipped down, the whispery sensation tickled her skin and her belly tightened with excitement.

"I need you. I want you." He whispered in her ear again, his hot breath teasing. "Do you trust me?"

Erin inhaled deeply, taking in his tantalizing scent. She ran her hands up his arms, testing the unbelievable hardness of his muscles. "With all my heart."

He groaned, the sound desperate and full of desire. "Thank you, God."

Seconds later his hands slipped into the back of her panties, and he tugged them down her legs so she could step out of them. As he cupped her ass, squeezing and stroking, he dove in for another kiss. His tongue took ownership, thrilling her as the driving movements reminded of her of his thick, hot cock moving back and forth inside her.

Oh yes, oh yes, oh yes!

You want more, lass?

Yes. Yes.

Erin responded with all the love inside her, tangling with him in a tongue-thrusting kiss.

His breathing came fast and frantic, as if he ran a race to the finish with her as the prize as the end. Tears of sheer happiness welled in her eyes as well as a driving need to scream out to him that she loved him. Still, it stuck in her throat, waiting for the nudge that would push her over the rim.

As Lachlan broke their kiss, she ran her hands through the thickness of his hair, cherishing the texture and relishing his arousing male scent.

Without more preliminaries, he dropped to his knees. "Part your legs."

She obeyed. He was going to lick her, and the idea sent a rush of arousal running down her leg. *Please lick me.*

He responded with a husky moan. As he nudged her legs further apart, she felt the heated brush of his breath against her swollen clit and labia.

"Oh, shit." His breathy curse startled her, then he added, "This is so beautiful. All plump and slick."

His words, laced with predatory hunger, filled her with pleasure.

He swept his thumb over her sensitive skin and she gasped. "Oh."

Warm and deep, his laugh vibrated in side her.

She loved him so much.

As he dipped his head, she felt the first hot lash of his tongue over her wetness. She gasped again. When he nestled closer between her legs and set to serious work, Erin thought her eyes would cross and her breath leave her body forever.

"Mmmmm." He murmured against her as his tongue dipped into her body and he held her there, pushing and thrusting his tongue in and out of her tightness. "Mmmmm."

In and out. In and out. In and out.

Then he did the most mind-boggling thing of all. He began to tease her anus with gentle touches of his middle finger, his tongue still at work flicking over her labia and clit. He tormented her for a long time. His tongue fucked her with ruthless touches that made her jiggle against his mouth in anguish. Sighs, moans and soft grunts parted her lips. Beyond caring, she let her feelings take the fore.

Her head rolled from side to side, her body supported by the wall and his hands as he feasted between her legs. Although feasting didn't quite describe it.

No, his tongue was a conquering invader.

When he parted the soft, hot folds over her clit, she knew what he meant to do next and her breath caught. He flicked his tongue over her clit, a fast movement that made her sob out in sweet ecstasy. Again her hips jerked in his grip, and unable to keep still, she reached down and grasped his head in her hands. Erin thought she would die as the continual movement of his tongue caressed her ultra sensitive labia and clit. Then, slow and with exquisite gentleness, he eased his finger into her anus.

She couldn't think. She could scarcely breathe.

Heat slammed into her clit, and Erin writhed against his mouth. His hot breath puffed against her wetness as he licked her insistently and moved his finger in her ass.

As his lips latched onto her clit and he sucked, Erin let out a startled oath of incredible bliss. "Oh, shit. Shit!"

Without remorse he suckled that tiny piece of flesh until she could no longer stand it. He inched his finger up her anus a little bit farther, moving with a back and forth gentle thrust.

"Lachlan." Her breath shuddered out of her lungs. "Please do something. Please."

He released her clit for a second.

She shivered.

He licked.

Heat sliced through her cunt, building, building, building.

He licked again and moved his finger.

Erin keened, ending on a screech as orgasm roared through her unmercifully. Fire erupted through her lower limbs and up her body as she wept in ecstasy. Her muscles clenched as he held her.

He sucked her still tingling clit deep into his mouth.

She couldn't help it; she let her cries rip as the second teeth-grinding climax burst.

As her body shuddered and quaked, he sucked and sucked and sucked until a third orgasm flamed high up inside her cunt, and Erin thought she would come unsealed forever. By the time she came down from the plateau, her breath sluiced through her lungs. As she panted, dazed from passion, he released her and picked her up in his arms. No more time for play.

This was serious.

When he set her down by the bed, Erin hadn't regained her breath. Lachlan helped her slip off the bra. He chucked it across the room. Naked, she lay back on the bed and watched as he wrenched off his shoes, then removed his pants and briefs. As his rippling muscles glided over her softness, even in the shadowed room, she saw the heat in his eyes that proved his passion and emotions ran high.

As his sinew-thick thighs lowered between her legs and his cock touched her, his voice came harsh with passion. "Now."

With one smooth thrust, he wedged through her aching folds, burrowing deep.

Filled to bursting, she moaned and started to thrash against him. Her hands clenched his back and clasped desperately at his wide shoulders. She found Lachlan's tight butt and dug into his cheeks. Wrapping her legs around his hips, she pushed up in counter to his movements.

He growled and slipped his arms around her so they were plastered together without an inch of skin to part them. His hips plunged and thrust until his motion caught her up and lifted her into the heavens.

"Oh, Lachlan." She cried out at the exquisite sensation of having his spike-hard cock drilling inside her.

"Fuck," he growled and yanked out of her.

"What?"

"No condom." His chest heaved with fast breaths. "We've got to have one."

"Some in the bathroom, top drawer on the right," she managed to say as he headed that direction.

She heard the drawer slide open and the ripping of a condom package. Seconds later he settled between her legs and took her with a stabbing thrust that made her cry out and arch up against his body.

He kissed her as he stirred his hips, grinding into motion. As thick, hot cock rasped against her sensitive walls, she whimpered with excitement. As the seconds lengthened, he kept the gentle thrusts long and deep, back and forth. Each languid movement of his body sent a myriad of sensations through her hungry body. A body desperate for a skull-splitting orgasm.

Again and again he sank into her until she didn't know where Lachlan started and she ended. Ebb and flow moved between them, and it felt to Erin as gentle as a breeze and as never-ending as a wave against the shore.

As the tender, exquisitely slow movement of his body inside her escalated, she could no longer keep her frantic longing from showing.

Erin told Lachlan exactly what she must have. "Harder. Harder!"

"Yes," he growled and hammered deep.

She countered his actions by thrusting her hips upward. His hips moved frantically, his cock plunging so hard and fast inside her she abandoned trying to resist the climax.

Her orgasm erupted, sending hot, gushing sensation to her cunt. She screamed as he kept the fire burning with each demanding shove. His completion came seconds later, and she reveled in the ecstasy as she felt his cock swell inside her, and heard his guttural shout of satisfaction. Lachlan's entire body quaked, his arms tightening almost painfully about her as he reached the last plateau.

Chapter 23

"This is right," Lachlan said as they nestled in each other's arms.

She laced her arms around his neck and rolled until she lay on top of him. She moved against his hair-roughened skin and delighted in his physique. He felt like a god of love, mesmerizing her with his animal beauty, and the command of his need.

And he was right. Nothing felt more right in this moment than holding him and snuggling near his chest. She listened to the strong, steady beat and savored their time together.

Amazingly, she felt arousal emerging again. She grinned down at Lachlan. "I'll be right back."

She left the bed and came back with the entire box of condoms. She saw that he'd removed the other condom.

"Good idea, sweet lass. Just being inside you unprotected for that short time—damn it, I could have made you pregnant." He put his hand to his forehead, worry laced over those strong, handsome features. "I'm sorry, lass. I wasn't thinking."

"I know. Neither was I."

"Forgive me."

"There's nothing to forgive."

He grabbed her hand and held it in a tight grip. His eye held a seriousness that burned to her soul. She supposed she should have felt fear, but the idea of having his baby stirred nothing but a melting sensation inside her. She wanted him even more.

"We'll be all right." She slipped her hand from his hold. "I want to pretend nothing exists in this world but you and me in this bed."

"Whatever you want." She walked away. "Where are you going?"

"Finding toys." She rummaged in her dresser drawers across the room and came back with two items. "I hope you like this."

"What is it?" His voice was hoarse with desire.

"Wait and see."

Without hesitation she straddled his body. His hands came up and clamped onto her hips, the hot caress of his callused palms touching her skin a welcome torture. Before his wandering hands could distract her, she grabbed one of his big wrists and looped the long, thin silk scarf around it. She anchored his left wrist to one wooden bedpost, and then his other wrist to the other bedpost. After tugging on the scarves enough to make sure they secured him without being too tight, she crawled off him long enough to flick on the small light on the nightstand.

She'd never liked making love with the light on before. But with this handsome male animal, naked and with a new erection as bold as day, she loved that she could see details.

"Oh, lass, I think I see now." His soft, rumbling laugh made her grin.

"Do you?" she asked, imitating a thick Scots accent. "You've been very bad and deserve punishment."

"What did I do?"

"You made me desire you more than any man I've ever known."

His smile widened. "Good. Punish me then."

"Hmmm," she purred.

Her libido took note of Lachlan's potent body laid out before her like a prisoner awaiting torture. He defined the word striking. Broad shoulders, powerful arms, hairy chest roped with muscle, a trim waist and narrow hips. Those long, strong legs shaped to perfection. And oh, what lay between those thighs.

She couldn't help but look at the undeniable evidence of his desire. Hard and ready, he epitomized the meaning of all male. She adored the way his cock stood up just for her, and that she owned the power to make him want her this much.

The fact that he was so virile, so *up* to the challenge, made her want to slide a condom on him now and fuck him into the next century.

Instead, she waited and allowed him to take in her naked body. She decided there and then he would get the show of his life. As she smiled, Erin knew he would be begging her to screw him before this was over.

He's the most gorgeous thing I've ever seen.

Thank you, lass.

She blushed and wondered if she'd become accustomed to his ability to read thoughts. "Stop it, will you? I want to devour you without every thought being on display."

He shook his head. "Remember, I can't help it. Besides, the way you're gazing at me now, no man would be able to resist."

His chest heaved with deep breaths as he watched her through lashes half-mast with desire and hunger raging in those mysterious eyes. Having him under her control felt empowering and arousing and she loved the way it turned her on. Under his weight she'd felt protected and cherished, and as his hands and mouth had started an aggressive exploration, she knew he cared for her deeply.

This time she would show him exquisite pleasure, and he would love each minute. She leaned over him and dangled her breasts in front of him.

He licked his lips. "Sweet mother of Nessie."

She laughed. "Like what you see?"

His eyes flashed with a combination of frustration and building arousal. "Damn it, lass. You know I do."

She laughed again, keeping the sound sultry and as enticing as possible.

He breathed against her breast, not touching, just waiting. "Erin, you can push a man too far."

Feeling powerful, she lowered her body and rubbed her breasts against his chest. Shivers ran through her. "Then what happens?"

"He might fuck you until you can't stand."

Desire licked over her body. "Oh, please do."

With an earthly growl, he lurched upwards and enveloped her nipple with his mouth. A startled gasp left her throat. He circled that nipple with his tongue until she whimpered. Darts of pleasure shot through her breasts as she allowed him to lick and suck. She knew no other man would do for her, no matter how much time passed, or how old she grew. Whether he recognized it or not, magic held her captive, giving and receiving and showing that love could take her higher. Lachlan's touch continued, his tongue licking in a way that sent hot arousal flickering through her skin like fire. His tongue danced against the sensitive point of one nipple. Heat gathered and spiraled out of control as he took her on adventures her body never knew before. She pulled back from him.

When she turned around and positioned her cunt right over his face, he breathed deeply. "Oh, sweetheart. Bring that closer. I want to taste it."

His words, deep and compelling, sent new shivers of fine delight through her senses. She complied, reaching down to wrap her hand around the base of his cock and enclose the rest of his long length in her mouth. His hips jerked and he moaned. She lowered her hips so his lips could reach tender flesh. When she started to suck him, his tongue flicked over her wetness and moved across her clit. Each touch brought exquisite feelings to the fore, mixed with a deep emotional longing.

"Lass, if you don't stop—"

She let him go.

Despite being tempted to let him spew down her throat, she ached to have him inside her. She reached for a condom and rolled it down his engorged cock, admiring the satin over steel hardness. She made sure she put in on slowly so she could torment him.

His breath hissed inward as she finally rolled the condom all the way to the base of his cock. "Damn."

Erin realized being tied to the bed was driving him crazy, but he loved it. Erin turned about again and treated his nipples to long laps of her tongue. She eased her wetness over the tip of his cock. He arched up and tried to impale her on that long, hungry flesh.

"Uh-uh." She winked. "We'll fuck when I say so."

The low growl in his throat sounded animalistic, and the hum of it made her womb clench. He strained against the scarves and his lips parted to reveal gritted teeth. "Come on, lass. Put a poor man out of his misery. I want you so damned bad, I can't take it."

She leaned down to suck his nipple again and allowed her hands to trail over him in erotic exploration. She palmed his hard pecs, and then down to the sinew of his thighs. As she cupped his balls in one hand, his hips twitched up with a motion that mimicked sex.

"Sweet heaven," he muttered. "Please, lass. Fuck me before I lose my mind."

"You asked for it."

She impaled herself on his cock with a slamming movement that made him groan, and her gasp with excited fever. Big, solid, and swollen, his cock felt deeper and harder than the last time. Marveling at the feeling of him filling her, she started the motion, unable to wait a moment longer to experience everything with him. Their dance surged and flowed like the ocean. Each thrust seemed to go to the heart of her, allowing her to forget not only danger, but that she'd ever been without this man.

Lachlan groaned and shuddered. His movements picked up, rushing with her to a conclusion with no beginning and had no end.

His hips pushed up and his cock wedged high inside her. At her moan of pleasure he gasped, "Ride me harder."

She decided she would give him relief rather than torment. Erin gave Lachlan his wish, sliding up and down with a fluid motion that made him groan with excitement.

"Watch me," she said.

She cupped her own breasts and tweaked the nipples, rolling them and stroking the hard peaks. She'd never done this sort of thing during sex, and the ravenous expression in his eyes said he liked it. The feeling of her own fingers stimulating her breasts sent sharp, extra pleasure all through her.

His hips pounded upwards, and she took him with ever deepening movements. Each thrust brought her higher until her breath seemed suspended. Dizzy with love and sexual excitement, she came down on him faster, working her hips against him in a frenzy.

An orgasm ripped through her, cording her muscles and tightening her burning channel around him. He cried out, a sharp, guttural tribute as he came. Lachlan trembled against her, his hips still working to move his cock in her pussy. Small sparks of orgasm continued inside Erin, and she whimpered as the movement of each solid inch inside her made the pleasure non-stop. Bliss built to indescribable strength, pulling her apart and then bringing her together again.

After a few seconds to regain some of her strength, she untied him. He drew her down into his arms.

She relaxed in his arms for a few moments before she spoke. "This isn't over. I mean, the vampire isn't gone. He'll be coming back."

Lachlan kissed her forehead. "You're right. I have a feeling he has a few more tricks up his sleeve before he leaves Pine Forest." When she shivered, he held her tighter. "I promise you I won't let him touch you again. But I won't kid you either. We've got a fight on our hands. He's clever and he'll try new things in an attempt to take us off guard. That's why I don't want you to be alone again until he is destroyed."

"What about my work at the library?"

"I'll be with you there…everywhere."

When she sighed, he kissed her again, a deep, languorous tasting that showed their passion wasn't finished for the night.

He propped up on one elbow, his gaze tracing fire everywhere it touched. Joy started somewhere in her heart and blossomed outward until she felt like she might burst with the news.

"Is this real?" she asked. "We've barely met."

"But we have forever to learn." His wicked grin gave her lascivious ideas.

She sighed.

"What's wrong, lass?"

"I was thinking about Gilda. I got off lucky with this vampire, but I think worse happened to her. Do you think he bit her?"

He shook his head. "Doubtful. She'd probably be dead if he had. Or he took very little blood from her."

As they settled into a companionable silence, she drifted into a dreamless world where only the two of them resided.

Chapter 24

Deep in his hiding place, the vampire paced the floor. Gloominess covered the empty tomb. Yet the hard, cold floor held no discomfort for him.

He cursed disappointment and pushed it aside. Eventually Erin would let her guard down and be alone. Tavish wouldn't be with her forever, nor could he guard her twenty-four hours a day.

Burning fire filled his body as his rage heightened. Though he'd left Lachlan Tavish for dead all those years ago, obviously he hadn't completed the job. With the strength of two and the love of a woman, Lachlan seemed to know what to do and when to do it. He hadn't expected Lachlan's interference or his ability to fight.

Hatred grew higher inside him for Tavish. Strength and honor made the Scot powerful. Surprise had been Tavish's ally. He never suspected that Tavish harbored extraordinary gifts. Ability to cloud the mind, fast reflexes, inhuman strength, elevated sexual prowess. The glowing eyes of a predator. And most maddening of all—the ability to sense a vampire nearby. No one he'd tasted before had gathered so many capacities into their body and used them for good.

Building frustration made him pace the floor faster. Tavish must be disposed of immediately.

Never mind that Gilda proved a luscious and more willing victim than he would have suspected. An unexpected delight, his tasty Gilda. Yet he burned for Erin, for the woman whose fire and life made him want her so much. If Erin hadn't come upstairs, he might have drained Gilda to her death. In a more secluded place he would have fucked Gilda, then perhaps done the same to Erin.

At the same time he couldn't help but feel some self-loathing for not finishing Tavish in the library and then taking Erin. Throwing his head back, he howled as if in agony and screamed like a banshee to the heavens.

Worst of all, Ronan Kieran would soon be here. Now he must dispose of two fighters before he might feast on young Erin and know the greatest carnal love of his Dasoria again.

A deep rumble shuddered through the earth, boiling and writhing like snakes or worms being cooked in a cauldron. Thunder mixed with snow once again.

He laughed, the sound more a screech than utterance of mirth. Soon Halloween would arrive, and then he would show the people of Pine Forest what true horror meant.

Therefore he would design machinations to rid the town of those people who would help Erin and would ruin the love he saw growing between her and the bastard Lachlan.

Love.

The vampire's blood chilled to arctic levels. Tavish might have fought him off for the time being, but his influence on sweet Erin would wear away as the sexual pleasure faded.

Oh, he had no doubt they went to bed when they entered Erin's home. He knew it in his bones. He could hear the sighing and the moaning and even the savage male sounds Lachlan made as he took Erin.

But their happiness wouldn't last long. A plan already formed in his mind how he would work his way back to them. He would have Erin for his own and use any means to get her.

* * * * *

Two days after the attack on Gilda and Erin, Arabella's Coffee Shop on Main bustled with lunch goers, and the constant murmur of animated voices almost sounded too loud for Erin's nerves. She settled into the booth and dreamed about hot soup to ward off the cold snap that arrived in Pine Forest that morning.

Outside the warmth and brightness of the restaurant, the town seemed subdued, the revelry that often accompanied the Halloween season muted by a heavy feeling. Not only that, but she felt a strange coldness surrounding her that even Lachlan's protective touch couldn't remove. Molding around her heart, the icy worry demanded her attention when all she wanted was to forget the odd events of the last two weeks.

More than that, she hoped Gilda would look better today than she had in the hospital yesterday. Gilda had tried to hide the trauma of her situation, and although she denied she'd been raped, Erin knew there was more to the story than her friend was telling.

Lachlan slid into the booth next to Erin, his arm going around her shoulders at the same time. He leaned in close, their lips an inch or two apart. "So, lady, wanna come home with me?"

His irreverent grin made her laugh. "Lachlan Tavish, people are looking."

He didn't even glance around. "Do you mind that so much?"

No.

"Good," he said touched his lips to hers for a gentle kiss.

"There you are," a female voice said nearby.

The moved apart, but this time Erin didn't feel embarrassed or compelled to hide her feelings for Lachlan.

"Gilda," Erin said. "How are you?"

Lachlan stood. Erin saw his concern for Gilda in his eyes as he hugged her. "How are you? Feeling all right?"

"I think so," Gilda said.

Dressed in a black felt hat, scarf, and long coat, Gilda looked ready for a funeral rather than a cheery meeting with friends. Her face showed strain, her eyes not as bright and her mouth showing a half-hearted smile. Her gaze landed on Erin and Lachlan as she sat down in the booth, and this time her smile touched authentic. "What about you?"

"We'll survive," Lachlan said with a gentle grin.

Erin shrugged. "Still a little dazed, I'll admit."

Gilda removed her hat and coat and put them in the booth beside her. "That makes three of us."

Lachlan's eyes appeared sad and Erin marveled that this big, strong man harbored deep, tender emotions hidden beneath his tough exterior. "I'll see you ladies in about thirty minutes. I've got some things I need to pick up." He started to walk away, then turned back. "Don't either of you leave before I get back."

After leaning over to kiss Erin, he left the coffee shop. Erin watched a few women gawking at him as he left.

Gilda's old sense of humor appeared to resurrect. "I can see you've moved way beyond friendly."

Erin knew denying reality wouldn't work anymore, and why should she pretend that Lachlan Tavish didn't possess her heart? She looked Gilda in the eye. "I'm in serious trouble here."

Gilda's small laugh made the awkward revelation okay. "I'm glad to hear it."

An odd ache filled Erin's heart. "I'm not sure Lachlan feels the same way."

Gilda made an impatient noise and reached for Erin's hands. She gathered them in her own, her eyes serious and dark with emotions that half-frightened Erin with their intensity.

"How can you say that? He saved your life that night. And I've seen the way he treats you. That man is deeply in love, even if he hasn't said so yet."

Those reassuring words relaxed Erin, and she squeezed her friend's hands before she released them. "It's just so amazing; even if he said the words, I'd have trouble believing it right off."

"Why?"

Erin looked at her empty coffee cup and then at the waitress heading their way. "How many women do you know that have a gorgeous, kind, strong, incredible man treating them like a queen? He's so protective and tender and—God—he makes me feel so amazing, Gilda. I've never known anyone like him."

She wanted to say more, but the waitress arrived and took their coffee and lunch orders. After the woman left, Erin decided she'd be one hundred percent honest with Gilda.

"You're right. I can't imagine Lachlan being this solicitous with a woman he didn't care about very much. I'm used to different behavior from the men I've known. It's taking me awhile to get used to it."

Gilda's grin returned, and other than dark circles under her eyes, Erin never would have known that Gilda suffered an attack last night. "Well, start getting used to it now."

"Yes, ma'am."

Silence settled over their table, and Erin itched to ask Gilda the details of her attack. Not because she suffered morbid curiosity, but because she knew Gilda bottled up feelings inside her. She could sense a tension in Gilda's tight actions, in her somewhat clipped speech.

"What happened that night?" Erin asked.

Gilda remained staring at the table, studying her nails in visible fascination. "I wonder if they'll grow longer and stronger? I always did want long nails."

Confused, Erin let that statement percolate for awhile before she continued. "What does that have to do with last night?"

Gilda's earlier calm seemed to erode as her eyes took on a dark, despairing look that sent ripples of alarm through Erin. "That son-of-a-bitch bit me, Erin. The bastard put two holes in my neck." Gilda jerked her turtleneck collar aside for a second and displayed a small adhesive bandage on the lower right side of her neck. "Just like the other women. But you coming upstairs might have saved me. I'm still walking today." She gave a small laugh, sarcastic and full of self-derision. "The walking undead."

Disturbed by her friend's bizarre statement, and worried on top of that, Erin took a deep breath and let it out slowly. "Does it hurt?"

"Not at all. It only stung a little when he bit me, and not even much then." She laughed softly and lowered her voice. "A vampire bit me and I didn't even feel it much. Can you believe that?"

Again her friend's continuing line of thought made Erin take pause. "I know you're upset about what happened. That's why I'm here. I wanted to offer my ear if you want to talk. Lachlan understands all this, too, Gilda."

Gilda glanced around the room, her gaze assessing as if she thought someone might be listening in on the conversation. "This isn't something a person gets over."

Seeing the devastation in Gilda's eyes made Erin's heart sink into her stomach. "With time, and maybe counseling —"

"No." Gilda's eyes hardened with assurance, with some horrible knowledge Erin didn't understand. "I've done something awful."

Wondering if her friend needed psychological help right this minute, she considered asking Gilda if she'd like an appointment with her doctor. Instead, Erin took a deep breath and decided to start at the beginning. "What happened when you went upstairs?"

"You *know* what happened."

"Tell me what happened and maybe the event won't hold so much power over you."

"It will remain with me forever because it changed...me." Sadness etched Gilda's voice, and she closed her eyes.

Erin felt tears well up, but she fought them back. "How did it change you?"

Gilda opened her eyes. "You have to promise never to tell Tom."

How can I pledge never to tell him? Swallowing hard, Erin made the decision. "All right."

Gilda leaned over the table a little and lowered her voice. "The vampire caught me the moment I went upstairs. I couldn't move, couldn't fight. I could see him and yet I couldn't. He was like this dark shadow and hovered over my body and held me prisoner with his invisible touch. I couldn't cry out for help." Gilda's body shuttered. "I knew something horrible would happen because of how I felt. Like I had no control over my body."

Erin wished she knew comforting words to tell Gilda, but all she had was the truth. "It was kind of like that for me, too."

"Could you speak?"

"A little."

"Move."

"Some."

"Maybe you're stronger than me. I couldn't speak or move."

Erin wanted to give Gilda solace, but the woman seemed intent on punishing herself. Gilda's solemn eyes matched the regret in her voice. She circled the rim of her water glass with a slow movement, her gaze following. "Something else strange happened. It filled me with such relief that I couldn't resist it and didn't want to."

A crawling feeling went over Erin's neck, as if a spider skittered over her skin. Involuntarily she reached up and rubbed the back of her neck. "Go on."

Gilda stared out the big window to her right, watching as clouds slid over the area. People's breaths frosted in the air, and they added quickness to their steps as they rushed around town. "He seduced me, Erin."

"What?"

Gilda stopped touching the rim of her glass. "Seduced me." A soft, sarcastic laugh issued from her. "He made me feel more excitement than Tom and I have ever had together. More sexual pleasure. And I couldn't resist it. Everything inside me seemed to respond to him. I could feel his touch on each hot spot in my body."

Gilda put her head in her hands for a second, then glanced around again at the small crowd. Erin did the same. No one seemed to pay attention to them, but Erin knew people had heard they'd been attacked and must wonder. Curiosity would soon draw one of them near to offer sympathy to one or both of them.

"Did he seduce you?" Gilda asked in a broken voice.

Erin stared at her friend for a half minute before she said the truth. "No."

Erin noticed the dark circles under her friend's eyes had actually gotten darker with the emotional pain. "Well, he seduced me with caresses on my breasts...over my hips...the way he kissed." Gilda's voice dropped yet again, until Erin almost couldn't hear her. "It wasn't human. I knew so many things in my head while he was touching me." Her voice broke, and Erin saw pain edging toward the surface in Gilda's face. Gilda's lips trembled. A hard swallow started her next sentence, then a blush filled her face. "I knew that he wanted to take me. Right there in the children's section, for God's sake. He wanted to make me...climax. The monster wanted to shame me and wanted me to feel desire for him in a way I'd never experienced with another man. Erin, I betrayed Tom."

What could she say? What did one woman say to another, a good friend and a person you knew would never intentionally hurt their spouse? "You didn't have control of your body, Gilda. Whatever happened wasn't your fault."

"I couldn't stop it. He sank his teeth into my neck, then he stuffed his hands inside my panties. He...I came."

Erin rubbed one hand over her face, as if the action would erase the stupefaction she felt coming over her in sickening waves. "Listen to me. You didn't betray your husband."

A little of the tension eased from Gilda's face. "Telling you helps a little. I can never tell Tom about this. Ever."

Erin stayed silent for a long time, mulling through the confusion in her own mind over what to say and do. She tried to remember the last time she'd felt this helpless to assist a friend or to dissolve uncertainty in her psyche.

Lunch arrived before Erin could think of words of comfort or answers. Gilda ate her Cobb salad in silence, and Erin dug into her Monte Cristo sandwich as if she hadn't eaten in days.

The powdered sugar on the sandwich tasted more delicious than anything she could remember, and Erin realized seconds later she wolfed down the meal with uncharacteristic greed. She stopped chewing for a moment and watched Gilda.

Gilda's actions mimicked Erin's; Gilda looked shocked as they stared at each other. "We're being pigs." Gilda suddenly smiled. "Never knew getting attacked by a vampire caused such an appetite."

Deciding not to be disturbed by their desire to eat fast, Erin put down the sandwich. "I didn't eat much breakfast this morning either."

Gilda laughed. "What? No breakfast in bed?"

"Not yet," Erin said wryly.

They continued the meal, albeit at a much slower pace. Erin savored the flavors, dipping her sandwich into the strawberry jam with relish. Maybe Gilda was right about a vampire attack making the victim hungry. Then again...

"I wasn't seduced or bitten," Erin said.

"What?"

"I wasn't bitten by the vampire."

"You're certain?"

"Absolutely." Erin felt momentary relief, then instant remorse. How could she be happy about her good fortune when her good friend suffered? "Lachlan got there before that could happen."

"Don't feel sorry for me." Gilda stabbed lettuce and olives onto her fork.

Erin started as if Gilda had poked her with a cattle brand. "Are you reading my mind?"

Gilda chewed thoughtfully, then answered after she swallowed. "Of course not. What makes you think that?"

Erin put her sandwich down again and picked up a large steak fry. She toyed with the idea of not telling Gilda about Lachlan's telepathic abilities, then realized she'd gone too far to retreat. "Because Lachlan can read my mind sometimes."

Gilda's eyebrows tweaked up. "Oh?"

Erin sighed and contemplated the wisdom of telling more. After a long minute, she decided to go for broke. "Did he tell you about the vampire that attacked him?"

Gilda sat up straight, her eyes widening and salad perhaps forgotten. "When?"

Erin cleared her throat and started from the beginning, explaining how the vampire killed Lachlan's parents. She told Gilda what Lachlan said about the vampire overall. She also told Gilda about Ronan Kieran.

"Another vampire willing to kill his own kind?" Gilda asked.

"According to Lachlan, some vampires are good, and some are evil."

Gilda sighed. "Just like humans."

Gilda absorbed the information. "I should have guessed about Lachlan. Tom and I talked about Lachlan's uncanny abilities. I mean, he seems extraordinary in many ways. But he's not blatant enough with it for most people to notice. I suppose if he reads someone's mind he doesn't always blurt out what he's seen."

Without waiting for that thought to go any further, Erin said, "Part of me can't believe all this is happening. I wouldn't have believed it a week ago and now here I am. It's incredible." After taking a sip of her hot tea, Erin continued. "Are you feeling any better about what's happened?"

Gilda pushed her almost empty salad bowl aside. "Very little. I think I just need time."

More guilt piled onto Erin's conscience. "I'm sorry. I shouldn't expect you to get over it that fast—"

"No, no." Gilda waved one dismissively. "Don't worry, honey. There's nothing you can do about it. But you're the only one I'm telling."

"What about Lachlan?"

Gilda took a deep breath, her gaze filled with new pain. "As long as he won't tell Tom."

Erin nodded. "I'll only tell Lachlan enough to give him some idea of what happened to you. No details."

Gilda's relief came out as a sigh. "Good."

Lachlan returned to the restaurant a few minutes later, and once again women's gazes followed him across the room. Erin couldn't be jealous. Women would probably flip over Lachlan even when he reached gray-haired old man status.

As he settled into the booth next to Erin, a shocking realization came to mind.

If I'm thinking about being with him as an old man…oh, boy.

But could she give any more of her heart to him? What if he decided to leave Pine Forest? What then? His gaze snagged hers for a moment, and the reassuring grin he gave Erin made her wonder if he could tell she worried about their future.

It's all right, lass. His mind whispered, deep and as soft as his physical voice, and she wished they could be alone so she could show him again how much she cared.

Gilda's gaze danced between them, all signs of stress erased in the moment. "What are you two planning for the rest of the day?"

Lachlan threw Erin a conspiratorial glance. "I'm sure we'll think of something. My number one priority is keeping Erin safe."

Gilda reached over and patted his hand, her small fingers pale and insignificant against his big hand. "There's some nasty weather coming in. Since we have a few days off it's a great time for renting movies and eating pizza."

Tom appeared at the entrance to the eatery, his face holding apprehension. He seemed almost shell shocked.

"Tom's here but he's not coming in," Erin said.

Gilda swiveled around, caught sight of her husband, then started to leave the booth. "I'll talk to you guys later."

With a weak smile and wave, Gilda headed toward her worried husband. Erin felt her own frown growing and wished she could stave off slow-building depression.

Lachlan slid his arm around her, and the warmth and comfort made a significant difference to her comfort. "You all right?"

She snuggled closer to him. "I will be when I can stop worrying about Gilda."

Erin spied those deep flecks of gold igniting in his eyes, growing until she knew desire mingled with his restraint. She felt him tickling at her mind, his wish to read her thoughts came through strong.

His palm slid over her shoulder in a soothing, repetitive gesture. "I know it's difficult, but you must try. It's the only way you can survive. You've got to think of yourself right now."

"What about you? What's this doing to your mental health?" She gave him a frail smile.

"I'll probably be bloody insane by the time this is over."

Weariness worked in between her strength and determination to keep positive. "What do we do now?"

His dark hair brushed over his collar, and the dark, soft-looking sheen made her want to hustle him home. She wanted his skin against hers and the connection of his mind with hers.

Ronan should be here tonight. He'll meet us at your house.

I don't know, Lachlan. Another vampire —

He's come to help me protect you, lass. I can do a lot to keep you safe, but Ronan has forgotten more things about killing vampires than I ever knew. His fingers slid over hers in a comforting touch, his gaze locking with hers as he answered mentally. Don't be afraid.

She eased into relaxation, the barest nervous sensation stirring inside her. She winked and smiled mischievously. "What do you want to do when we get home?"

"There's a few interesting things I learned in Scotland that I'd like to show you." Lachlan's wicked, hot breath spilled over her lips as he leaned near.

She played innocent, even though her heart sped up and she felt a tell-tale prickle of arousal deep in her belly. "Oh?"

"Oh, yes," he whispered against her lips.

Chapter 25

Pounding edged away Erin's deep, pleasant sleep. She jerked in Lachlan's arms, awaking with a gasp on her lips.

Lachlan's arms released her, and he sat bolt upright. "He's here."

Her hear thumped loudly in her ears as she surveyed the room. In the semi-darkness she couldn't see much. "The ancient one?"

Lachlan slipped an arm around her and his palm slipped down her naked ribcage in a reassuring caress. "No. Ronan."

Her fear didn't ease off. "How do you know?"

"I heard his voice in my head."

She sighed. "Of course." Another pounding came at the front door. "Couldn't he have called first?"

"Yes, but he hates telephones. Besides, he can't even break in. We have to invite him inside, remember?"

"How could I forget? There are only about fifty different things about vampires to remember."

"He's a little crude at times."

"Crude as in rude?"

"I have to keep telling him to watch his language around the ladies." Lachlan slid off the bed and reached for his jeans. She heard him rustling around. "After hundreds of years of living he's often a little impatient. He forgets that humans savor life here and there. Women like his sorry ass, though."

She imagined a lady's man, suave, sophisticated and witty with the rough edge of a barbarian added in for flavor.

"Witty, maybe," Lachlan said, his voice filled with amusement. "But that's not why women like him."

"His vampire allure?"

"No."

"His fancy clothes?"

"I can't remember the last time I saw the man in a tux."

"His big dick?"

"Sweetheart, how would I know that?"

She shrugged. "Well, that would be one reason some women might like him."

Lachlan laughed again.

"Okay, are you going to make me guess?" she asked.

"No."

"Spit it out, Tavish, before I come over there and screw it out of you."

Lachlan's bellow of laughter was almost drowned out by Ronan's door pounding. "Oh, lass, I wish you could, but I don't think even we have time. If we make him wait he'll waken the dead."

With a sigh of resignation, Erin went to the closet and searched for a pair of flannel pajamas and her robe in the closet. She dressed quickly in the chilly air.

When she came back to the room, he'd turned on the lamp. As the low light illuminated the room, she saw he stood in nothing but his jeans, unbuttoned at the top. Well…that made her mouth water. He then slipped a sweater over his head.

Erin followed him to the front door, her warm fleece robe tight against the winter night. When he turned on the porch light and opened the door, she at first couldn't see the vampire. A dark shadow, not entirely substantial, stood near the open door. Erin stepped back behind Lachlan, fear shooting through her like lightning.

When the shadow stepped closer, his form evolved and changed at once into a man. "Sorry, Lachlan. I didn't mean to scare her. Didn't want anyone to see me around the neighborhood."

Amusement mixed with devil-may-care in a velvet rich voice. Laced with a husky Irish accent, his potent and sexy voice brushed against her ears. His voice drew her forward a step. She did it without thinking, an involuntary motion like steel drawn to magnet.

Lachlan moved back from the door and gestured inside. "Come in and show her that you're not an animal."

Ronan moved into the living room.

"Don't lie to her now." Ronan's big hand came down on Lachlan's shoulder. "Because I am an animal."

As the vampire turned toward her, Erin appreciated right away why women collapsed at his feet in a faint. It had nothing to do with vampire powers, either. While she loved Lachlan, the vampire before her would defy any woman not to do a double take.

Something over six feet, he stood taller than Lachlan. As he caught her gaze, she almost gasped. Ronan owned the brilliant eyes of a fallen angel. Deep and dark, his gaze burned with uncanny knowledge accumulated through hundreds of years. His hair, a tossed combination of lush chocolate and reddish waves, dipped over his collar. A short cinnamon-brown heard and mustache angled from his sideburns downward.

Ronan's black leather jacket made him look rugged and ready for anything. He'd left it open and revealed a thick red wool sweater and jeans with black boots. His look said casual and yet sexy with a capital S. No wonder women ate this man up.

Lachlan clapped him on the back and smiled. "What's it been? Five years?"

Ronan's his rusty, deep voice touched her ears. "Four, since our last hunt."

"You've hunted vampires together before?" Erin broke into their solitary conversation, curious about the ghastly adventures they'd accumulated.

Once again Ronan's attention turned onto her, and the weight of his attention bothered her. A niggling fear dawned inside, even thought she knew this handsome man wasn't a monster like the ancient one. Despite this, he was still a vampire, and part of her didn't like that.

Ronan put his hand out to her. "Pleased to meet you. Lachlan has told me about you."

Firm and strong, his grip reassured her as she shook his hand. She dared look into his eyes, and saw kindness laced with his unholy origins. Perhaps she could trust him. "And he's told me about you. Do you think we can stop this…this ancient one?"

Down in those eyes she saw disturbing uncertainty. If a vampire hunter of great strength didn't have the confidence, what would they do?

"That remains to be seen," Ronan said. "No one has managed more than a slight injury to him."

As if he saw her fear, Lachlan clasped her elbow and urged her back down the hallway. "We don't have long. Get dressed."

As she allowed Lachlan to lead her to the bedroom, she dreaded the next few hours. After they closed the door, Lachlan spun her into his arms and kissed her with voracious passion. He tasted and explored as he plunged his fingers through her hair. When he released her, their breathing came hard and fast.

"What was that for?" she asked breathlessly.

"In case I don't get to do it again."

"What?" She heard the hurt in her voice and it speared her heart. Physical pain would have been preferable to the sting of stark terror that began to build in her mind.

"The ancient one is coming."

Shivers ran through her frame, and he held her closer. "How soon?"

"Within hours.

"But if we stay here and don't invite him in, we'll be safe."

"Are you going to stay in this house forever? Never going out? What if I can't be with you one day and he comes for you? What will you do?"

Tears trickled from her eyes. "This is a showdown, then? Are we challenging him to a duel?"

He nodded. "We have to hurry, but no matter what happens, I will always have a piece of you here." He took his fist and tapped it against his chest. "There's nothing I want more than to tell you I'll survive this, but I can't."

The very idea of this powerful, amazing man fighting to the death made everything inside her rebel. She reached for him, tossing her arms around his neck. A sob broke from her throat as his arms held her tight against him. "Please. Please be careful. You have to stay alive for me, you understand?" Erin pulled back a little so she could see him through her tears. "Promise me."

Lachlan tried to remember if he'd ever felt this afraid and yet this determined. Perhaps not. At this moment he wanted her love with a fierceness that tore through every doubt he had. "But if it takes my life to save yours—"

She beat once on his chest. "No, damn you! Don't you understand? I haven't said it out loud, but you know it. You have to know it." With a voice broken in fear and sorrow she whispered, "Oh, God. Why didn't I say it before? I don't know how you did it in just a few days, but you've turned everything upside down and inside out and now there's only one thing I know."

He reached up to cup her face in his hands, his lips brushing away her tears as they fell. He leaned his forehead against hers and closed his eyes. "What?"

"I love you. I love you."

He'd waited a long time for her to say those three words, and although she'd said them in her mind many times, nothing beat hearing them come from her lips. He smothered her next attempt at words and kissed her with passion that said forever and always. Heat pounded in his groin, and he burned to sink his cock deep into her wet channel and feel her cunt clench around him in fierce climax. Sweat dotted his forehead as the need started to build.

Erin saw the glow in his eyes turn furnace hot. Everything he thought lay bared for her to see. She didn't require mind communication to tell that this man cherished her and wanted her fiercely.

"I thought maybe if I let your love carry us, I wouldn't need to say the words," he said. "Because if I said them, I'd have to admit it was true. With my fiancée, I told her I loved her not long after I met her. She always said she felt the same, but she never repeated those three words."

"She was a fool. She didn't say that she loved you, not even once?"

"No. With you I reacted to memories rather than to what was happening here and now. God, how I regret that."

"You love me?" she asked with anxious hope.

"More than my own life, I love you." He illustrated it with another deep, tongue-thrusting kiss that left her trembling with renewed hope in her veins. "I love you, I love you."

When those precious words left his mouth, she buried her face in his neck and snuggled one more minute into the safety she found. "I love you."

Lachlan kept her close for several moments, and she drank in his masculine, clean scent and the strength she felt in his hands as he caressed her back. "After this is over, if we survive it..."

"Yes?"

"Marry me."

Joy ripped through her and tears filled her eyes for what seemed the hundredth time in an hour. "Lachlan." She sniffed. "Oh, Lachlan."

"Is that a yes?"

"Yes, yes, yes."

He laughed softly and his arms tensed around her. "If there was time, I take you now." His voice thickened with passion. "I'd rip your pajama pants off, tear open my fly, and just fuck you mindless. That's how much I want you. Nothing else but my cock buried in your pussy."

His erotic words, spicy, made her cream her panties in one incredible rush. "Let's do it."

His gaze was incredulous but fired up by the idea. He rolled his hips against hers and his erect cock nudged her cunt. Reckless or not, foolhardy or not, their bodies wanted each other.

Then she remembered Ronan in the living room, and thought about how crude it would be to make love while he was in the living room. Granted, the door was closed, but—

He'll understand, lass.

Are you certain?

A feral grin touched his lips. *Yes. And if I don't have you right now, I'm going to come in my pants anyway.*

She reached for his fly. "Can't have that."

He got to his fly first and tore at it while she removed her robe and pajamas in a few, furious movements. Without second thoughts slid backward onto the bed. She lay with arms and legs sprawled wide open.

"Now," she said.

"Now."

Nothing fancy. No foreplay. No inventive positions.

Only raw sex.

"Condom," he rasped as he started to reach into the drawer.

She grabbed his hand. "No."

His eyes widened. "Erin."

"If you die, I want something of you inside me."

"We can't be certain—"

"Give me this one thing. A part of you to take with me, no matter what." Tears welled in her eyes again. "It will make me stronger."

She saw lust build in his eyes. He knew the risk, the danger of coming inside her. She saw the moment the idea of making her pregnant fired his sexual hunger into overdrive. His pupils widened, his nostrils flared the slightest bit.

With a last yank he freed his cock.

Framed by his open fly, his masculinity stood hard and thick and asked for her touch. The sight of such perfect, aroused male flesh made molten thick heat explode in her cunt. When he touched her between the legs, she gasped at the tingling, mind-splintering desire erupting inside her. She must have him or die trying. Erin knew her slick heat bathed his fingers, and he tested her readiness with one dip of his middle finger into her slit.

She moaned. "Lachlan."

She whimpered with raging, instantaneous desire as he climbed on top of her and lowered his hips between her legs. With one incredible, driving thrust he speared her to the womb. A strangled cry caught in her throat, and Lachlan kissed her to mask the sound. He stilled for maybe a half second. He drew back.

Rammed forward.

As she groaned in stunned ecstasy, his hips plunged. Plunged again. Began a rolling, twisting, insistent fucking that shattered and shook her to the core.

This was blinding, never ending love and promises. Whatever happened from this moment forward, their love would be sealed in this last act of ultimate pleasure. As her slick channel wept, she felt herself getting wetter, as his naked cock slid and probed and danced inside her with a friction that felt so astounding she knew she could die now and have no regrets.

Her cunt pulsed and contracted, tickling and teasing, burning and expanding. She moaned again and again and again.

Then she knew it for what it was. She'd never experienced a climax that started from the first thrust to the last, and she knew it happened because of the love between them.

Come, lass. Fuck me.

His hips churned against hers.

Faster.

Harder.

As she caught his rhythm in her heart and mind, all thought left Erin. Sensation piled upon sensation. Heat, motion, heavy puffs of breath against her ear, the sound of his male yearning. Her breathy gasps of bliss.

Almost weeping with blazing desire for final release, she grabbed his ass cheeks. Braced on his forearms, he thrust inside her now with a hammering cadence that forced agonized groans from his throat.

He jabbed deep inside, hesitated, thrust, withdrew. A strangled moan of desperation came from his throat, and he slid his hands under her ass. Cupping her butt he thrust wildly, with a bestial rutting that sent her orgasm into the last stratosphere. She cried out, supernova heat erupting up through her as his hips gave a last plunge.

His entire body shook, and she felt his hot cum shoot deep inside her. One pulse, two, outlined by a shuddering moan as he collapsed atop her.

I love you.

His husky intonation in her mind left her floating on a wave of bliss so shattering she wanted to hold him and demand they stay here forever. They could live on love and sex.

Instead she told him mentally, *And I love you.*

Lachlan moved off of her and drew her into his arms, his body quaking with aftershocks. They didn't have long.

With gentleness she inched from his arms and sat up. No more time for subtle touches, lingering caresses or the melting enjoyment of afterglow. With despair and reality taunting her, she went to the closet and found a pair of jeans and a turtleneck sweater. As she dressed, she realized Lachlan had put on a windbreaker.

"Won't you be cold?" She slipped into her hiking-snow boots and laced them.

"If there's a fight, the last thing I need is bulky clothing."

Resigned, she spotted the strange gun lying on the dresser. "Will you carry it, or shall I?"

"You, lass. I want you to have something for defense in case anything happens to Ronan or me."

She took one last glance around the room, remembering with an ache in her heart that they'd loved here and maybe never would again.

When they returned to the living room, Ronan sat on the couch with a nonchalance that said he either didn't care what would happen, or he had the satisfaction of knowing what to expect. She couldn't help but blush under his steady gaze.

When Lachlan stood by her side, Ronan grinned.

His hard eyes gave way to twinkling amusement, and the sensual curve of his lips over straight, white teeth said he'd heard. Everything.

Erin gulped, embarrassment making her face hotter.

Ronan's gaze danced from Erin to Lachlan, then back again. "Fortified for the fight?"

She cleared her throat. "Um…yes." She stepped forward, a challenge in mind. "How are you going to help us?"

Ronan closed his eyes, and for a second she imagined him flying across the night in his mind, searching the town for the ancient one. Could vampires fly?

Yes, lass. Lachlan's voice answered in her mind.

When Ronan's eyes popped open, he contemplated her and Lachlan with grave attention. Ronan stood and walked toward them, and she backed into Lachlan.

Lachlan's arms went around her waist. "Don't be afraid."

"A vampire assaulted me the other night and you're telling me I have nothing to fear. How do you figure that?" She couldn't keep the sarcasm out of her tone. "This isn't something a woman deals with every day. When Ronan comes near, I can feel some force that compels me to run away."

Ronan put up one hand in conciliation. "She's right, Lachlan. She's been toyed with by a vampire. When she meets another vampire there will always be a little fear." He frowned. "Were you bitten?"

"No." She said the word with haste, as if speaking more quickly would make the statement truer. "No."

Relief seemed to alter Ronan's expression for a second, and he gestured to the doorway. "Midnight comes soon. Let's greet the beast."

Chapter 26

As the graveyard came into sight a few miles outside Pine Forest, Erin felt her entire body shiver with unrelenting fear and cold.

Silvery moonlight spilled across the black iron gates, their spikes defying anyone to enter.

Lachlan pulled his Lexus to a halt near the gates.

"The graveyard?" Erin asked as she stepped out of the driver's side of her car. "Dare I ask why we are here?"

She'd tried to get them to tell her earlier, but they said they should wait until they arrived. They stood outside the padlocked black iron gateway into the graveyard on the outskirts of town. Glad for her boots, she stepped through six inches of crusted-over snow. The crunching noise sounded loud, intrusive on the quiet of the forest. She winched, half afraid the vampire would be disturbed by her tromping around.

An occasional breeze rustled the pines around them, and she pulled her hat down over her ears. Neither Lachlan nor Ronan seemed effected by the cold. The two tall, strong men looked invincible. Black shadows in the night, they might be shades or other monsters in the eerie scene before her.

Her insides started a trembling born of cold and mind-numbing fear. Erin drew a deep breath and tried to jam her fear back into a manageable state.

She'd mentioned flashlights, but Lachlan and Ronan objected. They could see in the dark, and although she couldn't navigate as well, the brightness of the moon made it easier to see. They couldn't risk the illumination of a flashlight attracting the ancient one. The vampire probably already knew they had arrived.

Ronan looked into the star-filled night. "He has a crypt here."

"You're kidding?" She stared at the men in surprise. "But, there aren't any empty —" She realized what he meant. "Oh, I see. Does he toss out the other body, or just —"she gulped, "live with it?"

Ronan responded to her uneasy question with a grin, then his gaze shadowed again. "He often lives with it. He doesn't want anyone to suspect where he is. If he left the body outside someone would investigate. If anyone has found it before tonight, he has probably killed them by now. Any talk of someone missing? A groundskeeper here, perhaps?"

Lachlan shook his head. "Not that I know of."

"What do we do first?" Erin asked.

"We'll search for the crypt," Lachlan said, and he put his hands on her shoulders and squeezed with a reassuring grip. "Search for a broken seal."

Determination broke through her apprehension. She wanted to get this over with. "Let's go then."

"Wait." Ronan put his hand up. "We'll go individually and look around."

"No." Lachlan's objection shot out without hesitation. "I won't let her do this alone."

Ronan looked around the cemetery with its hilly areas and tall stands of pines. When he turned back to them, his eyes flashed with a golden fire. "It will take too long to cover ground if we go in a group."

"There won't be many tombs in a small town cemetery like this," Erin said. "But it's hard to say which one he'd pick. We'll have to examine them all."

Lachlan turned her toward him. "You're not going to walk around this graveyard alone. I refuse to let you do it."

Irritation found its way through her. "Lachlan Tavish, since when do you order me around?"

Lachlan's eyes sparked, a sliver of red in that golden glow. Now she knew what he looked like when he was blazing mad in darkness. "Since I fell in love with you. I'm not going to let you out of my sight."

Ronan stepped closer to them, and she could barely see the frown on his face. "He is probably right. You are the weakest one physically. If the vampire came upon you first..." He shrugged.

She might be eager, but she wasn't stupid. "All right, all right."

She heaved a breath and decided she would conquer her fear before her nerves broke. With bravery formed of a desire to get it over with, she stepped forward.

Lachlan reached for her arm and held her back. "I might be able to break that lock, but I doubt it."

He nodded to Ronan. Without a word the vampire grabbed the padlock, and with a flick of his wrist, the metal broke with a squealing protest of twisted metal.

"Wow," she said softly.

Lachlan smiled. "Yeah."

Dasoria.

The whisper tickled in her mind. Automatically she turned to Lachlan. "What did you say?"

He shook his head. "Nothing, lass."

"I heard something."

"The wind," Ronan said.

As Ronan swung the gate open, Lachlan and Erin followed. She felt the metal of the gun tucked in her waistband and hoped she didn't have to use it. Yet she knew she would. What choice did they have? They could run. But they couldn't hide from the monster that stalked the night.

Uncertainty made her stomach pitch and roll. Nausea filled her and burned her throat. She stopped.

Dasoria. You are my light and my love. All is gone without you. Come to me.

Lachlan put his arm around her shoulders and brought her close again. *Damn it, she looks so pale and frightened.* "What's wrong? Headache?"

Her silvery eyes reflected back at him. "He's speaking to me in my head again. He's calling me that strange name. Dasoria."

"What does that mean?" Lachlan asked Ronan.

Ronan shook his head. "It's an ancient name."

"Why would he call her that?" Doubts slammed through Lachlan, his fear for her well-being making him falter. "He's near, Ronan. She feels his evil."

Ronan also stopped and came back to them. "I sense him, too. You can detect the ancient one with physical symptoms, Erin? His evil is a tickle in my mind, but to a mortal it probably hurts like a bitch."

She laughed weakly. "That's about the size of it." She winced and turned paler. "It's getting worse. What can I do to stop it?"

Lachlan felt her starting to shake in his arms from cold or fear.

Ronan flashed Lachlan a wary look. "She may not be strong enough."

Erin stiffened in Lachlan's arms, and he soothed her by running his hand up and down her back. "If you don't want to go on—"

"No." She pulled back from Lachlan's embrace. "You know we have to. I'm surprised you could back down so quickly—"

"No." Anger made him reach for her arms and he drew her closer. "No. I won't lose you."

"I'm strong." She moved out of Lachlan's embrace again.

The tilt of her small chin, and the pissed-off glint in her eyes, made his heart thump with a mix of admiration and fear.

He loved her bravery at the same time he feared she'd be hurt or worse.

Her defiance gave Lachlan a surge of hope. "If we don't take her with us, the ancient one is sure to make a last bid to take her from me. I can't let that happen."

Ronan's stoic expression gave away nothing. "Then we go on."

Lachlan saw the momentary panic on her face, a chink in her bravery lapsing. Like a child, she feared he'd leave her. He couldn't stand it any more.

He kissed her forehead, drew her closer, and absorbed the comfort he found as her arms encircled his waist. He took her familiar womanly scent deep into his lungs and closed his eyes. When he looked at her again, he saw the paleness in her face deepen and her eyelids flicker. Lachlan resigned to fighting the dread he felt in the pit of his stomach, knowing he would be strong for her or die trying. Nothing—nothing, he swore, would happen to the woman he loved.

"Lachlan," she whispered weakly. "Oh, crap."

"Shit," he growled as she slipped into a faint. "Don't do this to me."

As her body went limp, Lachlan held her up while Ronan placed his fingers to her temples. Several moments went by and nothing happened.

"Damn it," Ronan said.

Alarm bucked through Lachlan, and he tightened his arms around her. "What's wrong? Why isn't she waking up?"

"I don't know. Usually this will work in a few seconds."

"Bloody hell."

"Exactly, my friend. She's in a weakened state. Perhaps it wasn't a good idea to bring her here—"

"And who did you think I would trust to keep her safe?"

Ronan's smile lacked mirth as he kept his fingers on her temples. "No one but you. I can see that. But she was attacked recently by the ancient one. Even though he didn't get the chance to drain her blood, she's weak."

A spike of misery made Lachlan growl, "Then make her strong. Give her as much of your strength as you dare."

Ronan did as told, and Lachlan felt relief stir inside his soul as Erin's hands warmed and her eyelids flickered.

"That's it, lass. Open your eyes and speak to us," Lachlan said gently.

Within seconds her eyelids popped open.

"What?" she asked softly, her voice frail.

Lachlan held her tight in case her knees buckled. "You fainted. How's your head?"

"Better. Much better." She smiled weakly at them both. "What did you guys do?"

Lachlan kissed her nose. "Ronan is a powerful bastard. Gave you some of his strength."

She smiled. "That means I'm ready to kick some serious ass."

He gazed into the sky with boldness written in his voice. "Stick that in your hole, you ancient fucking bastard vampire."

Ronan's smiled sarcastically at his human friends. "Sure, and it's a good thing I'm such a nice bastard. I think the ancient one isn't going to appreciate the vehemence. Erin, my power should sustain you for awhile. If you start to feel ill again, let us know."

Erin couldn't see Lachlan's expression very well, but she felt the desperation in his touch. Disoriented and feeling feeble, she realized she couldn't quite focus. At least her head didn't hurt and her stomach didn't feel as if it might lose its contents.

She moved out of Lachlan's arms and tried the strength of her legs. "You'll be with me the whole time. I'll be all right."

"We'll all go together. There is strength in three," Ronan said as he changed his mind.

As they walked, Erin felt a new confidence. With a powerful vampire and a man who loved her by her side, she couldn't fail. Though the back of her mind screamed with terror at the idea of battling the evil vampire, adrenaline pumped through her veins and kept her feet moving.

They searched the small graveyard, and from time to time Erin felt the slightest twinge of trepidation. Trees creaked, their needles whispering, the wind causing strange sounds in the forest. All around her she felt eyes watching.

Ghosts, lass. They're speaking to you?

Yes.

Ignore them.

As they worked their way through each row of headstones, they tried the seals on the vaults and found them secured.

At last she saw a huge crypt at one end of the graveyard. A wind, subtle as it stirred against her skin, warned them not to come closer. Evil penetrated the very ground here, and a few steps more would bring all three of them into unimaginable danger.

"There," Ronan said as he started up the hill.

Dasoria, come to me. Leave these cretins and join me as my beloved.

As the ancient ones voice grew in power, she recognized it as the voice that had taunted her so many times. This voice had tried to deceive her on many occasions into thinking it belonged to Lachlan. *I'm not your beloved!*

You are! You are the reincarnation of my love, the beautiful vampire Dasoria.

Erin felt a trembling sickness attack her stomach. "He thinks I'm the reincarnation of a woman named Dasoria. A vampire woman he loved."

Ronan and Lachlan both stopped.

"He's deranged," Lachlan said with shock in his voice.

"Fecking right," Ronan said with a snort. "Vampires don't reincarnate. Once they are finished…they are finished."

"You can't hear what he's saying?" Lachlan said to Ronan.

"Wish I could."

Despite the fear that added to her illness, she knew down in her soul the vampire used this to make her helpless. Easily done when the spirits of the dead and past deeds soaked the ground. Though Lachlan and Ronan could detect the presence of the vampire, Lachlan would be preoccupied with Erin if she fell ill.

It might get him killed.

Unthinkable.

She wouldn't allow it.

Whatever she did, she couldn't let Lachlan know she hurt from the inside out. She would fight the illness with her last fiber. As she tucked her hand into Lachlan's, they marched behind Ronan, she made a vow.

I won't fail you, Lachlan.

You couldn't fail me.

As she looked at him, his gentle smile obliterated all fear in one moment. She saw a deep love in those eyes she knew would never waver. In the darkness, under the pall of terror that surrounded them, she saw the vague shimmer of tears mixing with strength in his glowing eyes. It was the evidence of the one thing that made it possible to break through the pain.

Lachlan Tavish's eternal love.

"Let's get to that crypt. Vampire or no fecking vampire," she said, borrowing Ronan's term.

Ronan laughed and Lachlan squeezed her hand.

Ronan's walk looked confident, as if he could care less that a thousand year old vampire waited for them at the top of the hill. As they came closer her head started to throb again. She dismissed the pain by putting one foot in front of the other.

The stone crypt loomed, coming closer, closer. Gnarled trees stood sentinel, awaiting their first attempt to disturb the unholy master of the crypt. A light wind, whispering against their bodies, came to an abrupt halt.

She swallowed hard, her mouth dry, heart pounding, wits stretched to the highest degree.

Steady, lass. Breathe deep.

Yes.

Lachlan pressed her hand gently once again.

Erin could barely make out the intricate carvings on the stonework, and she ignored the name and date caved into one side.

Ronan came to a stop and reached out for the seal. "It's broken."

That's it, Dasoria. Come to me.

Pain spiked her head. "Oh, God."

She grabbed her head in both hands, the pain almost sending her to her knees. Weakness made her waver, her arms trembling as she gasped in misery.

Lachlan reached for her, slipping his arms around her once again. "Damn it all to hell." As his arms tightened around her, Lachlan roared into the darkness, "Fuck you, you stinking vampire! Pick on someone your own size, you filthy, rotting corpse!

After his outburst, a strange silence came over the area. No wind. No rustling of trees. As if the heart of the forest stopped beating, or the world held its breath.

Ronan stood stock still, not even attempting to help. "That should get his attention."

Thank the heavens for Ronan's calm. Erin felt the rage eating away at the man she loved, and she grabbed at his shoulders for support. "Don't give into the anger, Lachlan. That's what he wants. Don't you see? That's what the ancient one wants."

Lachlan's muscles coiled, hard and ready to fight. "I don't care. I'd kill him a thousand times over for you, Erin. I love you."

He loves me.

Though she'd heard him say so before, his last assertion buoyed her stubbornness and gave her the smidgen of strength she needed to persist.

"I'd die for you," he said, his voice hoarse with emotion.

Ronan reached for the seal again. "She's right. He'll use her against you, Lachlan. Shield your emotions. Use them to defeat him."

Erin shifted in Lachlan's arms, turning so she could reach under her sweater and grip the weapon.

Erin —

No, Lachlan. Let me go. When he hesitated, she tried again. *Trust me.*

Obedient, he allowed his arms to slip from her, and she confronted the burial chamber. She kept the heavy handgun at her side, ready to use it at a moment's notice. Tears ran down her face as the pain in her head ebbed, then spiked. Then ebbed.

Ronan's hands made contact with the crypt door, and with a mighty shove, he pushed and the stone cracked. With an agonized groaning the rest of the crypt door fell inward. As it crashed down the crypt steps with an ear-crushing noise, they waited. After an agonizing silence, Erin couldn't take it anymore. Her insides might be rattling with fear and her body not as strong as she wished, but she wouldn't wait for the ancient one to take anything from her again.

Okay, you foul creep. I'm here now. Come out, come out wherever you are.

The vampire's voice whispered in her mind. *Dasoria.*

Yes.

My love.

No! I love only one man. LachlanTavish. And I'll love him forever.

Not for long.

She gritted her teeth, wanting to rush headlong into the crypt and confront the darkness.

Ronan took the decision away from her, stepping into the black interior as casually as a man entering a party.

Lachlan took her arm and that small touch gave her a measure of comfort. She would conquer whatever lay inside the putrid, hateful night and emerge on the other side a new person. A better human.

Ronan grunted. "Fecking smells in here."

Lachlan snorted a note of disgust. "What did you expect?"

Erin hesitated as Lachlan walked forward and they took the first step down. "I can't see anything. How many steps are there?"

Lachlan stood to her left, and she sank into his grip with sudden appreciation.

"Only three. There's a bit more room in here than looks from the outside," Ronan said as he turned toward her. Again his eyes flashed, and she shivered at the uncanny sight. "Look out for the hole—"

Suddenly the ground shot away from her, and Lachlan lost his grip on her arm as she plunged. A scream tore from her throat, start fear ripping her system for the little time she had to think.

"Erin!" Lachlan's voice cried out.

The ground came up and slapped her hard as she landed on her right side, the impact cutting off her scream. Stunned, she lay unmoving for several seconds. She blinked and looked up at the hole above her. Lachlan and Ronan's eyes shone down on her from several feet up.

"Lass!" Lachlan's harsh cry pierced the silence. "Erin, are you all right?"

"Erin!" Ronan's call added to the pain in her body. "Speak to us!"

"I'm—I'm fine." Her voice cracked, and she shifted slowly to make sure nothing was broken. Other than a dull ache in her body, she felt unharmed.

Lachlan's hand went out to her, even thought it was obvious he couldn't reach her. "Don't move, sweetheart! We'll find a way to get to you."

Stubbornness and a fervor to get the hell out of there made her stand up. She injected lightheartedness into her voice, but the dry rasp in her tone made it seem impossible. "I hope you guys have a rope or something, because I can't jump high enough to get out of here. What I wouldn't give for vampire powers right about now."

"Don't even say think that," Lachlan said with unusual harshness.

She turned around to try and see in the pitch-black, half-perturbed at Lachlan's bossiness, but understanding his concern. She couldn't see anything and renewed apprehension started climbing her spine. "I don't know where I am. What is this place?"

"Perhaps a cave under the crypt, or a tunnel," Ronan said. "Maybe even a sink hole. It's very important you don't step in any direction. You don't know what drop offs you've got down there."

Fear shot up her back as she stopped moving all together, her muscles tightening with cold and trepidation. "You can't see what's around me?"

"Very little," Lachlan called back. "I don't see any drop offs in the immediate area, but there could be some beyond the circle of the hole that we can't see. Don't move."

Seconds later Erin felt it, the creeping discomfort of someone watching her not from above, but from the interior of her prison.

Chapter 27

Erin's voice quavered as she spoke. "Um…guys…there's someone down here with me."

Her legs felt like gelatin, rendered weak by nagging fright.

Before the men above could speak, a deep laugh echoed in the darkness around her. "Dasoria."

She twitched and tried to sense how close the ancient one stood to her. "No."

"Oh, yes," the ancient one's voice sounded in the area again, apparently tired of speaking in her head. "And you are mine."

She put her hands out in front of her, as if to ward off the trembling and the monster lurking somewhere near. "No, I am not."

"If you touch her, I swear I will hunt you down and skewer your fucking entrails to a tree!" came Lachlan's guttural warning.

Another eerie laugh, this one closer, trickled through the night. "She has two choices. Surrender to me, or see you both die."

Anger made her say, "Forget it, vampire! I'm not surrendering anything to you. I told you I belong to one man alone. Lachlan Tavish."

She meant the statement with all her heart, and somehow she knew that declaration, made aloud, owned power.

Ronan, who'd remained quiet during the exchange, finally spoke. "She's stronger than you know. That's why you didn't try and seduce her, wasn't it"

A low rumbling, like an earthquake, shook the area.

An earthquake? The earth trembled and lurched to one side.

Erin lost her footing and fell backwards, a shriek of surprise slipping from her throat.

"Erin?" Lachlan cried out again. "Erin!"

She landed with a thump on her ass and realized her back also came up against a wall. Trembling, she levered up onto her knees. "I'm all right!"

"Thank God." Lachlan's breathy statement sounded desperate. "Damn it to hell, Ronan, we've got to get her out of there."

A whooshing noise came from above, and suddenly a body from above sailed down toward her. Backing up against the wall, she flinched as the figure landed on its feet in front of her. She gasped as a hard hand gripped her arm.

"It's me." Ronan's voice calmed her. He looked around him, eyes flickering with that dark fire she knew so well in Lachlan's eyes. "I don't see anyone down here and no drop offs. The only way we'll get her out of here is if I toss her up to you."

Erin swallowed hard. "Toss me?"

She couldn't see anything but his eyes, but she saw humor glowing for one second in their brown and golden depths. "Sure, and it's a fine way to fly."

Ronan clamped his hands on her waist. "Now, whatever you do. Stand straight and keep your arms up above your head. That hole isn't that wide. I don't want to hurt you."

"You're going to toss me up all that way?" she asked.

"That's right." His grip tightened and with a quick dip of his knees, he did as he said he would.

She let out a gasp as he lifted her with an incredible power she felt through each inch of her aching body. Erin was flying, and she tightened her muscles and kept her arms straight out above her head like a diver going into a pool.

Powerful arms clamped around her, and she scented Lachlan's familiar musk as he caught her close. "Lass, you scared the shit out of me."

"You're scared?" Her voice wobbled as she buried her face against him and held on tight.

A howling came from behind them, so sharp and loud Erin felt it to the soles of her shoes. A scream echoed in the chamber, through the treetops and down through the dozens of headstones littering the fields down the hills.

Not the screech of a dying vampire, but the challenge of evil ready to battle.

"Behind us!" Lachlan turned with a movement so quick he disappeared in the semi-darkness, then reappeared in a flash. "Get out of the crypt!"

She didn't have time to see if Ronan had escaped the hole. Instead, Lachlan started toward the crypt door.

"Wait," she whispered.

As they edged through the doorway, Erin felt the cold around her increase. It pierced her clothing like an icicle dagger, freezing death and horror mingled with an eternal hell.

A form swooped down on them like a glider, all huge wings and hell-red eyes boiling at the center.

"Down!" Lachlan dropped and she followed, flopping to her belly.

Propped on her elbows, she drew out her weapon and aimed the gun toward the long slope of the hill, but in the darkness the bird-like figure had disappeared. What if the ancient one materialized as a gargoyle? A bat? From what Lachlan and Ronan told her, the possibilities could be endless. How did she fight something that may look harmless one moment, then turn on her the next? How did she fight a malignancy she couldn't see?

"Mother Mary," Ronan's voice sounded in the doorway of the crypt, and as she turned to look at him, he moved so quickly he went invisible. Ronan appeared to her left, lying on his belly as they did. "Where is the bastard? I thought he was in the hole with us."

"I think he was out here all the time," Lachlan said.

Ronan made a grunt of disgust. "Fucker threw his voice like a blinking ventriloquist."

A breeze wafted over them, stirring the hair around her head. Somewhere in her adventure falling down the hole, she'd lost her hat. Cold shafted up and down her body like the unrelenting hands of evil.

The stink hit her nose first, and then she knew. The ancient one stood in the doorway of the crypt. Behind them.

Ronan and Lachlan must have felt the presence of the archaic vampire the same time she did. She rolled to her back and pointed the gun at the solid black form with a demon's horrible eyes. Fire burned in the center of the vampire's stare, hell-deep and terror unleashed. Nausea made her want to retch.

The vampire jumped straight up and soared into the air as wings several feet long spread like a deadly canopy over their heads.

"He's coming in again!" Lachlan stood and with a lunge he leapt into the sky, his hands reaching for the terrible bird above them. A growl parted his lips as he latched onto one wing and hung suspended.

Frozen with horror, Erin watched as the form swooped and plunged, weighed down by Lachlan's body.

Ronan followed Lachlan's lead as he shot upward, his vampire strength carrying him twenty feet from the ground. With both arms he grabbed the creature's other black wing and cried out in triumph. Each flap shook the two men, threatening to toss them off.

She thought about shooting the obsidian creature.

No. She might hit Lachlan or Ronan. She couldn't do it.

Stop it, Dasoria. Or I will kill them both.

She hesitated, her fingers loosened on the weapon.

She heard Lachlan's voice roaring through her head, above the insane cackle of the vampire. *Shoot it! Erin, shoot it!*

Erin flipped off the safety.

Pain lanced through her head, and with a second to pray she wouldn't hit her beloved or Ronan, she pulled the trigger.

An agonized scream tore through her skull, this time the voice so that all could hear. "Dasoria!"

The bird faltered, wings still. It started to plunge to earth.

"Lachlan, no!"

Erin scrambled to her feet, the weapon clutched in her fingers. As the evil shape drifted, she saw Lachlan and Ronan dangling from the great wings. She tracked the path of the drifting monster, and followed, racing between and around gravestones. To her surprise the creature still whispered in her head.

Damn you. The whine, high-pitched, cut through her head like glass shards. She stumbled, almost fell. *Damn you to a black existence. You betrayed me.*

Throwing all caution aside, she ran harder, toward the decent of the bird. One figure dropped, and she screamed.

Lachlan! She tried to get a response from him. *Lachlan!*

Nothing.

Dashing like a madwoman toward the figure, she saw the crumpled form lying among bushes near a tree. Mangled.

"Oh, God. Oh, please, no."

She dropped to her knees by the body and recognized Ronan. He lay sprawled on his back, eyes closed, arms outstretched. One leg twisted at a strange angle, and blood matted the front of his hair.

Another shriek slammed into her head and she fell to her side, writhing with the agony. *Damn you all to hell!*

She rolled over and saw Lachlan swing and jump. "Lachlan!"

He cleared a tree and then she couldn't see him. The bird turned and came her way.

Her breath rasped in her lungs, her heart pounded almost out of her chest. Before she could lift the gun to take aim, the dark figure dropped upon her. A horrid stench, like the mouth of a rotten sewer clawed at her throat. Her eyes watered and she choked, and through the haze she saw the red eyes pin her with hatred more forceful than anything imagined in her worst nightmares. Putrid and poisonous, the vampire breath cut off her air.

No, not a bird.

A gargoyle with the talons of an eagle and the hideous gaze of a monster.

Darkness started to fall over her vision.

Die bitch. Die for making me search for you hundreds of years.

With a scream of hatred, she spilled all the anger inside her, mixed with the pain of loosing the man she loved.

As claws pierced her arms and lifted her up, she wailed. The ground under her feet disappeared as the vampire took her into the air. With her last strength she knew what she must do. The beast climbed.

Ten feet.

Twenty.

The man she loved was dead. What did she have to live for?

She drew the gun up between their bodies and pulled the trigger.

*   *   *   *   *

Pain lingered in Erin's body as she became aware of her surroundings. She blinked, her eyes focusing on the stars above her head. She was so tired.

Taking a deep, cleansing breath, she tried to determine the damage. The pain that remained wasn't sharp, so maybe, just maybe she hadn't broken anything.

Then she remembered Lachlan.

And her heart thumped painfully.

"Lachlan," she whispered, and a sob started in her throat. The sound that came from her sounded more animal than human.

Erin heard footsteps hurrying toward her, and the heavy breathing of a man.

"There she is!" Ronan's strong voice hurt her head, but at least the drumming in her skull was a dull roar in comparison to earlier pain.

"Erin!"

Was she dreaming? Had she heard Lachlan's hoarse, frantic voice? Staggering joy penetrated the last of the fog in her brain.

A thud and someone dropped to their knees next to her. Eyes glowed in the darkness.

Despite pain she sat up with a yell, her gun at the ready.

Powerful arms encircled her and another set of hands grabbed the weapon and yanked it away. "Thank God. Easy, lass, easy. You're safe."

"Lachlan?"

She felt his lips on her forehead, his mouth peppering her with searching kisses. "Oh, lass, I thought I'd lost you." His voice, husky with emotion, heaved with a shaky sigh. He caressed her, his hands searching her body for injury. "Are you hurt?"

"No, I—I don't think so."

Ronan's laugh, deep with amusement, rumbled over her head. Lachlan spewed a language that sounded like Gaelic, but it made the vampire laugh harder.

"I'm sorry," Ronan said as he tried to sober. "I'm sorry, but I can't help but find this funny." In the semi-darkness she saw he held the gun. "She fights with the world's oldest vampire and when she's dumped onto the ground, even then the little wench doesn't lose her weapon."

She felt Lachlan's lips move against her cheek, and she knew his lips twitched in a smile. "Screw you, Ronan. Don't call my woman a wench."

"Your woman?" she asked in mock anger, profound relief making her dizzy.

Lachlan's lips covered hers in a tender kiss. She returned the message, her heart filled with love for the man holding her so tenderly.

When their lips parted, she looked at Ronan. "I thought you were dead, too."

Ronan shrugged, then she saw his vampire eyes narrow with pain. "Broke a rib or two and my left leg. But they mended in a flash. The perks of being a vampire."

When her mouth fell open and she said nothing, Ronan continued. "Now you, you fell damn near twenty feet." He sat on the ground with a thump. "Fell farther than I did and didn't break a thing. It's a bloody miracle."

Falling.

She remembered the black gargoyle, and with a jolt horror slammed into her. "The ancient one."

Lachlan's arms tightened around her. "You shot him twice with the silver. I was running toward your when you got him the second time and he dropped you. He crashed into the woods just beyond." He nodded in the direction of the forest past the graveyard.

Ronan got to his feet, still clutching the gun. "I'll search the woods and make sure it's finished."

Lachlan lifted her into his arms and marched back to the car without another word to Ronan.

She nestled into the security of Lachlan's strong arms. "Should we let him go alone?"

"He can take care of himself."

"I can see that."

"I'm taking you to the hospital."

"I'm all right."

"We're getting you checked out. " Lachlan looked down on her as he walked. "I could understand if you didn't forgive me, though, lass."

Incredulous, she clung to his jacket and the hard body beneath it. "What?"

"I didn't protect you."

"You did. You fought for me. Just as I fought for you. We saved each other."

Warmth, infused with passion and love flowed through her as his eyes showed love and unswerving devotion in a searing glance. "You're right again, lass."

A niggling of darkness brushed her soul and she had to ask, "What if the ancient one isn't dead, Lachlan?"

He didn't answer her.

* * * * *

The gentle sound of soft classical music filled Erin's living room. Three days had passed since the midnight battle in the graveyard, and now this evening they celebrated surviving a battle with the oldest vampire on earth. She listened to the deep laughs of two of her favorite men, Lachlan and Ronan. Gilda, Tom and Mark's voices mingled as Tom told another joke.

As she finished dumping the bag of pretzels into a big bowl and filled another container with chips, she marveled at everything that had happened in those three days.

Gilda and Tom came to accept that vampires existed. Gilda gave Ronan a mistrustful and wide berth every time he came near. Although Erin assured her she could trust him, Gilda couldn't stand to be too near the powerful vampire. She kept looking at his mouth, expecting to see long teeth. Ronan guaranteed Gilda that his teeth only grew when he fought or intended to bite. He hadn't feasted on a human, he insisted, since the American Revolution.

One thing they could all count upon, they couldn't feel too secure.

Ronan and Lachlan didn't locate the ancient one's body, nor any sign of a vampire turned gargoyle. Maybe the old vampire lay wounded in a secluded region, but for the time being he didn't stalk the area. Ronan checked the crypt daily and saw no evidence of current occupation.

If they could be certain about the ancient one's present location, Erin would be more comfortable. At least they'd inflicted some damage to the cursed creature, or he would have attacked by now.

Ronan maintained they should have another plan of action for when the ancient one returned and Lachlan agreed. Their party for celebrating their survival would be a caucus with a battle plan in a few minutes.

A scratching noise at the window made Erin's breath catch. She glanced out and caught the steady movement of a pine branch tapping against the window. With a deep breath, she stabilized her nerves.

She no longer suffered headaches and didn't hear the ancient one's voice in her head, and that should have made her happy. She knew she'd need the reassurance of Lachlan's arms around her. Erin didn't like insecurity, and even more, she loathed dependence. With the ancient one out there, what choice did she have?

You'll be all right. Her own voice echoed in her head, an attempt at poise she needed time to resurrect.

Two hands slipped around her waist, and she jumped.

Lachlan's warm laugh tickled her ear as he nuzzled her neck. "Sorry, I couldn't resist."

"Beast." She clasped his forearm and sank into the treasured bliss of his embrace. Tilting her head to the side so he could nibble, she enjoyed the tingling sensation as his lips traced her skin. "What are you doing?"

"Trying to see what's taking you so long. Everything all right?"

She turned in his arms, clasping those hard biceps that would cradle her through the day and long into the night. "Just thinking."

"About the ancient one?"

"Unfortunately. What are we going to do, Lachlan? You and I know he's not dead. Ronan said as much."

"We'll make sure to keep on guard. I don't know how long we have before he comes back."

"A day or two, most likely. Maybe a week." Ronan's voice broke over them as he entered the kitchen. "Sorry, I couldn't help it." He tapped one ear. "Vampire hearing, you know."

A wry smile touched the vampire's lips, and dressed in dark, silky Italian-made shirt and expensive looking wool pants, he looked more like a sophisticated European businessman than a vampire.

Right on queue Gilda and Tom entered the kitchen. Tom hovered around Gilda most of the time now, his gaze watchful. Gilda remained jumpy, and Erin wished Gilda would tell Tom about what the ancient one did to her. She worried because she could see the pain eating Gilda alive. Then again, what purpose would it serve in the long run to tell Tom she'd been seduced? Hurt feelings? A rift between them? In the end, they would have to work out any problems on their own.

"I smell something cooking." Tom reached over to snatch the chip bowl.

Lachlan slapped Ronan on the back. "Ronan's brain."

"Ah, that explains everything." Gilda retrieved the dip bowl. "Are we having the party in here, or what?"

"Let's go to the living room where it's more comfortable." Erin led the way, realizing that the party turned into a strategy session as well.

Mark sat in a chair across the room, more absorbed in a book about vampires than in the actual conversation. To everyone's surprise, the smart boy launched right into research. He wanted to help his mother and his friends. He didn't look up when they entered the room.

While they settled onto the couch, Ronan took center stage and paced in front of the television. "We know the ancient one isn't dead, but we've given him something to think about. He knows he isn't dealing with easy pickings."

"But no one is safe," Gilda said, a glass of wine halfway to her lips. "If he's still alive, he'll be back."

Ronan nodded and stopped pacing. He crossed his arms. "True. That's why we need answers. When I was in Morocco I found out one thing…"

When he paused, a dismayed expression on his mouth, Lachlan finished the thought. "That you have to fall in love with a woman to defeat the vampire."

"What?" Tom said, his face a study in incredulousness.

Gilda and Tom hadn't heard this part of the story.

Ronan hesitated, his eyes saying he thought the whole concept idiotic. Instead he launched into an explanation and ended with, "Yusuf told me I had to find a woman willing to pretend to have a relationship with me. Since I haven't a clue whether he told the truth, I'll have to do more research. There's a seer in Ireland I must visit. I'll fly out tomorrow night and find out what I can. In the meantime, everyone be careful."

"What about our jobs? We can't afford not to work," Gilda said, her tone a little icy. "Are we just supposed to sit around and wait for you to come back with a solution?"

To his credit, Ronan didn't seem effected by her animosity. "No. You can do whatever you want, but obviously if you go to work you'll need protection."

"Fred won't understand this," Erin said.

"Are you sure?" Tom picked up a chip as he spoke. "Most people in this town accept the supernatural to some degree."

"To some degree is the operative term." Erin snuggled into Lachlan, safe under his arm as he slipped it around her shoulders again. "Fred may put the breaks on the vampire idea. With Danny Fortesque still hovering around, it may look suspicious. And I know Danny doesn't believe in vampires."

"Maybe I can talk to Danny and Fred." Lachlan stared down into Erin's eyes, the grim, determined set of his jaw telling her he would make Fred understand. "They don't want to put your life in danger. I'll be at your side if you go to work, so we'd have to explain to them anyway."

Erin nodded, unsure how it would turn out, but willing to try. "Tom, you wouldn't have to go to the library with Lachlan there. You could still go to work."

Tom didn't speak for a moment as he chewed a pretzel. After a few seconds of pondering, he turned his troubled gaze on them all. "I don't want to leave her alone. Not after what happened. I won't be able to concentrate until this is all over. If I'm not with her…"

He let the thought linger, and Erin saw by the solemn expressions around the room that everyone understood.

"That's it then," Erin said. "We'll have to hang tight until Ronan gets back. Hopefully with some answers."

Late in the evening, after everyone left, Lachlan and Erin lay in the bed, content to hold each other tight in the darkness.

Erin sighed. "What would I have done if you hadn't come along?"

"You'd have been fine."

She heard the forced cheerfulness in his voice and propped on one elbow to look down on the most handsome man she'd ever seen. She trailed her index finger through the hair on his chest and considered his assertion.

"No, I think I'd dead. Or at the very least, the undead. Do you think we'll understand this Dasoria business someday?"

Lachlan drew her head down so he could kiss her nose. "Maybe, if we catch the bastard, he'll give us some answers. Ronan will find clues in Ireland."

She tried to feel his confidence. "A couple of weeks ago I wouldn't have dreamed this in a million years. I can't believe how my life has changed."

Lachlan stared at her for so long she wondered what he was thinking.

That I love you, lass. That's what I'm thinking.

She smiled. *I love you.*

Erin shivered with sweet delight as his hands slipped down her back. *We'll get through this.*

I know.

In the meantime...

Lachlan swung her about, rolling until he trapped her beneath him. His eyes held molten sexual promises that wouldn't be denied.

She smiled in satisfaction. *You aren't going back to Scotland anytime soon, right?*

Not without you. You're mine forever.

Forever. That sounds wonderful.

He moved just enough to cup her stomach and circle around it in soothing motions. *We survived. Do you regret not using a condom the other night?*

"No, Lachlan. If you hadn't survived —"

He caught her mouth in a kiss. "Let's forget about what might have been, and concentrate on the here and now."

She grinned. "And I suppose..." She slid her hand down his thigh then up to where his hard, more than ready cock resided. "...that this is the here and now."

She clasped his cock and started a long, slow stroke.

He gasped. "Oh, yes, lass. Here and now."

The End

Coming Soon!

Just when you thought it was safe, the ancient one comes back. Stay tuned for book two in the DEEP IS THE NIGHT series, NIGHT WATCH:

Inheriting a haunted house in notorious Pine Forest is the last thing Micky Gunn wanted, but escaping the Shadow People who haunted her world drove her toward the town and new terrors. When the Shadow People follow her, things go bump in the night, and weird accidents occur, Micky decides it's time to stop running and to fight back. Mysterious, gorgeous cop, Jared Thornton came to Pine Forest to investigate his Aunt Eliza Pickle's mysterious death. When he discovers that gutsy Micky is in danger, he vows to protect her against the shadows that haunt her, and a thousand year old vampire determined to silence them forever.

About the author:

Denise Agnew welcomes mail from readers. You can write to her c/o Ellora's Cave Publishing at P.O. Box 787, Hudson, Ohio 44236-0787.

Also by DENISE AGNEW:

- The Dare

Why an electronic book?

We live in the Information Age—an exciting time in the history of human civilization in which technology rules supreme and continues to progress in leaps and bounds every minute of every hour of every day. For a multitude of reasons, more and more avid literary fans are opting to purchase e-books instead of paperbacks. The question to those not yet initiated to the world of electronic reading is simply: *why?*

1. *Price.* An electronic title at Ellora's Cave Publishing runs anywhere from 40-75% less than the cover price of the <u>exact same title</u> in paperback format. Why? Cold mathematics. It is less expensive to publish an e-book than it is to publish a paperback, so the savings are passed along to the consumer.

2. *Space.* Running out of room to house your paperback books? That is one worry you will never have with electronic novels. For a low one-time cost, you can purchase a handheld computer designed specifically for e-reading purposes. Many e-readers are larger than the average handheld, giving you plenty of screen room. Better yet, hundreds of titles can be stored within your new library—a single microchip. (Please note that Ellora's Cave does not endorse any specific brands. You can check our website at www.ellorascave.com for customer recommendations we make available to new consumers.)

3. *Mobility.* Because your new library now consists of only a microchip, your entire cache of books can be taken with you wherever you go.

4. *Personal preferences are accounted for.* Are the words you are currently reading too small? Too large? Too...**ANNOYING**? Paperback books cannot be modified according to personal preferences, but e-books can.

5. *Innovation.* The way you read a book is not the only advancement the Information Age has gifted the literary community with. There is also the factor of what you can read. Ellora's Cave Publishing will be introducing a new line of interactive titles that are available in e-book format only.

6. *Instant gratification.* Is it the middle of the night and all the bookstores are closed? Are you tired of waiting days—sometimes weeks—for online and offline bookstores to ship the novels you bought? Ellora's Cave Publishing sells instantaneous downloads 24 hours a day, 7 days a week, 365 days a year. Our e-book delivery system is 100% automated, meaning your order is filled as soon as you pay for it.

Those are a few of the top reasons why electronic novels are displacing paperbacks for many an avid reader. As always, Ellora's Cave Publishing welcomes your questions and comments. We invite you to email us at service@ellorascave.com or write to us directly at: P.O. Box 787, Hudson, Ohio 44236-0787.

Printed in the United States
21246LVS00001B/13-15